MUTINY

MUTINY

LINDSEY COLLEN

BLOOMSBURY

First published in Great Britain 2001
This paperback edition published 2002

Copyright @ 2001 by Lindsey Collen

Permissions:
Translated and adapted excerpts from Henri Favory's *Sirpriz* in *Tras*. Ledikasyon pu
Travayer, 1984 and an excerpt from Henri Favory's *Bef*, Ledikasyon pu Travayer,
1983, with kind permission of the author and publisher.

The moral right of the author has been asserted

Bloomsbury Publishing Plc, 38 Soho Square, London W1D 3HB

A CIP catalogue record is available from the British Library

ISBN 0 7475 5772 1

10 9 8 7 6 5 4 3 2 1

Typeset by Hewer Text Ltd, Edinburgh, Scotland
Printed in England by Clays Ltd, St Ives plc

Dedicated to the memory of my brother John (1952 – 1975)

PART I

We lie in wait like snakes, to be honest. We quite con-sciously rein in our own instinct to act like wild buffaloes and to stampede.

We aren't *that* stupid.

This is the first time in the forty days I've been in this place that I see a fissure in *their* armoury. I must admit I had been looking in *different* places for a breach and that I had been more inclined to expect a crack to start to show in a more *physical* place.

Who would have thought of looking in a *state of mind* for it?

I take note of this hair-crack in the mental walls of their institution. I am mildly pleased. Just in case it's a fault line.

Right there in the eating hall at breakfast, one blue lady glares at another, raises one side of her upper lip, baring a yellowed eyetooth, and snarls; then she reorganises her lip only to spit on the ground right next to the other blue lady's left foot. Illegal, that. *Spitting.*

What sub-section of what section of what Act of what year?

We've got to *get* them on the technicalities as well.

Fighting amongst them*selves*, they are.

We hate these women that guard us and guard the gates and guard the whole edifice. And we itch to raise our hands in violence against them. Strangle them with our bare hands. But we know the retaliation of which they are capable. And such wanton acts on our part would at best make things go round and round in a downward spiral.

Then, this particular one, the one that got spat at, who is called Blue One-One for some reason, flares her nostrils in wild defiance. A strange thought goes through my mind: *She's just as much imprisoned as we are.*

I think this thought and then I smile a nasty smile. *Tough luck.*

We, us

P risoner means any person – against whom any judgement or order of imprisonment given by any court of competent jurisdiction, other than an order for detention in a reformatory school, is in force; or a person arrested and detained on suspicion of having committed an offence. [*Prisons Act (1888) Section 2*] 'Detainee' means – a convicted or an unconvicted person detained in an institution. [*Reform Institutions Act (1989, which repealed the Prisons Act of 1888) Section 2*] – Copied down in the Prison's Library.

M y first night inside, forty nights ago, I am thrown in like a little old rag-doll, falling on to the floor of a cell with two old prisoners in it. One of them, I find out later, is the famous Tiko. Infamous, rather. Or notorious.

Like the opposite of a birth.

When there's overcrowding, they *three* us. They're raking us in now by the dozen. Paid as they are *by the head*, as they put it.

Why am I remembering all this now? Why now? Is it that I'm expecting someone new to be thrown in on us today? Like I was on them then? Someone like you? Maybe.

A second coming? Why do I waste my time writing it down? And yet I must. Write, write, write.

These two women in the cell I get pushed into are not that *old*, it's just that they have been inside a long, long time. Tiko five years, the other one fourteen. *Old* prisoners.

Before I can even pick myself up I hear Tiko say, 'And what's the cat brought in now? Look at this skimpy little bitch! God short of cloth when he got to cutting you out, then?' Only one second passes.

'Most bloody likely, skint bastard,' I answer, dazed. My instinct says *don't give in, fight them.*

'So?' Tiko goes on, looking at me from head to tail with clear distaste.

They sit on their bunks on either side of me, in outrage. Tiko nudges my back with her rubber prison sandal in disgust. 'What d'you *do*, then?'

M y eyebrow pencil, itself, is nearly finished now too. I have
been sharpening it with a bit of an old razor blade, and it
is down to half an inch in length and getting quite hard to use.
I've decided to keep what's left of it *in case*. In case I need it
urgently for drawing lines above and below my eyelashes, in case
I need it to keep panic at bay. I will hide the stompie back in my
hair. I try to feel relieved. *Maybe I will manage.*

I hope very soon to get a proper pencil to write with. Long and
elegant. It may make the words flow honeysmooth.

I will have to wait. And to pay for it. It isn't up to me *when* I
will write again. And in some ways it isn't up to me *what* I'll write
next time. It isn't up to me *when* I will do anything I want to
again. I am pinioned in space *a live butterfly specimen* and doing
time. That's what everyone calls it. *Doing time.* I believe that time
will be doing us if we don't watch out.

5

*H*olding communication with prisoner: Every person – not being a prison officer or guard entrusted with the charge, superintendment or direction of prisoners and not being on military duty at the prisons – who holds any communication with a prisoner inside the prisons . . . shall commit an offence. [*Prisons Act (1888) Section 35(1)*] No person shall unlawfully communicate with a detainee or cause or induce another person to do so. [*Reform Institutions Act (1989, which repealed the Prisons Act of 1888) Section 61 (2)(d)*] – Copied down in the Prison's Library.

She, her

I am here now. Night is here too. I sit in my cell. In my hand is this short stub of an ordinary pencil, badly bitten, scratching across the top page of a pile, roughly torn out of some jotter. My cellmate gave me them. She's only remand, that's why she gets pencil and paper. Of a sort.

I'm in my cell. It's the cell I got moved to thirty-nine days ago, where I've got my own bunk. It feels like my own cell, or *our* own, I should say, because I share it with *her*. *Her*. I've got used to it now and it even begins to feel like home to me. I've got used to *her* too.

And now, night has come back again. It always does. Even when we get the call of the wild and want to bay, and even when the blue ladies start milling like that. Even then, night comes back. Eventually. But it doesn't bring any relief from the heat. Not a breath of air moves. The window is high up.

I share my cell, as I said, with *her*.

Who is *she*?

She's called Leila.

As I write, the perfume of a Raat ke Rani engulfs the room. Where is that shrub? Outside up on the hill in the wild? Or in someone's garden in the housing estate? Loyal queen of the night emitting her fragrance? For free. Not just duty free. Even free for prisoners. In the dark of night. When not a breath of air moves.

Then, it passes on.

And the smell of rebellion returns.

Look at her, as she breathes tempestuously from her bunk. I can tell she isn't asleep yet. She is still nervous and withdrawn.

She twitches. She grabs at her blanket seeking comfort, and then throws it off violently because of the heat. There's a dim luminous light in the cell, a cell which is never completely dark and never well lit either.

One month I have been sharing this cramped space with this dull child.

A dull child, but a wild child, she shies away like a horse, and is silent.

Her presence is heavy and, in some ways, regrettable. But she's young, so I am giving her her time. She's grown up in bad times, her mind cramped by the inevitability preached at the youth, and her body nagged at constantly by endless photos of model-bodies everywhere. So I wait for her.

In any case, I am otherwise occupied now, or should I say *preoccupied* now. I am right now lying down here, waiting for word.

Of course, instead of saying *I am waiting for word* I could say that I am *awaiting the word*. It would sound more *auspicious* that way.

But I am just *waiting for word*, as it turns out.

Nothing special.

It is quite ordinary, even scientifically verifiable, this *waiting* of mine. We can't just break out in open revolt when the urge takes us. It won't *work*.

That's why I'm waiting.

Arrangements have been made. First I sent word to Boni through my work friend who visits me on Thursdays. I call her a work *friend* because she visits me. But, she's only an acquaintance really. My only direct link with the outside world. I asked her to ask Boni for *contacts*. Leaning my head down to speak through those holes so she, my friend, could hear me and then not being able to look at her through the thick Perspex at the same time. Not that I fully understand what *contacts* are. Or what I would do with one. I worked in the same firm as Boni all those years and I never made a move towards her, never tried to get to know her or join in the movement. Right until the last moment, when it was too late. I just always felt Boni was there, in case. I took it for granted, the movement, as though it, too, was there all by itself. Boni, I thought, would keep things going for us all. Not even realising that what happened to my brother could happen to me. Not even taking in what Boni said to me – and she wasn't even in the union committee – *Ride carefully now you're secretary.* Anyway, the message I got back from Boni was that I must not expect other people to think for me any more – I replied the next Thursday that I'm only a computer engineer after all – but she added that there *will* be a message. So I wait. For a signal of some sort. There will be one, of that I am certain.

I also know that this particular message is due fairly *soon*. Whatever *soon* might mean these days. I am on the lookout for it from now on, anyway. Which doesn't mean I'll stop doing my own preparations. Oh, no. Not on your life.

I'll tell her, I think. *Yes, I'll tell her.*

Now *this* is an act of faith. A sudden decision, it is.

And so I lean over all of a sudden on to my elbow, into the half-darkness between our bunks and I whisper loudly into the heavy air that surrounds her, 'Hey! I've got a secret to tell you.'

My voice rasps around our dim cell. *Sibilants scraping the walls.* A night whisper always impregnates the air.

'What?' she asks. She is lying on her back and then she lifts herself on to her two elbows behind her, interested.

Then she adds, frettingly, 'You gave me a fright, you know!'

Child prisoner. Resentful. Always so near to a sulk. And so tall.

She turns on to her right elbow and peers at me in that pale light. She sucks her left thumb like a child. There's scorn in her now though. She takes her thumb out of her mouth and says, 'What you on about? What's *wrong* with you? Need your head read?' Then she leans forward stunned. 'Hey, you look all funny. You've gone mauve! Spooky. Colour of the dead. Look at yourself.' I feel her shudder.

The air of rebellion is getting into her language now. She is awakening from her cussed dullness. This pleases me.

A space is empty between the two of us. Dingy. A depressed little gap between the two bunks in our cell. And indeed, I notice, *mauve*. The dim walls are mauve. The dull grey blankets have gone mauve. I feel myself shudder too.

15

She has no idea mauve means a cyclone.

There is even a kind of warning in her, against me. In the position of her body and in the way she, too, shines mauve.

But she leans on my experience.

She's got to. She hasn't got a choice, although she's been in here longer than me.

'Lean a bit closer,' I whisper in the heat of that night. My hair is stuck to my scalp around the edges of my face and neck. In flat little ringlets. Sweat runs down between my breasts, inasmuch as they exist, like a river. 'Lean this way, so they don't hear me, come on.'

She does.

I lean out and hiss the words almost into her ear hole, *'I'm expecting a messenger soon.'*

She visibly flinches at the word *expecting,* I notice.

'A messenger? For god's sake.' she says, 'You joined some religion?'

Lucky we are whispering like that.

Because at that very moment, as we are both leaning over into the middle of the cell, and as I am hissing the words at her, the electronic door swings open.

They don't knock, you know, and they haven't got noisy keys any more. We weren't listening carefully enough. We try not to be surprised like this. We don't like it. Especially at night and all. Especially these days, of all days. Especially tonight of all nights. With this smell in the air. We shoot back on to our bunks. Snakes withdrawing from where we had slithered out to.

Blue One-One switches on our glaring fluorescent light from the switch out in the corridor. It flick, flick, flickers and then holds its shrill glare, from behind a mesh of iron slats in the middle of the ceiling. I cover my eyes. She stands there, Blue One-One does, admiring the feeling of her own authority. Then I feel her lean in and I hear her chucking a blanket into our cell, on to the empty bit of floor between us. A coarse prison rug. Like ours. That's all.

It falls silent on the bare cement. Grey of course. The cement and the blanket. Both are grey.

'You getting company,' Blue One-One bellows. 'Told them to

16

send a circular to all magistrates about the fucking place being fucking full.'

'No need to *swear* now,' I say, petulant. I've got a blue lady on another technicality. In the middle of the night. Criminal Code Section 296, *using injurious expression and invective*. I happen to have picked up that bit of information in here today. *Direct quote*. Good.

'Ninety-third fucking inmate in a wing that's like a furnace for thirty fucking six. Matron got her numbers upside fucking down.'

Then, out of the blue, she focuses on me, and adds something, 'Probably another allegator,' she says, sneering, 'like *you*.'

I am *in*, you see, for *allegation*. Not for making one, oh no. An allegator, like me, is someone *against whom an allegation has been made*. It sometimes suffices for more than just the arrest and detention, and bleeds into judgement and sentence as well.

'Probably,' I reply, just to get her back. 'Probably.'

'Shut up!' she snaps.

And the door closes behind her. Electronically.

I understand that door. I know its every trick. It is shut now. But there is a potential problem if she were to try to open it again too soon. I happen to know.

'Shut up yourself!' I say therefore.

'Well!' I say. 'Well I never did!' It is like a visitation. I turn it into headlines, 'Blue lady brings in grey blanket. Blue One-One brings in grey one.' We have a need to draw things out. Otherwise time slows down. Closes in. Shuts down. Otherwise, nothing happens.

'Is *that* your *messenger* then?' She points at the blanket. 'Runner for gods, flops down dead,' she picks up the headlines game, must have played it before somewhere. 'Second coming of the Lord fails. Prophet comes down again in vain. Ghost blanket brings in message. Is that your silly *secret* then? Company? A *visitor*? Under our roof, my dear? In our house? At night like this? Spooky rug moves in.' She is even sarcastic now. Then she turns on me, 'You already knew before? *Some secret*.'

And then, before *you* even arrive in our cell, she turns on *you*, 'What kind of crime can *you* have committed to be thrown in at night like this anyway? Some surprise! She must be a really bad girl, this one.' She goes on staring at the blanket.

'I am indeed expecting a *surprise*,' I say. 'Surprise, surprise. Any minute now. In fact, to be more accurate still, we are both *expecting* a surprise. You and I are. Because I've *told* you. So you're also expecting it now. Like it or not. And what's so innocent about *your* crime, then? What is so good about *you*, girl?' Again she flinches at the word *expecting*, but it passes. I certainly flinch myself.

It's both of us now, *waiting for word*. Expecting a visitor.

'When are we . . .', she submits now. This is appropriate. Then she balks again at the word. Suddenly I know for sure. *She is also pregnant. Or thinks she is. Lucky I'm not still engaged to that creep any more. Washing my father's feet at our wedding indeed!*

'Soon. Like I say, *any second now.*'

Silence. We wait. Our eyes are used to the light now.

'What exactly is a surprise, then?'

She is now beginning to use this kind of open question. Another way of making time pass. Of pulling colours into the cell. She turns it into a question-and-answer game. She switches over to it. She who was so lacking in playfulness before. Slots into it now. Just like that. 'What is the nature of a surprise? Is it a-something that you know about or a-something that you don't know about, what is it? Or is it this knowing-but-still-not-knowing, that makes it a surprise? Knowing that there is a-something very specific that is not known? One person hiding it away from another? And also showing it?'

She asks this question, and then before I can answer her, even if I wanted to, that is, which I don't because I'm sick of her stupid game already, she goes on, 'And what particular surprise could this one be?' She pretends to go into some sort of reverie, thinking and guessing to herself.

I answer, though, 'Buggered if I know.' I hate this neon light on me.

We both laugh. It's only a game after all.

But then she changes her mind and does something.

She stands up and bows to me. By way of an answer to her own question. Then she swings her arms around. She's got a wide audience. A wide skirt as well, that spins out around, then settles down. Maybe bright red, layered. An appreciative audience, which she acknowledges with a subtle hint of a movement of her head, as if they all sit at a certain distance from her in semi-circular rows, clapping wildly. They are spellbound. I lean against the wall on the other side of my bunk, and watch her, spellbound too. It's near ten o'clock. *Not a time for pumpkins to turn into princesses yet?*

But, look at her, 'Ladies and gentlemen,' she assumes the intonations of a street merchant selling her wares.

She mounts a bicycle. Wobbles slightly. It's a twenty-two-inch wheel and she's a tall girl. Then she's off. With a hat on. Wide-brimmed Panama hat, and she holds it on with one hand, as she pedals. Its ribbons fly on both sides of her head. Are they *scarlet* ribbons to match the skirt? The other hand on the handlebars.

Because we have this spotlight glaring in our eyes, we must have theatre. It stands to reason.

'Monkey on a pumpkin!' I chant and laugh. 'Monkey on a pumpkin!'

She wobbles on purpose.

Ladies and Gentlemen. For you tonight, I have a big surprise!
Surprise! Surprise!
Abracadabra! Look who's here!
You haven't seen me for many a year!

Look what I've got for you, my dear?
For you, I've got a big surprise!
I sell surprises to everyone, you know!
I'm here today, I'm gone tomorrow!

Ladies and Gentlemen, rise
And shine! Surprise! Surprise!

Crackers, packets, baskets, boxes, bursting open with
*   surprises!*
All ilk, all kinds, all makes and sizes! Cry your eyes out,
*   convicts!*
Weep great big tears, kids! Mothers cough up!
Where's the dough then? Spend, Mom, spend!
What's the point in saving!
Surprise! Surprise! Right down to the bottom of the box.
Joob-joobs and jelly beans, buttermilk suckers, lollipop ladies
and tigers' eyes, cough drops, paper hankies, doilies, kitchen
mops, loo rolls, sanitary wear, tampons, towels, brooms and
mops, hand cream, kajal, hair dye, tikas, nail polish, deodor-
ant spray, bells and balloons, whistles, balls, marbles, goons,
mirrors, hairclips, brooches, badges, bangles, bracelets,
chains, watches, rings and jumka.

Abracadabra look who's here!
Etcetera etcetera etcetera!
Surprise! Surprise! Surprise!

I applaud wildly. Speechless.

She claps her hands and laughs, sweat darkening her brown prison clothes' armpits. She's pleased for a moment. Then she flops back, her lanky self all sullen again, flat on her back on to the blanket on her low bunk. I think she's going to retreat into her carapace, but she doesn't do that yet. Instead she starts to laugh again. With a slow cackle coming from her side of the cell, then winding down like a long ago record.

This adds to a kind of disappointment in the air.

She thinks I'm kidding. Or dreaming. Or going off my head. Maybe there isn't a *real* surprise after all. Maybe it's all just a game we're making up to pass the time in our cell, to give us a break from the sweltering heat and to keep our spirits up.

But then again. There is the blanket. A physical proof.

She knits her brows, and sits up again suddenly and smiles. One long eyebrow draws a rough black line over both her eyes. Pale brown calf-eyes. Huge lashes like Luxmee the cow's, goddess of plenty. Soft, sweet eyes. But eyes that can turn harsh just like that. A tooth missing somewhere in that lopsided smile of hers that makes her seem generous and carefree. No more than a big child. Then suddenly she takes to sitting with her knees wide apart on the edge of her bunk, her hands on her thighs, but not the way women usually sit. Instead she's got her thumbs on the outside of her thighs with her fingers facing inwards. She leans forwards and she demands information.

I can't tell her everything. I'm not going to tell her about the particular message I'm expecting. Not yet.

So she carefully pretends not to care. Not to care a whit. She hums. And picks at her eyebrows where they join in the middle. But I can see she has got *expectation* in her, now. She smiles her crooked smile at me again.

Good. *Of things to come.*

She falls into the worst subject. 'I'm hungry,' she says. 'I'm starving.' These words drive me mad. *Hunger* aches in any case. Hers like mine. But I avoid telling her to shut up.

An instinct leads me now. 'What you want to eat then?' I ask. 'No problem. I'll cook you something. I'll cook you *anything*. Anything you like. Anything in the whole world. In the whole wide world. Free choice is yours. But. There is a *but*. It has to begin with the letter "*a*", otherwise I won't make it for you and you'll just have to go hungry. Starve to death. That's all. Name it. You'll get it. And, you get to keep the recipe. For free.'

She looks up at the ceiling half-exasperated, half-thinking. Everything she does is ambivalent, she's *that* young.

Now she is thinking up a dish, I can see. Anyone could. Concentration in her every movement. So, I wait. Then, I add something. 'Hold it! There is another condition attached. Hold it!'

'A what? It's only fucking imaginary,' she says. Sometimes she's so literal.

'We can't talk about being hungry all the time, that's what. You can't and nor can I. We've got to *ration* ourselves. That's the condition. OK?'

'How often can I talk about food then?' She is so rude.

'Only *rarely*. Accept?'

'Aubergine,' she says, '*Aubergine and potato, smothered*. I'd do anything for some, even the smallest little bowl of it. I'd eat it with a hot farata.'

Poor child, she can't bear to think of anything sweet. Bitter brinjals, bitter eggplant, *aubergine*. What a choice.

'Did you smother someone, then?' I ask.

'Il*legal* question!' she fires back.

A *ubergine and potato, smothered.*
      Now aubergines are vegetables that love being cooked in oil. *She lights up at this.* They also hate being boiled in water. *Aubergines come alive in that cell.* So however you cook them, you need *oil.* No use growing an aubergine bush in a pot in here, for example, because there isn't any oil in this cell.

So, to make aubergine and potato smothered, you need to start by putting some oil in the bottom of a heavy-bottomed pot. Not too much oil, because by the end, you shouldn't see any of the oil, because what there was will have gone into the aubergines and potatoes. And not too *little* either, otherwise they won't cook properly.

Recipes are instructions, too. Like the criminal code. Telling you what to do and what not to do. Predictions, conditions, instructions, orders.

When you're choosing aubergines in the market, choose ones that don't sound too hollow and don't feel too light relative to the others. *I shake one next to my ear rhythmically as if it were a musical instrument.* The dense heavy ones are the ones that haven't gone to seed yet. The ripe seeds don't taste nice.

Aubergines, which is why this dish may have been chosen, can be bitter.

This edge of bitterness is what can be nicest, if you take good care of it. Aubergines grow on a sturdy plant that can survive in dry places, but if it's too dry a season, they can get to be too bitter. Anyway. If you suspect them of being too bitter, you have to soak them in very salty water for about half an hour once you've cut them up. The bitterness drains off in brown water, when you strain them afterwards.

And if the skin is too tough – you'll notice it – then you might have to peel the aubergines first.

So you take your tender, young aubergines one by one and cut them in half along their lengths, and in half along their lengths again. If they are fat roundish ones, you'll need to cut them into eighths.

Then you cut across the middle.

Sprinkle salt on the white insides of the bits of aubergine so that it can draw out the bitterness, while you are peeling the potatoes. Cut the potatoes into bits the size of the end joint of your thumb. If they are new potatoes, you don't even need to peel them.

Heat up your oil. When it's piping hot, take one dried red chilli, and remove its seeds – the seeds are very hot, so you can throw them away – and put the chilli in.

Drain the aubergines and the potatoes and while they are still dripping wet, throw them into the piping hot oil. It'll make a big noise, sh-sizzle-sh-sh. Add just enough salt, and put a lid on, one that closes really tight.

Then listen. The vegetables are cooking in oil and steam. When you hear the noise quietening down in the pot, wait a while, the potato needs to stick a bit so that it tastes roasted not just steamed.

Then from time to time, when the potato has browned, stir the whole thing carefully.

Then turn the heat right down to let the vegetables cook right through.

In any society they say that the first writings are laws and recipes. So they say. Coincidence that I'm doing them too? Then stories. Some society. Her and me. Some writing. On scraps of Corotex toilet paper and torn off sheets of jotter paper shoved into crevices.

A nd this is how another of our games gets started. Concentrate all out on food. Tell recipes to lighten the weight
of the boredom, talk about food to quell the pangs of hunger that
gnaw at the pits of our stomachs, talk to tame the obsession with
eating. Hunt and gather. Sow and reap. Prepare and cook.
Conserve for hard times. Pickle and stew. Dry and salt. Keep
the required seed, the very best. It is knowledge in concrete form.
Store knowledge for later. Share it.

Then forget about food. Ban the subject altogether.

I crack no joke about her choice of vegetable. Of all the
wonderful dishes beginning with an '*a*'. An aubergine.

Although she's old enough for rude jokes. And has heard
things in here that would make a sailor blush.

A nd that's how we come to be lying flat on our backs sweating away here in cell number 14a of Block D of the Borstal Prison with the lights on, waiting. And me filling up torn off pages of jotter paper with tiny script, inbetween. And filing it in holes in the cell wall.

The bunks are a bit short in the foot, because it was a reform school before. A borstal. Shorter in the foot for Leila, although *she* could have been at the reform school she's so young. Then they made it into the Women's High Security Electronic Prison without changing the bunks. She always has to sleep with her legs bent or her feet sticking out over the edge of her low bunk like she is doing now, one or the other.

'*Any second now.* What does that mean *now*, anyway? You said she'll be here any second now.'

Smart ass, I think. She is referring to the fact that today is the day they announced changing the length of a second.

They even *told* us. They actually announced it like an ordinary piece of news. That's how docile they think they know that we are. They put it over the intercom at breakfast, along with news of rioting in Londonderry and in Seoul and in Bangalore, *as if these mutinies were new even to me,* along with news of air crashes, electronic break-downs, hard-disk crashes, bankruptcies, meteorological satellite implosions, damages the Supreme Court decides that workers owe their employers, rising prison populations in the United States, security-programme-collapses, mergers, warehouse fires due to arson, massive prescribing of anti-depressants, and the numbers of deaths due to religious strife here and there, *all this sounds to me who doesn't usually listen to the radio like the careless signals of impending doom,* along with news of serial murders, gang rapes, drug deaths, mysterious abductions and intercontinental paedophilia rackets, along with the sugary mug of tea reeking of vanilla that we pick up from the tin-topped table for breakfast, along with the hunk of bread with its margarine so thin we have to dip the bread into the tea to get it to go down, along with all this, what do we get? What do they give us? They give us this news. News given out at the exact moment that they give us our two beautiful bananas. We get given two every day. *Give us this day our daily bananas. Fruit of the gods. Grown in its own perfect wrapper. In abundance. What Eve actually found and tasted. What Adam accepted.* They gave us the news, with the two bananas. Sweeten the pill. As if to say, take it or leave it. Take it lying down. That's what they want us to do. That is what until now we are doing. *The length of one second will, as from 00 hours tonight,* they announce, *become 0.439 per cent longer.*

It has an immediate effect.

Our dining hall is seething with rage. Our sentences will all be 0.439 per cent longer. Every bit of prison work paid by the second will bring us in less money for when we get out. Rage is like a haze in the air or a mirage on a hot bit of dry road. Palpable. And it is only breakfast-time. Imagine what it will be like by dinner.

We already know.

Remember what it *was* like by dinner. It was in a state of impending. *Impending.*

And this is only the women's prison. Imagine what it must be like in the men's section or in Alcatraz.

And this is inside. Imagine what it must be like outside. The workers must be furious. The investors couldn't cut wages, so they put up prices. Then they couldn't put up prices, so they sacked people and closed down whole enterprises. Now they can't do that any more, so they decide to get time lengthened.

We sweat and we wait.

I t is *still*. What I mean is that in our cell there is *silence* now. Leila is right really. What does *any second now* mean anyway any more?

Maybe it's eleven o'clock at night for what it's worth, and there is still no wind at all. Just this tiresome light and this resentful blanket lying here.

I strain my ears to hear if they're bringing *you* down the corridor yet, and then I cringe unwittingly. Against the possibility that they come and drag someone *injured* in. Clubbed. Or culled. Battered. Bruised or bleeding. It's the time of night for that kind of thing and the dread of it is unnerving me to the point where it becomes an illness of the mind. Who are *you*? You, who will lie on this blanket? I can't get out of my head the image of what they might bring in when they bring you in, after the police have been at you. They have so much power over us. Try as I will, the picture will not be wiped out of my mind: *The picture of an eyeball out of its socket, being cupped in a hand. And a mouth wide open, crying out aloud, and knowing the eyeball can never be put back again.*

So I try to listen for the sound of the sea instead. Maybe the reef is up.

I can hear something. Something just as tireless, just as relentless. Droning on and on. Changing slightly, purring, roaring, growling, bursting, humming, droning, changing gear. Cra-cra-cra-crack. Pr-pr-pr-purr.

But I don't think it can be the sea. That would be too nice. I think it's only the traffic on the bridge. Shame. Pity them going back and forth. Shame, shame, shame. Sentenced to moving like that. Activity without end, day meeting night and night meeting day, formless action, shapeless activity, purgatory.

Mindlessness.

What if they've beaten you *mindless*.

It's getting too late for an ordinary new admission. Thinking about the sound of the sea has kept my thoughts busy for no more than a few seconds. Now I'm haunted again. How might they bring you in? I am almost caused to fret like Leila does. I don't like it. Just lying here, staring at the ceiling, waiting for the next victim to be thrown in at us.

Then the worst thing happens. I start to get strangled with fear, enclosed again, totally trapped in my own panic about the death of my brother, Jay.

I'm convinced they will take him from the men's section and come and throw his body in here cut to pieces or just lifeless, or worse still that they are killing him right now in the men's section and hiding his body somewhere. I press the prison blanket to my eyes to keep these pictures out, but of course how could that help?

I am now possessed. I am taken over, inhabited by this dread. Dread of my brother's death. It invades me, as if I were a passive medium. I try to clear my head and to relax my muscles one by one, but my mind is not under my control any more. It's slipped out.

I try again, by an effort of will, to conjure up the memory of the feeling of the *surprise* in all its glory, *please come back again!* Oh, for that feeling that was here just a minute ago. The cell was full of it. But it's gone now. Evaporated into thin air. The aubergine is also smothered.

The theatre is closed down now and in its place is a lunatic asylum which I now inhabit along with the seething crowds of my own fears.

I reach for my eyebrow pencil and for the first time since I'm inside, I outline my eyes. In some desperate attempt at keeping the devils away.

You in the plural

P lanting cannabis: Every person who plants, grows, culti-
vates . . . gandia plant . . . shall commit an offence and
shall be liable to penal servitude. [*Dangerous Drugs Act (1986)
Section 33*] – Copied down in the Prison's Library.

13

I'll tell her about Jay, that's what I'll do. I say:

'He's not a poet or even a singer, my brother Jay, and when he's outside work, he runs with the pack. Or *rides*, I should say.' *Ride carefully now you're secretary,* Boni said to me.

'Is he handsome?' *I pretend to ignore her question. Are you handsome, Jay? Are you and your friends handsome, Jay?*

I say, 'I call them *you lot* or just *you*. You.'

Funny that. 'You in the plural' often doubles up like that with 'you in the singular', 'you' doing for both, or alternatively, in other languages, 'they' can double-up with 'you plural', the same word doing for both. Funny that. And it causes no problem. Like he, she and it. One word, two words or three words, depending on the particular language. No problem for grammar. But you have to have those words.

'With the pack or not, he's vulnerable, my brother Jay, and death is unreliable. And I might *lose* him. I'm so scared, Leila.

'He's my twin brother.' *So I tell about him. The time goes so slowly when they make us wait. Causing me, for one, to slip back into listening to the grammar of my own words, concentrating on the tune and not the lyrics of some song. Stop it, I say to myself. Reflexive that, 'I say to myself' not just 'I say to me'. Stop!*

'Jay is just as big-boned and tall as I am small-boned and short. Anyone can tell I was the runt of the litter. Mother only just managed to give birth to us and then she died. Sometimes father told us she died in childbirth, a long and difficult delivery, and other times he said a coconut fell on her head and killed her. On

34

the spot, he says. On other days he said she died by drowning, in very shallow water.

'So that's partly why I worry about Jay so much. Because death is so fickle.

'And we *lost* our father, too.' The words *lost lose loss* pull at my chest, a dragging pain. Power of a word. 'The father we once had went missing another way. He exchanged his soul to the devil for something. Maybe a piece of land from Dr Bythee. So I worry about Jay. What if *he* also gets exchanged for something. Or what if he corrodes? Iron turning into crumbling rust? What if I *lose* him? What if?

'Yes, he is handsome, Leila.

'I close my eyes and I hear him getting nearer. He tunes his motorbike, a musical instrument. 500cc's. It's getting nearer. Close your eyes, too. Can you hear his motorbike getting nearer? Ah! There he is. He switches the engine off. And before he even gets off his motorbike – his helmet's still on – I hear him. *Tor-wing, tweng tweng, tor-wing, tor-weng.* That's the sound of his stolo-stolo.

'It's afternoon. *That afternoon.* His guitar in a bag he's had the tailor make out of denim, swinging over his back. I ride a 100cc one. It's after work, the afternoon of the night of the concert.

'Then he takes his crash helmet off. A shock of tight curls springs up, then springs up again, and again, making it seem as though he's got layers and layers of crash helmets. Like those dolls, one inside the other.' *Like phrases in sentences.*

'What work does he do?' Leila asks.

'Storekeeper's assistant behind the bookshop at the university. When it's quiet at work, he reads a book a day. Stolo-stolo to his lips. *Tor-wing, tweng tweng, tor-wing, tor-weng.* Educated that way.

'After work he rides around with The Boys on Bikes. They wear leather jackets. Jay doesn't. He wears his long white etamine kurta that flows down to *below his trousers' knees.* They let him be. Personally, I regard them with suspicion, this pack he rides with. *You lot*, I call them. But, maybe I'm just jealous of them.

'He says, "Can I practise for tonight? I'm nervous." So he sits on the back step of the square double-storey house I rent in the middle of that bleak rich man's morcellement. Rent*ed*, I should say. Haunting guitar notes, he plays, notes that contrast with the words. Blues guitar notes that rise up out of an almost sega beat. The Boys on Bikes call him *Cherubim*. And as he sits on the back steps in that late afternoon sun, the outside edges of his wild, dark curls give the aura of a halo. Maybe that's why.

' "Oh, Jay, sing it again, Jay!"

'So he does.

' "It's perfect," I say. But then sisters are biased, especially twins. "Where does it come from, Jay?"

' "Oh, the ionosphere. The nebulae." He picks up the strains of the notes and plays them in different ways as he talks. "I have found the ripples of the big bang as they spread out through the universe and my notes ride on their backs, a kind of *surfing*," he laughs, "Orion on the back of the Dolphin." '

As I lie in the cell, I see him, my brother Jay scattered like guitar notes all over the universe. A cherubim in nebulae. *A chill goes over me and I try to control an impending bout of dreadful visions. They await me, like a pestilence.*

'Let me sing you that song, Leila. Let me sing you that song.'

I sit up on my bunk now trying to remember the words. I can only remember the tune at first. But I hunt the words down in my memory until I find them, because I need this song, I need it to keep the images at bay, the dreadful pictures of him being mutilated.

All is one
Won, won
(Then strange blues notes Jay plucks from his guitar)
More and more and more
More more
(Another note, also strange)
Makes the
Other
The the the
*(Here there is a silence of a very precise length,
followed by a blues tune, pure and innocent.*

36

Then a pause)
O-ther change
Sea change
The break
Of a chick from the egg
Ebb and flow
The stars move out
But are held in
(A rhythm begins to build up and repeat itself,
the guitar as percussion,
more and more, into a sega beat and
then silence, again of an exact length)
Jailbirds turn
To seagulls
And shriek
(These last six words are sung in falsetto)

'How was *he* to know that he would be arrested. Let alone *me*. He *did* sing at the concert that night, Leila. A nightingale.

'Jailbird now. Him first, like a warning to me. Wings clipped.

'Before his famous song, Jay posed a question or two – interspersed with a bar or two on the stolo-stolo – *tor-wing, tweng tweng, tor-wing, tor-weng* – about a dinner he and I had peeped at as children and at which we believe we lost our father. *Who owns and controls the party you're in,* he asked, *and why? Tor-wing, tweng tweng, tor-wing, tor-weng.*

'Then he sang his song.

'The concert was on the beach at Swazi. Jay says the moon passed overhead *very low* that night, and it was worth it.

'The police came around the next day and arrested him for planting six little gandia shrubs on his front porch.

'So I am infested with fears that the prison guards will tear his tongue out.'

Which brings us back to fear. Fear of the state our new roommate will be when she gets shoved in.

So, I say to Leila, 'Or should we try and get some sleep. In case they're not bringing anyone in after all.'

Sleep is far away now. And restlessness has moved in.

And she says sometimes she gets scared at night. Even when the lights are on. Time goes so slowly she says sometimes it's as if it's eternally left grinding to a halt. As if it'll never end. We're trapped for ever and ever.

I am silent now. Jay haunting me. Fear of his mutilation. Fear of his death.

'I'm scared sometimes,' she says, 'and I don't know what of. And I get visions I don't want to see.' *I don't know what she gets visions of. I dread to think of other people's visions. In case they're worse than mine.*

So can I please give her another one, exceptionally, Leila asks, another little something to eat. Just to nibble on, to chase away the fear, this time beginning with '*b*'? Can it be now? *Now?* She almost pleads.

Please?

Even *bitter*er than aubergines, she makes her request more specific.

How can I not? I need to as much as she needs me to.

B *itter gourd rings, crisp fried. I choose something bitterer. I summon up the muse.* You use the ripple-skinned bitter gourds when they are still dark green or just starting to turn a bit yellow at the pointed ends. Whether they are about four inches or about eight inches long, you just cut them in half, across. A curious bitter perfume comes out at that moment. It stays on your hands. With the back of a spoon you gouge out all the seeds, which vary from white when the gourd is tender to the most intense red-pink when the gourd is ripe. I had a jacket that colour once. And a tablecloth. Only I didn't know they matched. You also gouge out the white pulp stuff around the seeds and throw it and the seeds away.

Then you cut the gourds into rings that will have a hole in the middle. About two or three millimetres wide. Put them on a tray and sprinkle them with salt. Again the salt works for you, it draws out some of the bitterness, and it will also help the bitter gourds to fry really crisp.

Then you put your oil for deep-frying on to the fire. Preferably in a thick-bottomed pan, or a round-bottomed wrought-iron karay that sits on gas easily. What the deep-frying means is that all the bitter gourd rings will have to have enough space to be able to float fairly freely in the oil once it's hot. *Freely. The word jars. A bitter gourd moving more freely than we are.* So you may need to fry them in two or three batches, depending on how many people you're cooking for.

While the oil is heating up, you put newspaper on a tray. When the oil is hot enough, a haze coming off it just before it gets smoky, you quickly rinse the bitter gourd rings in a strainer or colander to get the bitterness off and shake the excess water into the sink a few times. Then you put a fair-sized handful of the rings into the hot oil.

It makes a hissing noise, and you let the oil heat up again, before turning the heat down a little, so that the bitter gourd rings can fry quite slowly. You keep turning them over with a big metal spoon with holes in it, if you've got one.

When the bitter gourd rings turn pale brown, and go very light, and start to make a tink-tink sound against the spoon, this means they're ready to take out.

Use the metal spoon to drain all the oil off because you can keep it. Put the drained gourds on to the newspaper, so that it absorbs any extra oil.

The rings go crisp and dry.

You can serve them immediately or when they are cold. They are either a snack (on toast or in a roll) or a vegetable dish. Because of the strong taste, servings are small.

She asks how many years it'll be before she will be able to get her hands on raw bitter gourds and try cooking them. She looks at her hands. Big generous hands.

But that's a question I say she shouldn't ask because it will cause useless gnashing of teeth and renting of prison garments.

She says it doesn't matter if she doesn't get them because they are foul bitter things anyway. Hardly a treat.

Sour grapes, she mutters to herself.

How could she even mention sweet things like gulab jamuns and ras gulas or cheesecake and ginger biscuits or apple pie with cinnamon or sucking sweetened condensed milk out of a hole in the top of the tin.

Because if she did, she might cry with the longing.

She says she doesn't mind how long they give her.

But of course she does.

Then it strikes me maybe this longing for bitterness is pica. Be wanting to eat the walls soon. Cravings made madder by the prison. Be scraping her teeth on the grim cement.

Then she says she has never known such a *stillness* as this night.

40

She hopes it doesn't mean anything bad is going to happen. *It smells rotten*, she adds, *as though the place itself is corrupt*. As though you can only know this truth, when everything's really quiet and when you really concentrate. She closes her eyes. *And when they have locked you up under one of their laws.*

Then she slowly tilts her head backwards, stretches her chin into the air, her long, crookedly cut hair falling back like a mane behind her, looks up at the light behind its filthy grid, as if it is the moon, keeps her eyes closed tightly and, instead of baying, she sniffs loudly.

'Yes', she says, '*corrupt. From here, just *here*,' she says, 'I can tell.' There is no trace of the smell of the Raat ke Rani left. Nor of the ripple-skinned bitter gourd we cut.

Only the smell of the corruption. '*Corrupt*,' she says again.

Then, when silence settles over us, begins to smother us again, she starts to shiver. Like a wet horse. Sweating in all that heat, she trembles. I can't stand it. She's a huge filly going mad in these cramped quarters with me. *Please, please, don't go and fall to pieces. I can't handle it.*

I feel balanced on the edge of a cliff, myself, on the verge of a fall.

So, I have to offer her something so that, in turn, she can give me something to hold on to. For my vertigo. It's like that in here. Fragile minds. Arms striking out at one another, then clinging on to one another.

T reating: Any person who – (a) corruptly either before, during or after an election, directly or indirectly gives or provides, or pays in whole or in part the expenses of giving or providing, any food, drink, entertainment, or provision to or for any person for the purpose of corruptly influencing that person to vote or refrain from voting; or (b) corruptly accepts or takes any such food, drink, entertainment, or provision, shall be guilty of treating under this Act. [*Representation of the People's Act 1958 Section 64(2)(a) and (b)*] – Copied from the Prison's Library.

'*C* orrupt.' I too say the word aloud. '*Corrupt.* When you say that word you know,' I say, 'its very sound stirs something in my mind. *If only my mother hadn't.* Could she have saved my father? But my mother, *our* mother, Jay's and mine, was already dead and gone. Without us ever knowing her. She is as vague in our minds as the cause of her death. Because of twins, result of a falling coconut, or due to dangerous though shallow water.'

Leila listens again now and the shivering slows down to the odd shudder. She pulls at her split ends. She picks at her eyebrows. Rather she do these things than that morbid shivering.

I go on, 'My mother, whichever way gone, is pure and gone. Burnt to ashes, ashes floated out to sea in a small earthenware jar. Not even her dead body corrupted. When Jay and I were ten, soon after going to look at the cows in the cow factory, but that's another story, and just before we became members of the Bicycle Party, which is what I'll treat you to now, in a minute, we went to Porlwi to the Civil Status Office and in the death register, under her name for cause of death we found that it reads: *"Natural causes, breathing stopped."*

'So much for official statistics, Leila.

'Our father outlived her.

'When I close my eyes hard, I can still hear him whistling as he fixes someone's pipes. Plumber, he is. Fixing people's water systems all day long. A nice profession, don't you think?'

Leila goes pensive, then screws up her nose. She's scared to interrupt in case the story goes away, I can tell.

'He provides water, gurgling clear, catch it in the cup of our hands water and throw it over our hot cheeks water. He plans and brings water that with a single flush and a U-bend, carries off our excretions as sewerage, waterborne all gone, without us even wondering where it went.'

Leila is completely calm now. She casts a glance at our slop bucket. But I just go on. Not to be drawn into detours about kinds of lavatories.

'*I can always find him by the whistling*. Jay and I are the envy of other children, a father like that, a father-and-mother in one.'

'You said you'd tell about the Bicycle Party!' Leila loses her patience, reprimands me.

So I do tell.

'One day, an afternoon it was, like a dark cloud, a man from the government party appears, blocking out the sun with his girth, and calling my father by his surname *Bhim, Bhim*. After that, he disappears from view. *Blows over*.

'Then a group of villagers hold a *meeting*. Jay and I stand on a rock by the window, peep in' – I stand up in the middle of the cell and act the children breathless with excitement, peeping – 'into someone's half-built house. That's the venue. As though the house, half-built, isn't private property *yet*. Father is in there, inside. We can see him. The meeting hasn't started. He whistles. Sees us peeping, signals his pleasure in his eyes. We see men come in, and women. They bring their own chairs, benches, pirha, mats.' In the cell, I draw up a chair and sit, enthralled waiting for the meeting to start. 'And when the meeting starts, Leila, they all talk *in turn*, and they all listen to one another.

'We never saw anything like it before, Leila. Never. They *care*. About everyone. They think and talk calmly. *What is this?* Surly uncles now pleasant, talking in dulcet tones, domineering ones attentive, even kind. Fickle drunkards now almost serious, listened to. Women usually silent, throw back their sarees from their heads and speak their minds. Together they all come to *conclusions*.

'We never saw anything like it before, Leila.

'A ten point programme for the village elections starts to take form. More meetings are fixed. Jay and I attend. Through windows. We give our hearts to that party. Symbol chosen for the ballot paper so that everyone can vote even if they can't read. A *bicycle*. And this is how I begin to learn about everything in the world, Leila. From the Bicycle Party.'

She sits up on her bunk, all ears.

'Campaigning starts. Adults, like children, find that they too can be light-footed, move swiftly, act, run, play. Gone is drudgery.

'The usual lethargy drops off them and the depression that they drape themselves in lifts away. They group together and paint the village red and yellow – the Bicycle Party colours – they do cut-outs of bicycles and climb up and hang them up from telephone wires. Jay and I join in. They put up Ahuja loudspeakers on top of shop verandas, each orator downs a tot of raw rum in one movement of the head and right arm then speaks into a microphone to huge crowds assembled under mango trees to listen. Even father is an orator. He introduces the programme. Its meaning. Applause. Denounces the outgoing team, symbol horse, about the over-priced tenders they allotted for planting bougainvillaea bushes on the roadside. More applause. Talk of a better future. We hear wonderful phrases *taking our destiny, land, creating our own future, food, freedom from drudgery,* and we hear practical points too *better pay for piece rates, shorter hours of work, lower prices in the shops, water rights.* Jay and I try to link the two. All this in the Bicycle Party. How could I ever forget?'

Leila stands up and wobbles on to her bicycle again, this time showing off a full-size wheel. Then she sits down. 'That was just an interlude,' she says. She pushes her hair back behind her ears, all the better to listen to me with.

'*The man from the government party is nowhere to be seen.* The grown-ups have forgotten him. Father is no exception.

'But Jay and I worry. Like children do. That's why you sometimes worry, Leila.' *She's no more than a child, herself, I think looking at her listening to me in this mauve-coloured light.*

'One of the twelve candidates desists at the last minute. Why on earth? Father says maybe he was *corrupted.* The word jars in

45

my ears, I who have never heard it before. Past participle. Done. Happened. Over with. As if it means the man is for ever ruined.

'So, after Nomination Day, we ask people to vote for eleven bicycles and one elephant, elephant being the symbol of an independent candidate we are in an electoral *arrangement* with. Arrangement, because the deadline set for registering alliances is already over. The twelfth one is gone. *Corrupted*.

'Campaigning speeds up until it's a forward-moving, hurtling feeling.

'We *win*. All eleven Bicycle Party candidates and the elephant.' Leila applauds now.

'Firecrackers, victory speeches, thanking the electorate, marching through the streets singing. Banners waving. The councillors elect father Village Council President, carry him on their shoulders. He whistles on.

'Within days the sharks cruise in, as people put it. *What sharks? Cruise in where?* Jay and I ask.

'We see them. A battleship-grey car with tinted glass windows draws up outside our rented house. The man from the government party is back. With the minister's district agent. *In person.* Not just a message or a letter. They just sit there and press the automatic button to make the windows come down, don't even switch the engine off. Just hoot and wait. They just put their elbows out of the car windows, fingers strumming the roof of the car, signifying power.

'We wait and stare. No red and yellow pennants on *this* car. Father will never walk over to some young men who sit glued to their car seats. Who hoot and wait. Who leave the engine ticking over.

'But he does.

'He leans down to listen to them.

' "*We have come in person,*" they say. "*Come to Dr Bythee's Friday. Off-shore banker who supports us. All village presidents in the district will be there. Other than opponents, of course,*" they say darkly, rev up and speed off, leaving dust in our road. And in our throats.

' "Father won't go to Dr Bythee's," Jay says. "*Doctor of what?*" Jay asks father. "*I don't know,*" he replies.

46

'But Father seems to be going to go. We smell it. He doesn't speak much, nor whistle.

'Friday, he just puts on his best clothes, checks no one's watching him and sets off on his own.

'We, at a distance, follow. Spy on our own father.'

Leila is completely caught up in the story now.

'Dr Bythee's huge gabled mansion looms up at us. We find a way into the middle of the eight-foot red-leaf hedge. *An off-shore banker. I see him sitting at work on a Lilo, anchored out at sea, drooling into a cash register that lies next to him on the Lilo.* Meanwhile, Father and all the other village presidents are left, fish out of water in the yard in the hot sun. We see them. Twenty–thirty of them. From time to time, the men stick their heads out forwards, as if their gills are constricted. They are obliged to skulk. Like menials, they wait. Embarrassment. Shame. One kicks at the gravel in the driveway with the toe of a brand new shoe bought for the occasion. Three huge cars then drr, drr, drive in. Disappear. Then, quite by magic, three men appear high up on the front veranda. They look down at the men. They wave, signal the men in.'

At this point I get up again from my bunk and show Leila how the men walk up those stairs, their arms not even swinging.

'The stairs seem very steep for them. They go up so slowly, the higher the slower. Their feet dragging as if clogged with heavy mud.

'Lambs to the slaughter.

'We skirt around the hedge' – I'm the twins again – 'until we are opposite what seems like the window best for peeping through to see what's happening inside.

'Whisky in cut glass. Round table. Big hands, rough and sad. Clumsy boots on Persian rugs.

'Each man takes a seat regretfully at the enormous oval table. Napkin, what to do with. Cutlery frightening them. They are made to wait again. Humiliation in the air.

'Dr Bythee comes in, arms outstretched in hypocritical welcome. Even children can tell. Rudely, calls aside three village presidents. Raises them from the table. Rudely, whispers to them. Then, with them at his side, he announces, "I'm sure you all agree, this year the president of the whole district will be our friend . . ."

'Silence.

'Father lowers his head. Cringes.

'What has he expected. A debate? An election? Why did he come, what is this?

' "We thought maybe," Father begins. But he is silenced. By what means? We do not know.

' "Let's leave it to the P.M. and his alliance leader, shall we? Don't want to make a *meal* out of it." The word *meal* reminds them they are being treated to one. Dr Bythee disappears.

'Servants in white livery bring in trays heavy with luxurious food.

'Then the Prime Minister, followed by his colleague from the governing alliance, strides in, congratulating everyone on the exemplary manner, democracy, civilised traditions, that have led to the choice of the fine new district council president, Mr ——.

'Glasses down and clap. Then glasses up again, a toast.'

Silence in that cell of ours now.

'Horror. What a few *minutes* can do. When did they start, these minutes here at this haunted house? And will they ever end?

'Jay and I kick stones all the way home.

'Soon afterwards, Father buys new clothes like all the village presidents do – their station demands – and he acquires a small plot of land. The others do too. And he loses his whistling. Becomes lost himself. We can't even look at him any more. Jay says, *"I think he got corrupted."* I think so too, though we are still hardly old enough to know what the word means.

'So we *lose* him. More lost than the ashes of our mother at sea.

'And so I was left with Jay. Left just with the love of the Bicycle Party. The way it made grown-ups turn wonderful, causing them to stand up like that, proudly, to play, to think and to act.

'So, Jay and I leave school early, go out and look for work. Then we are free to leave home. Don't have to watch him rotting any more.

'Fear now.

'I suffer fear now, of losing him, my twin brother. And not

hearing his stolo-stolo ever again. Nor his mouth organ. Nor his guitar strings. Unless I get a grip on things. I flex my fingers slowly, practising for getting a grip. Quite literally.'

Leila shudders. *Don't start that again,* I think.

L '*esclave qui aura frappé son maître avec effusion de sang sera puni de mort.* Any slave who raises his hand to his master causing effusion of blood shall be punished by death. [*Code Noir 1723 à 1835*] – Copied down in the Prison's Library.

A *ssault* *on* *public* *officer*: Any violence where directed against an agent of the civil or military authorities and where committed whilst such officer, agent or person is performing his public duty or where committed in relation thereto, shall be punished by imprisonment for a term not exceeding one year and . . . [*Criminal Code (1838) Section 159*] Where the violence used against the functionaries or agents mentioned in Section 159 has caused effusion of blood, the punishment shall be penal servitude . . . [*Section 160*] – Copied down from the Prison's Library.

I only told her, Leila, my secret because of something I saw happen in the Court House today. I only told about the past because of it. First I heard her *say* something. She said it to Blue One-One. I *over*heard it, to be more precise. She was up for her fortnightly remand, for the seventh time, handcuffed to Blue One-One, and I was waiting to hear what *new* allegation they have cooked up against me. I was also handcuffed to a blue lady. So that is howcome we were both in the Court House today, with about thirty other prisoners, mainly women. And male police officers brushing past us, threatening us. However many women prisoners they bring in, each with a blue lady, it is the *male* policemen who set the scene in the Court House.

'*What case you in for, koko?*' Blue One-One asked her, *koko* in the sense of *sweetheart*. Blue One-One asked the question seductively, I thought. She was, as usual, dripping with jewellery, drenched in make-up with her hair starched and dyed and her false teeth glimmering. Extra-terrestrial, I thought at the time. Had she used her bonus money for plastic surgery to change her nose? Blue One-One, profile to me, waited for an answer. She is the worst blue lady, I thought to myself.

And I distinctly heard Leila reply: *Wounds and blows on police officer.*

She must have said that because Blue One-One lolled her eyes around. I noticed this, and then she looked Leila right up and right down, as if this prisoner who had seemed so ordinary with her hair cut crooked, had just there and then turned into a miraculous materialisation of a very young Virgin Mary at the

Court House. *Admiration*. She showed deep admiration. Wonderment. Devotion. Hero worship. Momentary, of course. She must previously have been under the mistaken impression that this young woman was just another drugs-and-prostitution or theft case in on an eternal remand like the others. Well. My roommate also noticed that Blue One-One was impressed, so she added, as if for effect, the following words: *With effusion of blood*.

Overkill, I thought. Although she was only, technically speaking, quoting Section 160 of the Criminal Code. It was just a plain fact.

Their admiration for one another was mutual, I noticed. I sensed the trap being laid for *her*. She is too young, Leila is. Blue One-One's make-up, her jewellery, her cheek, her chilly look, all these things impressed *her*. I feel alarm. *These women must be in the pay of. A mortal danger to. Blue ladies are private guards they are, and they are run by.* They may hate their bosses, but they seem well nigh owned by them.

I arranged to brush past Leila to warn her.

'Careful. She's in their pay. She might offer protection from men police in exchange for sexual favours,' I whispered to her, using archaic language for want of better. 'Tread carefully.' Maybe it was the intimacy of that warning.

Because I then witnessed her lose her innocence on the spot. Yes, my roommate just sloughed her innocence off. Like the scabby long extra skin it had become on her. And on her lip I saw curled the snarl of a wild creature in captivity. Her crooked mouth preparing to bite. Young as she is.

I told her my secret not so much because I had found out that she was in for assault on a policeman, not even because it was with effusion of blood, but because of the exact way she sloughed off her innocence like that, in public, and stared serenely around her.

M *utiny*: Where a prisoner commits mutiny or incitement to mutiny, the Prison's Board may, after inquiry on oath in presence of the prisoner, if it finds him guilty of the offence charged commit him to a confinement in a punishment cell, with or without forfeiture of one-third rations, or on bread and water diet for any period not exceeding one month . . .; or in the case of a male prisoner, order the infliction on the prisoner of corporal punishment . . . which shall not exceed 18 strokes of a cat-o'-nine-tails or other similar instrument, or of a light cane. [*Prisons Act (1888) Section 43 (I)(a)*] Where the Board finds a detainee guilty of an aggravated prison default, the Board may punish the detainee by ordering his confinement in a separate cell for a period not exceeding 30 days, and loss of remission, privileges and earnings. Except as is provided for in this Act, no detainee shall be subjected to punishment or privation of any kind. [*Reform Institutions Act (1989 which repealed the Prisons Act of 1888) Section 2, 36 and 37(4)*] – Copied down from the Prison's Library.

'It's the *possibility* that's important,' I say to her, again speaking with a sudden decision to speak. Another act of faith. An act of will, will to overcome the invading spirits of my own mind.

'What possibility? The possibility of a *surprise*?' Rude, she is.

I lower my voice and beckon to her. She leans over again, her head reaching into the middle of the cell. Near my head. Now in the bright light, she listens, 'The possibility of *mutiny*,' I drop this slowly.

'What?' she says. 'Keep your voice low. You'll get us both on bread and water if you don't watch your tongue. You mad or something?' She is such an *old* prisoner, although so young, although still waiting on remand. *Rotting*, as she puts it, *on remand*. I know with a certainty I can't explain, that her remand is potentially *corrupting*. The word haunts me.

So I don't watch my tongue.

The spirit of this night is still there. The milling and the sniffing in us is so strong it moved out of us into *them*, into the blue ladies. The spirit of this night is not gone; it can be invoked.

I try.

'The possibility of us rebelling. Of breaking the monotony. Of getting out of the rut we're stuck in.' And then with the full effect of the shock this word evokes, I say it, in a soft whisper-who-dares, 'You know. Why don't we *mutiny*.'

The effect of this *verb* is what gets her. *To mutiny*. When it was a noun, she only feigned shock.

'You're not allowed to say the word *mutiny* in here,' she

whispers in delight, 'It's a *hanging* crime. Rebellion by prisoner, it's called. A felony.'

I take no notice.

Where do such thoughts come from?

'Let's train,' is all I say.

'Right!' she says, half in jest, 'Right!' She stands up on her bunk, showing she's ready for it. Ready for training.

'Let's go then!' she adds.

She is so impatient now. So immediate. So ready for action. Can she be the same dull one? She is like two opposites.

'The light's on anyway,' I say. 'You win.'

So I draw the new grey blanket aside, pull it on to my bunk, so as to free the middle ground. We both stand up in it.

Raring to go.

But standing. We have this ritual. We stand. We wait. Otherwise the time would go even slower. *Have to divide the time up into parts.* A time for standing. A time for clearing our minds of debris. A time for casting out the flotsam of prison fantasies and the jetsam hurled at us by blue ladies. We breathe deeply. There are times of late when we get here, to this point, and we collapse with giggles.

But not tonight.

We start with the usual. Heat or no heat. March on the spot singing the song, starting on the left foot on the word '*had*':

> I had a man and thirteen kids and they . . . (*here we do a double skip instead of marching, to get the left foot forward in time for the word 'left'*) . . . left
> Right left right
> Serves me jolly well . . . (*another skip to get the right foot synchronised*) right
> Left right left right
> I had a man and thirteen kids and they (*skip*) left
> Right left right left
> Serves me jolly well (*skip*) right
> Left right left right.

And so on.

This she had learnt from her grandfather, a batman to an English foot soldier in Tobruk. Made fun of marching drill then too, hiccuping as they got to a particular word, enraging some sergeant major in the desert.

Then when we are sick of this silly tune, we start to warm up. Sweat is already pouring off us. We run on the spot. Our weight forward on our feet. Concentrating as if we are running a marathon and life depends on pacing ourselves. Run, run, run. We breathe carefully, run run run. We use our arms efficiently. Run run run. Now kicking our feet out behind us. Moving our shoulders to accentuate our stride. On and on and on. Until we start to get out of breath, and then this becomes the signal for us to break into a sprint, on the spot, knees lifted higher now, lifting right off the ground, more and more, faster, faster, faster, until we are exhausted.

At this point, another sign, we start to count:

> Left right
> Le-e-e-ft
> Right left
> Righ-ay-ay-t
> Left right
> Le-eh-eh-ft

And on the drawn out vowel sound, we run at the wall opposite the door, and jump as high as we can, tired as we are, touching the wall as high as we can reach under the window. Then we fall down again and chug on the spot, building up to another jump.

Then we fall on to our bunks and smother our laughter in our blankets. We could die of heat.

Then we lie on our backs again looking at the ceiling.

For the moment.

But tonight, there is *still* this uneasiness in me. In Leila too. Our laughter has a false ring to it, even through our blankets.

'Our visitor's late,' Leila says. She bites her nails. They are already bitten to the quick. Has she caught the feeling of dread from me, or did she get it all by herself?

I listen carefully. I hear nothing but the restlessness of the traffic. And nearer to us, the restlessness of blue ladies. 'They are shuffling about,' I reply. 'They want to unsettle us.' *They* prefer us to be unsettled. To be unconfident, diffident, concerned, even a bit paranoid. I believe they are paid to be slightly sadistic, but I have no proof of this.

'Sure worked.'

It is late. The noise. Sudden. Eerie. It is the casuarina trees. The sound is worse when we are listening for something else. It is a high-pitched call. On a single note. We hear it again. Two trunks of two different casuarina trees that are so close together that they scrape together to make that sound, shrill, like the bleat of a sick lamb, or the cry of an alley cat, or the scream of a child having a nightmare in the heart of the night and sitting up clutching her pillow. There isn't a breath of wind. Is there some secret shift, in the depths of the earth's crust, that moves the trees' deepest roots which, in turn, make the trunks chafe and shriek like that?

We have no idea that this signifies an approaching cyclone.

From where we are lying on our backs, we can see the square that is our sky.

No breeze comes through it.

A freak heat wave is bringing summer in straight away, as if it's in a hurry. No more winter wasps flying in, moving in, making listless yellow clumps like floppy mushrooms up in the corner of the cell, then dropping off the wall, only to loll about in listless swarms on the cell floor, and then, too lazy to sting, just dying. Docile and without any future, they just give up and lie down on the cement floor and die. Then they dry out, light as a bit of amber-coloured tissue paper. For Leila to collect.

She collects them. That's what she announces to me, when I first come into her cell. 'Winter', she says, 'is gone. Summer', she says, 'is here. No more wasps committing suicide in front of me,' she says. 'Cheers me up no end. *I keep them, the dead wasps,*' she says, '*in memory. A bit of something that isn't grey.*'

In memory of *the previous girl*? The girl in here, in my bunk before me, left such a heavy presence. Killed herself, they say. Mopey-Sue, they called her. Tiko hated her, hated her for *giving up* like that. Leila just talks about the wasps instead. Yet the presence of that past girl is always here. Like another person in our cell. The dead don't move on immediately. They get into the turmoil of our heads and the tangled roots of our hair.

And so, Leila and I lie on our bunks night after night as the heat builds up. A whole *new month* has passed.

'Yes, she is rather *late*,' I say. I make *you, the new girl,* sound like an ordinary visitor. 'Thoughtless of the new girl, hey Leila? Being *late*.'

We have gone back to words like *late*, *summer*, and *soon* and *beginning of the cyclone season* and *before the sun comes up*. Today's announcement about what is happening to seconds at midnight tonight, is not the first of its kind. They have been issued one after the other by the World Trade Organisation. So as to increase productivity. After wage cuts and price hikes, after staff compression and closing down whole factories, they started on the time. We have grown accustomed to this phenomenon. We could, it would seem, be expected to grow accustomed to *any* phenomenon.

If we don't watch it, that is.

And, like the wasps, die in clumps, and dry up unnoticed, and turn into amber-coloured tissue paper.

Time has, of course, changed. It has either slowed right down or speeded right up, we can't work out which, by now. Which is how we return to these more *relative* words. *Early. Late. Next. Before.* The countable aspect of time has definitely been weakened, stage by stage.

I wonder now why I told her my secret at all. Look how disturbed she is now. Agitated. And we have lived happily together without any questions, without any shared secrets, without expectations and dreads, without pasts, without crimes, without futures, we have lived in the present for a whole month. It had been a binding contract. It specified quite clearly its terms: 'The present tense only.'

I have broken that agreement now. And, after speaking of the past, of Jay and of the Bicycle Party, I have gone and spoken of the future.

Until now, we did only our daily training and our escape plans. Our escape plans are part of the *present*. Escape is one thing.

Everyone dreams of it. To want to hide away somewhere, to be a runaway. Run away to another enclosure. But *mutiny* is of course another thing, quite another thing. The exact opposite of running away.

But now, with this talk of mutiny, the future expands out in front of us. Like infinity. *Is there another second after the last one?* Words go wild in our minds. Possibilities. And no doubt we will start hurtling back into our pasts. *Was there a moment before the very first moment?* There's no stopping us now. We will skid in all directions.

W hen we were lying here at night in the past, tired out by our training, it had become a kind of house rule, before the word *mutiny* was uttered, that we use part of this time for making getaway plans. In low voices. Even in whispers. Plans for the present. *Traditions get built up so quickly.* Not plans for the future. Dreams for the future are castles in the air and we had therefore declared them not allowed *null and void* for our games. We don't want to cause ourselves distress. But to get out of our present state of imprisonment, we look for chinks through which we can make escape plans. Escape, escape, escape.

We have *got nowhere*, however, absolutely nowhere. The walls are thick and grey. The door is sealed. The window is high up.

But, we go on. We persevere.

And now with the word *mutiny* still echoing around the cell, our old exercises get a new urgency to them. So, we play on.

I say, 'Tonight, let's . . . let's look at different *times* for actually getting out of the prison building. OK?' She agrees.

So I begin, 'At night time, there are less guards on duty than in the day for a start. Have you counted them? They are probably sleeping most of the time too.' I am doing what we call *the launch*.

I don't tell her that I know all about the electronics of the place. Not yet. I keep it to myself. She has no idea that I spend ages piecing together all the electric circuits in the place in my mind, again and again running through the electronics in my head, in the meantime. In the meantime.

'True,' she replies. 'Are we planning for everyone who wants to get out to get out together, or just the two of us?' She is clarifying and testing the plan.

'Let's say everyone. It's darker at night and there are less people outside the prison walls.'

She doesn't say anything. She just studies her unevenly hacked split ends. She is lolling. A horizontal hulk.

The game stops, fizzles out. It just ends. It's all over now. We realise the old game is dead.

As from tonight all that is gone. Shrivelled up and gone.

We have sloughed that off too.

Leila and I will never plan a *simple* escape again. It's mutiny now. *What have we gone and taken on? I am frightened to write the word down on paper.*

I/me

'Tell, she says, tell. Why d'you put on that stupid eyebrow pencil? Why are you in here? You can tell me now. There are no more rules against it now. *Why? Why? Why?*'

I might as well tell her.

Conjure it up in here. The night seems auspicious for the telling. The waiting is in any case driving me mad.

So I say to myself, '*Tell her, Juna, tell her.*' And this is how I begin.

J ust at the very moment, Leila, that I realised it was *inevitable* that they were going to arrest me – me being alone with all those plainclothes men stalking around like caged panthers inside my burglar-guarded house like that while out the window I could see that lone blue lady sitting there in the back seat of one of those four plainclothes cars out on the road with the car door yawning wide open just the other side of my neighbour's pomegranate tree looking straight ahead of her like only *they* can – I panicked. I panicked about *two* things: What if I had to go out without my mascara on and what if once I was out my nose began to run. *Ridiculous*, I know. But true.

'What an opening,' she says, 'go on!'

So there I was standing at the back of the big downstairs living room imprisoned in my own house early in the morning *in a state of panic*, looking out.

So, I made an announcement.

'I have to go to the bathroom *first*,' I said, '*then* you can arrest me.' *Conditional*, I thought. *First this, then that. Could in another context mean just one before the other. Thinking such thoughts to keep the panic down. First not being, then being. Or being, then not being. Between stillness and motion, motion and stillness. Between freedom and imprisonment. Imprisonment and freedom.*

I waited. *I surprise myself sometimes. Even at the time I said it, I surprised myself. I never thought I had it in me.*

On the back of the dining room chair looking outwards in front of me was my bright red-pink linen jacket with its black curved collar, sitting there all pert, ready to go out to work all by itself. And my dark glasses to stop the ends of my hair from flicking into my eyes when I'm riding the motorbike were open on top of the diagonally laid bright red-pink linen tablecloth, also looking out. *Never realised they matched, my jacket and the tablecloth.* My high heel sandals stood, dark brown leather with shiny black edgings, where I had eased them off my feet the night before, so tired I was, next to the table, one in front of the other, as if already walking towards the door where I should be picking up my black crash helmet by now – one of those silly ones, that looks more like a baby's chamber pot, that I wear because of the heat in the traffic jams in Porlwi – from the coat hook and going out the front door to work as usual. *Ride carefully now you're secretary,* my workmate Boni had said.

'You know Boni! How?'

So, you know her too.

How do *you* know her, Leila? Yes, she works where I used to work. But I never took trouble enough. I never tried to get to know her. To learn from her. I lost something. A chance I was given. I regret that.

'I don't really know her. It's just that she helped me. Helped me give myself up,' Leila adds. 'Go on!'

There, on my chair, there in front of me was my computer language expert's clothing. There right in front of me. That's my job. That's my clothing. The outer layer of it anyway. A red-pink linen jacket – no more than a waist length bolero – with a black curved collar and high heel leather sandals seem to suffice to keep everyone quiet on the subject of *formal dress for work.* That's how I get my pay, I'm a computer language technician. I am by profession an *interface* between electronics and human language. Making circuits out of meanings. Only no such *profession* actually exists. Which is why they had to buy what they call an autodidact like me. Who may not dress right. If she didn't leave her outer layer in place from the night before, ready for work. *All the lonely people.*

The police went on thinking about my condition. My *if.* Only everything was different by then. Especially *time.* It seemed to get stuck for a few seconds. That was all. A minor hitch in time. *A stitch in time saves nine.* While they considered my *condition.*

I thought of Jay.

He's been through all of this. Why didn't I share this with him properly before?

But, I was still waiting for the police chief to reply. *Will he let me go to the bathroom first?*

Then he, dressed in his white safari suit, stuck his head through into the bathroom to make sure there wasn't any window I might be able to escape through – he sized me up for thickness, flat as a lizard, he found. There *wasn't.* Even *I* could never have slid myself through any of those slats. *Why was he dressed in white, which? Dirt would he have to avoid, what? Was he underneath this bush shirt shroud?* I shuddered to think.

I saw him sulk for a moment and then recover in time to say, 'No objection.'

Just as if he already had me in court. *Time warp.* He and I, lawyers in opposing teams already at that stage of the trial. Like children in our aunts' high heel shoes. Standing up and saying, 'Objection, Your Honour.'

Only I wanted to kill him. *Slit his throat.* The thought made me balk. I never had a thought like that cross my mind before, never in my whole life. Before that *slit his throat.* Always a first time. *First this, then that.*

No objection, indeed! So I went in and closed the door behind me.

Funny that, I felt safe in there, just standing leaning my back against the door, feeling the *slit his throat* subsiding. A kind of momentary happiness. Enclosed as I was in a small cell with good plumbing.

Shows how fast my needs were shrinking.

I leant over and stripped off four segments of toilet paper. Pink, it was. Two-ply. Tough Corotex. In case of my nose. Then I quickly grabbed the two-inch long eyebrow pencil off the glass ledge, licked the end hard, stood on tiptoes to see my eyes in the bottom part of the mirror, and drew a rough line above and below one eye and then above and below the other. Done.

Now, I can manage, I thought. *Maybe.*

I stood there, listening to my own heart beat. Blood straining in my arteries at each pulse. Funny I never heard it before. Internal plumbing. One-way valves and y-joins. Interconnected pumps and pipes. Squish-blub. Squish-blub.

All alone, I felt.

Alone in the world. I saw a razor blade on the glass ledge. *Slit his throat.* Jugular, I thought. So many of them out there.

From now on, they'll make me dance to their tune. I must prepare myself. Their beat. My fiancé'll be pleased I broke it off last week, relieved anyway. His razor still on my ledge. Just in time, he'll say. Imagine him engaged to someone doing time. Worse than a girl refusing to wash her father's feet on her wedding day.

It was then, at that very moment, that I *knew* that I *already knew* that I was from then onwards up against *enemies.*

There were those men *out there* outside the bathroom door. *Them against me.* And the blue lady staring ahead of her like that on the other side of that spindly pomegranate tree. My brother Jay already locked up inside.

So I was glad to be free of anyone inbetween them and me like *he* would have been. My fiancé. Funny that, took talk of our *wedding* to show me what I hadn't seen. *Wash my father's feet,* he insisted. So that put an end to that. *Undoing a stitch in time saves undoing nine.*

Leila can't help it. She interrupts here, can't let me go on without a comment. *'So you had a fiancé!'*

I signal with my finger to my lips. Shush.

'*You broke it off?* Do you regret it?'

No. No. I did cry though, I admit it, Leila. I was disoriented by his absence. He had become a part of my routine, a habit. He would stop by at my house on his way home from the bank. Every day. Dinner together and watch television. I felt alone without him, at first. More alone than lonely. I went to work with swollen eyes and a red nose every day. But, now, not at all. No more mourning for him. It's all over. A kind of relief. For a narrow escape from something constricting. I said I wouldn't wash my father's feet at our wedding – it was to be in two months' time – and he just flew into a rage. But there were other things. He didn't like me riding the motorbike, not one bit. He wanted me to resign from being secretary of the new union, that's for sure. Our paths seemed to start to move apart just when marriage was trying to force them together. Have you got one, a fiancé?

Silence.

So, anyway, where was I? We can come back to that another time. I was in the bathroom, wasn't I?

'Hurry up, please,' the chief called. 'Hurry up, please, it's time.'

'Hurry up,' one of his men relayed.

'Hurry up!' another lower ranked one echoed.

Oh, no! What, I thought, *is happening to me!*

Giddiness. Where's my mascara? Pull self together. Got tissue. Nausea. Control panic. Ride carefully now you're secretary.

I didn't understand anything about my arrest.

Neither reason nor procedure. Neither motive nor charge. To me, it was a bolt out of the blue.

I am a person who doesn't understand very much about anything, come to think of it. Except for computer systems and what I call the common map of *all human language* – they hold few secrets for me – everything else is very hard for me to come to grips with. Any number of things are bolts out of the blue to me.

I feel hurled into the world myself.

Just like they have hurled me into this cell.

As if I'm a bolt out of the blue myself.

Anyway, on an impulse, I hid my two-inch eyebrow pencil in my bushy hair on the right side of my head somewhere above my right ear and below my right temple, and instead of blowing my nose on the four segments of pink double-ply toilet paper or slipping them into the pocket of my grey cotton trousers, I rolled them up finely like a cigar and folded them in two and found a place for them on the other side of my head in a similar position.

Then I swore at the mirror in my bathroom for its being fitted like everything else in the world for people much taller than me. And once again I had to stand on tiptoes just to see my own head, and in particular to check that both hidden objects were invisible from any conceivable angle. My hair was cut like it always is in a perfect globe. Like Jay's. *He is already behind bars, why didn't I learn more from him, instead of just visiting on Thursdays.* But the hairstyle makes *my* head look huge on top of my thin, stunted body. Mascara on. Nose not running yet.

They wouldn't notice a thing.

Satisfied that an eyebrow pencil and a few sheets of toilet paper could reassure me, I pulled the chain and came out of the bathroom with my hands up in the air – just like Jay and I used to do when we played cops and robbers.

One of those plainclothes men saw me and stopped wandering around my house, was actually drawn into the game – and came up to me and prodded my pockets.

'Couldn't you arrest me for something more *ordinary*,' I said in a new harsh tone of voice I'd never heard coming out of my own throat. I swallowed. *Humans can't swallow and breathe at the same time – talking takes precedence over swallowing while we breathe – and I felt I was having to choose all the time now.* 'You know, like robbery, or larceny?' Was I hoping this kind of talk would somehow stop him searching in my hair?

'Your *mouth!*' he replied. I didn't feel a thing when he cursed me or my mouth like that. *I have cut the actual swearword he used to save myself the memory of it.* Normally I would have been mortified. My cheeks would have smarted with humiliation. The charge that word had for me. It used to be as immediate as an electric shock from a length of wire keeping cows in. No longer so.

All of this is to say howcome I got the eyebrow pencil and how I got arrested, I say.

By now Leila is wide awake and fallen into silent reverie. Picking furtively at the ends of her hair. She is making her mind work hard. Overtime.

She looks out into the cell differently now. As if the space between us is no longer so bare. *Let her be.*

So, I write. Huddled over the stub and the jotter pages, the elementary tools I have for writing these very words, words in sentences that will maybe one day be gathered up into pages and made into a book. Printed maybe in a lithe typeface, and bound maybe into a beautiful cover. Words that will fall into and jump out of the grammar that I, as a human being, have the power to breathe into them. *Magic.* Words about events that the world gives birth to, events now being nudged this way now that by us, its conscious inhabitants. Words that can transform our small cell. Bring light and shade into it. Colour and texture. Emotions and thoughts. There's no predicting *what words I will write* nor *in what order exactly.* But I can predict one thing. More than half of the words that I use will correspond to no outside object or event, nor to any description, nor to any action, but will be necessary only for the grammar of what I'm writing down. *Of, than, any, more, the, or, but, no, for, to, only, nor.* A *feeble* prediction. But one within my scope.

Not being used to writing with a pen and paper let alone an eyebrow pencil on toilet paper, having spent twelve hours a day for the last twelve years of my short life in the company of computer keyboards, the very first letter on page one came out big and splodgy.

This is what started the tradition that I will maintain throughout my scribblings, of a big first letter on each new scrap of paper. *Drop cap.*

I also felt obliged, from the very first note on pink toilet paper onwards, to number the bits of paper I get hold of, as I write on them, so that there is some semblance of order in them at least, and also some proof that I, myself, am imposing my will on any bits of paper that come my way. I put the number on the top right hand corner, so that it is clearly visible without wasting any space.

It is my intention to – *I will, I shall* – collect parts of the Criminal Code as I learn of their existence. Some are already included. There are prisoners in here who know whole sections off by heart so getting hold of them won't be any problem. And there's the austere Prison's Library where I copy bits from assorted parts of the Criminal Laws.

What I believe, stupidly no doubt, is that if only I can get to *understand* this code – its whys and wherefores, say – then this will make me understand everything else. My imprisonment here for a start.

There's the question as usual of its *language*. Not which

language the Criminal Code is written in, but of *language* itself. *Any* language. *Grammar.* The *structure* we use to build different meanings. The cruel limitations of grammar in all languages. Its invisibility to all its speakers. Its hidden structures within structures. Boxes in boxes. *We can all with the greatest of ease take any itinerary we choose in our mother tongue, we don't even give it a thought, all of us can, and yet we haven't got the foggiest idea about the map nor its topography. Even the most educated of us, except perhaps some advanced linguistics students.*

I will write in these itineraries. But so often I see them. They spring to view for me, as if I were *some advanced linguistics student.*

After eyebrow pencils and runny noses, my next obsession. *Grammar.* The grammar you and I already know without knowing we know it. The grammar little children can *emit.* All of them. All by themselves. Even if their elders are obliged by some catastrophe – like slavery, say – to make do with some make-shift contact language. Grammar comes out of the next generation's little children's heads. Ready-made. In all its human perfection.

It's a fact that my profession has caused this particular *deformation* in me, this persistent wonder at human language. I try to control it. But the grammar of a sentence can almost make me lose concentration on its content. This is a fault. Sometimes I wish I hadn't ever spent all those hours as a child on Tuesdays at the *L'Alliance Française* reading Noam Chomsky in translation and on Fridays at the British Council reading Derek Bickerton. I should have gone to secondary school instead. *Curiosity killed the cat.*

Nor done all that fiddling with the electronics after hours, for that matter, day after day, night after night. But then again, *that* would have implied having somewhere else to go after work on Mondays, Wednesdays, Thursdays and Saturdays. Maybe if I hadn't ever seen that man in the dairy laughing like that. Maybe if my mother hadn't died like that before I even saw her. Maybe if I hadn't joined the Bicycle Party like that. Maybe if my father hadn't gone to Dr Bythee's like that. Maybe if my aunt had balls.

By now, lots of things fall into the category of *it's a fact.*

It's a fact I am puzzled about the *grammar* of the Criminal Code for a start. The Criminal Code is deceptive. It seems to vacillate from one thing to another. Sneakily. So different from its underneath. One minute it seems so clearly to be a *prediction* of what will inevitably happen under certain conditions to anyone found guilty of doing something – like when it seems to say, 'If you are found guilty, you will be locked up.' More than a prediction, this is a *condition*. Or a *cause*. And then at other times, the same law reads like a *statement* by benevolent elected law-makers to magistrates and judges in the context of a benign doctrine of the separation of powers, saying, 'If the judicial arm finds this kind of thing going on, it forms part of its scheme of duties to find someone guilty and lock him or her up for it.' Sometimes it all just sounds like *definitions,* for example, 'If you set fire to something for nothing, this is arson.' The next minute it reads more like a *threat* from someone very powerful to others unknown – To Whom It May Concern – 'Hey you! You who live in my realm, don't you dare do such and such, because it is hereby written down that you must not. Or else you've got it coming to you. From me and my mates. For ever!' *The same state that drops a bomb on the middle of a market place can arrest a drunk beggar in another market place for disturbing the peace.* And then, subsidiary conditions are often hidden elsewhere. Ignorance of the law is, for example, no excuse.

Whatever the grammar of the thing, I am locked up. The effect is absolute.

And my ignorance is cruel.

But, I have my implements. First I had the eyebrow pencil and the toilet paper. The toilet paper being two-ply made eight sheets of paper. I never used them for their original purpose once I got in. Inside, my nose has simply stopped running. I haven't got any fear left in me of being without toilet paper. Inside, these old obsessions get domesticated, then tamed. And as this happens, they get hounded out by the bad new ones that have taken up residence in me. *Monsters. Prison monsters.* But I could at least write with the materials of my previous obsessions. After a fashion. Until I got better tools.

So, as well as noting down snippets from the Criminal Code, I shall write down childhood memories, *I shall, I will*; this process might hold me in one piece; in some peace; I feel my personality, or lack of it, starting to break into bits, warring bits, already since my incarceration began, bits that I have to struggle to keep together in my cell around my name: I am Juna Bhim *born* motherless to a plumber, *brought up* a twin cow-keeper who stole cane tops, then *converted* at puberty to electronic fiddling, *promoted* as adult to self-taught computer-language-technician bought and sold for millions, reluctantly *elected* secretary, now *turned into* convict. And never quite knowing the reason why. *Ride carefully now you're secretary.*

I feel other bits of myself drift apart or collide with one another: The stunted little body with the big head, the one driven by obsessions and the negotiator, the lost one looking around her for threads to pick up, the rebel, the bearer of remembrances of things past, the dreamer of worlds to come, the player of games, the one who refused to wash her father's feet at a cancelled wedding, the runt of a litter of two, the one who left the little red-pink linen jacket with the curved black collar no longer to ride the motorbike carefully or otherwise, the one who worries about them maiming her brother in Alcatraz, the one who rented the double-storey square house in the morcellement outside of Granbe from Anita who's abroad, the hungry one. Hungry.

That's another thing.

In here, I am hungry. And thirsty. All the time.

Driven nuts by food. Or lack thereof. *If only I had access to the stored up nuts of a squirrel.*

Maybe I will write about milk too. Rich and creamy. Frothy, just out of the cow's udder. And food. *Milk of human kindness.* Of which I was deprived at birth. Food of a vast variety. *Food for thought.* They control every crust of dry bread we get in here. Thirst. Thirst to be quenched by opening up the throat and stopping breathing and pouring in delicious sweet gurgling milk. *Thirst after righteousness.* Hunger. Hunger to be stayed by tasty morsels of bread and a little something. *Hunger for truth.*

The old *Prisons Act* was on the statute books for one-hundred-*and-one* years, an old prisoner tells me at breakfast. One hundred *and one*, she repeats, as if one hundred may have been understandable even for an old colonial law, but that extra *one*, no. Joke was on us though, she says, because when it was repealed, it was replaced by the *Reform Institutions Act, same thing*, she says.

I found out right at the beginning that it isn't enough for me to know *only* the Criminal Code. Ignorance is no excuse. This law is only one of many. On its own it wouldn't tell me who these blue ladies are that guard us, for a start. Nor where such prison officers came from either.

The scope of my own ignorance-is-no-excuse becomes a bit clearer to me, when this old prisoner is telling me what she knows of the history of that law at breakfast.

P rison Officers: No prison officer shall be a member of a trade union. [*Prisons Act (1888) Section 8*] No prison officer shall be a member of a trade union. [*Reform Institutions Act (1989) Section 8*]

Every prison shall be under the charge of a Keeper and such other officers as may be necessary. [*Prisons Act (1888) Section 15(1)*] In every reform institution there shall be an officer in charge. Every officer shall wear the blue uniform of the Service, and be provided with a baton; and may be provided with such firearm, weapon, ammunition and other equipment as may be necessary. [*Reform Institutions Act (1989) Sections 4 and 6(a)*] – noted down from the old prisoner's quotation.

They, them

T he blue ladies are restless tonight. And *restive*, as well.
      I saw them watching us at the evening meal. Watching
over us and watching *out for* us. And *watching* us. I can't get over
it. They suddenly appeared armed with teargas canisters this
evening, for some reason, dangling around their hips. *Orders*,
they say. As if it were a reason.

Instead of marching like they usually do, instead of marching
like they are supposed to when they are on duty, *left right left
right, abou-out turn, left right left right, atte-ention*, etcetera,
they walk around slowly, as if in a daze, *sniffing*. Distinctly
sniffing.

Yes, that's what they do.

They tilt their heads backwards ever so slightly, and then, as
they brush past each other, they flare their nostrils and sniff one
another. They *mill*. Something abstract about them. Refractory.

I can only think they must be picking up *our smell*.

They must be detecting this smell in us, this smell of mounting
rebellion. And it's getting under their skin. The scent of impending mutiny is slowly overpowering them. There are so many of us
inmates jammed in here, each with so many pores emitting their
own particular smell, that's why. The blue ladies can't quite place
what it is, this smell. Or even where it's coming from. But it's
catchy. It arouses in everyone who gets a whiff of it an aura of
discontent. Disaffection. Contagion.

So they've probably got it too now.

Something like a troop of animals *about to* set off headlong
and to stampede, but not yet, not quite yet. Just the moment of

the presentiment minutes before the stampede actually starts. That's what we smell of.

For us the feeling is harmonious.

But as for the blue ladies. They just don't know what's got into them.

Maybe they think it's only the heat. Or the overcrowding, and the overwork. Or the intensity of their required vigilance. Causing this trance-like milling. They've got this premonition that they *need* to pick up the scent from each other without ceasing.

They move around with their weight tilted forwards on to the balls of their feet like that, instead of the usual slovenly style with their weight spread evenly over the whole of the sole of the foot, dragged along the length of the day shift, shuffled across the breadth of the night shift, day and night after day and night.

Something makes them now suddenly push the strands of hair back from their faces in this distracted manner, causes them one by one to turn their heads around backwards, to raise their noses up towards the ceiling and to draw air in surreptitiously, like foxes, and to *sniff*. Trying all the while by a sneaky elongation of their necks to make their nostrils reach beyond the range of the smell emitted by their own deodorant.

I hadn't intended to write about them. But then again, I haven't got much choice about what happens here nor when it happens. All order and proportion is lost. I must deal with things one by one. Forty days and forty nights have passed. And right now, I find myself watching them. And I've got my stub of pencil and a few sheets of paper, bigger than I've ever had before. A4 duplicating paper. Yellowed and musty smelling. I try to smell where it has been. In some cellar? In case the suppliers block it during a strike? Forgotten in a bonded warehouse? Stolen by a storekeeper, sold to a dhall-puri vendor, turned up in prison, in exchange for.

L eila is speaking fast all of a sudden, like a squall. I look up. She's speaking about someone. Making this someone materialise in our cell. I push pencil and paper under my blanket and listen to her, 'She said to me, "If you could just pop them into my embroidered cotton bag – I brought it along specially for you – for your *valuables*. *Slip* them off and *drop* them into it. Stops the police getting the satisfaction of ripping them away from you, doing an inventory, and getting the upper hand on you."'

'What are you talking about?' I ask her. 'Who said this to you? Who?'

Leila starts in on a story so abruptly that at first I'm left behind. Lonely.

'Who is this *she*?' I ask Leila.

'Boni, that's who. Boni said: *Go on, slip them off, and pop them in*. When Boni said that, at that exact moment, I realised I was trapped. An animal in a noose. Surrendering.' She begins to bring her life into the cell.

'"*Take off my bracelet you mean?*" I asked her. I couldn't believe it, Juna, I mean I was so innocent, I didn't know anything. "Yes, of course, your bracelet, your earrings, your watch. Get your money out too. I'll keep this little bag for you, till you come out," Boni said. Of course, Boni's got no time for *valuables*. You could hear it in her voice. But she will keep mine for me.'

Leila had felt *the arrest*.

She felt panic. She says she looked at her bare arm. Put a hand to her bare earlobes.

'I thought of Mantee,' she says. 'She was young when she came to live in our street with her new husband. Not much older than me. Maybe a year later, it was, her husband had an accident and died. I close my eyes now and I can still see her. She is standing there next to his laid out body, when all her relatives and all her in-laws start tearing her jewellery off her piece by piece. Right there in front of everyone. Before the funeral. Stripping her. As if to say: *Teach her.* As if to shout at her: *Going and becoming a widow like that!*

'So now. *Pop. Slip. Drop.* So that I wouldn't break when I got locked up.

'Boni said nothing unnerves them more than you turning up at the police station without your valuables on you. She said it sticks out a mile you aren't the pleading type, not one of those anything-to-be-given-bail-at-once types. I didn't really want bail anyway.

'Boni folded the cotton embroidered bag up and put it deep into her *tant,* one of those with a woven cover. It was on her lap. In the bus.' So Leila says.

And everything goes all quiet in our cell.

'So, that is how I *know* Boni,' Leila says now, breaking the heavy silence, silence that *awaits an arrival, still awaits an arrival.* The past is rushing inwards now. Bringing premonitions with it. Has my threat of a message given her a premonition?

She gets up, and stands in the middle of the cell, shaking the new blanket that has landed between us. Shaking it out as though she is spring cleaning in a big, modern flat. It floats up in the air, straight, like a flying rug. It's so airless, the blanket hovers. *The airlessness doesn't make us think of a cyclone.* Then the blanket falls. Now she is laying it down in its place between us, straightening it out on the floor between our two bunks. Now she is crawling over it carefully, folding it in half. Perfectly. At right angles. Smoothing out all the wrinkles. Then she sits back and looks at it. Then, quite suddenly she starts shaking her head. She picks it up again, stands up with it in both hands, and shakes it out more carefully, lays it down again, flattens it, folds it in two, kneels on it, squares it up and smoothes out every single crinkle. This time when she sits back, she looks positively critical of it. So there she goes again, picking up the blanket, shaking it hard, lifting it outwards, and starting to lay it down again. More perfectly. More smoothly. Not a single wrinkle left. Then she scrunches it up and starts all over again. *More* prison obsessions. She is getting on my nerves, but I control my desire to shout at her. To clout her. To wring her neck. Instead, I must let her be.

Since I found out what Leila's *in* for, and since I told her a secret, the atmosphere has changed in here. Another thing: I am scared. Scared of the word *mutiny*. Scared out of my wits. Shitless. I feel my heart beat-ger-beat, beat-ger-beat loudly in my ears. Fear makes the roots of my hair taut. I feel more perspiration prickle and then sting as it gathers into drops.

There is this intimacy now. And regret.

'By doing that, Boni helped me,' she goes on. She stops doing her stupid housework at last. She stands up as if the spotlight is on her now again. I am relieved. It's just another of her games. Her turn to act. She bows in a matter-of-fact way. Maybe she will offer me something beginning with a '*c*'. I can't bear to think of such things as come flooding to mind, my stomach aching for them: Chocolate pudding, chocolate milk-shake, chocolate-coated ice-cream lollipop, chocolate cake, chocolate-chip biscuits, chocolate liqueur, chocolate fudge, hot chocolate, chocolate ice-cream.

'No joke,' she says. 'Such a *little* thing she did for me. It meant so much to me. That's *what*. It's something to do with computers, isn't it, where you both work.' *Wish I had got to know Boni better. Why was I such a self-centred fool? What did I expect life to bring to me? On a platter, too? Ride carefully, she said, now.*

'She *heard* they were looking for me, heard through the grapevine – everyone in the underworld knew, and they spread things around until they got into the underground – and she knew I would have to give myself up sooner or later. So she came to see me at my boyfriend's hiding place, don't know how she knew where it was. She said she would come with me when I went to give myself up. To help me. And she did, did help me.'

So that's it. *Probably found this one too young to ask to be a messenger. Who would she have been contacting inside then? Is that person now outside? Don't blame Boni for hesitating with Leila. She is too young.*

85

Who has Boni given the new message to now, to be brought inside to me?

Why are *you*, whoever you may be, so damn late?

I ward off the monsters that accompany this thought.

'Then Boni handed me a fifty cent plastic bag, she did, in exchange for the cloth bag and in it there was a green face cloth, a bar of pink soap, a yellow toothbrush, a tube of toothpaste and a copy of *L'Express*.

' "You're *remand*," Boni said to me. "Allowed these. Always remember that. And newspapers and pen and paper. And food from the outside." That's how I got the stub and jotter pages. "One look at you and the blue ladies will know that you can look after yourself," Boni told me. "Even if it isn't true." '

Leila's bit of theatre is drawing to a close now. I feel a sense of mourning somewhere deep inside my chest. I mourn the end of each play.

She is back at the blanket. Is picking it up and is shaking it again. This time mechanically. Nervously. She is straightening it out again. Really smooth and square. *House proud*.

Then she pulls herself together.

'So that's why I am preparing a nice bed for our visitor,' she adds, 'because Boni was so good to me. When's our secret coming true then?' Her mood has got confident again. And generous. I can see she is trying to break out of the prison mode of useless repetition. Even at her age, she gets it, and even at her age, she resists. She sits quiet now.

'I'm glad I told you about our visitor,' I say.

P *rison discipline*: The Commissioner of Prisons may impose a penalty of confinement in a light punishment cell with or without forfeiture of one-third rations, or on bread and water diet, on any prisoner who commits any of the following offences against prison discipline [including] – using articles prohibited by prison regulations; talking with another prisoner without authority; wilfully giving or causing unnecessary trouble. [*Prisons Act (1888) Section 41*] A prohibited article means an article which is not issued under the authority of the Commissioner or may not be introduced into or removed from an institution or be in the possession of a detainee. Every detainee shall be subject to prison discipline and to the provisions of this Act or any regulations made under this Act. [*Reform Institutions Act (1989) Sections 22 and 2*] – Copied from the Prison's Notice Board.

I write. On paper. With pencil. Prohibited articles.

I eat most of the more lyrical bits. This is also illegal. I get so lost in thought when I'm deep in writing, I don't hear the blue lady coming until it's too late to roll it up and stick it in a hole in the wall. So I stuff it into my mouth instead and swallow it. Yeah, there are holes in the walls here. Nooks and crannies. I suppose someone or some string of someones before us have dug the holes for keeping something else in. Probably gandia. Or bits of razor blade, or matches. Or god knows what, but not paper. Maybe it was the children in the reformatory just digging for nothing. *Borstal*, it was. Digging with their nails, I suppose. To make at least an attempt at resisting their confinement. So anyway, I eat most of the more lyrical bits.

Shall I look for them, the lyrical bits, in the slop bucket tomorrow? Or are my guts too good at digesting the lyrical bits, them being written on Corotex or jotter paper? Other than the odd bit of tomato peel, I suppose it'll all be crap. Human digestion is a wonderful thing.

By now, I have forgotten about my *valuables*. I can tell you.

Even Leila has forgotten about hers by now too. We *accompany* one another in the cell. Keeping monsters out of our minds.

'S till not here, your new friend,' she says, as if it were my fault, and I reply with a stinging rhyme.

> *Patience is a virtue.*
> *Virtue is a grace.*
> *Grace is a little girl*
> *Who didn't wash her face.*

I am hurled back into the spiteful songs of a girl child. It is partly my impatience, of course, because I just can't wait to see *you*. I am in expectation, even before knowing who *you* are.

I *love* visitors. I've only got one friend who comes on Thursdays, my colleague from work, and who I speak to downwards into those holes while I try to look upwards into the thick Perspex at the same time. To see the effect of my words. And when she speaks into the holes on her side, I see only the top of her head – she hasn't got dandruff – and not the expression in her eyes.

'Look!' I say pointing at the cell window. Must keep her spirits up. And mine. I'm standing on tiptoe on top of my bunk, opposite the window. There are the tips of three bright green lakoklis leaves trying to peep into our cell. The fluorescent light from our cell window brightens the green of those leaves, turning them into an almost blue colour. *Or is it mauve again?*

'OK, let's have a closer look at this matter,' she says it with such gusto.

I'm game. And time drags so slowly along. I look at the door though, meaning we will have to listen carefully, because we are expecting a visitor.

She stands up and puts her legs wide apart back to the wall under the window. Anyone watching us would know we have done this before. Many times. She cups her hands together next to her right side and bends her knees up and down in a buoyant way.

I put my hands on her left shoulder, my left foot in her stirrup, and we go a-one, a-two, a-three-ee, and I leap out of her hand, and up at the bars on the window, and just manage to grab hold of them with two monkey hands. Then she positions herself under me, and I climb tiptoe on to her shoulders and stand on them. From here I can see out. *I don't climb up her, stirrup to shoulder, she's not reliable enough yet.*

'What can you see tonight?' she is impatient.

'Much the same. I can see the billboard for *your* insurance. It's still there. Shall I read it to you again?' She calls it *her* insurance, for some reason.

'Oh, please do!'

We like this.

'First there's the little letters at the top. *We care because you pay us to. And then we pay you, too!* And then big it says *Secure Life*. There's the baby swinging in the *julwa*. It is still smiling. Yes, maybe you are right, maybe it is a boy baby. He is innocent.

'All the leaves are still,' I say. 'Dead still. There's a kind of premonition in the tree. There is not a breath of. *Oh look!* Now that's funny. There's this one, yes just the one, leaf, a single lakoklis leaf, it is slightly detaching itself from the rest, and it's starting to move. I can't believe it. It is slowly swinging on its silver-mauve stalk, to the left and to the right like a pendulum. The movement is getting heavier, as though it is following a beat, Leila. You won't believe this but *all the others* are still dead still. And it is moving like the dull tick tock of a metronome now. All on its own. Tick tock, tick tock. You can't believe what it looks like. The others are all staying absolutely still. The mad leaf is beginning to twist and turn and to swing back and forth, to and fro, front and back, side to side. All the other leaves around it are still unmoved. Unmoving. And now, the one leaf is speeding up.

It's going out of control, it is in complete defiance of what seems possible. It is beginning, this one leaf is beginning to shake and to dance and to gyrate in a most frenetic, wild, abandoned way. A solo. And the other leaves are all still staying dead still. It is as though they have decided to transfer their energy, some kinetic energy, all the energy they have, from the root of the tree upwards, along themselves, into that one leaf. As though it comes up from the root. And then all the other leaves, without motion, hand the energy along silently.'

At this point we both jump slightly, and almost lose balance. I grab for the bars. We have heard the sharp cry of the two trunks scraping together again. She says, 'Can you see the two trunks?'

I crane my neck this way and that.

'Yes, I think I can. It must be those two big trunks out there.'

'But is there any wind?'

'No, none.'

I lift my weight off her shoulders, suspend myself from the bars, and she knows to step back now. I push away from the wall, and jump down in front of her.

'So!' This is the way she announces that she will be asking me a question; she says 'So!' I look up from my writing. It must have been the metronome-like movement of the leaf suggesting it to her, passing along some message to her, 'Does your sentence get longer or shorter when they make the seconds longer?' But for a moment I think she is talking about *sentences* in my lyrical and un-lyrical writing. But she isn't.

She asks this rudely and it's to do with my imprisonment.

'Same as yours,' I reply.

We flare up so easy.

We have, at this point, the two of us, to some extent already given up believing in the sacred assumption that you can count time as if it were bottles of space.

She and I lie and wait. We lie in wait. The sweat isn't drying on us, and we look at the sets of little notches on the wall in that dull-bright electric light now making every detail inside our cell clear to the naked eye. The notches are all, for some reason, clustered together in one corner. Like the wasps she keeps stored away under the corner of her bunk. Huddling there even in death.

We look first at our own set of notches. We also engrave ours in the same corner. We try to make them really straight and dignified and equal and equidistant from one another. Paying the respect due to each day. Without success. Forty suns have risen since I was closed up. When I arrived here we started notching. Thirty-nine times, because once I slept in Tiko and the other bank robber's cell. Then Leila's cellmate died. Poor

Mopey-Sue. And they moved me in. Now each time the sun comes up, we notch.

Then we look at all the other previous sets of notches. Some sets are higgledy-piggledy. Some rise slowly with the passing of every day, signifying hope. Others shrink, and look like despair. Maybe death row. She stands up and goes over and counts the longest set of notches again.

577.

When these 577 were etched in, time was probably still considered to be divisible into equal bits. You can see from the confidence with which they are etched. A sudden jab and a short line. We notch with a hairclip she smuggled in and which she hides in her messy hair. Some of the previous prisoners' notches are no doubt equal to later ones' notches. Others aren't. And now notches, our notches, are even more worthless as far as general comparisons with all the other sets of notches go. Even our fortieth notch, the one we will do tomorrow morning, will not be equal, in any absolute sense, to our thirty-nine other notches. And it will give this away to future eyes in this cell.

But we have decided to go on with the notching. We will still mark the rising sun. We will not be deterred.

She's expecting a heavy sentence. Effusion of a police officer's blood is costly by any system of weights and measures.

'So!' she says. This means yet another question. Her tone is furious.

'So! When did this all start, this changing of the length of time and so forth?'

Young people feel the rage. They feel it more. She is starting to shine now, with sweat and rage and the lilac-coloured light. *Leila is lilac*. I wonder whether to say this aloud, and decide against. I just sing it to myself: *Leila is lilac*.

'How can they change the length of your sentence like that? It isn't fair! It just isn't.' She is cross.

So I pass the time of night by telling her about the economics of it. First the elongation of the year, then of the month, then the week, then the hour, then the minute.

Then I sing a jingle, or a *generic*, as they called it, that was popular at the time of the first elongation:

Every year a lea-eap year
Every year a lea-eap year
Use it for your profit
Be blessed with good cheer
Every year a lea-eap year
Put it in your pocket.

'Where is this supposed visitor anyway? Or. . . Or, do you think she's getting the treatment from the blue ladies?' Then she says quietly, 'They were all acting so weird earlier on. Sniffing one another like that. Did you notice?'

So, she noticed them too.

Today, with the announcement of the change in the length of each second, they can have no idea what is welling up inside us at this very moment.

When I look up to answer her, I see that she has fallen fast asleep. Fast asleep.

You in the singular

D *efinition of the state of Mauritius*: Mauritius includes – (a) the Islands of Mauritius, Rodrigues, Agalega, Tromelin, Cargados Carajos and the Chagos Archipelago, including Diego Garcia. [*Constitution of Mauritius Act (1968) (Section 111, as amended for Republic status in 1991)*] – Copied down in the Prison's Library.

I t must be around about the time that they are actually
changing the length of a second that *you* come along. Round
about 00 hours. A hushed midnight, when anything could be
happening.

You get hurled in at us.

Leila wakes up with a start.

Just like that. In the middle of the night, you come flying in.
And land with a soft bump.

You arrive. A granny materialising in our cell.

Literally shoved in by rude hands. Literally falling. Dropping
in, as Leila puts it. And you drop on to the blanket she has laid
out so carefully again and again, on the floor between us. Soft
flesh, you have, and the reticence of an old, old lady. And see-
through bones. We allowed you in somehow.

Oh, it's *you*. So this is *you*. I study you quickly before the blue
lady turns off the light. A déjà vu? Then I stare into the darkness,
but see nothing. I strain, but it is still too black.

Not a déjà vu, no.

I have actually seen you before.

Recently. Yes. *Today?* Yes, I saw you earlier on today. Where
did they keep you all day then? Are you beaten and bruised? On
the way back from the Court, it was, when we were in the prison
lorry, so many of us herded in and squashed down, I overheard
you tell your blue lady something. It was Blue One-One again. In
charge of *you* on the way back from Court. A line or two of a
story of some sort. She wasn't even listening. But I was. You were
so intent.

' *"The Islands are closed."* That's what they told me at the ship's desk,' you said to Blue One-One. 'I with two babes-in-arms at the time,' you said holding them in your gesture to Blue One-One, one on each hip.

'*What?*' you said you replied to the official. '*But look, here's my boat ticket. What you mean closed?*'

'*The Islands are closed,*' the official said to you, '*Can't you hear me? Are you deaf or something? Next!*' he shouted, looking out of his hatch right past you at the woman behind you in the queue with her ticket in her outstretched hand too. '*Next!*'

Now you have arrived here. On the mat, as it were. Between us. In our common land. There's a strange feeling in you. That you are brimming over with something. You are all overflowing with feelings. I have never picked up such vibrations. You quiver.

'I am a messenger,' you say.

'Doesn't half look like it,' Leila says.

The only bits left are factual stuff, so superficial that when I am writing them, at the very first footfall, the first movement outside the door, when some blue lady touches the electronic pad, I hear all this and it warns me and I roll up the bit of paper really tight and stick it in one of those holes in the wall in time. For all the intense bits, it gets too late, and I have to swallow them whole.

Anyway. Factual bits.

I clinched a deal this morning. Before breakfast. In exchange for one of my two bananas a day for seven days, I will get a pencil. Full length. HB. Bananas are more than gold in here. Together with coconut and a rare stick of incense and the low call of a conch some prisoner blows into in the middle of the night, bananas are holy.

So today when they told about the seconds being longer, I was already eating only *one* of my two bananas, because I'm paying for the pencil. And I felt the loss. Sacrifice of the sacred fruit. For the means of writing words.

Must get Leila more pen and paper and outside meals and newspapers. Remand prisoners' rights. Boni said so. Boni makes facts more real.

C *onfession*: Where the accused admits the charge to be true, his confession shall be recorded, and judgement delivered according to law. [*Criminal Procedure Act (1853) Section 75*] – Copied down from the Prison's Library.

Y ou are lying there, just like the rug that was hurled in before you. Just like your precursor. Dark grey and without much life. You don't look much like a messenger to me either, I must admit. The light is off now. And once our eyes get used to the dark, everything is mauve again. But you lie there in the heat and in that airless gloom in our cell and you say, 'I am a messenger.'

So I say, 'I am the one the message is for.' I give you my name. 'I am Juna. Juna Bhim,' I say. 'Have you got a message for me?'

I stare at you as if you are an oracle. You don't move an iota. And yet you are like a mother. Someone's mother. Someone's grandmother. Maybe *her* grandmother, Leila's. Or my own dead mother, back again after her breathing stopped.

'What's your name, if I may ask?' I ask you. I offer to cover you with the blanket although it's stifling hot. Your fingers restless on the edge of the blanket, moving this way and that, uneasy and continuous almost imperceptible fidgets, in the pale light. *As though you will die soon.* The thought goes through my mind. *Or be reborn.*

The trees scrape together, calling a lost soul, again. I shudder.

Then I see something distant in you, and the way you lie there. *You don't care.* You are not like a mother at all. Not any more, maybe. You have become abstract and distracted and you just don't care any more. You just arrive and lie there and say you've got a message, and move your soft fingertips like that, each a butterfly, utterly indifferent to the things around you.

You are far away.

I start to get the distinct feeling that you are some kind of guardian angel. *Sent in* like this. And I don't like it one bit. I don't want an indifferent guardian angel. I don't want any guardian angel. I feel resentment building up. *I am being invaded.* Your very presence begins to threaten my autonomy. I start to wish you had never come. You pull your scarf off your head and your short curls, whitish mauve and springy, some plaited and standing up, some curling any old which way catch the light. They never used to let us keep our scarves. Now they give us enough rope to.

'They call me Honey's Mother. My name is Gracienne. Mama Gracienne. Mama Gracienne Townsend. Yes, I've got a message for you. But I'm worried. I've got a worry. I think they have caught the one who gave it to me. I think they have captured her. I think they have got her in here somewhere.' As you say *somewhere*, you move your hand around vaguely, so that light catches your passing palm. Caught in a spider's web, flailing around looking for another caught one.

You *do* care, after all.

'Who? What is it? What word do you bring? Who have they got?'

You then stay quiet.

I am patient.

I wait.

She isn't. Leila is not patient. She doesn't. Leila can't wait.

She interrupts the silence. Just like that. She changes the subject. She asks you, 'What case you in for then?'

Criminal thoughtlessness.

Anger and impatience stir in me. What with all this rising need to rebel. I force myself not to waste any anger on her. A child.

'Confession,' you say, 'I'm in for *confession*.'

'To a priest or something?' Leila snaps.

'No,' you reply.

'Confession to what?' she goes on insistent, persistent.

'Confession to murder.'

I can't believe what I'm hearing.

'Who'd you kill then?' Leila is not put off. She is relentless now, 'Who'd you kill?'

'My daughter.'

'Your own daughter.'

'My daughter, yes. My own.'

'Did you *do* it?'

'Yes, I think I did.'

'How old was she? How did you kill her?'

'Oh. She was your age,' you say, turning to look at me as if I had just come into focus. 'Yes, round about your age. Or maybe around *yours*?' You turn your gaze back on Leila now. Do you now remember this daughter of yours when she was Leila's age, too? And at the first steps she ever made as well, all at once? 'She was called Honey. Everyone called her Honey.'

'How did you do it?'

'I don't know.'

'When did you do it?'

'Oh. Some time back.'

Silence falls on the three of us. Confused and confusing.

'A loon,' Leila announces. She says this falling back on to her bunk, kicking her legs into the air almost with glee. 'We've got a loon locked in here with us. Some new girl.' She does the screws loose sign with her hand.

Leila is so rude.

I go in hard, and tell her to lay off you, and stop cross-questioning you in the middle of the night. For god's sake you haven't even given the message and she's in after your blood like that.

I talk to *you* then, I turn to you, and I say, 'You don't look as if you would hurt a fly, Mama Gracienne.'

She feels the criticism as if it were a blow, Leila does. Her eyes burn under her joined eyebrows, in shame and anger. Her crooked lips quiver in a lopsided smile. She may not be able to control herself.

'Don't let yourself go!' I shout at her. 'Hold on to yourself. Just because our convention has broken down, just because past and future have come in, it's no good you just falling apart like that and attacking this poor woman. A bit more *retinue*, please, girl!' She hasn't got any pity in her, that girl. Once the taboo is broken, there she goes, flying straight into the past. Worse still, into *your* past. Head first, and digging into it. Squelching around in it with her fingers. Nails bitten to the quick and all.

So I shout at her.

While I'm shouting, you raise your hand, Mama Gracienne, into the air, and tilt your head backwards and say, 'I can smell a cyclone.'

'Loon,' Leila mutters. Then she shrugs, says she's sorry. She's very sorry, and she's very sleepy too, she says. She goes quiet. And like a puppy that's suddenly overtired, and as if to prove her youthfulness and her innocent guilt, she keels over and falls asleep again. Fitful at first, and then peaceful.

We hear Leila breathing, regular and even. It is not feigned.

The answers come to those who *listen*, I think, nastily, even if not to those who stand and wait.

Then *you* speak to me.

'You must go to the hospital, Juna,' you say, '*to the hospital.* Boni said so. Tomorrow.'

You came into the prison so differently. You came in bringing the message through, giving yourself up. Softly. Repudiating some old silence. Did you make some vow in Honey's name? When did your inaction turn to movement like this? And cause you to start drifting like the remembrance of things past into our cell? And why should a mother decide like this to confess?

The Confession. That's what Leila calls you. That's what you are. The Confession. Gracienne Townsend, the Confession.

And we are letting you in. Into our cell, and into our lives. She and I let you in.

She sleeps there. On the other side of you, there she lies. Leila Sadal. *The Effusion of Blood*.

And me, Juna Bhim. *The Allegator*.

I haven't got much time now. Only till morning.

Leila is still asleep. Still deep in the sleep of a child, peaceful and restless at the same time, completely immobile for ages and then suddenly moving her heavy limbs. From time to time she grinds her teeth loudly. The sounds she makes all rasp around the cell walls.

You sleep too now, Mama Gracienne, lightly, more like a grandmother than like a mother, unconfident even in sleep, exhausted by your confession. Constant dozing off, only to open your eyes, whites showing wide awake, without warning, and then dozing off again. Your hair mauve in this light.

And there's me, lying here with tasks and responsibilities bigger than myself. I am so small.

Little.

I look at my minute wrists and miniature hands in that palpable dark light. And the two warts on my hand, even they are little. I hate those two warts. There they sit next to my left thumb, uninvited. I turn my hands over quickly and back again. Even the nails are thin, transparent, the moons at the quick are a pale mauve. Then there are my stubby square feet. I buy shoes from the children's department. Hips narrow, thighs hollow, breasts lean and milkless, collarbone covered in tight skin.

We, a family, closed into this cell.

This thought makes me smile.

For us here and also for my first family.

For my dead mother, whether through twins trying to rush out together feet first, or a large coconut falling sixty foot on to her head, or drowning in the tub she washed clothes in, for a lost father, whether his soul was sucked out of him against his will and spirited away by Dr Bythee's chauffeur in a dark grey car with retractable fins, or whether he exchanged it freely for a small plot of land, and I smile for a brother jailed whether for singing a song at Swazi beach or for growing a few shrubs of a plant with a dark green starful of pointed leaves.

Now *this family*.

Can we *mutiny*? The three of us?

And others?

Are we capable of it? Us of all unlikely people? You, a mother confessing to guilt, me a computer language expert turned Allegator, she, I turn and look at her, a dull teenager, an Effusion of Blood. I feel tenderness for her. If she were my daughter I would look at her and be ashamed of her size. *Outsize*.

Which *hospital* do you mean, Honey's Mother? Which hospital can it be? Not much point in asking you, how would you know? In any case, surely you would have specified if you had known. Which hospital *could* you mean?

I'll have to work it out myself, I think almost aloud.

Tomorrow will soon be today.

If they send no word as to *which* hospital, I must assume that it will have to be the one they take me to for *general* things, complaints of a kind that would not take me straight to a *specific* hospital, not say, the Ear, Nose and Throat Hospital in Vakwa or to the Moka Eye Hospital, or to the Cardiac Unit at Kandos.

In this way I start thinking about what complaint I'll need to mimic. I realise that I must resign myself to the fact that *they* will probably incidentally find out about.

None of their business anyway, I hasten to add.

I fall into a fitful sleep.

The sound of the sea is all around me. Waves crrre-cre-cresting and breaking. I am swimming a slow breast-stroke in warm sandy-bottomed seawater. Tranquil, still waters, running deep. I swim into a deep navy blue cave in the coral, just inside the reef where the water is otherwise turquoise and translucent. When I dive under, I open my eyes and I see that the sun is cutting the sea into shafts, slicing the water into wedges, and lighting up the plankton, dot-sized fairy lights. Each dot emits a mauve colour, pulsing like a celestial body. Nebulae, I mumble under the water, causing bubbles to escape and rise up in a sudden flurry. Nebulae. I swim around in the cave now, as if to check its size. It is the size of our cell. I am however pleased to discover that there is only *one* opening to it. An *octopus house*. I am the octopus. This is my house. I can go in, as octopus are wont to do, and use one or two legs only, pulling bits of coral and shells and sand up behind me, closing my only door, watching my two exposed legs, while all my other legs are safely hidden on the inner side, protected from passing eels. Eels are known to sneak up on the blind side of an octopus which is concentrating on its front door – piling shells up conscientiously with one or two legs – and to attack through the back door and bite a neglected leg right off. So in my dream, I begin to close myself in, just like an octopus does, into a cave with only one opening. I swim up to the opening of the cave which is like the window in our cell only a bit bigger and a bit lower and I dive down and stretch my hands way out of the cave and pull bits of dead coral towards the mouth of the cave building them up on the sill of the cave window. Two barnacled rocks, some old sea-polished bones, a handful of dead shells, a bleached sea-urchin, a few stringy bits of greenish seaweed. I do this to block up the entrance in such a way that I can open it up again later, and then when there is a tiny hole left, I pull up handfuls of fine white sand from the outside, leaving a small hole to withdraw my arm in by, depositing one last big cowry shell in the hole from the inside. I feel house proud. My housework has been well done. But I have difficulty swimming backwards away from the hole. I realise I am not so much like an octopus as like an eel, myself. I have sloughed off my pock-marked ugly suckers, I am smooth and symmetrical, with no limbs any more. The handless maiden. I can't swim backwards at all any more. I feel pleased at this helplessness. No feet left to be washed. No hands to wash with. Secure in the five walls of my house. Proud of my clean front yard. Neat and tidy for all the neighbours to see. But then I realise that the foam from the waves breaking on the reef is slowly filling up the gaps between the bits of coral and shells and sand so that I can't breathe any more in there. I realise it is all my own fault. I haven't got any of my eight arms and hands left now. I'm walled in. The air is getting less and less. I start sweating with panic.

When I wake up I'm sweating in the heat of our cell. An airlessness worse than before has settled into the cell. I am scared to go to sleep again, in case I have more bad dreams. And in case I oversleep and miss my cue.

It's got to be *before* they give out the morning rations. More convincing that way. No one would forego her banana rations. Most people who play up do it only *after* they get their two bananas for the day. Such opportunism is noted by the powers that be. I'll only miss one banana anyway, because I'm still paying back for the pencil. But I'll owe that prisoner a banana for another day afterwards. Never mind that now. I'll have to begin before rising bell.

PART II

I start screaming at the first glimpse of daylight that manages to peep through the high up cell window.

Blue murder.

It's the only thing I can think of doing, really. Scream for all I'm worth. Scream my lungs nearly out. I've been given the message. And tomorrow has become today. And so I scream.

As I start screaming, I realise that inside of me, deep inside, there is a vast scream that wants to be screamed. I scream, cry, wail, shout, yell, and, as the sound echoes back at me, I scream again, and I begin to feel that I'm not going to want to stop screaming ever, that I'm going to want to go on and on and on screaming, for ever and for ever. I feel that the air in the cell is getting used up. As though there is foam forming in the cell window. As if I may get silenced by it. As if I am a mutineer at the bottom of the Black Hole of Calcutta. As if death may come and fetch me like it did Honey. So I scream and scream.

You sit up, lean over and shake me. You of all people. You get a hold of my two shoulders and you shake me.

Of course, you get a bad fright. Leila does too.

You are terrified. This is only too obvious. You, who have only just arrived inside. I'm sorry. I didn't mean to scare you. You, waking up for the first time like this in a strange place. A very strange place indeed. Inside the Women's High Security Electronic Prison that used to be the children's reformatory. And waking up to that pandemonium. I am sorry. But you brought me the message. I'm not saying it's your own fault. But you have got some responsibility.

Y ou only work out later in the day that it must have all been put on. Kick yourself. Almost laugh, you do, Mama Gracienne. Smile to yourself anyway. Quite a show, you think, and shake your head at your own innocence.

When Leila asks what the message was you say there wasn't one. But, you say, you can *smell* something in the air. You've got a premonition. You can feel the future coming at us. There's a *cyclone*, you say it again, a cyclone far away still, but coming nearer.

A *cute appendicitis* is diagnosed from the sick bay itself. So, they don't give me any breakfast. In case I need an operation.

I am to be transported to hospital. They put me into what looks like an ordinary prison van from the outside, but it is fitted out like an ambulance on the inside. With a dilapidated drip stand and a rusty medicine box.

Inside with me is a blue lady. Not one I've ever seen before. A new blue lady. New to me anyway. She is handcuffed to me. Such a silly thing for them to do to themselves let alone to me. We make up a clumsy eight-legged creature in a small cave. I am used to this. The system of tagging us with the electronic thing under the skin fell into disrepair or disrepute at some point. *Upkeep charges* or something, they said. I am particularly interested in what exactly happened to that system. It was always riddled with difficulties. Back with the handcuffs now. *Low-tech*, they call them. On with the *low-tech* then, love, she says. In her free hand, she clutches a handful of paper money, all scrunched up. A kitty of some sort. Tamed money.

The van sets off. Through the criss-crossed windows I see coloured signs. Billboards I didn't ask to see. I see Leila's insurance sign close-up. *Secure Life.* Buses with advertisements painted on them flash past in front of my eyes. Motorcyclists' helmets go past with their sound effects. I hear the bridge rumble first, then see its supports. See the sea through it. Dull silvery-blue-grey. We cross the bridge. Rumble, rumble, shudder, shudder. A big pantechnicon behind us. Oscillations start. Wonder if an army of marchers could manage to get the oscillations to go wild, out of control, and cause it finally to break if they were to do a left-right-left-right on it. *Must remember to pretend to be sick still.* From time to time anyway. And try to look out of these squares of wire that enmesh the windows at the same time, in case I miss something. Now, as the sun comes out, I see only a sun glare through the windows. Inside the van is dark. My pupils are too wide open for this light. It is hot in here, too hot, even though the van is moving. It's as though more and more hot air comes through the thing, pressing down on us, a single creature with eight limbs. Instead of the air cooling me, it makes me hotter. Like a bellows on hot coals. I can't get away from the heat. And I'm tied down, tied down to this blue lady. Traffic sounds get more busy. Hooting and revving up of engines. Stopping and starting. Exhaust fumes. Then a long stretch at an even speed.

All of a sudden, the driver starts to shift into lower gears, bringing the pleasant feeling of deceleration. I can hear traffic all round, so it isn't the hospital yet. It's somewhere on the way to the hospital. There's a dog nearby, and it barks. Another dog joins it. Are they barking at us? Moving in on us in a circle, all pointing their muzzles at us, putting their heads back, and barking? Don't blame them. Imagine the smells that come sneaking out of this van of ours up their snouts and into their brains. I try to pick up the smells myself. I put my head back and sniff. First is the smell of blue soap. Some antiseptic in here somewhere as well, probably in that rusty box. And then alongside this, the smell of imprisonment. Illness. Panic. Unwashed balls – it must be used for men prisoners as well. The perspiration of humiliation. I think I can smell blood, dried blood, and the faintest hint of urine. Old urine. And, is it possible, I think, I believe I can pick up the smell of approaching rain. *Is it possible?* And then the smell I'm trying to keep out of my olfactory field, the smell of all the blue lady's lotions and potions. You name it, she wears it. It stinks. I hate her. Hate with a dull, harsh hatred. What could I do to her? I can only think of one thing. I could let out a large turd. That's what I think. There she would be handcuffed to me and my turd. Right next to her. I too can define the smell of the place. Must remember that.

I wonder what I'm getting reduced to now. An animal would not have such a thought.

The van is pulling up outside a little shop, I see it through the mesh. I smell some old alcohol, probably from the tavern part of the shop. A dark and rebellious smell. *Useless* rebellion. The driver gets out and comes around, unlocks the back door. Yes, *she* is locked in as well. She unlocks herself, freeing herself of the handcuffs. She rubs her wrist as if to clean it. She seems to count her four limbs. Then she counts her money, and after that in a swift move, as if she's done this a million times, she handcuffs my wrist to the leg of the seat, a kind of bench we're sitting on, in that Black Mariah. I have to lean forwards now because of being handcuffed to the leg of the bench, so I can't see out of the window any more. Suddenly, before she even gets out, it starts raining heavily outside, unevenly and in waves, big drops making a loud noise on the top of the prison van. It is all encompassing, this sound. Deafening. It brings with it the fear of being tied down in a flood like this, head between my knees, and the waters rising. What would she do? What would the driver say? Unlock and untie me, or leave me to drown? Head down in the rising tide of floodwater?

He lets her out, and locks the door after her. The rain goes on. I control the panic by laughing at myself. *Might as well be the eel.* The handless maiden of my dream.

She disappears, I can only guess, into the dark shop. I know how dark it is when you first walk into an old shop like this one. How intimate. Darker when it's raining, because of the door being pulled half-closed to stop splattering. The driver gets back into the driver's seat and only then does he point the rearview mirror downwards slightly, and look at me in it. The pelting rain subsides all at once to a quiet drizzle, just as quick as it started. As if speaking to his own image in the driving mirror, but in fact looking directly at me in the glass and catching my eye, he says abruptly, 'She's gone to buy lottery tickets. I've got a message for you.' Lucky the rain has let up like this otherwise I wouldn't be able to hear a word he says.

'Already?' I say.

'There are two key words: *The eye.*'

'Eye hospital?'

'No,' he says.

'Eye of the needle? To get into heaven? With my arm tied to a bench like this I probably wouldn't get through the eye of a needle, would I, however poor? And what if there are floods? Will you untie me?'

'You're getting closer now. Not the eye of a *needle*. The eye of a *cyclone*.'

'Cyclone?'

I am halted in my stupid *badinaz*.

'There are fishermen who say there is a cyclone coming. *The way the airless winds move around. The heat has been calling the cyclone, they say, and often they are right.*

'The message I bring is: *Take this cyclone as a sign! That's all.* There's the man who sweeps the weather station offices. He overheard them saying it's true, the fishermen are right, there *is* a new cyclone forming. It's up near Diego Garcia right now. Not on the meteo broadcasts yet. A monster, he says they say. *Megasystem* is the word they use. Should be given a name by tomorrow. It will be Cassandra. Third cyclone of the season.

'I have seen the sky go *mauve*. Mauve enough to beckon a cyclone.'

The driver checks if the blue lady is coming back yet. No.

'The north winds', he says, 'have brought all this hot air from the equator and left it lying around.' How mauve the lakoklis leaves shone last night. Leila was mauve and guarded against me. *Leila the lilac.* And Mama Gracienne smelt it in the air. The mauve in the plankton in my dream. Pulsating. And just now, a passing fear of floods, waters rising while I am nailed down.

'Now, for the message.

'*Contain* the general rebellion. Wait. Everything is in the *holding on*. Don't let anyone waste her anger on useless acts of protest. No hollow gestures, please. The secret is to wait, and convince everyone *to wait*. When you hear a formal cyclone warning, you go ahead and look for trustworthy women. Able. Bold. Calm. Choose your own list of qualities. Make *an agreement* if possible. Look into their eyes.

'When you hear a Class Two Warning, *run through* all the

ways a mutiny could take place. And getaways. As if it's in play. Ludic. Not just the itineraries of escape and mutiny, but the *map* of a mutiny. In whispers. Remember that some of the old recording systems they used to have everywhere may still be in operation. So stick to riddles. Guessing games. That kind of thing.

'When you hear a Class Three Warning, you start actual preparations, as if for all the ways and means of taking power in the prison, and all the escape routes you have thought of, all the links between inside and out. Use *what if*s. And *and if*s. Contingencies. In this eventuality. In that eventuality. Throw lots to predict the different options of the enemy. Guess all the different things *they* might do.

'But if and when you hear a Class Four Warning, be quite fast. Ruthless. Choose one strategy to take over. Everyone who wants out, out. The rest of you, run the place.

'Now if the cyclone passes right over us, there will be the *eye*. Only then. Only if. In the eye itself, will there be, definitely be, general mutiny.

'If the eye doesn't go right over us, there will be partial prison mutinies, some getaways and then the repression will be immediate. But if the eye does pass right over us . . .'

'Why then?' I ask.

'It's a good time. The police, army and private security men will be exhausted. They might feel an instinct to pillage. Let pillaging engulf *them*, not us.'

I am honoured and scared.

Too much depends on me.

'It's all up to you.'

'I prefer getting orders. Instructions, directions. Recipes for escape.'

'That's just too bad, isn't it.' An *affectionate*ness in his voice now. 'Because you won't be getting any. You should be sick of orders by now, and if there were recipes, *they* would know them too. Oh, here she comes back with the lottery tickets. One last thing', he adds. 'We did get a message in to Alcatraz. So he knows, your brother Jay knows. They've got a whole pack in there. That's what they call themselves. The *pack*.'

'Jay?'

'He's well.'

'What if the eye doesn't come over us?'

He glares. What kind of listening am I doing, he means. His eye then goes blank in the rearview mirror. Turned off.

So I let my head fall down. Tune out.

I start moaning, and writhing in my seat again because she is at the back door of the van, hurrying against the drizzle. By now I actually *feel like* moaning and screaming, so it comes out convincing. In the face of all the responsibility that has been foisted upon me, I scream in fear. It isn't fair. I can't do it. Why me?

I realise I am scared of getting out.

The very thought of freedom provokes a kind of vertigo in me. Choices creating voids on all sides of me. *Liberté-é-é* the word echoes into the gigantic open spaces of unknown possibilities. *This is an experience I don't need.* I am happy locked up.

I start holding on to my right side again. As if she is risking my life by buying the lottery tickets. She looks back at me suspiciously and mumbles *little runt.*

Her lookout.

He locks her back in again.

The doctor says lean over and presses hard on my pelvic basin while I lean over. She doesn't say anything, but forces out a fake sigh. Doesn't even mind that it rings false. I hate the smell of hospital floors coming up at me, when I'm bent in two like that. But worse still, this police doctor smells of a rich breakfast, maybe bonito curry. Her expensive suit, whose edges stick out and *show* all around her white uniform, is of a military cut. She is a police officer first and foremost, this one, and then only after that, a doctor.

She is far too used to working with the dead, I think. Autopsies and postmortems and formaldehyde. Yes, that's what she smells of, too. Formaldehyde. What does she preserve? She smells of the murdered ones, their severed limbs, of the accidental deaths, suicides, deaths in detention, abortion deaths. Such silent patients. She is not used to speaking to them. She doesn't work for her patient, dead or alive. She works for the police who give her instructions. She assists at whippings and testifies that patients have not been beaten in cells, never. She signs forms in exchange for money from the authorities. Certifies things. Perhaps she has just examined a rape victim, found dead in a cane field.

She looks as dead as her patients.

Then she speaks. Robot-like. I realise she isn't speaking to me but to the blue lady, pointing at a form for her to sign. *Piece rate claim form.* I realise that the prison management company will give her an extra payment for this consultation. Then the doctor says to my blue lady. 'Up the pole. How long's it got in?' I flinch. As if a pole entered me. But of course the *it* is me. *He, she or it.*

'One allegation, three years. Up for another one. Concurrent, I should think.'

'Addict? No need to waste a scan on her, anyway.'

'No. A *political* allegation.' She says this snidely. With distaste. As though it were just that much less palatable than a drugs allegation. As though it stinks. As though she has to control an instinct to spit. As though she wouldn't touch me with a *barge pole*, she who was tied to me, making up a single octopus with me, only half an hour ago. 'Hardly get any pure *drugs allegations* any more compared with this flood of political *trash*. Especially in the men's prison.'

'Don't exaggerate,' I say, as if I were invited.

'Pleased with yourself then?' the blue lady asks me. I wouldn't grace her with a reply. So she goes on and on. 'An allegator up the pole?'

'Already *knew*, Mrs *Blue*. What's it got to *do* with *you*.' Again, the tunes of spiteful nursery rhymes come back to me. So pathetic, I have become.

W ait for the eye. Like another time bomb. From the outside.

I am expecting, already.

For the first time, I am pleased about being pregnant. I wonder
if it's just to spite them? No. More like *to be outside* their control.
Young girl out of control. The marvels of *the inside.* I don't even
know when the countdown started. Don't even know how many
weeks a pregnancy is any more. Let alone months. It came down
to *less*, I remember, every time they lengthened time. It saved on
the maternity leave payments or something. She, the prison
doctor, didn't venture to suggest how many weeks or months
I am by any manner of measurement of time.

Not that it matters any more. I'll still be on the inside. And time
is so elastic inside. At least, I managed to untie myself from the
future father. Small mercies. *Should have been quicker on getting
an abortion before they arrested me.* The thought comes back.
The *if only, if only, if only.* As if I had the choice, them knocking
on the door like that.

I draw away from the fact that a child will grow up *inside.* But
then again, only if we don't succeed. *What a thought, I shrink
from it, as though my fingers could get burnt on it.* The time a
cyclone takes to come here is also variable. *It depends.* But then,
it always was.

As my blue lady and I, chained together for better or for worse,
go past the radiography department, which is now walled in
against some worse rays, I hear the piped music of a cyclone
warning theme tune.

Already?

It must be Class One. Don't get a minute's peace.

My blue lady says, 'You look pleased with yourself, short arse. Let's go listen to that radio then. Cyclone should cheer you lot up in those leaky cells.' Only because we're handcuffed together again, that's why she invites me. Like Siamese twins we are. Eight-limbed. I pretend I am not in the least interested in hearing that radio. Learn to keep secrets.

We catch bits of the radio announcement: *In the vicinity of Diego Garcia, twin low pressure areas observed for days. Northeast. First there is Cassandra, now a tropical cyclone, large diameter. Centred near 7 degrees south and 72 degrees east. Then there is Doorgawatee, already an intense tropical cyclone, small diameter. Centred near latitude 8 degrees and 71 degrees east. Very active system. About 1,500 kilometres north east of Mauritius. Both moving in a south-westerly direction. On this trajectory, heading directly for us. Picking up speed. Unstable general situation. Resembles a mega-cyclonic system. Doorgawatee may get absorbed by Cassandra. Or they may take different directions. Public advised to take all necessary preliminary precautions.*

Not a Class One yet. Twins. Because the cyclones are so strong, they are giving an advance announcement.

We huddle in the middle of our cell, together again, the three of us. The four walls press inwards, the floor slips downwards away from the ceiling, making the room tall. Like being in a chimney, us being small and lost, stuck to the bottom of some featureless space.

Sitting there cross-legged, pregnant with something inside of me, soon wanting to get out. *I hold it in. I don't tell them yet.*

Instead I say the doctor doesn't know *what* I've got.

'I'll say,' she says.

Then I say the doctor says it's either appendicitis or acute tenesmus and what I need to do is to fart a lot. So I fart.

They laugh.

It's the kind of thing you do in prison. Burp and fart and curse. For nothing. You can decide that kind of thing *all by yourself.* So you do it. Your choices are *that* limited.

Quite suddenly I change my mind.

I'll tell them. I'll announce it.

'I've got *news*. I've got news,' I say, 'hot news, from the outside.'

'*We've got company coming!*' I say. Leila is delighted, 'Another surprise?' she asks, pretending to ride a twenty-two-inch bicycle. 'More company? Another visitor? Another messenger without a message? Not much more space in our cell. Or is it the Permanent Secretary on his monthly?'

'A visitation.' I say.

'Well, well,' she replies.

This is also the kind of thing you do in prison, draw out the slightest bit of news into a massive feature story. Not that this bit is *the slightest*.

'Their names,' I say, and do the old cyclone announcement music they used to use on television till last year – the new jingle sounds more like gladiator music – and then as if introducing two famous Bombay movie stars or top-of-the-pop singers, *Cassandra and Doorgawatee.*

'Who?' she is mystified.

I change my tone, to one of genuine concern, 'Two *cyclones* are coming.' Then I slip again into *yo ho, yo ho*. 'That's who. Two cyclones are coming, *yo ho, yo ho*. Twins. Like me and Jay. *Twin cyclones*. Two visitors. Cassandra and Doorgawatee. You told me as much, Mama Gracienne, last night. At least you told us *one* was coming. So it's not completely unexpected news.'

Leila is satisfied.

She is pleased with all this disorder due to be arriving, and even more pleased that you had predicted it, Mama Gracienne. She is proud of you. 'What's in a number?' she says, she says to you.

You are a bit frightened by it, Mama Gracienne. Maybe you fear it's some form of punishment. Come to make you atone for your *confession*. Like a plague of locusts.

'I feel it coming,' is all you murmur, 'I feel it in my bones.' Each soft hand pulls at the elbow of the other arm. 'Things have been preparing for its coming. I can tell that this will be a strong one. Worse than Alix, worse than Carol, worse than Gervaise.' These cyclones are all from before I was even born. 'The only thing is,' she murmurs on, 'You can't tell whose side a cyclone will take. You can't tell beforehand. One thing I've noticed. There aren't any mosquitoes about. I wonder where they go and hide for cyclones?'

You *do* know that it's coming, you've been through so many. What infinite number of variables you must be weighing up that would need to be fed into the meteorological computer: The patterns of the heat, the humidity, the winds, the smells, the pressure. The behaviour of insects. The colour of air. The texture of the sky.

'Whose side *these two* will take, you mean,' I correct you.

'*Twins!*' Leila exclaims. A sudden squall in her now.

I turn to her ask her straight out if she'd like *two*.

'Don't mind if I *do*,' she says, pretending I am offering her something to eat or to drink. I, of course, can't keep Jay out of my mind. *What if* . . . But I fight the fears down.

A ny police officer may without warrant arrest any person who is reasonably suspected of having attempted to commit an offence. [*Dangerous Drugs Act (1995) Section 54*] Where any person is arrested under reasonable suspicion, he may be detained in police custody for a period not exceeding 36 hours without having access to any person other than a police officer or Government Medical Officer where the exercise by this person of the right to consult a legal advisor will lead to interference with evidence. [*Section 31*] Any person convicted of an offence where the street value of the drugs which are the subject-matter of the offence exceeds one million rupees, shall be sentenced to penal servitude for 45 years, and risk forfeiture of his possessions and those of any member of his family. [*Section 40(3) and 43(7)*] Any person who has been convicted of a conspiracy to commit any of the offences shall be exempted from penalty and absolutely discharged if, having revealed the conspiracy to the police, he has made it possible to prevent the commission of the offence and to identify the other persons involved in the conspiracy. [*Section 41*] – Copied down from the Prison's Library.

N ow that our contract is over, now that we no longer have
to stick to things in the present, now that we have let the
past and the future in, Leila has nothing to restrain her from
asking me all manner of questions. Mainly she wants to know
how I got to be an allegator in the first place. *Tell.* She says.

When I hesitate, summoning the story from all its storage
places. *Loud knocking at dawn, safari suits prowling, burglar
guards, words spoken, a breath taken, a trap sprung, panic felt
and flurried off, a streak of colour against a doorway, the word
'aghast', life never the same again, a niche to hide an eyebrow
pencil, if onlies, where to start, sandals already walking.* She says,
tell, again. *Go on.*

Hang on, I say. It seems so far away. So precious it's hidden.

Neither she nor Mama Gracienne has got the foggiest what an
allegator is. Not that I knew before I got to be one, either.

So I start by saying ignorance of the law is no excuse. Look at
me, locked up just the same as if I did know.

'Basically, it means,' and I falter for I know so little, 'it is
supposed to mean that someone has made an allegation against
me,' I say.

'Drugs?' Leila asks, 'It's always about drugs, isn't it?'

I say maybe that's how it started. Maybe it used to be drugs.
Drug-takers and drug-dealers making allegations against one
another to try to stop the torture. Maybe they did it to escape the
death sentence. Or when it was removed, to get out of the forty-
five years' prison. Or to incriminate the rival gang. I don't know,
I say.

I feel relieved to be telling them. Words lift weights from shoulders.

Allegators are so *unpopular*. I know this. I have found this out. Everyone hates drug-traffickers. Almost as much as people used to hate heretics. And witches. A witch was good for nothing except to be held with her head under water, feet tied together dangled from the bridge for three whole minutes, and if she survived it meant she was, effectively, a proven witch, so she got sentenced to burning at the stake. If she died, it meant she wasn't one. Tough luck. That's what I am, a *tough luck she's closed up anyway*.

From here, I must move fast, I think to myself, because I've got to get Leila's confidence *now*, what with the cyclone coming.

With you it's different, Mama Gracienne. You don't care what I am convicted of. But then again, *you* may not want to *mutiny*. You may want to *not mutiny*. You may not even want to escape. You *confessed*. You want to be in here with them guarding you. Inside. Of your own free will. Maybe you will still want to be in here with the four walls around you and no real windows, when the time comes for us all to take over and to *evade*. Who knows with you, Mama Gracienne?

Leila interrupts my thinking. 'Tell! Tell, then,' she begs, 'What did you *do*?' She takes up a position in the cell, as though she is the most dedicated audience in the whole world, waiting for a story, waiting to be transported out of these four walls by a narrative. Waiting with bated breath for the greyness to recede and to find herself surrounded by, immersed in, flashes of colour, unexpected sounds, and smells and textures so real that she lives them.

You, too, lie and wait.

I say perhaps we should start with an hors d'oeuvre. The day is long I say. Too long. We have to tease it out, like lambs' wool. We must take our time. Start with a starter. Or soup, maybe. An offering.

'You're doing it on purpose,' Leila cries.

'It'll help me get my thoughts in order,' I say. 'Soup will. It will soothe.'

C rab soup. You like crab soup, Mama Gracienne? Love it!
How do I make it? Ah, I'll tell you. I'll tell you *both*. Leila
laughs at this. *As if I could choose to whisper in Mama Gracienne's ear.* First you must make sure that as well as crabs,
you've also got some of the spices. Like for everything else, you
don't need all the spices every time. But for crab soup, you need
crabs.

*She pretends to hunt in the corner of her bunk. We haven't got
any, she says.*

Hang on, I say. In due course.

Well, instead of crabs you can use tek-teks, the little bivalves
that you can catch as they dig back into the sand when the waves
recede as the tide goes down. *But you must leave the tek-teks in
salt water in a bucket with a cover on it, so that they spit out all
the sand in them first.*

Otherwise you need crabs.

'I love crabmeat,' she says, 'it's so sweet. And tek-teks taste like
little oysters.'

*I've got her now. She's hungry. Baseline in prison that.
Hunger. Gnawing at her ribcage.*

Melt some butter in the pot, and then slowly brown chopped
onions. This is the first part that you have to concentrate for, the
browning of the onions. You can turn the heat off, if you want to,
when the onions are perfectly golden brown, through and
through, almost going crisp, so you can put your mind to other
things.

Then you need green coriander *down to and including the*

roots, which you need to wash well, because mud gets stuck in them. Take the leaves off, chop them up fine, and put them aside for sprinkling on top of the soup at the last minute, when you've already taken the soup off the fire to serve – otherwise the coriander leaves lose their taste and smell, if you let them boil away.

You need to crush into a nice paste *the following*: The roots and stalks of the coriander together with a piece of root ginger, some cloves of garlic and some curry leaves. You can add one chilli. (You can chop up some extra ones to serve in vinegar and salt at table, for people who like crab soup hot; if you make it hotter, you need more salt and sourness to match.) You make the paste by chopping up all the spices very fine with a chopping knife, then squashing them with a mortar and pestle, or rolling them with a cylindrical rock on a flat rock – or with the flat side of a butter knife, but it takes time.

This mixture, with some turmeric added if you like, then needs to be fried well in the butter and onions. You fry it for quite a while, stirring and stirring so it doesn't burn. Add oil, if necessary, so that the spices actually fry lightly. From the smell you will know when the mixture is cooked. This is the only other part you have to concentrate for. Coriander root is bitter if undercooked or overcooked.

Then you add water and the crabs.

It's important to clean the crabs first, whether you catch them or buy them fresh. You do this by tearing out their intestine parts and throwing these away. Then you carve the crab into bits.

If the crabs are big and their carapace hard, you can put them on a chopping board and hit them gently with a rolling pin, leg by leg and on the carapace, so that they are easier to eat later.

As the crab soup starts to boil, you can turn it down and leave it for fifteen to twenty minutes to get everything tasting nice. When you want to taste the soup, add the salt and some tamarind (or lemon juice) to taste; add it bit by bit, and taste each time, until it is perfect.

If it is too spicy, you can add a little water. But then you might need more salt and a wee bit more tamarind.

When it's ready to serve, sprinkle the chopped coriander leaves (no stalks) on top.

49

I t is only then that I tell you, Mama Gracienne, about our game, and how we have already done bitter gourds. I remember you murmur and mumble *margoz*. *Bitter times*. What was '*a*'? you then ask.

'Aubergines and potatoes, smothered,' Leila replies.

But the word *smothered* makes the atmosphere in that cell go all heavy.

You sigh, Mama Gracienne, and raise your hand to your mouth and seem to wipe it. And take a deep breath. You make Leila regret she ever said the word.

'No excuse now, Juna,' she says, relentless. 'You've got to tell now. What are you? What is an allegator?'

C onspiracy: Any person who agrees with one or more other persons to do an act which is unlawful, wrongful or harmful to another person, or to use unlawful means in the carrying out of an object not otherwise unlawful, shall commit an offence and shall, on conviction, be liable to imprisonment for a term not exceeding 5 years and to a fine . . . [*Criminal Code (Supplementary) 1870, Section 109*]

W hen they come to arrest me, they arrive calling out as if to wake up the dead. *As if,* I look from Mama Gracienne to Leila, *to awaken the dead.*

I've got them with the opening. Four ears tuned. The cell recedes.

Leila sits up and leans against the receding wall. 'Like you did to us this morning with your screaming!' she accuses. '*You* could have woken up the dead.' Then I see her shudder, tremble and almost back away from her own words. *Maybe she is remembering Mopey-Sue, her previous cellmate. Wonder how she found her, whether it was her who found her. Did she try to wake her up from the dead? Shake her? Scream at her? By hanging was it? Or slit wrists? With the other bits of the razor blade? Or drowned in a very shallow slop bucket?* Then the whole moment blows over.

'You nearly killed Mama Gracienne with your shouting.' *Mama,* I notice. Good.

But you, Mama, are smiling about something else. Time moves differently for you. *Bitter gourds!* you exclaim, as if you still can't get over recipes in jail. *Crab soup!*

The smothering has gone.

Then you also drag yourself up into a sitting position, your soft arms folded over your large soft tummy. 'True,' you shake your head in general disbelief, 'nearly did kill me.'

I must do your plaits later, Mama. They are in ruin. Make you look mad as a hatter.

Mama Gracienne and Leila are both learning to be good story

listeners, sitting there, calm and already amused and just waiting for my muse to settle in, helping me. The oppressive height of the ceiling is gone, and we are a triangle of concentration. Nothing else will exist except the story, now. And the story will expand outwards into infinity and will free us. Or so we think. Or we act as if we think it.

'The beauty of the story is in the listener,' I whisper to them, clearing my throat, as if this is a conspiracy.

'Get on with it, you're delaying on purpose, again,' Leila moans, knitting her eyebrows together, and now lying face down with her head cupped in her hands.

They listen maybe to forget the pain inside their heads. I feel *you* reaching into the past which is my past while you fit new things into it, and I feel *her* reaching into the future which is my future while she imagines its dim outline in the warm air of that cramped cell in front of her.

I start with this bit, I tell them, because that's how I remember it happening. This story, I say, starts very suddenly, as if on cue.

As I wake up, there is already this phrase in my head: *As if to awaken the dead*. It's like it's prefabricated. Hell's doors. They are calling. Loudly. Fear grips me. But they aren't calling me. '*Anita! Anita! Anita!*' They call my landlady's name.

Pounding on the front door. *I knock on the cell wall*. Like this. These men must *know* her, I think.

'*Don't break the door down!*' I shout. They sometimes get at you when you're still in your pyjamas.

I remember sighing. I remember I am overcome by a *petty* dread, a resentment, that these unknown men are spoiling the start of my day. *Start of the day* program booted wrong. Ruining the start of my *day*. Little did I know.

Jay's arrest hits me. A song, a few words, a few sprouts of leafery.

I think of the mess at work, a disk crash waiting for me. Bad enough. Then I get worried in case they make me late for the appointment I've got with the gynaecologist at lunch-time.

'Stop the *racket*. Knock! Knock! Knock! Want her to hear you from the other side of the bloody sea?'

They're probably collecting some debt she owes. 'Want to wake up the guards at hell's gates?'

I look at my watch. I remember this. Looking at my watch. It's a smart one. I just press a button and I know the time in any country where there's a company or a government department we are doing a data retrieval contract for. *They've got that watch of mine in a flat plastic bag, sealed and signed for, downstairs. Waiting for me. In the hold of this hulk.*

Seven o'clock already.

Overslept. Damn. If I'm late, by the time I get to work, it'll be night-time in western America already, then what? Here I am, here I may be. But my work is *over there*. Why? They say I'm cheaper. I was bought from my previous company for two point four million. After a medical. I earn an immense hourly wage plus the rent allowance – for that cold double-storey house of Anita's – and medical insurance that would cover anything. So long as I go on working for them.

I feel bound to be honest with them. Especially with Leila. She looks unbelieving. Disbelieving. Can I blame her? I can hardly believe it myself. That's what the state does to us. Puts us in a state of disbelief.

I put my turquoise candlewick gown on, and go to the window. *Wonder where they've put that gown.* That house won't be waiting for me any more, that's for sure, wonder who's in it now.

A troop of plainclothes men. *How many came to arrest Jay, I wonder?* Even then I already think of them as *plainclothes men.* Leaping out of four plainclothes cars, leaving the doors yawning open. Big men. Some already standing there like orang-utangs. Moneylenders' men? And with them is *a lady in pale blue clothing.*

Bodes ill, I think to myself, bodes ill. Funny that thought.

There she is, sitting out there in one of the cars. With the door wide open. Looking straight ahead. Just sitting. I can see her through the spindly pomegranate tree in front of my neighbour Agnes' house. Not even interested enough to see what happens next. I mean how did she know I wouldn't take out a gun and shoot her?

The blue lady *perplexes me.* Her presence there. And yet I wouldn't have known a blue lady from a blue-arsed-monkey at that time.

The men are still shouting, '*Anita! Anita! Anita!*' Some of them are still banging away at the front door.

I stick my head out of the only window without burglar guards. I'm upstairs, just above them. I look down. They all step back and look up.

'She isn't in the country. She's away. Abroad somewhere.'

A pack of them after me. This is the first time, the very first time that I get a whiff, the slightest smell, of being *hunted down*.

But it passes.

'Open up the door! What're you hiding in there anyway?' One even tries to provoke me by shouting, 'We're coming in to *get* you.'

Now I smell fear in myself. In my own sweat, I smell it. But I still push it aside easily, shove the fear into a corner and get on with life.

I open the window again, lean out and shout, 'I am *not* Anita! Repeat *not*. I am not *Anita*. Stop making such a noise! She's out of the country. Listen to me! I'll call the police, if you don't watch it.'

'Open up!' one shouts.

I make pleas for calm. I try to make them see reason.

I begin to realise that these men are acting on orders. They are not going to listen to me, ever. So I get dressed quickly, pulling on my ordinary work clothes: light grey cotton slacks and light grey cotton bodice. I'm still in the flat sandals I wear around the house. I brush my teeth, pull a comb through the outer edges of my hair, and I go down and open up the front door, lock by lock, and then swing it wide open. I stand there with my hands on my hips. I feel very short and very thin and very little. But I bar the doorway as best I can, a doorway which seems to stretch out like an infinitely wide gap now.

I stand in the prison door to show how.

I still firmly believe it's some gang that's been charged with collecting debts from my landlady. Bailiffs. Bruisers. That type of thing. *A case of mistaken identity.*

Then they just push me, and push past me. I go reeling across the room.

When I look out past them, there are others coming in. Again I see the woman in a blue dress, sitting in one of the cars behind a spindly pomegranate tree, heavy with grenades. Impassive.

Like in a nightmare, I can't stop them. I am powerless. I don't even understand the premises on which they act, nor the premises from which they come.

Then, at around about this time, it dawns on me. These men are the *police* after all. Some branch or other of the police. A division or a section or a squad. Or the security company that has some policing contract, *same thing*.

It comes as a blow to me. Won't be able to report them to the police.

So, I follow some of them around, asking, 'Who is your boss here? Have you got a warrant?'

Like sleep walkers, they are. They don't dig into things, or even open cupboards or turn anything upside down or anything. They don't actually touch anything. Almost as though they will be coming later with a man with a little electronic briefcase to look for fingerprints. They walk around, sometimes even moving backwards, as though they think they might find a lot of suspects hidden in different rooms of my house. Suspects who might jump out at them and scare them.

Their hands are ready to take guns out of their pockets. I can see it.

I better watch it.

They are dangerous. But they also manage to look unconvincing, like bad actors in a slow TV serial made by beginners.

I identify one of them as their leader, as their chief. He addresses me.

'Sorry about getting you up so *early*,' he says. As if only the time of day is odd.

Speaks quietly. Sober. Dulcet. The worst type, I think, calm as can be. As though I had experience in police *types*.

'We are the drugs squad, as you know, Mrs ——? The Granbe branch of the drugs squad, Mrs —— Good morning to you, Mrs —— I really do apologise for getting you up *so* early.'

At this point, I get shit scared.

I protest.

But at the same time, I realise I sound stupid. Weak and ineffectual. But I must try, so I do.

'I am not . . . Anita. She doesn't live here . . . any more. I don't know who you are, so get out of my house.'

The *drugs* squad.

The horror of this sinks into my early morning brain. *Drugs?* It hits me. Clamp-downs and raids, clean-up campaigns, calls for bringing back the death penalty, closing down of pharmacies, *these people are killing our children*, enquiries into lawyers' visits to clients in prisons, newspapers full of it, *merchants of death, stamp them out*, doctors struck off the rolls, school children's bags searched, teachers going hysterical on television. *Eradicate them, vermin.* Customs posts tightened up. *Imported vices from the decadent.* Special squads set up. *Vigilante committees* protest against them. Neighbourhoods sealed off. Nightclubs closed down, suspects held incommunicado.

Will *this all* be turned, like dogs, on me?

Now what?

He raises his eyebrows. That's all. As if he is straining to keep his temper with me. As if I am so ungrateful he can't bear it.

'We have come to *arrest* you, I am afraid.'

'Me? What for?'

'Oh, it's just an *allegation*.'

'What you mean *just an allegation*? Where's your warrant? You come here shouting someone else's name, and now you say you going to arrest *me*. I am going to telephone a lawyer. This is absurd. I can't believe it.' I find I am capable of this outburst, and this is a consolation. Small.

'Oh, you know *lawyers*, do you? Which one? No need to raise your voice, Mrs . . . What *is* your name, by the way.'

I do not rise to the bait.

I notice that knowing a lawyer is proof of my guilt.

My audience-of-two cackle. The joke is always on lawyers. We are all three gripped by my story. Even me. I wish it was a made-up one. I wish it had a happy ending. I wish it had an ending full stop.

'Here's my drugs squad card,' he goes on. 'I don't need an actual *warrant*, as you know. Anyway you're coming with me of your own free will. Tell you what, I'll do you a favour: You can telephone a lawyer. No one else. Do be quick please. Don't want to delay anything.' He means bail, when he says *anything*. 'A favour,' he repeats, 'just for you, Mrs . . .'

I give them my name. It's the law. Juna Bhim. *And I've never been called Anita*, I add. They already have my address, I point out.

'You tell me not to delay you. I tell you frankly, you can go any time you like.'

He smiles patiently. Meaning *the things he has to put up with*.

I look up the number of a lawyer. Wife answers. Out of the country. So sorry. Meanwhile they all mill around the house, slowly and still not touching things. I look up Jay's lawyer, the one I helped him get. Child answers, she's out of the country too. I ring a third, home number. No answer. Left for work? I telephone at work. No answer. Must be on his way. Cellular number now. *This telephone may be switched off.*

The slow pace of a nightmare takes over completely.

'You seem to know a lot of *lawyers* then, don't you?' He goes on again.

'Allegation for doing what?'

'An all-e-ga-tion is an all-e-ga-tion,' he spells this out like elocution. E-lo-cu-tion. 'The prison is full of allegators these days. Mainly male, though, I must admit. Mainly male. Quite fashionable, you will find.' He is already mentioning *prison*. And making guesses as to how I might find things in prison.

'Before I go with you, you have to tell me what exactly I am alleged to have done. It stands to reason. You are the *drugs* squad, you say. Allegations are to do with drugs, aren't they?'

'Conspiracy,' he says in a matter-of-fact tone. Then he says 'Conspiracy' again, this time as if it's got a death penalty. Then he repeats this as though it is quite an ordinary thing again. 'Conspiracy.' A run of the mill thing for him.

'What d'you mean *conspiracy*?'

I'd never heard such a thing.

'Conspiracy', he says. 'Conspiracy.' Echolalia, he's got.

'But conspiracy to do what? You can't just stand there and tell me you are going to arrest me for an allegation for conspiracy.' He stays calm. Like a piece of rock.

'Conspiracy with others *to commit an unlawful act*,' he says. I remember it as if it was yesterday, him there in his white safari suit looking like a maggot. 'It is an offence, you know, Section 109, to be in one.' *An awful act? No unlawful act.* I check on his men quickly. Just in case I'm misunderstanding everything. They are all dead serious. Blank. Faceless men in faceless clothes. Dangerous. They might *kill*.

I. Must try a counterattack, I. Mustn't give in, I. Must hold out, what. Is happening to me?

Then I feel my heart get squashed like. I feel I'm in a vice grip that I can't move out of, like. And they are slowly tightening the vice. They locked up my twin brother Jay only a month ago. For singing a blues song. *Doom.* I feel doomed now. I know they're after me. It's all over. *Don't be stupid*, I say to myself, *it's got nothing to do with Jay*. As if imprisonment were hereditary. As if twins could be jailed because of their genes. Or for congenital reasons.

'I think you are being ridiculous. I think you are all ludicrous. Making fools of officers of the law, that's what. Making an ass of the law itself. What unlawful act?' I ask. '*You* have to say. You have to name it, name the act.'

He looks bored. Infinitely bored.

It flashes through my mind that this is Candid Camera, and all these people are part of a television crew and they are filming from one of the windows and that this man is going to say *Smile, you're on*.

But it isn't and he doesn't.

Instead he acts as if I am putting him out. Causing him trouble. 'Oh, we are not accusing you of *committing* an unlawful act. You misunderstand the whole nature of our provisional charges, Mrs . . . You have taken part in a *conspiracy* to commit an unlawful act.'

Snared, I am. Snared now.

Snared in the middle of a maze, back leg caught, trapped inside a puzzle with interlocking parts that I don't understand.

He replies, the chief does, 'Allegation for conspiracy to commit the unlawful act of planting drugs on property of another.'

The next lawyer I telephone I get. She doesn't *do* drug related offences, she says, putting the receiver down quickly before she gets herself infected.

I panic now. My nose starts to run. That's when I realise I haven't put my mascara on yet, Leila.

I telephone my work friend. Ask her to find me a lawyer. You know the woman that comes to visit me on Thursdays, that one. She agrees.

'Who're you speaking to?' the police chief interrupts sharply.

I cover the mouthpiece, 'A friend. Where can she get a lawyer to contact me? What's your name and rank, *Sir*?' Sir. Leftovers of submission come back so easily to me.

'Porlwi Drug Squad. Rungtoolall, District Superintendent of the drugs squad.' District Superintendent came *in person* to arrest me. Maybe I'm alleged to have planted whole toises, whole perches, whole arpents, even whole hectares of the stuff. I am horrified. *Oh no.*

But I still stay calm. 'You told me Granbe.'

'We'll be taking you to Porlwi,' he says. As if only the capital itself will do for this grand felony.

'It's *Friday* today, for god's sake. They want a confession,' my friend says. The shocks keep coming at me. How is she so clever? I'm the one who has the experience of a brother in jail.

I don't know what day of the week it is any more in any case.

I live in the present now. Vacillating between being engulfed in a panic that strips me of thought, and being in the grip of a prosaic but firm belief that there must be some very *simple* mistake here.

'And on whose property am I supposed to have conspired to plant gandia, Superintendent Rungtoolall?' I feel compelled to ask these questions.

'Oh, so it was *gandia*, was it?'

So then I shut up.

'Here?' I round off the conversation, pointing at the buff coloured vinyl squares on the floor to make the point. I notice a flowery pattern to them.

He looks down at them. He looks so hard, it's like he's expecting a small gandia plant to be nuzzling its way out between two squares. To join the other flowers on it. Or, as if he is about to give orders for the squares to be levered out at once in case they're hiding some key evidence against me.

'No, not here.'

That's when I ask permission to go to the toilet. And that's when I fetch my eyebrow pencil and those four bits of pink toilet paper rolled up in those two holes in the wall under Leila's bed. *My scribblings make them laugh. They think it's rubbish and they aren't wrong there.*

I don't even bother to put on my red-pink linen jacket which is hooked over my dining room chair, nor my high heel sandals next to the table. Nor my dark glasses I use for the motorbike. I can still see them, my dark glasses, sitting there as if staring out from the red-pink linen tablecloth.

They usher me out, make me lock up my house, and take me to the far side of one of the shining cars. They shove me in, and on to the middle of the back seat. Sandwich me. That's the first time I see a blue lady close up. She just goes on looking straight ahead of her. Her make-up holding her in place. Like a corpse. I try to look into Agnes' house to see if she is up, perhaps signal something to her. Don't know my other neighbours.

'Don't know your neighbours?' Leila interrupts.

'Go on,' you urge, 'go on.'

All four cars rev up and drive off fast in convoy.

At the headquarters, a man in uniform leans over sweeping the yard mournfully with a scraggy broom. I remember this, as if it was yesterday. Funny, the things you remember. And I remember that Rungtoolall's *face*. I'd recognise him anywhere. Anywhere in the world. Even if I just heard that voice of his, I'd know it.

Up the stairs and into a bare room smelling of dust and fear.

I remember my Thursday visits to Jay when one week I'd rather lip-read than hear his voice and the next week I'd listen to his voice, ear to the holes, without being able to see the expression on his lips or in his black irises.

They sit at wooden tables, the policemen, and start filling in ledgers and typing information on to computers. An out-of-date network system, I observe to myself sarcastically. Useless. Worse than useless. Chalk on slate would be better.

They question me laboriously. Name. Address. Place of work. *Electronic Creations Ltd.* This *worries* them when they write down and type up my place of work, and they begin to fidget. But not *unduly*. Do they think I might disapprove of their computer system, or do they realise how much I might have cost my company to buy?

There are notes in chalk on a blackboard on the wall, as well. I try to glean a clue from them. They make no sense to me.

Chalk and computers. Scraggy brooms and fast cars.

There is coming and going in the corridors, to and fro. I see lots of scruffy *little* people, who must work as informers. No taller than I am. Thinner. And badly fed. An *underclass*. Excluded ones. Perhaps in drugs.

My friend does find me a lawyer and he does turn up. I am relieved. But not for long. Never be off your guard with a lawyer.

'I hate lawyers,' Leila says, 'hate them.'

The first thing I notice about this lawyer is that he has the distinct aura of not believing a word I say. I am his client, remember. I will pay him a fine sum, remember. My friend will have assured him. But, *he suspects me*. He can't make head or tail of what's going on, therefore he concludes it's me at fault.

I start to wish. If only I was arrested for something simple. An ordinary offence. That a common or garden lawyer would understand. *Wounds and blows*. He could deal with that. Or *receiving. Disturbance. Abortion. Foul language in public place. Not* some offence that makes a lawyer jumpy. *Not* something a lawyer can't see the logic of. Not *allegation*. Not *conspiracy*. If only.

As it turns out it isn't the kind of *planting drugs* I think it is. Now that's a surprise. Never jump to conclusions. Never.

Mama Gracienne and Leila both lean forwards. They want to know what kind of planting drugs, in that case?

Not conspiring to *cultivate* anything at all. But to plant drugs *on someone*. On their property, on their premises. To *set* this someone *up*. Set up some person I've never heard of. On his hotel property. Never heard of his hotel either. Conspired with people referred to as 'others'.

They say that on such and such a day, at such and such an hour, I was at home.

At some point while I'm there at the drugs squad headquarters, they bring a man in, in front of my lawyer. This man is called Imran. I don't know him from a bar of soap, he comes in and identifies me.

'Yes, that's her all right,' he says, and points at me, 'That's her. I know for certain. *Mo konn li tre byen.* I am not making a mistake. She's called Anita,' and he goes out again. When they say *tre byen*, it means you're known for something bad.

I can see Mama Gracienne and Leila are starting to lose faith in me. They aren't believing me any more, either. As bad as my lawyer.

He, this man Imran says in his statement that he came to see my neighbour who is, he says, a friend of his. Agnes. The only neighbour I know. The one with the spindly pomegranate tree. Agnes was supposedly out. I was supposedly in. We live amongst rich people's concrete houses that they come and live in for weekends, just behind the tourist bungalows up north. *I add this by way of explanation.*

Anyway, there I supposedly was, cleaning my supposedly blue motorbike. I've got a red one. I supposedly talk to him, this Imran. I invite him into *her* house. I go and open the door, which he says is unlocked and I let him in, and I follow him in, and it is there, in Agnes' house, that we supposedly sit down and hatch the plot, which is the conspiracy, or part of the conspiracy.

I supposedly advise Imran in detail exactly how he is to set up a certain Balmick, who, it turns out, is his boss and who runs a hotel. I am supposedly in cahoots with the competitor of this man Balmick, someone called Ameen. Ameen has also got a hotel in the area. Two rival hotel owners. Is hotel a euphemism for something else? I don't know. Until now, I don't know. But I have made enquiries, and these two hotel owners do exist and they do own things referred to as hotels in that area I lived in. *Lived, past tense.*

I remember feeling a sudden regret, *damn it*, for not knowing the area I live in better. Too much of my time at work, my mind always on electronics and computer language systems. *Damn it* that I don't live in some other area. A village like L'Avenir, for example. Where I come from.

I never clapped eyes on this Ameen before he was brought in for the 'confrontation' a few minutes later. He says he doesn't know me either. Small mercies. Is he also as innocent as I am?

My lawyer tells me I am accused of organising for Ameen to give Imran some fixed quantity of drugs which he will use in order to set up his boss who is Ameen's competitor. Five hundred grams of brown sugar. Plus *used foil papers*. Such attention to detail, I think. Only to find out this kind of thing is specifically referred to in the law as part of *'drugs paraphernalia'*.

Goes to show.

I, for my part, will supposedly pay the sum of 2.5 million for him to do this planting. I begin to realise that I am accused of being a *servo*, I'm supposed to be some kind of a ringleader. Worse than a drug-peddler. A leader of a gang of drug-peddlers. I am supposed to have access to amounts of drugs and amounts of money that will automatically define me as a *drug-trafficker*.

Then, the conspiracy goes on, we aim to inform the police about the drugs, Balmick is then due to be arrested. If he gets charged with being a drugs *dealer,* then Ameen won't have a rival any more. Imran will have 2.5 million.

But they don't bother to say what *exactly* I stand to gain.

My neighbour is also accused. So they tell me. Agnes. Is she also as innocent as I am? My lawyer advised me not to get anyone to contact her. *In case they slap on charges of tampering with witness.*

So, they lock me up.

Until my court case. Which comes quickly, *fast track*. Yes, I got *fast tracked*. Danger to the public.

My lawyer digs out clippings about the same plot being hatched last year by the drugs squad. So he *complains*. Says the police thesis doesn't make sense. Says why am I giving the 2.5 million? What's my interest? Says who are these fools who supposedly try the same thing on this Balmick twice? Calls for a *nolle prosequi*. To stop prosecution because there's no case.

Anyway, it's a drugs related charge, so they pass me through *fast track,* which means they rely on one allegation by one Imran.

The police tell me I'm lucky to have a lawyer. Next time round, people like me will be barred from having a lawyer for thirty-six hours after arrest. Because by then I may well have previous, so they won't do me any *favours.*

My lawyer works hard. All three lawyers do. Ameen, Agnes and I each have a different lawyer. The state witnesses are Rungtoolall, Balmick and Imran. My lawyer cross-questions the first one. The police prosecutor jumps up shouting 'Objection, Your Honour!' My lawyer persists, 'But you and your men called the name Anita, Superintendent!' He pulls his black gown from shoulder to shoulder. Looks around at the sparse audience. He even produces the newspaper cuttings about the earlier conspiracy case trying to show that the police had only just made a carbon copy of some existing plot, so short were they on imagination. The Court thinks the cuttings not relevant to this particular case. *Not material, my learned friend,* as one of the magistrates puts it. My lawyer struggles on.

Guilty, the two magistrates say.

53

*S*entences: **Death:** (1) Every person sentenced to death shall be hanged by the neck until he is dead. (2) Sentence of death shall not be carried out on a public holiday. [*Criminal Code (1838) Section (10) (1) and (2)*] **Penal servitude:** (1) The punishment of penal servitude is imposed for life or for a minimum term of 3 years. (2) Where in any enactment the punishment of penal servitude is imposed without a term being specified, the maximum term for which the punishment may be imposed is 20 years. [*Section 11*] **Imprisonment:** Where in any enactment the punishment of imprisonment is provided for an offence without a term being specified, the term for which imprisonment may be imposed may exceed 10 days but shall not exceed 2 years. [*Section 12*] The Court may inflict that punishment with or without hard labour. [*Criminal Code Section 5 (2)*] – Copied from the Prison's Library.

[Death sentence no longer exists, suspended by the National Assembly in 1995, replaced by forty-five years' imprisonment.]

Y ou believe me, Mama Gracienne, when I tell my story
about being an allegator. I can see. But does Leila? The cell
is stuffy and getting smaller. And hotter. A strange silence comes
down. Reflective, we are. Something dawning on us. The *state* we
are in. Look at us. Look at our wrists. Locked up. If what I tell is
true, then what does this mean? How innocent are we all?

Compared.

'Why did they call *Anita* then?'

I don't know. I just don't know. Was it a mistake in their
conspiracy against me? Or was I a mistake in some other
conspiracy?

'Then what?' Leila says.

Then they sentence me.

Three years.

No, I don't know what time they're measuring on.

Now I hear, they've got a *new* allegation on me next week.
Wonder what I've gone and done now. I'll have previous now. Be
a recidivist. I can get up to forty-five years.

There's silence while my story goes on sinking in.

L arceny *of produce of the soil.* Any person who fraudulently abstracts, steals, takes or carries away any crop or other produce of the soil, whether the same had or had not yet been detached from the soil, shall commit larceny and shall be liable on conviction to imprisonment and *wacha-wacha* . . . *[Criminal Code (1838) Section 302]* – Copied from the Prison's Library.

Allow *myself* a memory. *Reflexive.* Let it in. In this heat and listlessness. A little memory. Leila is locked into herself still. I can't tell if she's dominated by thoughts or feelings or visions or what. It's as though she has left the cell. Mama Gracienne has fallen into a trance. Left me alone in here. *Let them be.* I'll bring in a memory. A short sweet memory where the sun is about to dip down behind the drunken diagonal black mountain behind the village of L'Avenir, and our cow likes *variety.*

That kind of memory. The sky is solid red-pink behind the mountain. They've been burning cane again.

Has this memory got conjured up by the blank inside pages of the new forty sous exercise book I've got hold of to write on? Some piece of homework left undone when I was ten?

I let it in.

Or is it that same red-pink colour of the sky, my jacket against the tablecloth the day of my arrest? Didn't know they matched.

Or is it just the sore lack of variety I see before my eyes inside here? Grey, grey, grey. Sensory deprivation.

It's the dry season, and our cow is still insisting on rich dark green lush soft lakasya that we have to climb up aloes to get at with a worn thin sickle, served with a handful of shiny dark brown lakasya seeds from our turned inside-out pockets *and* bitter elephant grass from where the marsh has gone dry. She still wants sourish donkey grass cut from around the underneath sides of rocks *and* dog-tooth with its sweet hidden stalk end even if the grass itself has already gone dry and yellow, tasteless as straw. All of which we have got for her and served with a bucket of water – coarse sea-salt rich in iodine already stirred with a wooden spoon into rice-water strained by our father's hands off this evening's meal – but it won't quite do.

She *also* wants cane tops. Dessert. A sweet tooth, she's got.

Otherwise, if we don't give her any cane tops when she knows very well it's cane cutting season with the smell of that smoke in the air, she gets restless at night and she moos. She might moo so much and so loud that we end up going out and finding her a bull, *a tall, dark, handsome bull,* and bringing him to her *likiri* in the night, only to realise that that's not what she *mainly* wants right now, thank you.

She wants cane tops.

So, Jay and I are walking fast down the coconut palm alley towards the sugar mill, each with a sickle balanced on our left shoulder – worn like this they keep devils at bay – and I with some liana around my neck for tying the bundle of cane tops up with afterwards. We are on our way to a plot of *obscure* sugar estate land beyond the smoking mill chimney where we can cut cane tops unseen by the armed watchmen, and from where we can head back home again afterwards under the cover of the sudden darkness that will envelop everything once the sun dives down. Again unseen.

We are unsuspecting. Jay is playing his stolo-stolo, cupped in front of his mouth, as we go.

Tor-wing, tweng tweng, tor-wing, tor-weng.

But we check that our father isn't coming after us. Which means that now and then we are actually *walking forwards and looking behind us* instead of looking where we were going. Because what if our father catches us like this, wandering off, when we haven't even washed our arms and legs yet, after raking up six months' cow dung piled up ready for selling by the lorry load to the cow dung men tomorrow after school? What if? *Our father's a plumber, so his twins have to be clean.* Clean by sunset. Water and soap galore, knees and elbows scrubbed with bits of coconut fibre till it hurts. Our father being our mother as well. And, after going to the toilet, wash our bottoms and then wipe them. With toilet paper, ends of rolls taken from clients with western sit down lavatories when he gets clients which isn't often because the times are bad. Sometimes he rages and beats us and scrubs us even harder with the coconut fibre. *Maybe a skilled workman balks at his children being driven back on to the interstices of the very land of this mother earth that god knows when we had all been driven off of.*

So, our father is the reason why we are walking along, looking *behind* us like that.

Wsh . . Thud!

So loud we jump. Spinning round to face forwards, stopping dead in our tracks. Silence.

Then we step back.

In front of Jay, just at the very place where he's going to be in one second's time if he takes one more step forward, there is, already inert on the ground, so still it looks innocent, a huge green coconut that has fallen like death in front of him. Ten pounds from sixty foot up.

'Nearly only one twin left,' says Jay. He smiles at me. He is a *cherubim.* He just cups his hands around his mouth again and goes on playing his stolo-stolo, as if to say fate can't make him scared *that* easy.

Tor-wing, tweng tweng, tor-wing, tor-weng.

But it makes me shudder.

He is the twin that looks twelve and I am the one that looks eight.

We are somewhere inbetween. Sickles on our left shoulders. Smelling happy of cow dung. We haven't joined the Bicycle Party yet. Nor have we gone to Porlwi to find out what our mother really died of, yet. Nor has our father got into the position where he exchanges his soul to the devil for something else, perhaps a house. Nor have we had our hair cut like Angela Davis yet. Or like Sai Baba.

'Don't talk like that, Jay,' I say.

Jay, with the outside of one foot, slides the huge coconut over on to the edge of the shallow ditch that the canal has turned itself into for the dry season. And leaves it in the shadows there.

So we can pick it up on the way back.

For us, the twins, there is a mysterious and treacherous providence in the fall of a coconut.

Which decides us to do something that we have been wanting to do for months. Dying to do. We forget about our father. We postpone the cane tops. We touch our sickles lightly for good luck. *Let's go to the cow factory. Just in case we die.* (There is the shallow water in the ditch right next to us that we could get drowned in, for a start. The water glints dangerously in the setting sun.) *In case we die before we see the cow factory.*

We set off on a detour. We will go see those *cows* that the sugar estate keeps all locked up in a long concrete house, see them with our own four eyes before we die.

We have heard it said that the cow factory's like a *hotel* inside, only it's got lights on, day and night. Can it be true? How would we know, we haven't ever seen the inside a hotel either. I *still* haven't. But I can't speak for Jay.

We have to climb over two barbed wire fences to get to the dairy. Balancing our sickles delicately on our shoulders all the way. When we get there, the window is too high for me, so Jay climbs up on a rock just next to the window, and looks in. He is so quiet as he looks in, so tense and so clearly horrified that I catch all his feelings without seeing a thing.

'Holy cow,' he says.

He turns and looks at me.

He jumps off the rock, takes his sickle off his shoulder and mine off mine, and puts them both down quietly on the rock, and stands square, back to the wall and lets me step into his cupped hands, and climb on to his shoulders so that I can see in through the open shutter.

There *is* bright electric lighting inside. Harsh light. I wait for my eyes to get used to it.

A vast factory stretches out in front of me. I stare and stare. Wonder and horror going on welling up in me.

There are hundreds of cows and they are all lined up and penned in. Facing each other. Just standing there in the middle of all that concrete. Not knowing why.

What makes it this particular memory that comes back now, when I let a memory into our cell? All those cows penned in there? All those years back?

For a long time, I can't think of anything to say.

The animals look quite healthy, after all.

And yet we feel distressed. Both of us. I feel Jay's distress in a droop in his shoulders, through my feet.

Then I notice that there is one young man inside. I signal Jay to stay quiet, and I watch him. He is moving an electrical appliance on wheels nearer to one of the cows standing in there, and applying four tubes to her udder. Then he applies similar tubes to three other nearby cows' udders. He must turn on a switch then, because we hear the sound of a motor, and the four cows get milked. Milk rises in separate measuring jars. All electronic.

Meanwhile each cow's fodder is in a tray in front of her. All the cows stand, chewing cud. All concentrated food. Brown and smashed up. The smell of molasses.

And of cow urine. All their urine runs down a cemented canal at the back of them and out somewhere. Special plumbing for cows.

I look for bulls, but I can't find a single one.

'*Holy cow*,' Jay mutters under my feet, 'poor, poor Luxmees.'

I still don't know for sure what he was referring to, but I get the distinct feeling then that he was referring to the dairy being a prison for cows. *Now, of course, I am certain.*

At the far end there is an office with a huge glassed-in window pane and inside it I now see a second young man. He is sitting in front of a computer screen. All sorts of electronically fed information is coming from the cow shed via electric cables into his office.

I jump down and ask Jay if he saw the man in his office.

We pick up our sickles, hook them back over our left shoulders, go around to the other side so that we can peep in through his office window. *Looking into an aquarium. Seeing the man pinned down to his seat like that.* Then, instead of seeing things about cattle on his screen or accounts for the sugar estate farm, we find that he is playing a kind of game. All by himself. On the screen is written, we can see it clearly, '*X went to town to see Y.*' Then he types in, '*Intention, clear. But result, unclear. Did he see him or not? Grammar inefficient.*' He writes '*X ti al anvil, li ti zwenn Y.*' He leans back in his chair, and lets out a wild laugh. Head back and happy. Self-contained bliss. But the sound doesn't carry outside his glass cage. Is he laughing about grammar?

'Poor *devil*,' Jay whispers.

Again I don't know for sure what he means. Maybe the loneliness of this modern cow keeper. Maybe his laughter in aspic. But I know one thing. I envy him that laugh.

Or is Jay just worried that he is playing all by himself? For a twin, it's hard to understand such a thing.

We are disturbed by this visit. Slightly agitated. Half wish we hadn't come.

So we leave. Jay puts his stolo-stolo away. We have to run now. It's pitch dark. And a frightening place, the estate. With armed guards. And worse still with *nam trene* that lure the careless to join them across the border, in death.

We quickly go and cut the amount of cane tops we need, cut, cut, cut, then tie them in a tight bundle with the liana off my shoulder. I stick my sickle into the cane tops. Then we both lift the heavy bundle up into the air, and at the exact moment when it hovers up above us, not knowing whether to go on going up or to start coming down, I slip under it, my tightly plaited hair cushioning my scalp. I make sure the balance from side-to-side is right, and we set off to go fetch the hidden coconut.

I am obliged to swagger wondrously just to keep the bundle from moving up and down and jolting my neck. Which is why I still walk that way.

Jay gets out his stolo-stolo again.

Tor-wing, tweng tweng, tor-wing, tor-weng.

He plays it to keep any more coconuts from falling on our heads. But I, stupidly, feel safe with the huge bundle of cane tops on my head.

I just worry about Jay. He could be dead by now.

When we get home, father says, 'You'll end up in borstal, the two of you, stealing like that. Go and get scrubbed clean, no time for homework, straight to bed!'

That night as I'm lying in bed thinking about my undone homework and imagining the blank pages of my scrumpled forty sous exercise book, I decide that when I'm big I will imagine the link between all human languages and computers. Even then, to me it seems possible.

Much more interesting, I decide, than plumbing.

Now, in the whole world no more than a handful of us deal in my skill. We fall equidistant between the language theorists and the computer software people and the electronic technicians. We don't have much formal education either. None of us.

But then again, it's all relative. In here, my having passed the Certificate of Primary Education puts me in the top bracket.

While my ignorance about almost everything that almost everyone else in here knows remains quite patent.

U nlawful strike becomes lawful if trade dispute reported? An existing or threatened strike in any industry shall be unlawful unless a report of the industrial dispute out of which it arises has been made and 21 days have elapsed since the date on which the Minister received the report and the dispute has not been settled or referred to the Commission or to the Tribunal and if the strike commences within 56 days from the date on which the Minister received the report. [*Industrial Relations Act (1974) Section 92 (1)*] – Copied from the Prison's Library.

'But why? Is it all made up against you, or were they looking for someone else?' Leila just can't believe it. 'At least I *did* something,' she says.

The cell is so stuffy we could die. Sweat is pouring off our brows. Hard labour just being incarcerated in this heat.

Even before the accusation of *Effusion of blood*, she had the other charge of *Breaking in by band*, she says. She *did* something.

'Why do they want you inside? Who is it wants you inside? The police, or the companies or the government or someone else?'

'I'm not sure yet. Not a hundred per cent sure,' I say, *Ride carefully,* Boni told me, *now you're secretary.* 'All of them, I should think. It probably wasn't a case of mistaken identity, after all. Not wholly. The bit about them calling me Anita remains a mystery. The courts aren't here to solve mysteries, my lawyer tells me. Maybe the Anita part is just a mistake the police made. Maybe they haven't perfected their conspiracies against citizens.'

Then I tell them how the reason they are all after my blood is that I'm in the new wave electronic creations union. And I'm just beginning to be in a movement. But in this movement, I'm very new. I don't know anything. *I regret that I don't.* I think it's all because of the union. I'm secretary, you see. They needed a secretary, and they voted for me, the members did. I was just an ordinary member. I went to the meeting with a bread roll with potato salad in it, I remember. Holding it in one hand in a white paper bag, eating into it. I used to get so hungry sometimes, even outside. Someone proposed me, and my mouth was full, so I couldn't refuse, and then I got elected. Secretary. *Ride carefully now you're secretary.* That's what I believe, only I've got no proof.

Oh. I see, Leila says. She weighs this.

'But what have they got against this union?'

Here I explain about our court case. 'We have been preparing a case against the company. Arguing that there has been a slow drift back to slavery. Buying and selling employees like me. It started just with the sportsmen. Then some performing artists. Then us. We are called the computer creative technicians. My branch, as you know, is language generation, *grammar* you could call it, studying the hierarchical blocks we juggle so naturally, as we speak. The union is also bringing up the question of the payment in kind. Rent and medical insurance. The disappearance of the right to refuse overtime. We are obliged by law to accept overtime. The virtual banning of the right to strike. And so on. We have actually declared what's called a *Trade Dispute.* That's what they call it. It's a kind of threat of a possible future strike, that's all.

'The last secretary got a promotion to management. The president has had his passport taken away from him, on the grounds that he may be wanted as a witness in a car accident. An accident he never saw.

'Now me.'

I see on her face that she now knows everything I've said is true. It's all true.

'Our union is part of a worldwide web of unions, mind you,' I add. So that she doesn't give up in the face of it.

Mama Gracienne has given up on understanding it at all, ever. But she *believes* me. She has experience enough to tell a lie from the truth, and she can see I'm telling the truth, the whole truth and nothing but. Not those staccato versions they elicit from you in the box.

But Leila says, 'Prove it!' Doubt coming back into her heart.

'Prove what?'

'That you were set up?'

'Now I've got to prove my innocence? Do you think people should be free and equal?' I ask her. 'All people?'

163

I have managed to get around to the test line with ease. I wait, not daring to breathe.

'Yes,' she says. 'Oh, yes.'

I mouth the letter '*m*'. She knows what word I mean.

'As a matter of fact,' I say, and now I mouth whole words, '*I did the electronics for in here*.' I point to the doors, and then move my hands widely meaning the doors to all the cells, to the dining halls, sick bay, the generator, and the inside gates, and even the outside gates.

Leila is still letting it sink in. *Did the electronics for in here.* Then she smiles her crooked smile, flicks her uneven mane off her face, puts her head back and laughs. She laughs a long and increasingly deep laugh. Somehow if this is true, then all I've said is true. For her.

You also smile now, Mama Gracienne. 'In that case,' you say, 'I think we need to celebrate.' She raises a small glass of crude rum, you can see from how close together her fingers are. *Neat.* She throws it down her throat in one movement. Shudders at how strong it is.

I suggest it should be something special, something so tasty we could die.

Mama Gracienne offers. 'Can *I* tell something beginning with a "*d*"? It's from the Islands. Dried fish. *So tasty you could die.*

'I cooked dried fish for Honey, the night she died, so I'll tell it in memory of her. But I didn't cook it in homemade tomato sauce.'

D ried fish, crisp-fried like in Diego Garcia in homemade tomato sauce.

'Remember when you buy dried fish, that a half a quarter pound can feed a family,' you say.

I am comparing the grammatical structures you use for this recipe with those used in a statute. A recipe: Remember, *you say,* when *a,* that *b* can *c.* A statute might read: Note when *a* (a local authority is set up) that *b* (it) can *c* (govern those living in the defined area). *Why do I waste my time with such thoughts?*

Boil the dried fish for a while, and then drain it. This takes some of the salt out of the fish and gives it back some body. Then take the fish off the bone, break it up into flakes, almost splinters, throw away all small, silly bones, but keep big ones, especially if you get the one with the spinal cord in it.

Heat up a pan of oil for deep-frying until there's a haze. Then put the fish in. Water will steam off in a loud hissing sound. Deep-fry the shredded fish until it doesn't make the hissing noise in the oil any more and until it's light. Then pour the oil from the pan, through a metal strainer (not to melt a plastic one, Leila) into a metal container for keeping the oil, which is delicious, for later use.

Then leave the fish draining in the strainer.

Now, brown onions slowly in some of the oil you have used for the fish, add three sprigs of fresh thyme. When the onion is nearly cooked, add crushed garlic and, if you want to, one or two chopped up green chillies.

Then you chop up tomatoes (sour tomatoes are better) into

tiny, tiny bits, almost crushed, and put them into the oil and spices. The tomato then half-boils, half-fries in the spices.

Taste the fried shredded fish to see how salty it is. Then add some salt (but not too much) to the tomato, and at the last minute put the fried salt fish in. Take off the heat and sprinkle finely chopped fresh coriander on top.

Serve with rice and leaf soup, after a glass of baka dew.

Murder: Manslaughter committed with premeditation or lying in wait is murder. [*Criminal Code (1888) Section 216*] – Any person who is convicted of murder, or murder of a newly born child, shall be sentenced to [death – death penalty removed in 1995, thus] penal servitude for 45 years. [*Criminal Code (1888) Section 222*] – Copied from the Prison's Library.

You are lying in your bedroom knitting, you say, that night, the night you did it, or you think you did it.

You are knitting, knitting away and thinking. *Musing*, as you put it, just before putting your head down and falling asleep. You are thinking about this and that, putting the day in order in your head.

Everything is very quiet.

Honey is in her room. She's probably already asleep. Her boy is probably asleep, even before her.

You smile as you think of him. Same calm ways as his mother, as your Honey.

Honey says she is *dead beat* today. The factory work tires her out, mentally and physically, she says.

She operates a big cutting machine that cuts two hundred backs and two hundred fronts of shirts all at once, she says. So that the pattern in the material for the backs joins up exactly to the pattern in the material for the fronts, where they will get sewn together under the arms. So she tells you.

She only gets back after dark.

Then the evening meal.

There was, you say, nothing unusual in that. You convinced her to share *your* food and not to bother lighting her Primus and not to bother cooking for herself and the boy.

Not to tire herself out, you say.

Rice.

And pumpkin leaf soup with the rice water and browned

onions. And salt fish. Boiled first to desalt it a bit, and then broken into tiny bits, and deep-fried until they were crisp. The boy loves that. Some chutney with raw, sour little tomatoes and chillies and pickled lemon and garlic. You say this as though you can remember the exact tastes, as if they have all stayed in your mouth from that night onwards.

As though these tastes were a sign.

Or as though they remain as a proof.

This is all happening one evening some time back. Maybe this time last year, in terms of the weather, you say. It was hot and stuffy then too.

Airless is the way you put it.

That night was airless. Same as in this cell tonight you say.

The custard apple tree in front of your house has got new leaves on it, you add for proof. So many, you remember, you can't see through it when you look out of her window. As though the green of the forest is inside her room. And they are dead still, the leaves, that night.

Her boy is probably also asleep. Yes, you repeat this. Need to convince yourself that he knows nothing.

No doubt already fast asleep in a cot-like thing he sleeps in at the foot of her bed.

He is very bright, you say. An affectionate, warm child. Like her, you repeat, calm.

Their room is very neat. She keeps it that way. The clothes are all in a cupboard in little piles. Shirts. Underclothes. Trousers. Her skirts. Dresses. And their socks.

There is a calendar on the wall with a photograph of a grotto of some kind. Tall mountains behind, with snow on them. A religious grotto, you say. With a candle in it. Perhaps in the Alps. You sometimes pray to this calendar or to the grotto or to the candle. When you are all alone.

Pray that she and the little one will be safe. That it will look after them, the calendar.

Roderick is out at work, you tell me. Yes, her husband is called Roderick.

He works night shift at the electronics factory.

He prepares his own food if she's not back from the factory

yet, and today their paths crossed, as you put it. She got home just before he left. Their paths crossed that night. This is not unusual.

No, they don't fight.

Never heard a rough word between them.

They both take a drink, you say. That's all. Drink a bit.

And they laugh.

They are too carefree in their ways. For you, you say. Too carefree. Happy-go-lucky, you add. You say this.

You also say that you are not like this, that you left your happiness behind, long ago somewhere.

Maybe you buried it.

In the place your navel string was buried in. *On another Island*, you say. You left your carefreeness on another island. With your umbilical cord.

Was it when they closed the Islands maybe, I think.

But I don't know.

I don't understand what this means.

I heard you saying it to Blue One-One, *the Islands are closed*. A man said it to you.

Through a hatch, did he say it? These words mean nothing to me. Maybe you will tell me another day. Explain what it all means.

We will have plenty of time in here.

Perhaps too much time.

But I only say, 'What electronics does he make, your son-in-law?' Of course, I have to ask this, although I try my best not to. I just can't help it. I am too curious on this subject.

Tiny little plates, he says he makes. Soldering minute things he looks at through a magnifying eyepiece strapped to his head, soldering them to one another. Like a jeweller, he says. Only not jewels. Each thing has a precise other thing it has to be soldered to. He doesn't know what they make with the plates. He says he doesn't want to know either. They sacked a group of his friends who tried to find out. He said he told them not to be so nosy. He warned them. He told me he had. Not our business, he said to them. We just work here, he said. He thinks maybe it's for tanks or satellites or automatic things for submarines. Weapons, arms,

170

automatic ones. But maybe he is only a boy imagining things. Why do you ask?

'Just wondered. I'm interested in electrics, you see, and electronics. I also do that kind of work.'

Everything is quiet, you say.

You knit a last few stitches with the light on to get on to the ankle bit, two plain two purl, you say. Two plain two purl from now on you can do in the dark. You switch the light off.

Socks.

You knit socks. Socks for everyone. One by one. You knit in the day, and you knit at night. You knit with your eyes closed. You knit in the dark. The hotter the weather, the more socks you knit. You started knitting when they closed the Islands and you never stopped, you say.

This is an aside, you say.

If you had needles, you would be knitting right now, while talking, you say. *They'll never give you needles in here,* I say. But then again, maybe I am wrong. Maybe they will now. They have changed their attitude towards such things, Tiko told me.

I look, for example, at your scarf. I think of the prisoner in our cell before us. Mopey Sue? How did she do it? Cutting or hanging, I wonder.

Then I go back to listening to you again.

You hear Honey cough. Or is it a snort? Or is it just her snoring? In her sleep, you think.

So you ignore the sound.

Wait.

Listening.

Knit-knitting, knit-knitting hesitantly now. Not with the same rhythm. Checking two plain two purl again and again with your index finger. Losing concentration. But no concern in you, yet. A cough or snort or snore is the kind of thing that happens often. But still, you are alerted somewhere deep inside you.

Two plain two purl. Two plain two purl. But watchful. All ears. Suspicious.

Then there is another sound. This time it is a loud snort.

So you put your knitting down quickly and quietly, but with enough time to make sure the needles are stuck into the ball of wool carefully, and you feel for your slippers and patter through the lounge to her room.

You stop just outside her door, and listen with your ear almost touching her door, right to the wood of that flush door, you say.

'Honey! You OK, Honey? Sweetie?'

No answer.

She's asleep, and so is her little one. Because he doesn't answer either. He is big enough to answer. If he was awake, he would answer.

So, you don't open the door. You turn around, leave her. Privacy demands this, you say.

You turn your back on her door, and you walk slowly back to your own room.

But you leave your door open now though. In case.

You take your slippers off, but leave them just where you can put your feet back into them, if necessary.

You go back to bed.

You just sit there, leaning against the wall, your knitting on your knees. You wish you didn't knit and knit, not in the dark like this. Not in this heat.

But you don't even start knitting again.

You hear that sound again. You jump now.

Nerves, you think. Only my nerves.

But your heart is beating too fast.

Maybe it's just palpitations, you say. Because of the anaemia you've got.

You put your knitting aside for good now.

You sit bolt upright and you wait. You listen. You wait. On edge. Your pulse thumping away at your temple. A feeling of concern is rising in you.

But then again, she cooks separately. Most days anyway, and this means you have to respect a certain distance that goes with separate cooking. I don't want to interfere, you think.

You hesitate.

At the same time, you do your best to calm yourself down. You make yourself breathe really slowly, especially breathing out really long and hard, like the doctor said to do when you got that anxiety spell in the night for nothing once, and like your great-grandmother told you to do, when you got scared as a child on the island where there were so many ghosts they outnumbered the people.

Stay still, she said to herself. Ever so still. And breathe right out, long and slow. For god's sake, you mumble to yourself, keep calm.

Then you hear a sound so loud and so terrible, a sound so unearthly, so appalling, coming from deep down, deep inside a human being's chest cavity, your daughter's, your Honey's chest, that you shoot out of bed, tear out of your room, through the lounge, run barefoot up to her room, shove her door open, and find her.

You stand there.

One look, and already you know. By the light of the street lamp through the window.

She is already dead, you say.

Dead.

'How do you know?' I ask.

Your sweetest one. Your closest one. Your *last youngest smallest* one. Your Honey. Your only one. Only one left.

You touch her forehead.

Is she still warm?

You can't remember any more. Her nostrils and mouth are already sealed with a fine foam. Like the foam on a wave on the reef, you say. Foam you couldn't possibly breathe through. No living person, you say, could breathe through that fine foam.

Now this is when your story goes threadbare.

And it closes up on me.

And it shuts me out.

And you start to act shiftily. But I know. I know.

The child is still asleep, you say. Are you sure? Do you wake him up?

You feel tension in the air.

Dead.

Death has come into your house. Into her room. What does it mean? What are its consequences?

Her death frightens you. Frightens you so bad you don't know anything any more. Your throat is closing in on you.

173

Do you just lose your mind? Do you have a bad turn?

You panic.

You feel rigid. As though you were the one who is dead. You say this. In another world, you say. As though death had come to take you.

If only, you say.

But, you say that you feel lucid at the same time. Clear-headed, as you put it. The opposite of losing your mind, you say.

Direct, right there, in the middle of your mind's eye, you see your great-grandmother, your maternal granny's mother. You look at her, your great-grandmother. Then you move into her, you say. Does this make sense? Do you revert to being her? Or do you do what you somehow learnt from your great-grandmother to do? Under such extreme circumstances.

She knew about the danger of knowledge and of the inexplicable, your great-grandmother did. The danger of understanding and the deadly peril of any new mystery.

She knew the risk for the *witness*.

She knew about the dangers for the first on the scene. She taught you about all this.

The danger of the answer and worse still, the danger of questions. The ill-fatedness of the unexplainable. Your great-grandmother trained you. *Hide the unknown.*

And hide from it.

Hide from the knowledge of it, itself. Cover what you do not understand. Immediately and irredeemably. Cover it up. Like a cat does after defecating. Look left and right, sneakily, and cover it. Never try to know the unknowable. Step around it. Avoid it.

Never let a policeman in either, if you can help it, she had told you.

Never.

At times like this, never tell things.

Silence.

Pull the sheet over her. Pall.

Rather no one know. Not even you.

But you don't actually pull the sheet. You just stand there. Studying the foam for any sign of movement.

None.

You shake like a leaf. Then make a low lulling sound. Ululations. You go blank.

Under orders.

Like a zombie.

A female zombie.

Beware!

Be shifty!

Your eyes skim around in horror. The strange singing in you comes from another world.

Beware!

Sulk!

What will be the effect of any action? The song of the past gets sung slow, swing low, sweet chariot, sing slow.

Be sullen!

Show nothing!

Do nothing!

Just in case of catastrophe. Catastrophic effects may ensue. Quiet. Beware.

Beware.

Beware.

Careful, tread carefully. Give nothing away in your words.

Put the fingers of both hands together lightly in front of your face. Tilt your head forwards slightly. Look at your own hands. Hide all knowledge.

Now raise your hands, and hide behind them. Know nothing.

Except one thing.

You know, and you know with a deep and absolute certainty, that *anything* you do, *anything*, could provoke the end of everything everyone ever knew around you. You and everyone else could get snatched up, stolen, spirited away for ever, from everything you ever knew. Never to return.

Cataclysms.

Holocausts.

Mass deportations in irons.

Rough seas.

Be *silly*.

Pretend not to understand.

Go catatonic. Be a beast of burden. Embrace stupidity. It's safe.

Safer.

Assume silence. Silent as a tomb. A sepulchre. Confuse the others. Confuse yourself.

You are rock.

Rock forwards, rock backwards.

Rock.

You are stone.

So you crouch there now. You sob dry sobs. No one will ever know anything.

You stay still like that, you say.

You don't even go and call Aunt Paquerette, the neighbour who might advise.

You wait.

Checking.

You stand up and look now.

Petrified.

You stare.

No movement of the foam. No stirring or bubbling. You look at her child.

Her child still asleep.

Your child dead.

You don't know how long. Too long. No use asking you about new minutes and old minutes. What's the point?

So, why do you come forward and make this confession now?

You didn't do anything.

And they lock you up with me, an allegation, and with Leila, this young case here of effusion of blood of a police officer.

You say maybe you did kill her.

Maybe, you say.

But you didn't, did you? I know you didn't. You know you didn't.

Just because you don't know what happened to her. Just because you don't know why you acted like you did, doesn't mean you killed her.

So, at the time she died, you thought maybe you killed her? Or now you think so? Or when you confessed? Yesterday?

You say you don't know. Maybe just yesterday.

So finally you go and call Aunt Paquerette.

Who runs over to your place, and rushes up to Honey.

And touches her.

And says, but Honey's Mother, she's already cold.

In all this heat, she's already cold.

And then Aunt Paquerette catches it from you. The same thing. It moves into her and inhabits her too.

Or does this thing, whatever it is, like lightening, strike her, too? Separately?

Hard to say, you say.

You move as one. The silence. The throat-constricting petrification. You both stand there.

A deep and wild helplessness rises into all your joints, and makes them weak.

And then this passivity moves into your shared consciousness. You and her.

You want to be two *beasts*. Of burden. With no consciousness. With no knowledge. No responsibility for things you cannot change. No memory for things you'll never know.

No nothing.

Please, please.

Let us feel no more, you say you said.

And so it comes about that together, the two of you, in silence and hurriedly, change her into a new cotton night gown, a greyish pink, and you put some newly knitted baby pink socks on her cold feet, and you arrange all the bedclothes neatly. You put on a new pillowcase with yellow and orange genda flowers and a shrub of citronella of all things, embroidered on each of its four corners.

You do this really quietly.

Like in a morgue.

Whispering strange prayers and catch-phrases in some unknown tongue. Both of you. She caught the secretiveness from you, Aunt Paquerette did, you say. And then you doubt this again, all over again. Is it that you both had this knowledge handed down separately, but from the same thing? The same net thrown over the past, trapped like an animal, the same shackles and whips?

You both mumble and mumble and mumble.

Prayers you didn't know you knew come to your lips. *Back* to your lips. The same words to both of you. If prayers they are.

Maybe phrases or songs, maybe rituals or rites. Maybe ululations and variations on a tune.

Then the two of you pick up her child, fold him in your arms, and you run out, holding your heads falling backwards, away from the child, raising the alarm, and you go wailing in the street, crying out to the neighbours, 'Oh, what a terrible problem has come upon us!'

You both cry this strange phrase.

'Oh what a terrible problem has come upon us!' As though divine intervention. Something sent to haunt you, it haunts you.

You do not say the word death. Or illness. Or pain. Or loss. You say *problem*.

You do not say *happened to us* but instead you say *come upon us*.

'Come out! Wake up! Please. Oh what a terrible *problem* has *come upon us!*'

Or are you afraid of the priest? Could you both be *that* afraid of him? To hide Honey's death? To risk her life?

Could you have saved her life?

Dare I ask that question?

Is this why you confess? Could you have saved her? By calling neighbours and a nurse or a doctor at once? Mouth to mouth. Hit her hard on the chest. Cardiac resuscitation. Lie her head and shoulders over the edge of the bed. Physiotherapy to drain her breathing tubes. You know all about this, you do. So does Aunt Paquerette. Could she have lived? Your Honey? Maybe?

You don't know.

I can't measure all this. What is the priest to you?

What the priest could mean in your mind, or in your and Aunt Paquerette's minds, is unknown to me. I cannot guess the exact nature of his place in your hearts. Or your great-grandmother's feelings for a priest under the circumstances she and some priest must have lived under, unmentionable circumstances, circumstances of him owning her.

Perhaps *he* will think it is suicide, today's priest.

This is what he *will* think.

And it's this that is too much for you?

Was it suicide, Honey's Mother? And refuse to let the body into the church, leave it out in its coffin in the glare of the sun, to rot the faster, right there in front of everyone's harsh eyes? Only to be buried in the *Hindu Section*?

Do you think she drank something poisonous?

That foam.

Did it have any smell? Could it have been the result of Honey drinking poison?

No, she wouldn't. Loved life too much, to the full, you say. A hedonist, from what you say. Did *that* make you ashamed of her, her embracing of a passion for life?

Scared of the priest, are you?

Priests are against pleasure.

She loved pleasure, Honey did. She loved chocolates. Fluffy boleros. A drink. A joke. A laugh. A smoke. Sega dance. A surprise. Comic books. Jazz music. A hot stare. High heel shoes. Hot curry. Probably sex. *Nisa*. Maybe even nirvana. She was perfect.

The doctor comes.

You do send for him at some point.

Eventually, later in the night, you and Aunt Paquerette have some young man half-drunk go on a bicycle and call him. Tell him to tell the doctor that *a terrible problem has come upon us*. Which is what the boy on a bicycle does say.

The doctor comes quickly.

He knows you and he knows Aunt Paquerette too. *A terrible problem come upon you.*

He walks through the silent crowd of neighbours who stand ever so still. Hovering in suspense.

Words lost.

Whites of eyes showing all round irises.

He stops as he enters Honey's room.

In the lintel.

He takes one look, and you suppose he knows.

But he is a man of science. So he must check. He must check laboriously. And while he is checking, he must try and work out what has happened. With a small piercing torch that comes out of his bag, he checks in this eye, and then that one. Just in case. Some reflex closing of a pupil. Some sign. But by then it is late. Far too late. He even leans over to see if there is some smell in the light foam that has reformed between her teeth. Then he asks everyone to leave, except you and Aunt Paquerette. He looks into your eyes and into Aunt Paquerette's and then at both of you. His eyes, you say, tell that he knows the unknown, his eyes know the unknowable. He knows me, you say. For the doctor, all this is beyond his calling. But, he is close to you, you say. Close. Such a nice man, you say, as if this may take you away from your story. So he shares the moment with you. He asks if she has been ill.

Flu last week, you say. Nothing important.

He asks what she had had for supper.

Same as you, you say. Ate *my* food today, doctor, you say. Leaf soup and dried fish and rice and some tomato chopped up with spices into a chutney.

She pregnant, he asks, *been* pregnant?

Not to your knowledge, you say.

Where is the husband, he asks.

They've gone to fetch him at the electronics factory, you say.

He shakes his head ever so slowly. Ever so sadly. For what seems like ages. Has he felt what happened to you? And to Aunt Paquerette? Does he know already that the doors to knowledge closed in front of both of you, despite both of you?

He looks at you. His eyes ask a deep question. But you won't tell him anything. Not because you don't want to. You yearn to. But because you don't know what to tell him. You have no idea what to say because you don't even know what happened. You have your lost grip on things. He senses it. He knows it's all lost. All gone.

All out of your reach already.

Far, far away.

He calls Aunt Paquerette over close by. Speaks quietly to her over his doctor's bag. And she answers quietly. You don't hear what they say. You just see their lips moving. They stand like that, the two of them. Like in a trance.

Then he comes over to you at the foot of Honey's bed. Death's bed. He says he is sorry.

He says he is also sorry but he can't say what she died of, will therefore need to get a post-mortem done, do you agree? He asks you.

You agree. You nod your agreement.

So does Aunt Paquerette. She actually says the word *Yes*.

So does Roderick when he comes in. He can see it has to be done.

You organise the transport of her body to the hospital. Or someone does. You who know she is already dead and what's the point now. *But you want to know.*

They'll cut her body up for nothing, you think, but you decide you want to let them.

What does it matter if they replace her insides with bunched up bits of newspaper.

Maybe even open up her head, you think, and you shudder. And yet.

And yet, there is this part of you that persists, that wants to know after all. To know the truth. For sure. The modern part of you. Science. Trust in the doctor. The desire to leave the fear of the past. To move forwards. The part of you that could *maybe perhaps who knows* have saved Honey but didn't manage to.

A certain peace comes down on you when you know you will know.

Honey's body is out, away on a visit, a visit that will bring back knowledge. Certainty. A modicum of order. A glimpse of the enlightenment you want and need.

The absence of her body is the promise of a parting gift from her. Temporary peace comes down. Like a shroud. In order. In harmony.

In all our history, it is so temporary this feeling of peace and of the rule of reason, I say this to you because they are the only words I can find.

You go on telling me what happens next.

Then, you say, some blue lady interferes. At the hospital while they are sitting around waiting for an autopsy. She is there for some other case, watching over some prisoner, and she just interrupts. You know her vaguely.

She, this blue lady, comes forward and says she knows the

family. And she says no *need* to go through a post-mortem. She says you never know what time the body will be given back. The police haven't got a case anyway, she says.

So she gets some hospital doctor to sign some paper, and they bring Honey back, all the way back again. Bring her back again without any answers.

Just a death certificate.

With some nonsense for cause of death.

Burying another generation in mystery. Leaving you in doubt like this, in eternal doubt about her history. Her fate now sealed in non-knowledge.

And it is this that makes you go off your head a bit. Go slightly unstable, as you put it. Obviously it would, Honey's Mother. This is normal. You didn't do it. You didn't kill her.

No, I say, no, I *don't know* what she died of.

How would I know? I mean if you don't know and the doctor didn't know, how on earth could I know? We never will know now. The knowledge is buried with her.

That doesn't mean you killed her, does it? Yes, you did act strange. Very strange. But it doesn't mean you killed her. You go to sleep now.

You need some sleep. You need peace of mind. It's quiet in here. You'll like *her* too, when you get used to her. Leila. She's only a child really, a child gone a bit wild.

'I am worried about the one who gave the message to me. They suspected her of something, they wanted to get her, to get hold of her, and I don't know what they've done with her.'

There's nothing you can do now. Tomorrow maybe.

I get up and go and tuck you in. You are soft.

I take the scarf off your head. Rather not leave it in your hands over this particular night. Don't want to make one space more in this cubicle, so to speak.

Well, they won't get you this way.

I stroke your hair. I look at your hands. The fingers that knit. Two plain two purl. Making socks in this hot climate. Maybe they'll give you needles to knit with. I'll watch you if they do. I'll get you to teach me. You can teach me and her.

'There's a strange smell in the air tonight,' you say. I sniff carefully. Yes. What is it, Mama Gracienne? I hear a bat beyond the prison shriek.

'Definitely a cyclone. A bad one.'

I can believe it. There is something ominous and inexorable about this night. A warning in the silence and the calm.

Far away dogs growl and snap-bark.

Then I look across at *her* on her bunk. The tall heavily built Leila.

She sleeps, stretched out full length, legs jutting out, one pointing in at the other. Her eyelids are mauve and the palms of her hands phosphorescent. Still fast asleep, sweat glints off her tilted brow. *Must get her more pen and paper and brought-in meals.* The careless disjointed way she lies makes her look like a fashion model, posing, blown up on a billboard somewhere. She looks very public. Her prison clothes haute couture. Her badly cut hair lies askance, the latest in vogue. Her expression, even when she's sleeping, insolent.

'Just look how sweetly she sleeps. You didn't do it, Honey's Mother.' I shake my head at Leila and at Mama Gracienne.

T hen I take to screaming again.
     Again I take you and her by surprise. Both you and her.
Again. Again I find myself enjoying the scream. Needing the
scream. Wanting to go on screaming beyond the edge. Again the
blue ladies catapult in and whisk me off to sick bay.

They have been expecting me there. In case I have an ectopic,
they say. It is written into the doctor's report: *Observe for query
ectopic.* So I get myself under observation.

And I observe as well, needless to say.

S o here I am in sick bay. A blue lady comes in with razor in hand, and stands at the door making a signal that my time is up, and that she's going to cut my throat. She draws her hand across her throat in the notorious gesture of a threat disguised as a warning. *Nothing arbitrary about the grammar of gesture.*

She does it again.

I signal back that she better come in fast and get on with it.

Then I say aloud, 'You don't want to make a mess. Go on, put a sheet of plastic down for the blood.' She smiles and by way of reply shows me the little vacuum cleaner she is carrying in the other hand. 'Not to worry, sweetheart. High tech.'

'I am not your sweetheart.'

'You've got lice,' she says, 'and I wouldn't really have a sweetheart with lice, would I now. *Allegator!*' She spits the last word out with disgust. Then she struts over to my bed, pulls my head down roughly, as if I am some animal she owns, puts my head under one arm and she proceeds to shave my head with the other hand. A gust of wind whistles through the sick bay, disturbing the peace.

From time to time, she shouts at me, telling me not to move suddenly like that, for god's sake, when I have been still as a statue. She's covering herself. When she's finished, I just sit there in that dead stillness, waiting for her to get out of my sight. A strange passive rage is in me. There is not a breath of air.

When she moves away, I feel my head, hoping stupidly for neat contours of skull and scalp, perhaps some new beauty in myself, but instead I find my head to be full of little tufts and unevenly shaved bits, and obviously a dozen cuts, each oozing its own trickle of blood. I didn't really have lice at all. They just do it, cut your hair if they want to. I see the blood on my hands now.

'Nice, isn't it,' the guard blue lady turns around and says. 'Nice and clean.'

'Oh, beautiful. My hairdresser is such a talented woman. Just what I always wanted.' I turn my head this way and that, blank eyes of a model on the catwalk. *Their cold gaze is also probably hatred.*

'You're not sick, stupid bitch. I'm watching you! Put a foot wrong and it'll be bread and water for you. Up the fucking pole, and all.'

A gust of wind gets into that sick bay and whips around it like a warning to that blue lady with the razor. Her nerve wavers, I see her glance over her shoulder and let the razor droop. The gust subsides, and just as she relaxes, another comes in and tears around a little longer looking for things to lift up, and a blue lady's conscience to disturb.

The weather is now starting to *deteriorate*. How far can it? *Worst there is none. That far.*

Gusts start coming in series now, trying to blow things around in the sick bay cell, before quieting down again. The quiet more threatening each time. The gusts more sudden and stronger each time. But the gusts find nothing to blow. Not even hair. Everything's nailed down in here.

Only this blue lady nurse to rattle.

I can hear the outside, where gusts make leaves and twigs flurry and scurry around at the foot of the walls. Large apparently stable things in the rest of the prison begin at the height of each gust to creak and to groan, like masts of long ago ships as they lean on the timbers and members below deck in a storm and frighten those seamen imprisoned on them.

Prison ships. Sentenced to the hulks. Hulks moored out of reach, out in the harbour of the city.

Everything gets into a state of *bouts* of agitation.

It's getting stronger.

Now when a gust comes, everything shudders and rattles in the whole place. Locks and window panes. And there is the sound of things banging all over the building. And these sounds echo about. *Not so solid after all. We had thought too, too solid.*

Then there is an eerie calm.

All shutters have to be closed. Loose shutters have to be tied down by the blue ladies. In sick bay they have tied down a stay-bar on a small opening above the window. A telephone cable that I can see out of the sick bay window goes mad during gusts, quivering like a serpent and then beginning to shake danger-ously. I could probably reach it with a hook and pull it in and use it. I know how to insert pins into the cable, ordinary straight pins, and use this wire, with the most elementary headset that I could probably make right here in sick bay. Rain comes along-side some of the gusts. Hard little squalls of diagonal rain, whipping at everything cruelly. Wetting everything, drenching things through and through, causing mulch to form on the ground, I can smell it, and making the air heavy with humidity. Stuffy and expectant.

I am here to try and recruit someone.

But there is no one else in the place. I've drawn a blank. I am the sole occupant of the sick bay. *I mourn for someone I haven't found yet. I miss her already.* And yet, it is, strictly speaking, not too important that I haven't found anyone in here, because I have asked Leila also to look for someone. Keep your eye open for someone, I told her. Someone who would understand everything. Someone bold. Who we can trust. Leila's young but by now quite capable.

One of us will hopefully succeed.

Here there is just the blue lady nurse, the Lady with the Blade. Sitting just by the door now, because the guard blue lady has gone off somewhere. Fidgeting this way and that, she is. It is as though, having shaved my head like that, she is left with a compulsive need to move her legs about now. She just can't sit still. She tries, but then fidgets again. She's supposed to sit inside, but I suppose she can't stand looking at me and my fine hairdo. Good. *Lady with the Blade. Death the Reaper.*

I need to go to the toilet, go to the toilet, go to the toilet, and I say it so often that she gets sick of locking and unlocking me. So she unlocks my hands from the bedstead for good, leaving the handcuffs dangling from my left wrist like a malformation. Like she's pawned my handcuffs for her own freedom. My slop bucket is just by the bed. They take such risks, these blue ladies. I could go and hit her over the back of the head with the slop bucket, knock her clean out. They know us too well, and not well enough.

I don't do it, of course, because the timing would make it a senseless act. But how can she be so sure?

I do need to go to the toilet quite often, as it turns out.

At least there is a radio here though, in sick bay. She's got it stuck to her ear, the blue lady nurse has. Tuned in to Indian film music. Loud. Must be blasting her eardrums clean out. Maybe the cyclone noises already scare her. I am pleased it's loud. This music will be interrupted from time to time to give details about Cassandra and Doorgawatee, who I need desperately to get details about. I wish I knew more about cyclones, instead of always having treated them like some kind of unwelcome interruption of my routine at school for six years and then at work for twelve, as some kind of inevitable visitation. *The details. Take care.*

I am thinking about who I could have recruited had there been someone else in sick bay. Who I could have hoped to recruit. Maybe she will walk in soon. Pure speculation. I reckon I could meet one of three kinds of woman prisoner in sick bay. Not *just any* prisoner will do though. For example it wouldn't help to meet someone who is genuinely ill, sick as a dog, and who will not be fit enough to help. Or I could meet up with a shirker, and she may shirk everything, not just prison work. She may shirk a mutiny or even a getaway. But then again I could just meet a third kind of girl. *Like the one I already miss before I've met her.* I may meet someone *curious*. That's what I'd like. That's what I'm looking for: A curious person. Someone in good faith. Someone with a sense of wonder. That's what I'd like. A girl who comes here just to see what it's like in sick bay, and to go back to her cell with this knowledge. Nothing more. Except maybe a funny story to go with it. That's what I want.

But we prisoners are all milling, building up readiness. Milling to fine tune ourselves. Right now, we are. The milling mode, the whole lot of us are in it. The blue ladies even pick it up from us. I too feel the urge to mill around and sniff others, to make sure we all act as one.

I haven't got anybody at all to choose from. I haven't even got company.

Left to my own devices, I muse restlessly. *When my milling is thwarted, it turns into seething rage.* One of the things I rage about is that I've got too many responsibilities.

I want more guidelines for this getaway or mutiny or whatever it is. I like some guidelines in life. I need more plans to be handed down to me. I won't say I need 'more orders'. But yes, maybe. More directives anyway. Now I am out on my own instead. I don't feel well enough equipped. I've never trained myself for this kind of duty. All I know is electronics and computer language. A bit about the union. Less still about the movement, so new and slow was I. I regret this most of all. What I know isn't enough. For one, I don't know anything about the logistics of a getaway. Let alone a mutiny. Why take power at all? Why not pull the sick bay blanket over my head and hide. What will I do with liberty anyway? *Rage, if thwarted, will become depression.* Then you get to like the *inevitability* of things. Of almost everything: Wage cuts, the weather, redundancies, illness, price rises, factory closures, time elongation, cyclones and false charges. Imprisonment itself becomes inevitable, if you get to like the inevitability of things, if you thwart your own rage. The reality then weighs heavy. *Adapt or perish.* Get used to *reality.* Learn to turn away like the others have. Jobless growth, no more than a statistic heard on the television and forgotten. All those millions of people who take pills against depression, just a little known fact.

I refuse.

I, now lying with a handcuff dangling from my left wrist inside the High Security Women's Electronic Prison, enjoy the rage I feel. And things have come to depend on me.

This is what makes me free. *Things depend also on me.* I am suddenly free.

A free woman.

It makes me dizzy. Free to think and plan and act. I am scared. Dead scared. I am scared of my own thoughts and my own impending, giddying liberty. I shake. Not so much scared of *escape*. But of *mutiny*. I am scared of authority as well, terrified. Even when it is vested in the fidgety wreck at the door, who has just made some ten or twelve cuts in my scalp, and then fallen asleep with a transistor radio on her bosom and her head on the transistor. *I wouldn't hit her over the head with that radio, because I need it.*

Doubt comes and I feel like receding into oblivion instead. If only I were not even a milling, sniffing animal, but one with a carapace, or some form of calm vegetable like an aubergine or bitter gourd say, or more inert maybe, like a cowpat, or perhaps even a rock, a nice plain basalt rock.

And then the next minute, when I think again about escaping, a kind of thrill and a wild dream rise in my insides, of running in open spaces splashing through shallow water, out to the reef, and diving down into the open sea, swimming. *Actions and routes and choices and maps and concatenating ideas and events.* But when I lie still, feel the dangling handcuff, and try to look *mutiny* in the face, she dances as if to tease me. She threatens, if I don't watch out, to swing me around until I get vertigo.

64

When she is brought in on a stretcher like that in the middle of the strongest gust yet, I don't even recognise her. Who'd be able to? *Ride carefully now you're secretary.*

From the bed next to mine, when she feels, blindly feels, me peering over at her from my bed, and when the gust subsides, she asks in a hoarse voice, 'Are you handcuffed, girl?' and when I say, 'No, the handcuff is dangling from my arm,' she says, 'Come over to my bed.'

'Oh, it's *you*,' she says. 'How did you get into sick bay? Come nearer. Can't you recognise me?'

I don't recognise her voice either.

They must have injured her larynx as well. As well as every visible bit of her face and body. Her eyes have disappeared in swelling. But I begin to recognise can't place it *something about the rhythms of her speech. I have heard those cadences before.* Where do I know them from. *They are patterns that warm me to her.* Ride carefully.

'What have they done to you? Who . . . are you, why? . . . are you here?' I ask, 'The police do this? Me, I'm fine. Nothing real.'

'Not the ordinary police,' she whispers. She *knows* me. Then adds, 'No police station in the area would take delivery of me. They won't touch me. *Beaten up too badly,* they say. Trouble in it. They think I might *peg*.' She leaves long silences. Time is no object.

Gusts rise and then die away in the silence. No stopping them now.

'Then there'd be enquiries and suspensions and loss of bonuses at the end of the year. *Don't worry, I don't intend to*. No, it was the *political arm* that did it. That's why I'm direct in prison, no magistrate or anything. I'm a Green Slip. They fill out a green slip to get me admitted straight into prison. Matron is scared to put me into a cell. She is observing me, she says. There'll be one of those doctors in soon, so be careful.'

'What's the political arm?' I ask, not wanting to pain her with too many questions, but feeling an urgent need to educate myself a bit, what with my new responsibilities. Maybe I will understand my arrest better, if I know about this political arm. *Can't quite place what I recognise. Ride carefully.* I must try to find out who she is. I look away from her.

I wouldn't mind looking at her if she was sick, or even if she was injured if it was by accident. *Feel faint.* But I can't stand looking at her mutilated body. Mutilation intentionally inflicted. *Dizzy.* Even the calm of her rasping voiceless voice causes me distress. *I want to retch.* Her wounds are a shadow over my heart, like I'm part of what did it to her. An accusation against myself for being so ignorant. *Ignorance of the movement is no excuse.*

'Political arm of the drugs squad,' she spits it out, rasping. Her pain, I begin to feel it.

I force myself to look at her face now.

Her lower and upper jaws on one side are so swollen that her face looks lopsided, as though she is reflected in a funny mirror. *Quizzical.* Her lips are black and bulging with uneven contours and with crusts of dried blood in each corner. Both her eyes are puffed up, closed almost completely, and they are quite different shapes, one from the other. One is more closed on the inside, one is more closed on the outside.

'Don't look so worried. Nothing's actually broken,' she says.

A bright green tree lizard, turquoise green, comes in through the air-brick on the wall behind her bed and looks at her quizzically. It's got bright red spots glowing in the turquoise on its back. Luminous. It stops there, just behind her. Does it feel the approach of the cyclone? Is it this that makes it abandon its perfect camouflage in the palm tree at the prison entrance? Come indoors and stand exposing its resplendent colours against a wall so white? At what risk?

Just like this prisoner.

'It's just my face that's a bit beaten in,' she says. 'And my throat. And everywhere.' She is also turquoise and red about the eyes. Her throat green and blue. Hers are the dirty colours of torture. But her hoarse voice is still so beautiful, as if singing a lilting stanza. 'They use the drugs squad because nobody wants to stand up for anyone accused of drugs. No lawyers, no newspapers, no do-gooders, no Rotarians, no unions. So the political arm of the police just attaches itself to the drugs squad. Easy. You still can't believe it's me, can you?

'You've come to sick bay to look for someone? I went to meet Gracienne. A friend said she was about to confess to a murder. The police suspect me, but *they don't know what of*. That's why they beat me up. They know I contacted her. But they don't know about the message.'

The way she said '*but they don't know what of*', the exact cadence she used, the tune she spoke in, made me recognise her.

'Boni, can I say your name?'

'Call me *Diya* to be safe. Not that I look much like *a little lamp* right now.'

It dawns on me now. *Leila* knows Boni, *you* know Boni too, Mama Gracienne, and *I* know Boni from work. And here she is now. She tries to prepare us. Inasmuch as we are preparable. Invisibly. *Ride carefully now you're secretary*, she said, and that was the only warning I ever got from anyone in the whole world.

'Can we check you bone by bone?' I ask. 'Let me just fill you in first. Mama Gracienne was put in my cell, so I got the message immediately. She's well. We are three'd with Leila, *the Effusion of Blood*. Mama Gracienne worries about you, she's got a sixth sense.'

Boni looks relieved at the news that *you* are fine, Mama Gracienne. You, the mother I have found. Inside. I, who was born without a mother.

'Yes I'd like it if you could check my bones. Be very quiet while doing it though, so we hear any blue lady coming. We don't want them to come and disturb us. They must not know I know you.'

The blue lady nurse by the door is fast asleep throughout. Her head on her loud radio. Even in her sleep, her legs are condemned to move restlessly. This way and that, micro-movements, fidgets.

'She certainly won't hear much,' I say. Lucky my handcuff is dangling from my left hand, so I just keep brushing it out of the way.

I check her right hand, start with the right thumb. It is unbroken. The nail is black and navy blue. May come off. And all the fingers of the right hand, and the hand bones, then her ulna and radius, OK. Her upper arm bone. Her shoulder joint moves fine. Collar bones on both sides whole. Her upper left arm, and down the arm. All unbroken. Bruised, but not broken. Then her ribs. Slowly. OK. Round to the back. Shoulder blades, fine. Hips. Two femurs. Knee cap. Tibia and fibula. All the toe and foot bones. All unbroken.

'They haven't identified me yet,' she said. 'Their ID machine is out of service. They put me in it, and it just read, "Mapi spooler has exited unexpectedly." So they tried again. Same thing. I know it's happened before, because one police officer said, "And where does he fucking well go each time?"'

A one syllable laugh tries to come out of her, but it's obviously too painful.

'So they fill in whatever I say. I say *Diya*. They write *Diya* down. They don't bother to put our faces to memory any more, so they haven't got anything to fall back on. Since fingerprints went out – declared obsolete they've got confused. Yes, I'm going under the name of Diya. I am thick. Little or no intelligence. On IQ, I arranged to get less than.'

Then she looks at me, 'Well! Well, I am pleased to see an allegator before my eyes. I bring good news. Relax.'

'What's happened to their ID machine?' This is a question I try not to ask. Professional deformation. I kick myself. It's so repetitive, every time I hear about electronics not working, whatever the situation, no matter how inappropriate, I feel I just have to know *why*. Even before asking about good news.

'Tartaric wasps' nests,' she says.

'What?' I ask, thinking that I'm not understanding the consonants that come from her damaged lips and tongue and probably even damaged teeth.

'There's tartaric wasps' nests in the whole central system.'
Then she makes a strange sound, and I realise it's her trying not to laugh it hurts so much. That wonderful musical sound is a laugh coming up from her tummy, bubbling out happily. Lucky the radio is loud.

'They have made their mud nests and laid eggs in them in all the circuits, and that's it. You should smell it. That waxy smell.'

'And what about backup?'

Then she makes an even funnier sound, as though she is crooning. Almost yodelling. More suppressed laughter trying to come out.

'How can you laugh? In your state?'

'Oh, it's only pain I've got now. Only pain. I just tune out of it. That's what's so nice about your checking me bone by bone.'

Then she goes on, 'You know what happened to the backup? It's all there. Loads. On disks. Sweet little things. The micro-disks that were in fashion. They have got everyone in the whole region on backup on them. Anyone who's ever set foot in the region is on their backup. But it's all on those micro-disk reels that fitted a system which isn't operational any more, as you know. Apparently they're trying to find someone with this system still operational to do a conversion, but they can't. You know, just like happened with all the early NASA data. It's on huge reels that computers don't use any more.'

What I do now is, I glance at the let-sleeping-blue-ladies-lie, I stand up and dip the end of my brown prison shirt into my water mug, and then go and lean over and with the wetted corner of it, I clean the dried blood off from around her mouth. Slowly and with care. The blood is dry, so I have to rub quite hard. I don't see her wounded parts separately from her any more. I only see her as a whole person now. Her *being*. I put some order into her hair, slowly.

'Like *your* hairstyle,' she mumbles.

'Oh, Boni. Oh, Diya, I should say. Oh, cyclone, come slowly, so you can be better in time. What did they do to you?' I hold her hand.

'You will manage without me,' she says, 'but in any case I will be better soon. My spirit is fine, and my body will mend. Not a time for the details, now.'

'Rely on me for the lock systems. Diya, Diya, Diya. I am practising and practising. That's what I'm good at. Electronics. I'm not experienced enough at anything else, Diya. I am not getting enough directives.'

I sound moany, I know.

'Why have they undone your handcuffs then? You've got to try and keep them off when it comes to the eye of the cyclone, if you're still here.'

'Because I have to go to the toilet so often.' Saying this makes me think of Leila suddenly.

'You helped Leila give herself up?' I ask.

'I heard she was "wanted". So I went to see her. We always need to get messages in and out of the prisons. But I found her so young I decided to just help her give herself up instead. You will have to go give her more details, then. Do you really have to go to the toilet so often?'

'Yes,' I say.

'Good?' she asks.

'Can't say yet,' I reply.

'Check the young one for the same thing. She is too young to be in here, and too young for *that*.' I already know.

'Two in one cell! You've forgotten to tell me the good news you've brought, Diya?'

'It's for *after* mutiny. I really like your new hairstyle. For the ones in the getaway. There are lots of bits of women's clothing in a pirogue under the bridge, on the side of the river opposite to the prison side. It is called *Sapsiway*, the pirogue is. White with a red line painted along its length. Mast also red. The clothes are in four plastic bags. Each have bits and pieces for about five people, but ten could share them and get some distance. Including sandals of various sizes. Don't tell until *you* are on your way out, or *someone else trusted* is. There is a small radio. Money for transport, for when buses start to run again. Now the river will be up by the time of the getaway. And all the pirogues will have been pushed up on to land. *Sapsiway* will be pushed up on to the higher land by the football field. The plastic bags will be tied under the front deck, to try to keep them a bit dry. Assume they will be soaking wet. *Wet clothes* is much better than *no clothes*. Do not leave prison clothes on *Sapsiway*. Anywhere else, but not on *Sapsiway*. And if I'm fit enough, I'll take half in the opposite direction. Towards Ti Rivyer.

'Remember, what is important is to *act* normal. A good actress would hardly even be spotted in her brown prison shirt, prison trousers and prison sandals. Tell the others too. It's in the walk, the way you hold your head. And,' she goes on, 'one last thing before our blue lady nurse comes alive again, and gets back to work.

'Put a hand under your bed. Here,' she says pointing. 'It should be on the left hand side. It's been in here for ages. Many messengers ago. Hope it's still in place. Can you feel anything?'

I wonder how she can know what's under my bed.

I look at her. A woman hidden in a swirl of bruises and grazes and lashes and swellings and gashes, and she can think and suggest and act.

It feels like a blade. The teeth of a small saw; I am marvelling. A hacksaw blade. I glide my hand behind the hacksaw, there's something else. A file. It's a file. A flat but heavy little file. Both are no bigger than pens. Can use the file to sharpen the blade too.

'I need a screwdriver for all the electronic plates.'

'Both tools have screwdrivers at each end. American one end and ordinary the other.'

The minute I know I've got two screwdrivers, I feel fine. 'Well, we should be away then. We'll come get you from sick bay?'

When the subject gets on to electronics, I gain in confidence.

'Oh, I'll be with you. Maybe I'll be out by then.'

I take the saw, and make a tear with it in the waist band of my prison trousers, and I thread both implements in. I pull my prison shirt down.

When I hear the familiar sound of the cyclone warning music, I shout across to the blue lady nurse, 'Wake up, Lazy! What if matron finds you sleeping on duty? She'll stick your name up on the notice board, then what? Your efficiency rating will fall, then what. Turn the radio up, then. Do us a favour. Who is this battered woman here anyway? What you do to her, then?'

She wakes up, and does turn the radio up. Even further up. Boni also wakes from the fitful sleep she was in.

It is the *Class One* cyclone warning.

Time has been unleashed now. It will start to move to the rhythms of nature. It doesn't matter how long anyone says any second is any more.

I try to memorise it all: *The cyclones are still both heading very fast in our direction. Most unusual to have two cyclones at the same time, acting in the same manner. Cassandra and Doorgawatee. Cassandra still large diameter, her girth is wide. Latitude ten degrees south, longitude sixty-eight degrees east. Doorgawatee smaller diameter. Eleven degrees south, sixty-seven degrees east. Both are now Intense Tropical Cyclones. At their centres, there are gusts reaching up to 280 kilometres per hour. They are approximately 1,000 kilometres north-east of Mauritius moving in parallel, at an accelerated speed of twenty-two kilometres an hour. General south-westerly direction. Seas will be very rough.*

'Pack up then, allegator, back to 14a Block D or wherever you belong. Your head looks a pretty sight.' It's Blue One-One again. Ubiquitous Blue One-One. In person, standing at the foot of my bed. Following me around. *You-bikwetis*, I curse her under my breath. Telling me where I belong. I loathe her.

She looks at Boni with contempt, as if she should be ashamed of herself, lying there in such a state.

I can't stand her. She is the one blue lady I hate the most. I feel this burning hatred and at the same time I am overcome by a regret. Because I am lucid enough to know how petty I am being to concentrate so hard on this one idiotic hair-starched and hair-dyed representative of law and order who I happen by chance to find standing in front of me.

But I can't help it.

I can't stand the sight of her. Nor the way she is looking at my naked head. Especially not when there's a cyclone coming. I can't stand the smell of her either. Blue One-One smells even worse than all the rest of the blue ladies put together, what with her wafts of deodorant, eau de cologne, mouth freshener, body lotion, talcum powder, hairspray, scent, each in turn, and then all muddied in together. Enough to make you puke. Especially with the smell of sick bay mixed in. Now I pick up the smell of nail varnish, emanating from her fingers. She must have just come on duty. Acetone. And boot polish, the distinct smell of boot polish, clear as a bell from the toes of her newly brushed prison guard shoes. A sneeze starts to build up in my nose, but I manage to control it. I get scared that my fear of a runny nose will come back again.

No such luck. No harmless worries are left in me. But an acute
sense of smell. Like a dog.

'Can't you pack it in?' I say. 'Wherever I go I see your face turn
up in front of me. I can't even come to sick bay without you
following me here. Give it a break.'

I know I have to keep the banter up. I can't say *why*, but I
know I have to. *Never ignore your jailer unless you absolutely*
have to. Try, by whatever means, to bring out what's human in
her. Her quest for recognition, her need for human company, her
love of some mongrel pet. Try to find a glimmer of something. An
old rusty yearning for knowledge, a flickering response to the
first few bars of a melody, a resentment about a childhood lost,
some faint memory almost gone now of hope, a hint of a smile.
Whatever. The quest, however fruitless, brings out your own
humanity in you. And in so doing heals you. I have found this
out.

'Nothing the bloody well matter with you, is there? No use
your staying here, getting on the nerves of this here bright magic
lantern, Diya. Blocking up much needed space for genuine
patients with genuine illnesses. *She*, for example, needs a bit
of rest all right. She fell down the stairs, as you can probably see
for yourself. Quite a flight of stairs in her house, isn't there then?
Know her by any chance?'

Blue One-One must be in *intelligence* these days.

Not very good at it either. And what with their internationally
compatible under-the-skin tag-system broken down, they probably have to start everything all over again. From scratch.
Without even up-to-date finger-printing any more.

'Never set eyes on her,' I lie. 'Surprised her own mother could
recognise her after what you girls have done to her.

'She's not a very talkative type either,' I continue. 'Must live up
top of all those stairs all alone. Or, lost her tongue when she fell
down maybe. Bit it off. Or did you girls cut it out? Doesn't want
to tell me a thing. Shouldn't think she'd be charmed to tell you
anything either. I believe she is a very beautiful woman. Under all
the stairs business. I think she may be influential, as well. Just a
feeling I have. May know people in high up places. May be the
daughter of a major shareholder of Prison Systems Inc., never

know. You ought to watch out for her. Don't you go believing that behind her silence and her blood-stained mouth there is not a human being. A human being who might just be able to get you into a lot of trouble.' I can't find any good in Blue One-One, so I have to resort to threatening her instead. Diya won't be able to look after herself much in the state she is in once I'm gone.

'Could you stop talking your baragouin!' she shouts at me. Blue One-One senses that I am threatening her and doesn't like it. Means it has worked. 'And shut your trap!'

Once I get going, I love telling her lies, and asking questions. 'Is she all there, do you think? Upstairs? I mean before you threw her down? Where did you get that smart bit of vocabulary from then? *Baragouin*, if you please?'

She doesn't answer me, but turns to Boni instead. She leans over her and shouts, as if she's speaking to someone deaf.

'You know *her* then, Diya? Do you know our pet allegator? Ever clapped your beady, closed up, swollen fucking little eyes on her? Such a clever one, our pet allegator. Talks too much, on the one hand, and not enough, on the other. Allegators are like lobsters. Shit in their heads. Which is why we shave them.'

Boni turns her head slightly, 'Who? . . . 'e? Talking to . . . 'e? Not shit in . . . 'y head.' She isn't very good at her m's yet. She's acting dim-witted as well. I can tell.

'Thick as two planks,' Blue One-One announces with satisfaction. 'She's thick. She's so thick it'll be hard to do the shrink tests to see if she's all there. Even if she was all there before, you never know now. You just never know. Quite some stairs.' She tutts and shakes her head. She is threatening me back. Tit for tat.

'True.'

I say this word to put an end to our conversation. It has the same effect as the words 'full stop' or 'period'. I have heard enough from Blue One-One on this subject.

Then I ask her to turn the radio up. To hear the cyclone warning again. She does this. It is blaring now. She does it not because I ask, but because she wants to know how much extra cyclone duty money she might get, depending on what class she gets to work overtime in. Essential services, they are, blue ladies.

The very few essential services left since the rest were privatised and called utilities.

We get to listen to the warning again. Learn it off by heart. I will tell the others when I get back. Draw the co-ordinates in my mind. Eleven degrees south, and sixty-eight degrees east.

67

S o when the blue lady guard reappears, Blue One-One gets up
and says, 'Let's go, allegator,' and she dispatches me off with
the guard. A gust disturbs everything in the sick bay, and in that
gust, I pretend to check I haven't left anything – as if I were
leaving a tea party or something – and manage during this
pretence to cast a farewell glance at Boni. The world in a glance.
I touch the hem of my shirt. The blue lady guard goes ahead of
me by mistake, it must be the cyclone making her act out a
different order. So, I have to overtake her. I must walk ahead, of
course, as if she defers to me.

This unnerves the blue lady. Unusual that. Wind makes the
corridors seem narrow, with leaves like mice scuttling down the
skirtings, and uphill.

She steps on the backs of my heels on purpose. When I nearly
fall over, she tells me to *watch my step*. I refuse to let her get
under my hair. I haven't got much left anyway for her to get
under.

You smile when I come in, Mama Gracienne. Then horror at
my hair. As if I was mutilated. Then check my body in one
glance, and relax.

A mother, pleased to see her grown-up daughter back home.
And you open your arms wide.

You and Leila play draughts, squares drawn on the floor and
little pebbles. It must be Leila's move, because she doesn't look
up. The blue lady doesn't even look in.

You wait for the door to close behind me. 'And don't you go
doing that to us again, mind,' you say. You tell me off for the

shouting and screaming. Put it on record. 'My nerves aren't up to this kind of thing too often. It's not funny any more.' Then you add, 'And with these gusts that press on and on, I get scared easily.' She says nothing about my hair, but just takes it in in one more passing look.

'Don't worry, we'll harness this one,' I smile. You laugh and Leila also laughs, laughs her head off, because she has seen my head. 'Who knows, maybe you will look this one straight in the eye.'

'Can we go up to the window for a quick look out?' I ask. 'See if I can see the cyclone.'

'You look a picture,' Leila replies. She is touching the ends of her own long hair, so crookedly shorn. She says nothing more about my hair, just shakes her head and laughs again.

She is game, of course. They'll play their draughts game again later.

We do a little warm up. That's our rules. *Rules is rules.* No lifts before warming up. *Both of us expecting. I look at the way she stands, the particular way she puts her hand on her hip. It must be true. A family that gets funnier.*

So then she puts her hands in the stirrup position. *I remember Jay doing this and me looking in at all those cows.*

I climb up by the window, steady myself on her shoulders. *Hold it just there,* I say. I work first the hacksaw blade out of my waist band, and put it on the sill, and then the file, and put it next to the blade on to the sill. Neatly side by side. I make sure they can't be seen from down there.

'Well?' you ask. 'Well?'

I feel giddy. The clouds race across the heavens too fast. Tear across. Rush from the east in lethal lines across the sky so headlong to the west that I almost lose my balance and fall over. I have to hold on to the bars to keep myself from keeling over. *Advantages and disadvantages of bars.* 'The purple is worse,' I say. 'Not just mauve like yesterday but pure purple and there are bits of naked branch showing here and there on the trees, because leaves have already been stripped off leaving some bark bare. Your insurance sign is still there, you'll be pleased to know,' I add.

I lift my feet off her shoulders, she steps back and I jump down.

The minute some specific action, like this peeking outside is over, there is a lull back in the cell. A silence. A yawning boredom. An emptiness so deep inside it causes a vacuum. Fear unsettles us. This time the vacuum draws Leila out. Nature abhors.

She says please can *she? Please.* Can she tell me a recipe beginning with '*e*'. One that Mama Gracienne told her last night. She's been practising it, trying to remember it off by heart for when she gets out. For *if ever* she. She wants to practise out aloud. I could hug her.

Hope it isn't *eggs*, I say. Of course, it isn't. It's marsh leaves, that's what. Three e's.

68

E dible elephant ear, it's called. It grows lush in marshes, edible elephant ear does, so you can wade in in boots, go cut some yourself before cooking it, or grow a patch by the tap in the yard, if you want to. It's also called bred sonz. *Am I right, Mama Gracienne? So far?* The new shoots coming out are best, rolled up like cheroots, they are. You cut each stalk and leaf a foot or eighteen inches long. *Is that right, Mama Gracienne?*

'Perfect, sweet one,' you say to her with your generous lips whispering her on.

First, you rub your hands in oil so that it's easier to get the purple dye in the plant off your hands afterwards, then you set about preparing the leaves and stalks. You start at the bottom of the stalk, snap off a two-inch bit, say, and there's a string left. You pull off all the stringy bits, like you do with green beans, only all over. You pull this way and that, and long bits come off. Then you break off another little bit and do the same thing. When you get to the leaf, you break it into pieces.

Put all the leaves with some salt to boil in a wrought iron round-bottomed karay or in an ordinary heavy-bottomed saucepan for about half an hour. (You can boil edible elephant ear leaves in a brand new iron karay just to cure it before using it, Mama Gracienne says, but that's another thing.)

Then you drain the bred sonz out, and throw the water away. If you don't do this first, then the edible elephant ear can make your mouth get itchy. Or so they say.

Now, you put oil into the karay or saucepan, brown quite a lot of onions, put in a few dried chillies. Then you put the drained edible elephant ear back and fry it a bit. Now the key thing is to add the right amount of salt and tamarind. The way you prepare the tamarind is you take a handful of them, peel them, also removing the three fibre strings, take the pips out by pouring warm water over your hands and working the flesh of the tamarind. You squeeze it and squeeze it, then strain the liquid into the karay or saucepan.

Now you have to let it cook another fifteen or twenty minutes. Then you start to beat it into a mash.

Serve with faratas.

'Let's sit down and eat it,' Mama Gracienne claps her hands together. 'You are both so welcoming.'

69

U ncontrolled juveniles: Where the parent or guardian of a juvenile represents on oath before a juvenile court that he is unable to control the juvenile and desires him [or her] to be sent to an industrial school, the court may forthwith order the juvenile to be removed to and detained in an industrial school until he [or she] attains the age of 18 or for a shorter period. [*Juvenile Offenders Act (1935), Section 18 (1)*] – Quoted to me verbatim by Leila Sadal.

70

L eila Sadal, the Effusion of Blood, is a wild horse girl. She could have been in this place when it was a borstal. *Young girl, out of control.* She still looks underage. Can't be sixteen yet.

Anyway, she tells us, she starts being seen with this boy, being noticed with this bad boy, a boy whose brother is a gangster. He likes her, she says, and I can believe it. She changes out of her blue checked school uniform, white socks and gym shoes, all of which she puts in her kit-bag on her back, and is seen speeding by in jeans, a leather jacket and high heels on the back of his motorbike, her beautiful hip-length dark brown hair flying out from the bottom of the crash helmet. Before it got hacked up, she says.

Trying to tame her, they were, to break her in, the whole lot of them from her parents, whose veneer of respectability was fast wearing thin, to relatives and teachers, who wanted to impress with their concern. And to bring her to heel. They were all in on it. A project. *Aprivwaz sa tifi la.* The principal tried hardest. Friends were ever so helpful to her parents. The whole lot of them, she says. Even an accountant who is an acquaintance of her father's stepped in. But her mother is the one who gets adamant. And nasty. She wants Leila declared *out of control* and locked up until she is eighteen and safe. No longer a threat to her family's reputation any more.

And the boy is *the same religion,* Leila emphasises. A proof that she wasn't just doing it all to annoy them. Because if she was, he wouldn't be. This is what *gets* Leila. The same religion, same community. She is the best in class in pure mathematics and quite good at computer science at the high school (and otherwise the dullest girl around – she says it of herself – wearing her hair long and pulled back into an orderly plait for school) and she still can't please them.

So they attack, go for the kill as she puts it, and she goes wild.

The order in which these things all happen is not clear. She starts smoking cigarettes, being locked up in her bedroom by her parents, playing pool in public houses, getting hauled in by the principal, taking drugs, eating unclean meat, getting small tattoos done on her arms, answering her mother back, frequenting an opium den and chewing gum.

Her mother wants her *put away*. For all or any of the above, she says.

Leila doesn't blame her in a way. Or so she says.

But her father *does* blame her mother. He, a quiet gentle man, draws back from the lynch mob that's after her blood.

Her father says she's only a child. *Zanfan, sa.* She will learn. He changes sides. He becomes sympathetic to her. Tender. And then, soon afterwards, he starts talking to himself, and praying to the Almighty loudly and in public, and one day, grabs hold of Leila and cuts her hair. He wants to have something to keep in case they take her away from him. He goes half mad, back on to hard drugs and loses his job in the cloth importers' warehouse owned by her mother's family.

So Leila's mother tells him to get the hell out of *her* house.

So Leila goes wilder.

Her poor father, she says.

Anyway, Leila and her boyfriend and a few of his friends do a big fraud on insurance, on Secure Life Insurance, *her* insurance, and split the money. Something to do with tilting an insured car down some remote cave in the north and claiming insurance for car theft.

'I've still got the money out there,' she says, pointing towards the lakoklis trees. She is starting to talk like old prisoners do, 'I don't waste my time getting arrested for allegation or confession. I invest in my arrest, you could say. For me it is worthwhile.' She talks big for a young breakaway. Talks just like Tiko herself, 'I've got my future to think of.' She is witty too now.

'Why d'you bother to get arrested at all, smart Alec?' I ask. 'You told me with your own two lips and your very own tongue that you think *"everyone should be free and equal"*. If I tell you there's arrest in that statement, what would you say?'

'Bullshit,' she says. So easily roused to anger. Her crooked smile a sneer. Her long brow dark and stormy. 'That's what I would say. *Bullshit.* I am equal. Everyone is equal. We should all be let out of this place. And I'll say it if I want to. And I'll say it again.'

'Well, I can tell you that *if* you say that, and if you *do* something about it, my girl, you will sooner or later be *done* with an allegation or something. That is what allegators are made of. Sugar and spice and all things nice. Like me. It's about time you just grew up and realised it.' I, I who know nothing. I, I, who have only just heard of the political arm. I, I who am elected secretary, the one who didn't ride carefully enough. 'There's more to the world than meets the eye, as they say. So, go on, tell us then, why'd you go and get arrested then?' Then I add a question, a rider, you could say, 'Why aren't you in *juveniles*, then?' I have just confirmed in my mind, just realised that she must only be about fifteen, even now. Maybe fourteen. And tall and strong as a horse.

'*Juveniles* refused me. They don't take Effusions of Blood.'

'All right, on with it.'

D *amaging property by band*: Any person who plunders, or damages provisions, goods or merchandise, or any other property committed by a body or band, and with open force, shall be punished by imprisonment for a term not exceeding 10 years, and by a fine. [*Criminal Code Section 352*] – Copied down from the Prison's Library.

'Y ou see, there's this woman, who is, they say and I believe it, in the drugs business,' Leila, suppressing a sigh, a sigh that is replacing a tear, relates this as if she is much older than she is, older than me, older than all the other prisoners, older than her mad father and even older than *you*, Mama Gracienne.

Relates rather than just *tells.*

I incline my head to one side, an acknowledgement, a sign of appreciation, a gesture that she's got the floor now.

Silence descends. I feel panic rising in me, and disappointment flooding over me. What if she stops telling us? What if I never get to know? What if I have to face the silence of the walls.

Mainly she's in drugs, she goes on.

Relief.

Then she sloughs off her dullness, which was such an outer thing anyway.

Her story.

'This woman's got this big house with thirty rooms,' she says. Leila ran through them with burning eyes. 'You should have seen the furniture she had on her closed veranda,' she says, 'and in her main salon, you wouldn't believe it.'

'Had?' I interject. *Always watching the tenses, we are. Like fear of death, they haunt us. My mother was a this. Did she stop being a this, or is she dead? It isn't clear from the grammatical structure. Nor is it clear even now whether childbirth, a massive coconut or treacherous water.*

'Yeah. *Had.* A chaise longue. Ottomans. Antique chairs of all shapes and sizes. Tables from India with ivory carvings set into the wood. Carpets with gold thread woven into them, not just on the floors, but on the walls, and plates made of silver and platinum set into alcoves. The door knobs in her house are made out of precious stones, set into silver and gold. The taps in the bathroom are gold-plated. Golden lavatory, she's got. Like the Pope's. The doormat's a real Persian, the one you wipe your feet on. Not to mention the jugs and vases, balancing on every horizontal surface. Everywhere you look. Giant porcelain urns from the east, China or Vietnam, with great fronds of filigree ferns coming out of them. And these beautiful veranda windows, hundreds of panes with diamond-studded glass from Venice.'

The child seeming so dull to the adults, so wild inside. And also so wild outside the enclosures.

'Anyway. Anyway, she, this lady, it turns out, also works for insurance. Not just for drugs, but also for insurance.

'What work would she do for insurance? you may ask. She does the *dirty* work for insurance, that's what. That's the answer. Ten out of ten.' Leila didn't know about this trade before she knew this woman in person. 'Do you know anything about it?'

I am moved by her telling. Her awakening. Her having been awakened but masking this. I ask myself where has the dullness gone now.

I say I have heard about it, but I don't have first hand experience of it. Nor do I want to. You, Mama Gracienne, you just shake your untidy plaits at Leila while your hands work slowly at the soft flesh of your upper arms, massaging it. You aren't *into* the story yet.

'She, this woman,' Leila says, 'actually works on a contract basis for the very same insurance company that we *did*. This woman works for Secure Life. So while the insurance company people paid up with a grin on their faces, after we had *done* them, it turned out it wasn't a grin at all, but a sort of rictus of fury, as my boyfriend calls it. *Rictus of fury*.

'He knows smart words because he's a rap singer. He bought the CD for the biggest dictionary in the world with money his brother gave him, and he does rap in three languages all at once.

'Which is another thing my family didn't like about him, rap songs. But that's beside the point.

'He's in the men's now. Alcatraz. *They*, this insurance racket,' she points vaguely to her sign outside, 'they wanted to *kill* us. Or at least to teach us a lesson. So a local contract was out. When they are in this particular situation, it is the insurance company's habit', she believes, 'to contact this particular woman, approach her, make sure she submits a bid for the contract. *Tenders* and all for their contracts. Because it's a transnational corporation, Secure Life. So it follows the rules. Equal opportunities for all. No corruption. And so on.'

She talks like a woman of the world, this one. This child who looked so dull.

'But, of course, *she* got it, the woman did. The contract was in her purse. Sewn up. And she was about to come around and do us in.'

Now Leila didn't know exactly what she had in mind. 'She does all sorts of things, they say, in these cases.

'Sometimes, for example, she sets you up with drugs.'

I shudder. *I must find out about this later.* I've got another charge coming. *Allegation for conspiracy to plant.* Won't help for the last one, that's done and gone, but maybe for the next one.

I am *alleged to be like this woman actually is.*

I feel as if I'm falling.

'Sometimes,' Leila says, 'she just poisons you, right off. But then there's the body to deal with. And a funeral which is considered messy. People say so. People say that she gets rid of some of these so-called *nuisances* by having them encased in cement and cast out to sea, or buried in the foundations of high-rise tower blocks. Sometimes, especially if you haven't got that many relatives, she threatens you or blackmails you into working for her as a sub-dealer or hit-girl.

'This, she is known to say, is more efficient. It's called *Making you into a Nikita*. Makes her more competitive on the world market, the woman says.' But, Leila didn't know what she had in mind for her and her boyfriend. She didn't know then, and she never found out.

Mama Gracienne, you just shake your head at Leila. Mondye, you mumble. Your soft hands move lightly around your neck, this way and that, as if you have lost something important that you usually wear around your neck, against such things as what your ears are hearing now.

But when Leila and her boyfriend hear the woman's clinched the deal and has got a contract all sewn up in her purse, a contract to come and get them, she and her boyfriend decide on a *pre-emptive strike.*

Leila picks up my admiring glance. Strategy and tactics, I am thinking. This girl is quite something. I listen in silence to the words Leila weaves.

'Maybe,' Leila says, 'I lacked experience then.' She is the first to admit it. Maybe she and her boyfriend will suffer her revenge for a long time to come. 'I've already started to as you can see. But then again, my life probably wouldn't be worth a sous if I were outside. The High Security Women's Electronic is doing me a big favour, as it turns out. Protection for free. Anyway, much as I try, I can't say I regret what we did. Not yet anyway.'

'What did you *do*, for chrissake?'

It's Mama Gracienne. *You* want to *know* now. Your interest has been aroused. Your calm has turned into impatience. Your resignation into curiosity. Your hands knead your forearms faster now, and your plaits all look like question marks above the head of a comic strip cartoon. Your head is turned around towards her, your eyes are completely fixed on her. You, who are usually so absent.

Listen, Mama, listen what she did.

Leila goes on. She and her boyfriend and his brother, and his brother's two friends went into that woman's house. It's on the bottom half of Green Square. People call that bit *execution square*. Where they used to chop the heads off male slaves and hang the female slaves to starve in public. That's where her house is.

She pauses in her telling.

Mama Gracienne, you know only too well how such places suck in everything, even silence. And the dead move into the living there, as a warning.

We listen. Me closely, you half-earnestly half-absently, now.

That's how Leila knows personally about all that woman's furniture and all her cut glass and all her hand-painted dinner sets.

She even knows about her silk pyjamas and designer label outfits. And that woman had more pairs of champal than Imelda Marcos had pairs of shoes. And all mod-cons in the kitchen. Micro this and macro that. Laser this. And super that.

So she and the boys went in there and broke it all up.

Into small pieces.

This big.

They pulverised the whole lot. As they picked up something, and turned it over in their hands admiring it, they just used all their might to smash it against the wall. Into smithereens. Whatever it was.

'At a certain point, we started to enjoy it. You know, as though we always wanted to break all those things. And all the things we had ever seen in rich shops in arcades and in advertisements in films and in glossy magazines.'

I go cold.

I recognise how I have started to enjoy screaming in the mornings. *The smashing up is the same.* I'm not sure I would have had the courage to confess as much myself.

'I got so carried away,' Leila says. 'Crash! Smash something to bits!

'Break something else!

'Hit!

'Slash!

'Kick!

'Punch!

'Tear into cushions and stab couches with knives from the kitchen drawer. The stuffing oozing out like entrails of a hare killed by a dog behind the power station.'

Leila muses at this memory of wildness. At her own story.

'Rent the curtains asunder. Rip them off those fancy brass ding-dongs they were hanging from. Until they half hung, half draped, half fell, like broken ghosts too lazy to go and haunt people any more.

'I actually threw an electric fan at a chandelier. It sounded like sound-effects in a French movie. The tinkling sound going on and on long after it had any right to do.

'And then, when everything was in small pieces, pulverised you could say, and I had been reduced to sitting there pulling buckles off shoes one by one, *inn des trwas tire vu deor*, and ripping baubles off belts, sitting on the floor there like a girl possessed by the spirits, I suddenly saw something.

'Something came to my notice.

'I saw those diamond-studded window panes. They looked so *cute*. I couldn't resist them.

'I stood up, as if to be a solo dancer on a stage somewhere.

'As if to take the floor under the spotlight.

'And with a preliminary jump on the spot, I started to high kick those windows out as well, and that was the mistake. That was our tragic error as my principal at school would have put it when I did literature.

'My tragic flaw. Seeing those windows and finding them so *cute*.

'Those windows. Now, most passerbys who saw all the little diamond-studded window panes popping outwards, *pop two three four, pop two three four, pop two three four five six, pop* – that was the toes of my shoes popping them out, I had those shoes that are the fashion right now, red ones with the metal toe bits that make a tap dancing sound, karate kick after karate kick, higher and higher, like I was a syncopated Moulin Rouge girl – they probably just nodded to themselves, smiled, and put their heads down and walked on. That's what I think. Because they hate her guts. Everyone hates her guts.

'Except her own son. As luck would have it, he, they tell me, was passing by. He is a man whose profession is waste removal – he gets all the big companies' sub-contracts – and he was driving past in his rubbish lorry, they tell me, having his workmen remove from the area surrounding his mother's house – execution square to be more precise – all the tin cans gaping with their lids bent upwards, dog shit, excuse my language – rotting potatoes going liquid in plastic carrier bags, expired brand name medicines with their instruction for use, broken umbrellas like so many dead fruit bats, dog-torn-open used sanitary towels causing shame, plastic bottles half-filled with dim-coloured substances, odd shoes, chipped enamel bowls, disposable nappies, and other nameless bits of junk that people take the trouble to go and heap up on to the ground there in front of her house – I don't know why people are like that – as signs of petty revenge, directed both towards her and to the place on the earth, as if to keep the memory alive that *that* was where the gallows were, special separate gallows for slaves.'

'But you were inside. How can you tell all this?' It's you again, Mama Gracienne. Now you even criticise her story.

'I know this off by heart,' Leila laughs. *The teller runs the tale. Who would have thought* she *could though.*

'Anyway, when *he* drove past, checking all the while that his workmen left no sign of rubbish on the pavement, he looked up and saw the windows pop, pop, popping out, or so they tell me, and he got on to his cellular and called her on her cellular.

'She was, as luck would have it again, sitting in the Inspector's office at the police station at the time, *inside*, when her cellular rang *ding dong ding dong* in her handbag.

'Again, this is what I happen to know.

'She was there collecting her rent or paying her rent, I'm not too sure which way the money goes. And her son told her over the telephone about seeing the window panes popping out like that.

'Anyway, they all came around at once in, I don't know how many, jeeps and police cars, screeching to a halt outside her house and armed to the teeth as you can imagine. In a matter of seconds they were out of their vehicles and were standing there with the big guns shouting "hands up!"

'This bit I saw. Just like in a cops and robbers film.

'Through one of the holes in the windows, I could see a constable under orders fumbling with a cartouche of teargas for us. "Prepare them something to cry about, Sergeant," the Inspector said in a stage whisper.

'By then we had smashed the whole place up. The pieces were uniformly small and sharp. Shards. Shreds. Shrapnel.

'So, we took one look at all of them. And we aren't stupid, so we all five of us put our hands up right on top of our heads, and stood dead still and everything. Sylvio Suntoo and his girlfriend, Patricia, Muttur's daughter – heard of them? – got killed like this for not giving themselves up quick enough.

'The police could see us because the curtains were only held up in one or two places and the window panes were almost all popped out. Our feet were firmly set in the glitter of broken glass. *Diamonds on the soles of our shoes.*

'And we intended to give ourselves up. All of us. Even me. Then I would have just got *breaking in by band* like the others. And my neck would have got broken when I got out anyway.

'But one of them said to me . . .' And here she falters a bit, and then, her voice breaking slightly, she quotes him verbatim, "*We know you, bit of filth father plumb loco, mother rich bitch.*"'

She stops here, and then repeats it.

' "*We know you, bit of filth father plumb loco, mother rich bitch.*" For some reason, maybe it's just too close to the bone,' and here she stops and runs the knuckles of one hand over the other's forearm, then changes hands. And just when we think she will talk again, she puts her head down a little, and lifts her arms up and runs her knuckles over the bones behind her ears, 'My father back sniffing brown sugar and then going and cutting my hair like that, like this,' her fingers run through it in front of her eyes so she squints at it. 'My mother back to her old sweetheart meeting him every week on the sly and lying to my father and to me, barefaced, and then her trying to get my father certified like only a rich whore could or would. Anyway.' She looks down and I think she's going to cry. She becomes the *child* she is, a big toddler, lips quivering just before the sound comes out, and when the crying starts, we won't be able to do anything about it. And then she looks at you and then at me. Instead she sighs. The terrible sigh of a young, young girl child who has – I suddenly know it – contemplated taking her own life. *Maybe that's why the one who committed suicide in this very cell before I moved in here upsets her so much. She got in first.* The smart of a tear in each eye. She tries to swallow them away, fails, and as she flicks her unruly mane back over her shoulder, her tears like dew from a lion's neck fly and hit the cell wall.

Silence.

We are waiting for her to go on, for *her* to go on. We show no sign of disapproval. It isn't us that sit in judgement. So we make no sign of anything. Nothing. If we say something nice, she will cry and we don't want her to cry. In case she never stops. So, we just sit and wait. We just listen. And we intimate by our quiet waiting that we accept all that she says, and we accept it as true enough and just enough. For us anyway. *Who are we to?* She is our cellmate and there can be nothing closer. At a moment like this. A magic second in an eternity of dull hours, passes on.

'I just went mad. And just like I had popped out all those diamond-studded window panes one by one, I started, I am ashamed when I think of it, to pop out *policemen's teeth*. With the toes of my shoes. One two three, I did. *Pop* two three. Blood was spurting from their mouths. Mixed with curses and teeth. Before they had time to. Then, when a fourth one tackled me, a full length body tackle the way they are taught to do at Mobile Force training, and pulled me to the ground, I found my head next to his, and, in my revulsion and fear and determination to defend myself, I got a hold of his ear in my mouth, and I bit and bit as though my life depended on it, as though I couldn't stop biting, and I bit so hard I bit a piece right out. I clearly remember having to spit it out, and spitting again and again, to make sure I had spat it right out.'

She stops now, and seems to still be trying to spit it out.

'Then they all started to beat me up and kick me, where I lay there on the ground. I remember tensing all my muscles, again as if my life depended on it, depended on my muscles being so taut no boot would get through them to any part of me that could be injured.

'There was a lot of effusion of blood. I'm the first to admit that. Mainly that one policeman's blood. The ear was bleeding more than the gums and lips. I don't know if they put that kind of thing in medical text books. But then things went all wrong. I heard an order given, spat out like it was a bit of ear, and the policeman with the cartouche of teargas fired it towards us. And I thought of Suntoo and his girlfriend and again I felt my life depended on what I did. The teargas so close by and in an enclosed space like that was ferocious. It started to burn my eyes and nose and throat like blades, but then we, all five of us, looked through knives for eyes and saw in real slow motion that all the policemen near us were much closer to the sizzling teargas bomb that span around like a snake than we were and that they were beginning to be badly affected, swearing, crying out blindly and flaying their arms and truncheons in the air like graceless dying spiders with too many limbs, too heavy to control. So the five of us spotted the chance, saw it like a fish sees a hole in the gill net. We saw it and headed for it. Once out, we slipped through all those endless rooms in that house, inter-leading without corridors, knocking over tables and potted plants, eyes stinging, right out the back door and, in one movement, like five segments of the same creature, over the wall.

'And as we landed on the other side, we adopted a new timing for our disguise. We walked calmly, slowly down the street parallel to the street at the front door, as if we had all the time of the day. Until we got to an alley that led to a public fountain to wash our eyes in.

'So that was how we got to be wanted. "WANTED" posted up with each of our photographs like terrorists in Italy, pinned up in all post offices and police stations. My photograph with my hair all crooked, I don't know where they got that photograph from. They closed in on all the others one by one, the place is hard to hide in these days.

'And so it was only me outside. *En cavale*, they said in the papers. Until I thought I'd better give myself up. Until Boni guided me through me giving myself up. When my charge sheet came through, I saw they only charged me for the one I bit the ear of. Did the prosecutors pretend the others didn't get their teeth kicked in? Says a lot for their laws, doesn't it? I should have been charged with four counts, not one. Funny that. I don't know why they didn't. I suppose they would have got into trouble with their superiors about so many teeth lost to just *one* young *girl* out of control.

'I got my money's worth so to speak.

'So, they did me for assault of a policeman with effusion of blood as well as for breaking in by band.'

I take her in my arms and rock her. And you put your arms around both of us, you do. And I feel she is my child, more than the beginnings of any child in my own womb, and I feel that you are my mother, more than the mother I lost before I ever had her.

Three generations sitting on the cement floor of a prison cell waiting while a cyclone approaches. Captured and held down.

Or maybe we are three babes waiting to be born. Funny triplets in a womb.

And then I say a funny thing. I say: *They won't rob us of this cyclone, they won't.*

Till now I don't know why I say this.

Nor do I know why it soothes both my cellmates. Mama you croon. She hums and hums. And I don't make another sound. Something lifts. *Cattle have thrown off their yokes.*

Bef finn kas lakord.
Enn bef.
Dis bef.
San bef.
Mil bef.
Milyon bef.

Once we are free inside, even inside the High Security Electronic Women's Prison, there is such *silence* in the world. Even in the middle of the build up to a massive cyclone. Free because of a decision to act. The decision to *mutiny*.

A kind of peace comes over us. Nothing else exists for us. I don't know how much time passes. Maybe only minutes. Maybe an hour. There are some violent outbursts of wind and rain, mounting to a fury, like a dog running after its own tail out there. Round and round. Then a calm, foreboding calm. Out there.

In here, peace.

The spell gets broken when, in one bit of quiet between two gusts, Leila announces she's got pangs of hunger. Her stomach is without let up. *I want. You want. She wants. We want. Food.* Again.

'Hungry,' she says. 'So hungry I could die. I can't stand it,' she says.

'Stop moaning,' I reply. *I suppose she is still growing.* And probably growing for two. She's already told her recipe, quoting from yours, Mama Gracienne, so it has to be me again I can only suppose, this time beginning with an f.

But, *no*, I'm wrong. Leila takes the initiative.

'*Fish*. I wish I had a piece of pickled *fish*,' she says. 'Can you make fish pickle?' She turns to *you*, asks *you*, Mama Gracienne. She knows you must be able to.

'I want to know how to choose and prepare the fish,' she says. 'And make the pickle. Nobody ever shows me anything.' She must mean her mother. *Nobody.*

So *you* show her how to make fish pickle.

Easy, you say. And I learn too. I always wanted to know.

F ish pickle: You buy fish, fresh or frozen. Or you go out fishing with someone, wouldn't that be nice, Leila? Would you like to come too, Juna? We used to go out fishing any day we wanted to on Diego Garcia. My man had a pirogue. Small but with a sail and oars. Be nice, the three of us in a boat? Not in the cyclone, mind. The sea will be tempestual. So, we'll have to buy the fish instead.

Tuna is good, or linn dore, the one with spots on it, or bonito which costs less, but is also delicious. Say, about five pounds of fish, while you're about it. Because it lasts. When you buy fresh fish, check that the flesh is still firm, and that it hasn't started to go soft.

First you cut the fish into big cylindrical slices. Be careful to use a very sharp knife so you don't crush the fish flesh. And when you get to the bone, you need to use a hammer, a short sharp blow to get through the bone without damaging the fish. Then take quarters off the bone. (Keep the skin and bone to fry up for the dog with the gills and other innards, but not the gall bladder, because it's bitter. If you buy bonito, you can carve the black bits near the bone out and cook them for the cat.) Then you slice the most beautiful bits about one inch square and one centimetre thick. (For bonito, boil the fish in water with salt and vinegar for ten minutes first and then strain it; for other kinds of fish, you don't do this.) Salt the pieces of fish lightly, and deep-fry them. (You can't deep-fry them all at once, so you have to do it a handful of pieces at a time, and this takes time. So, you think and hum a tune.) You deep-fry the fish quite slowly, so that by the time it is golden brown it is also fairly dry, but not too hard. (The longer you intend to keep the pickle, the drier and harder you have to fry it, mind. That all depends on your intentions.) As you fry it, and take it out, you put it in a big bowl.

Meanwhile you send boiling water through the jar you're going to keep it in, and let the jar get bone dry. When the oil you have cooked the fish in cools down to fairly warm, you put powdered turmeric into it, and then crushed mustard seed. And stir. You drop in lots of crushed cloves of garlic. And then, if you want to, you can add onions you've soaked in vinegar for a few days and then squeezed the vinegar out of. Then pour some of the oil into the jar, then place a layer of fish, pressing each bit down adding salt each time if necessary, add more oil, and another layer of fish, pressing it down. And so on. What you think then Juna, like some?

'Why do you press it down, Mama?' Leila asks.

To get the air out. And the fish and onions must always be covered with oil. Never leave air in your pickle. And another thing, whenever you fish a piece out of the jar afterwards, always use a clean, dry spoon – otherwise you might introduce mould into your pickle. Never let water into your pickle either.

'**Y**our basket's all wrong,' *you* say. 'Stupid! Look at its shape. Idiot!'

Our eyes are, for this one hour, not cramped by the closeness of everything. We are in a big room. Big enough to allow the walls to recede like they do now. And we work.

Wide space. A quiet moment interrupted by Mama Gracienne's spelt out criticism. Moving hands.

We are in the basket-making workshop.

There is space and light. Now there is low talk, humming, and whispering.

Working this way and that, we are. Our hands whirling fast, out and round and back, out and round and back. Each as if eight hands and arms spreading out like Doorga's, filling a circle around us with movement. Even *you* get harsh in the prison, Mama Gracienne. Criticising me like that for my basket, in the middle of a quiet spell. The gusts must be getting under your skin.

After the mumbling and humming and whispering, a quiet spell comes back. *Calm is a weave.*

I work on.

I begin at the same time to stare at the table in front of me.

My attention gradually gets drawn more and more intensely to the *legs* of that table. Look at them. Sturdy bits of wood.

More chinks in their armour, I think. *Legs can be arms.*

I am not concentrating on my basket enough. I pick it up and laugh at it. 'Mama Gracienne, you are right, it is crooked. All lopsided.' The rattanware refuses to obey my commands, used as I am to computer keyboards.

I swing it over my left arm anyway, by its handle, and I stand up. And lean my head over my basket, a long-legged sea bird, spying down into the water.

The calm spell lasts.

So I act on.

I put on the mask for mourning now, face lifted up asking *why*. *Why? After all I did for?* I am at a burial. I start pulling petals off a flower, one wild rose and then another, then frangipani after frangipani, then whole handfuls of marigold after marigold, its wicked perfume keeping insects at bay, and putting all the petals into the basket on my arm. Stalks I throw away. Some of the petals I sniff at and either love the perfume, yesterday-today-and-tomorrow flowers, or turn up my nose cruelly at it, jasmine buds smelt from too nearby. They all laugh at my theatre. Nothing funnier than a funeral.

The calm persists.

It is as though the theatre will last as long as this *akalmi*. Some sort of a contract between the other basket makers and me, me who they usually choose to hate. But at funerals, it's different. Respect for the dead.

Then I give them each a handful of petals, force it into their palms, one by one, palm by palm. And when we have all got a palmful of petals, clutched, we listen for the *om shanti*, and *om shanti*, then when we hear it, we throw the petals into the middle of the floor. As if on to the bamboo coffin. On to the body in the bamboo coffin laced with wreaths. *Om shanti shanti shanti.*

In a new kind of harmonics.

Om shanti shanti shanti.

Then four of us pick up the bamboo coffin and we set off at first in slow dignified manner, and then at a brisk walk, then on the trot, until we run, all the others after us. In silence. To the funeral pyre. We begin to laugh all of us, at the same time.

We are laughing, but we are getting crosser and crosser. Not with each other. With *them*. The anger builds up by itself now. Anger upon anger. End of all *their* business. Bear it off to the funeral pyre and set it alight in all four corners at once. Rage upon rage. Then dance around the fire. Round and round. *Are we going mad? What punishment do they mete out for this?*

A gust comes and blows and blows on everything, blowing away all the old ills. Coffins and cobwebs. Wreaths and wild rose petals. And theatre.

When the gust goes, we go back to our baskets. Weaving this way and that. Busying away. Hands and feet. Arms and legs. A certain purpose in our work now. Each one of us deep in thought.

The electronic button factory in the prison isn't working any more. Not just today. For weeks now.

That's why we're back to *low-tech*. That's what they call basket-making as well. *Low-tech*. We have no idea what has happened to the contracts that were signed whereby we were to produce buttons for the world market, nor do we care. Tiko asked Old Blue, the Keeper, what happened and she told her it was complicated. What we know is we had over half the world market buttoned up, so to speak. It said so, in the prison report in the Prison's Library.

'Look through the bars,' I say to everyone near me. There is a large barred window quite high up but not as high as the one in our cell, and we can actually see a bit of *hillside* at Latur Koenig. We watch this bit of hillside every time we come here. For some sign of a goat or a chicken or maybe, who knows, a person, perhaps a person we know. But we have never seen anything out of the ordinary. This is the only bit of earth outside that anyone can see from inside the prison. We know it off by heart. We look at it, the way you look out of the window when you get up in the morning. A habit, in a way, but also to check that everything is still there, in order.

Today it isn't.

The leaves, all of them, the leaves on every tree, on the bushes and shrubs as well, everything in our view from across the valley and the main road and up on the hill near the Latur Koenig are all *wrong*. All the leaves still left up, that is.

'Look at the trees.'

The prisoners all lean over and look up.

'What about them?' All the women are making their baskets abstractedly. Angrily. Anger continuing to rise, like flood water, levelling out all the time. Leaving no land dry. A lively, raucous fury, equalising us all. Ankle deep by now. They all peer up out the window. All of them. They are a picture of determination to *see* something.

The words *we are furious*, meanwhile, coming from our every movement. Anger from our every pore.

Threading this way and that. Weaving bits of bamboo this way and that. Holding the bottom of the basket with our bare feet, our legs taking the curve of the wicker, and working our arms without needing to look at our hands.

'Can't you see? They've all changed colour, every last leaf. All the leaves that are left on the trees have changed colour. Not really *changed*. They look as though they have changed because they have all *turned around*. They are all showing us their underside. Their *other* side. It means the effects of Cassandra and Doorgawatee are here. A kind of wind is blowing that is unknown to us, unknown even to the leaves of the tree. The gusts are now cyclonic. It's not just bad weather now, it's Cassandra and Doorgawatee. Welcome.'

'Who're they? Who on this earth are Cassandra and Doorgawatee?' one woman asks.

So I tell about the twin cyclones. We all look at the leaves. They are silver. Shimmering. Like so many shoals of fish. All in formation. Their colour all wrong. A cyclone coming, not just a funny wind. Not just the strange light. But the leaves are not the *right* colour. And then, when the gust passes, they all change colour back again, just like when a shoal of fish changes direction suddenly under sea.

When we all turn and look, when we prepare like this, is it not us who are the worm that has turned?

'Go sit on the ground by the window. Look up through the bars. See if you can see the sky. Look up at it.' *You*, Mama Gracienne, say this to me. You are so funny sometimes. You just give me an order. And I obey.

I listen to you. Just like that, I do.

I do as you tell me to.

You never say anything undue. Nor would you ever suggest I do anything excessive.

The only thing *excessive* you've ever done in your whole life is your confession.

I throw a bit of bamboo over on to the floor near the window. *I'm no fool.* Then I pretend to go pick it up. So no blue lady can suddenly snap at me, ask me what the hell I'm doing down there, report me, get me put on bread and water.

I go sit on the floor by my thrown down stick of bamboo. Then I check there isn't actually any blue lady already watching me. They are all three talking to one another. In excited vacuous vapid conversation. '*To kone . . . pa dir mwa . . . ayo! . . . to pa pu krwar . . . vre? . . . get sa! . . . abe, lerla? . . . kapav krwar.*' I scrutinise them for signs as to what they are up to. No good, I'm sure, up to no good at all. I look up and I speak to you.

'It's purple. Pale purple. The sky has changed.' I feel lost.

'Is it clouds high up or is it the blue sky you are seeing, Juna, tell me?' you ask.

'I can't tell,' I reply.

'Then, that means the cyclone will come here. If you can't tell, then it'll come upon us. Right over us. Maybe even the eye itself. That is the proof. That when you look at the sky, you can't tell if it's clouds or the absence of clouds.

'The eye may come.'

I slide back, eel-like, to my place. I sit still and look at the pieces of bamboo I am trying to make into a basket. Like me, a stunted, crippled creature. My basket *is* all wrong, like she says. Practice. I will need more practice. But then again, my mind isn't on it. I've got too much else on my mind. Eyes of cyclones. And gathering mutinies.

I stare into space in the corner. Tiko, who is next to me, clicks her fingers in front of my eyes, '*Penny for your thoughts!*' I smile, but go on staring.

'Don't you go and give up, now, for Christ's sake,' she shouts. '*Pa fer sa. Pa fer sa!*' She is thinking of Mopey-Sue, no doubt.

But I have started half-studying where the electrical wiring runs. I can't help it, when I stare into space I do that. I study the wiring. Sometimes it's the plumbing but right now it's the wiring of the place. It's usually *behind* the walls in here for obvious reasons, but they must have done some quick repair job once long ago and then forgotten about it, a temporary measure by negligence become permanent, because there is this *one* white insulated electric wire, flat as a tape worm, working its way from out of a hole in the wall up to the grid with the flourescent light behind it in the middle of the ceiling. A grid just like in our cell. Then I notice something, half next to it, half behind it. *Amazing.* Half next to the electric cable, half behind it, there is a pencil-thin mud-brown termite tunnel creeping up the wall in the shadow of the electric wire, almost invisible. I follow both the electric cable and the termite tunnel now. High up, the termite tunnel branches off on its own, away from the electric wire, so I follow its path with my eyes, now focused. It goes up to an old wooden beam that has stayed on, surviving the change over from corrugated iron roof to a concrete one for the workshop. The beam is painted grey to match the rest of the place. Inside that perfect mud-tunnel, I see them in my mind's eye, hundreds of termites, maybe thousands, tens of thousands, back and forth from an underground nest, secretly preparing, carrying mud up, mixing it with chewed wood pulp from the beam, gluing the mixture in place, and winding their way back, carrying mud up, perfecting their tunnel as they go, and then winding their way back down into the bowels of the earth underneath the prison somewhere. Then I know that when they get out at the top, they will build a big round mud ball, and when it's finished, they will lay eggs in it, eggs that will hatch and that will turn into flying ants and fly away, some of them heading straight for the lights and dying, others off to freedom, or I don't know where.

The termites have probably completely eaten up that wooden beam as well, to mix in with the mud. There is probably nothing but a skin of oil-paint left there. If I were to stick my finger into it, poke that beam, it would give, collapse without shame, like the taut plumped out skin of a perfect looking Mezon Ruz mango that has meanwhile gone rotten inside. And inside that collapsed paint, there will be nothing left but a hollow emptiness and films of fine dust. The termites will have *used it up*. Unseen.

I wonder if it's a structural beam.

Tiko snaps her fingers in front of my eyes again. 'Your thoughts aren't worth a sous anyway,' she says.

'I prefer the button pressing factory,' she goes on. 'But it's not working any more. It's modern there, you know, like a proper factory, robotized and all *electronic*. Did you know?' she is quite proud, the prison being her domain, 'in this prison we make enough buttons for the whole of the world's *shirts*, not counting fancy buttons, when we are in action. Not a quarter, not half but *all* the *shirts* in the whole world. *And*. And, did you know it is illegal? Unfair competition, according to WTO rules. Old Blue, the Keeper, told me. There's a tribunal meeting right now, WTO tribunal, I overheard Old Blue, the Keeper, say so the other day. A multinational button company is suing the government. We get paid next to nothing, they say. Not a level playing field, they say. We, it is true, work for a few sous a day. Most unfair,' she says sarcastically. 'But better than making fucking baskets. Anyway it's out of action now. Proverbial spanner. Seriously, it *was* sabotaged. A contract was out to sabotage it. Paid for either by a rival button manufacturing multinational or by some poor prisoners. You never can tell these days.'

I think of the termites again. Then, answering Tiko, I murmur *awful allies, they are.*

'What you say?' she asks.

'Know anything about the electronics of the factory?' I ask. Crippled by my professional curiosity, I am.

'Yes, I know a lot about its electronics,' she says, 'I was helping out when the button factory was installed.'

And then she adds, in a lower voice, 'You won't believe this but some idiot blue lady has put the electronics for the factory on a *network* with the overall electronics for the whole system, even security. Pity the factory isn't working. We could plan a getaway during the cyclone.'

Even Tiko talks like this.

'Easy to get in there? To the factory area and the electronics?'

'Yeah, not difficult.'

'How?'

She comes over and whispers slowly and quietly in my ear.

R *emoval* *of* *alleged* *mental* *patient*: No patient shall be received into any mental hospital, in Mauritius, unless accompanied by an order under the hand of the Magistrate for the district from which the patient is removed. The person at whose instance it is sought to remove him shall apply to the District Court, stating his desire to obtain an order for the removal of the patient. The Magistrate may make an order for the interim detention of the alleged patient. [*Lunacy Act 1906 (Sections, 14, 15 and 20)*] – Copied down from the Prison's Library. The new Mental Health Act (1999) isn't in the Library yet.

S tate Land Act: No person shall put up any building or other structure on any part of any State Land without express authorisation in writing, and shall, on conviction, be liable to imprisonment for a term not exceeding 5 years, and be removed immediately from any land occupied by him, and shall have any building or other structure on the land demolished. [*State Lands Act (Amended 1991)*] – Quoted verbatim to me by Leila Sadal.

When we get back to our cell, we find it gusty and hollow inside. How can this be? The cell seems more empty now. There's even an echo. I put my hands to my ears protecting them from the high-pitched sounds that seem to come from everywhere. The cyclone is beginning to create a vacuum inside our cell.

Leila picks at her eyebrows, angrily, and Mama Gracienne frets and casts glances at the sky, imploring.

Leila says her father's lost now. Lost everything. Even *her*, in jail now. She worries about him in the cyclone. *Except his soul*, she says. *Except his soul*. Her mother's family own the small cloth warehouse he used to work in. She says this as if it explains her whole world.

Leila's mother's family go to see expensive lawyers to kill two birds with the same stone: to get Leila put away until she's eighteen and to get Leila's father put away *for the time being*.

So her father wisely runs away.

He literally leaves home and decides to get a new job.

He goes and builds a shack on State Land at Kan Saplon, she says, ten foot by ten foot in second-hand corrugated iron nailed on to a sturdy frame of second-hand wood, and he makes up a new job for himself, preparing pickled cucumber and selling it together with fresh pineapple with salt and red chilli paste in a side-street outside the New Court House where the families of prisoners can buy some and give it to the prisoners when they come up for renewal of bail. She goes and visits him, sits on the step of his one roomed house, and listens to him talking about this and that. He seems happier now. He tells Leila he is saving money to send her to university where she will study mathematics, and be the first girl student to be Professor of Mathematics at the university. *When she says this, she looks around the cell, as if it explains everything.*

'Maybe we should get you a correspondence course,' I suggest. But she is pressing on undeterred.

'He puts down a cement floor, and polishes it with bright red Brito until it shines. His front doorstep shines too. Bright red. See your face in it. He soon gets running water and a tap in front of his house, so he doesn't have to carry water from the mosque yard any more, and he gets electricity. Then he gets a decoder so that he can tune into Sky News and Canal Plus, as well as the Mauritian channels. He also gets himself a smart tricycle built with a glass box on the back of it to show off his beautiful spirally peeled pineapples without a single eye mark on them, cut in four long pieces, each a long yellow lollipop with a comfortably carved handle made from the corresponding quarter of the once prickly pineapple leaves. The salt he keeps in one square Tupperware box and the red chilli paste in another. He keeps them separate because some clients want either more of one or of the other. The pickled cucumber, white tropical cucumber with the seeds taken out, is cut into nice thick pieces in two large jars of vinegar with spices in it, one in each side of the glass box, with a wooden skewer in each one for getting the bits of cucumber out with. 'Metal would oxidise,' she explains. 'And he's got a wad of see-through plastic bags for serving the raw pineapples and the cucumber pickle to customers in.

'He is, by now, sane again. And he is off all drugs and should have lived happily ever after, amen.

'Maybe he's just sad about the Mathematics Professor being in a prison cell instead.'

There is silence in our cell.

And the vacuum is getting worse as air is sucked out now, with each gust taking away a bit more air than it can draw in. Then leaving a calm spell more airless each time.

A new gust suddenly blows in a length of bright orange hair ribbon, cut into a v at each end. It whips through the cell window, and then hovers like a parachute, then curves down and lands on Leila's bunk opposite mine.

'Looks like your dad sent you that,' you, Mama Gracienne, say to her, 'How nice of him.'

And you get up slowly and go over to it, pick it up and tie it carefully into Leila's hair. She looks consoled.

Then two birds, a pair of bright yellow Cape Canaries, already flustered in good weather they are so highly strung, fly in suddenly. In a panic. They sit on the sill of our window. One sings distress. It is obvious that their nest is gone. Although it had been so carefully woven on the long and pliant end of a branch. Even though they had together stripped all the leaves off the branch making it less likely to break. Maybe their whole cluster of nests on that one tree is gone by now.

They sit on our sill and shiver.

P *rotest* *or* *demonstration*: Any person wishing to hold a public meeting or a public procession shall give written notice to the Commissioner of Police not less than 7 clear days before the meeting or procession. *Otherwise wacha wacha.* [*Public Gathering Act (1991) Section 3(1)*] – Copied down from the Prison's Library.

B ut a day comes when Leila's father and his neighbours start to hear talk. Talk of getting them off State Land. *Make way for development. A ring-road. Can't have advantage takers. Not fair on the deserving poor. Respect law and order. Hard on crime.* And then one day he gets home from selling his pickled cucumber and his pineapples, and he finds that the Ministry of Housing and Land Development has put up a *Notice to Squatter* on his house. Pasted it on to his outside wall. She saw it and remembers it in bits and pieces. *Whereas you, Leila's father, are in occupation of a plot of State Land of an extent of so many square metres situated at Kan Saplon without any right and have put a corrugated iron structure house thereon without the express authority of. Satisfied you are a squatter. Call upon you to vacate and pull down your house within five days. Otherwise five years' prison. Demolish your house.*

Who else has got a notice? This neighbour. That one. The word goes round. All of them in their cluster.

Fear settles in as if from outside. Terror rises up inside each of them. At night they cannot sleep. Nightmares of huge yellow bulldozers bigger than their houses torment them. With dull faced drivers locked behind heavy grids.

And her father starts to look haunted and hunted down. Glancing over his shoulder when he is selling a piece of cucumber. But he goes on working. He pretends to ignore the notice. What else can he do? He is not going back to her mother's house. They all ignore the notices. They have no choice but to ignore them. Where would they all go? They go to seek advice from priests and deputies and social workers and lawyers, to no avail.

And one day, while he is in front of the New Court House, pleased that he is selling lots of his cucumber and pineapple, and almost forgetting the threat that hangs over him, he overhears people, his clients and others, talking in excited tones about the police and bulldozers as if they are in action, and he distinctly hears the words 'Kan Saplon'. His chest goes tight. His head empty. He quickly closes up his big jars of cucumber, puts the top of the glass square back down, and he pushes his tricycle all the way home, mumbling to himself, and not knowing whether to hurry or to drag his feet.

When he gets nearby he knows, because there are crowds of people gathered on the footbridge over the motorway. They put that footbridge up after the last riots when yet another person was run over on the way to buy a few rupees of turmeric from the shop. That footbridge. Shiny cars are still tearing up in three lanes and down in two. Uncaring. Apparently oblivious. Callous. The riot police have made a cordon on the mountain like a necklace of blue sticks around its shoulders, their plastic shields catching the falling sun, like diamonds.

Five of his neighbours' houses have already been pulled down. He rushes past, past all the crying women, and past the shouting public and past the blocking police. They try to stop him, but press photographers are nearby and he just rushes through the policemen like a man possessed.

He gets there in time to see the men from the Ministry of the Environment and the Quality of Life carrying a table out of his neighbour's house, a schoolchild's exercise book still open on it, two closed. The Court Usher sits and makes list after list of what is taken out. *Table, one, with exercise books, three.* Her father sees them carrying out the small round goldfish bowl with a goldfish still swimming inside it. This is the last item. He wonders what the Court Usher wrote down for that? *Goldfish in bowl, one?* He starts to cry out. To weep and to shout. Why? Are you doing this, who? Are you anyway, haven't? You got a house of your own, doesn't? This make you want to cry? Where? Will this all end?

Then he curses them.

Endless wakefulness be upon you all!

Destroyers and cowering obeyers of orders!

He lays on them a curse of eternal nightmares every time their heads should touch the pillow.

One policeman hesitates.

Another wipes his eye with the coarse cloth of his military sleeve.

But the chief laughs, and uses his baton to push her father away. Swears at him, stands on her father's sandalled toes with his policeman's boots, and he pushes one of his men's see-through shields at her father's face.

Then the yellow bulldozer tears the corrugated iron like paper. *Worse than in a cyclone*, was all he could say. *Worse than in a cyclone.*

And then it was his house next. What it had taken him two months to build is broken down in two minutes.

Children stand, hands half lifted, eyes in tear-filled disbelief. Then they, the little children, comfort their mothers. It's mainly women and children. Her father is an exception, a man on State Land.

The next day, he joins the movement. The movement decides in a series of assemblies to act. To bar the *caterpillars*, as they call the bulldozers. Women, children and her father, together with young people from the movement in other areas who come to help. Together they all manage to bar the bulldozers a whole day.

But the next day, the third day, the bulldozers get out before dawn, and destroy the remaining seventy-one houses. Twenty-three were made in concrete. Years of savings and work, crushed in seconds. Quicker than the corrugated iron, he told Leila in the particular marvel that only recalled horror can muster.

Her father weeps for these women and children who had lost a house better than his.

Silence is back in our cell. What words are there left?

The gusts come to represent the destruction of houses.

Mama Gracienne, it is *you* who speak first. A question to Leila, 'But did your father keep his soul?'

Leila looks up at the pair of canaries. They are too upset, too highly strung altogether, so they cry out and fly off into the storm.

She shakes off her orange ribbon and reties it with a firmness long past her age. Her eyes glisten with moisture.

But she doesn't speak.

Not for ages and ages.

T aking part in riot: 'Riot' means an unlawful assembly which has begun to execute the purpose for which it is assembled by a breach of the peace. Any person who takes part in a riot shall commit an offence and shall, on conviction be liable to imprisonment not exceeding . . . [*Added to Criminal Code 1991 (Section 143)*] – Notice pasted up on Prison Notice Board. Pinned on top of it the day after Presidential assent to the law, that is on New Year's Day, 2000: Where 10 or more persons, who are present together at any place, use or threaten to use unlawful violence for a common purpose and their conduct is such as may or is likely to cause a person of reasonable firmness to fear for his personal safety, each of the persons using or threatening to use such violence shall commit an offence and shall be liable to penal servitude for a term of not less than 5 years. [*Public Security Act, Act No. 1, 2000*]

A riot breaks out and the people there, specially young boys, throw stones at all the rich cars going past, and when one gets stopped, they chase the driver out and turn the car upside down and set it alight. Tyres come rolling in from everywhere and the fire grows. A few more cars and a bus get turned upside down, like Matchbox toys, and set alight in their own petrol. Barricades on both sides of the motorway.

And in no time the army moves in, but can do nothing to stop the stones and tyres being hurled on to the motorway. The more teargas they send into the neighbourhood, the more people are driven on to the streets and into the riot. More barricades get set up, Leila says.

The odious police chief, the one who laughed, is standing arrogantly on the footbridge directing operations, when her father, a fine stone-thrower, aims a small rock at him, and it connects. Strikes him hard right on his arse. Applause and cheering is heard from everywhere and from nowhere you can prove.

The movement gets strong, her father says, more and more people join in. And no more houses are getting broken down. The government said that they were going to break down three thousand shacks on State Land, but they haven't. The movement gets so strong that the government is too ashamed to come and fetch his, her father's, corrugated iron ruins. The government just leaves them there.

So her father moves back under those sheets of tin. He is still sleeping under the debris of his own broken down house. And she can't help him because meanwhile, she's gone and got herself locked up.

So, she worries about him in a cyclone.

So there's nothing else I can do but tell her I'm sad. You, Mama Gracienne, you know what to do. You always know. You hold her two hands between your hands, and push her two hands together. Again and again, as the weather gets stormier and stormier. As we imagine the corrugated iron sheets being whipped about like so many sheets of paper.

Then you implore her.

Times are bad, you say. You implore her. What can we send to your father from where we are now? There is little. He is in a cyclone shelter now, maybe the government school at Pay. Maybe he is sharing food with other cyclone refugees. Maybe he would like a little . . . a little something from you. In exchange for the orange ribbon he sent in. You implore her. Something. To tell us something. Something beginning with the letter 'g'. You say you know she can make something that we could send to her father. If we can make it in here, we can send it. And if we can send it, he will get it. Make it carefully, mind, you say to her. How could *you* know to say that to her, to hazard such a thing, to walk where angels fear?

Leila says there's only one thing she can make, but she knows her father will love it, so could we say if it sounds nice enough?

Of course we'll say, we say.

'It's green banana chips: He loves them. You use ordinary bananas but before they are ripe. Any old bananas. You wait for them to be full size, though, but still absolutely grass green. Or you buy them green. To peel them you take a sharp knife and make marks in about five places right down the length of the banana, from the stalk end to the other end. Then you chip off the peel.

'*Do you think it would sell better than my father's cucumber and pineapple?*'

'*Who knows?*' you reply, not breaking her train of.

'Then you slice the bananas into fine diagonally cut slivers, which you put into a bowl adding salt and turmeric as you go along.

'Then you put a lot of oil into a frying pan, and wait for the oil to get hot, then deep-fry them. When they make a noise against your aluminium spoon, like Juna says, tink-tink-tink then they are ready. You drain them well, and then put them out on newspaper. You can eat them straight away or you can keep them in an airtight jar, and they last. Just like potato crisps only they're nicer.'

'*You can do the same thing with breadfruit,*' you add, Mama Gracienne again keeping Leila's train of thought tightly spun out like a spider does when making its thread. '*You peel it, when it's still green, then you cut it into quarters (or vice versa). Then you cut slices about four or five millimetres wide. These fry really quickly because breadfruit is a dry fruit. You shouldn't fry them too crisp, in case you overdo the nice floury insides.*'

'That's the only recipe I know. But I know my father loves it,' she says.

'Maybe you could prepare some for him to sell in a side-box on his tricycle,' you say. 'It sounds delicious.'

'Maybe,' she says.

Bananas, I think. A fruit that's also a vegetable. A vegetable that's also a staple. The most magic of all fruit, all vegetables, all staples. Boiled and mashed as a staple. Curried and fried as a vegetable. And made into crisps. Fruit eaten raw. Ordinary yellow and black bananas, pale pink bananas, dwarf ones, ones ripened on the tree that taste fluffy, zinzli ones that you can eat with the skin and all, giant ones that you can cut in half and still not finish. And fruit that you can cook: Make fritters of, banana cakes, flambé with rum and brown sugar.

And what a gracious plant, its leaves so wide and shiny that you use them for eating from instead of plates.

And so I bring myself not to think of the *eating* part any more.

I stand up and suggest we hold a panchayat. 'Yes, a panchayat,' I say.

'A what? To see if the Confession is guilty or not? In the middle
of a cyclone?'

Leila can still be so nasty sometimes. She never can let your
ambivalence lie. Even after she and you were so close only
minutes ago.

No respect for your age either, Mama Gracienne. Nor for the
fact that no one will ever know for sure what happened to your
Honey that night.

Maybe the girl just feels all empty now she's told us so much.
Mama Gracienne, you are the one who looks over to me to say,
let her be she'll learn. So, I just answer her.

'There's plenty of people judging *that.* We have got more
important business, now. Much more important matters. A *land
survey* to carry out. A new land survey.'

Leila and I have already done one before. For the two of us, I
insisted. But, in turn, she doesn't always acknowledge other
people. Like *you,* for example. She doesn't always want to
recognise your rights here.

'Now we have a new occupant to welcome here to our domain.
You, Mama Gracienne, are most welcome.' My arms, the way I
put them out, show that Leila and I are *both* welcoming you. I
speak on behalf of the two inmates who have been here longer, as
it were. The old girls. You just shake your head and smile at me,
as if I am mad, but you like it.

'We apologise, don't we,' I look at Leila, 'for the weather. You will need your own place. And we've got to decide together where it will be. You can't just lie where some blue lady threw your blanket in, can you?'

I strut around, a land surveyor, now.

I carry a long stick with red lines painted here and there on it, saying things like *the common land, feet nearer slop bucket than noses, decent sleeping place*.

Leila begins to join in – her heaviness lifting – *parcelling the sugar estate* as she puts it into common land for all, sanitary facilities, and a living space for each.

We are not short of time, so we stretch it out. We have to sleep somewhere, and walk somewhere and sit somewhere, and shit somewhere. Our possibilities are always limited, two bunks are firmly fixed to the walls. Cyclone or no cyclone.

She starts to laugh, 'Let us now organise our kingdom and praise the famous inmates that were here before us.' She is referring to an ex-prisoner called Hannah or Ammah or Emma or Hemma, it's not clear, who led the *silence strike* to get covers for the slop bucket. Covers, which have stayed on as a right.

You smile too. Then you chuckle. Then you say that when you got your land lease in Tamarin long, long ago, before Honey was born, you saw the land surveyor arrive with his red and white poles. But, at the time, you never guessed you would have the honour one day to share a bedroom with a land surveyor.

'Where did I put my red and white poles down again then?' I ask looking around our domain.

'Here, here, here,' they cry, both rushing up with the equipment.

Leila takes up the piece of chalk, a real piece that she keeps hidden in the corner of her bunk. Tailors' chalk. Blue, and hard and sharp. Don't know where she got it from.

Then we three sit on the floor close to one another. We think and talk this way and that. A full length conference from which decisions will emerge. Of the *let us* and the *we commit ourselves to* and the *we will* kind. We turn our noses up at decisions of the *thou shalt* or *thou shalt not* kind. Because we haven't got that kind of an empire, we say.

Nor do we want that kind of a one. We are of one sort:

Prisoners. And we want to be of one sort: *Free people*, Leila says. It's so easy. She sounds like someone in the Indian mutiny. Or in the French revolution. Or Mexican. Or English. Or Russian. Or American. Or Chinese.

We draw lines first with our fingertips. This is while we are thinking and while we are talking in general terms. She just holds the blue chalk, as a sign that we will put a light mark once we have decided. In the chalk lies the authority of our contract. We can afterwards decide to rub out any mark we decide to put in, but we can't just rub it out arbitrarily. All this we decide.

'Should you sleep between us on that bit of space you have been in these last nights, Mama Gracienne? On a more permanent basis, I mean? Take up domicile there? Or should you have a sleeping place along the width of the cell at the foot of our bunks under the window? Or are there any other options?' Leila presides. She, after all, is the old prisoner, young as she is, and she has got the chalk in her hand. She looks to you. *What did you mean the Islands are closed. What Islands? How closed?* Her father was ejected from his tin house, that I know. You who have had the experience of a previous land survey. Long ago in Tamarin.

I suggest maybe the space under the window, for the meantime. Because when Leila will have drawn the line, then you can stay there and it's yours, I say. You won't have people walking on you and on your space any more.

You seem not to mind. You appreciate that anyone cares.

But I see Leila getting concerned. A slight look of agitation. Her eyes flash warnings. *What about our training?* Is that what she is thinking? To her, any habit we have, any ritual, is far too fixed. I notice almost panic rising in her. Very labile, she is.

'Relax,' I say. 'What are the *possibilities?* Go on, let's generate them all.'

'You take my bunk,' she says to you, 'Mama Gracienne, go on.'

I am impressed.

'I'm only just fifteen. And it's a bit short in the foot for me, anyway. You're older and you're shorter!'

You smile.

'How sweet of you,' you say. I can see now in how you speak to Leila, in how you *let her be*, how your Honey turned out so nice. It's *you* that helped her turn out nice. You make Leila nice too. Even her. She is difficult. A child of sudden inside storms and unexpected squalls, who gets overwhelmed by all sorts of emotions that no one can even guess at. They call them *hormones* now, but everyone knows it's actually emotions.

She explains that we will need to use her own space for our training. Once you make her nice, Mama Gracienne, she gets nicer.

'From here and now onwards, when we *aren't* training, you have sole use of your bit,' I declare and she draws out a bed for herself on the ground. It tapers to leave a passageway to the slop bucket by her feet. She takes her blanket off her bunk, and puts it on the floor in her new space. She will naturally put her nose at the far end, away from the slop bucket.

Then she picks up your blanket from the floor, Mama, and makes it up into a nice bed on your new bunk for you.

She goes and sits on her blanket in her space, leaning against the wall at the foot of your bed.

Just in time, for each of us to shelter from the next gust, in our own place. It presses down on us. When it passes, we go on.

'Here is the common land. Between the two bunks,' I say. Symbolically I take the blue chalk from her and I draw a faint dotted line in the passage between our bunks to her blanket. 'The slop bucket will thus stay at the foot of my bunk.' It is at her feet too.

You curl up on your new bunk, with a place of your own.

You like it, I can see. Your demands are meagre. You have made your confession and you are here. Thank goodness they didn't throw you in with Tiko and the other bank robber, they'd have eaten you alive.

Leila lies on her new bed on her tummy, her feet bent up in the air behind her. Then she turns around. 'I like the view,' she says. 'If we all stayed in a row, it would be silly. Like birds on a telephone wire. Like this we can each see the other two. Oh, I've got a suggestion. It's an invitation in fact. Would you like to share a sip of champagne just to celebrate?'

We all chink together glasses with long stems, and put them, like chalices, to our lips.

'What year is this one,' she asks me, 'what vintage?' We lick our lips. I am the only one who has ever tasted champagne, so I am invited to explain its taste.

'Let's play what we wish we had to eat again, after the drink,' she asks.

The child gets more childlike.

If we aren't thinking about food, it's about crapping. If we aren't thinking about crapping, it's rude jokes about sex. All we've got left. Other than uselessly worrying about our brothers, our children, our husbands, our houses. *Thank god I chucked my fiancé out just in time. Washing my father's feet at our wedding, the very idea.* My brother Jay. I worry about him. I always have. Stupid because these worries bring nobody any good.

It seems best to let some of the obsessions out. Once in a while, maybe even on a regular basis. Don't cage them up too much or they turn into worse monsters for the dark you keep them in. I turn to Mama, 'Your turn. You wish. It has to begin with an "*h*".' Now it's already the eighth letter since we started playing this game.

We are always hungry, all of us. Not just her, the Effusion of Blood. Every single inmate. On the chunk of bread, we get margarine. But *only since the hunger strike in 1979*, the old prisoners tell us. Meat twice a week *only since then* too. And the *two* bananas. Inalienable right.

It's a fact. We *think about food* all the time. Unless we manage to confine it to the game. So we are bound to play it.

Even as the cyclone approaches.

Mama Gracienne says she knows how to cook hare. *This* I wasn't expecting. Game. *I wonder where she learnt enough of the alphabet to be able to play this game, I must ask her one day.*

Hare, salmi served with potatoes, sauté. When you've skinned it, it's worth hanging hare up for a few hours, like all game. Cut it into nice pieces and brown them in oil. *We had hare when Honey was teething. For old time's sake. I rubbed her gums with a clove.*

To brown hare, you need sizzling hot oil, and then you have to let the meat get stuck a bit, and only then turn it over, and then you let the other side get stuck too. But, not let it burn, the black bits are bitter. When you brown the meat, the juices get sealed in. Don't put salt on first either because it will draw out moisture and not allow the frying.

Put the browned bits aside for later.

Now parboil peeled potatoes, already cut up into quarters. Parboiled means bring to the boil in salted water just covering the potatoes and boil just until the outside layer of each piece of potato changes from a translucent colour of raw potatoes to the creamy opaque white of cooked potatoes. The inside of each piece of potato is still hard and raw. Then strain, keeping the water for stock. *Honey loves potato stock. Loved. Till she was grown up.*

Now for the salmi. Game needs spices, like cloves and cinnamon, and game needs time, time to stew.

You, who confessed like that. Do you need time? Time for thought? Prisoners are in frozen time. Or humans in aspic.

You brown a lot of onions in oil, slowly. Small strong tasting purple onions are best for this. Put in a lot of green thyme, whole sprigs of it, and some finely chopped mint. Then, when the onions are brown, put crushed garlic in. More than usual. Add some crushed cinnamon, and also one piece of bark. Add three or four cloves. (Not too many, because when they boil, they get bitter if you use too many.)

You worry so much about feeding us something bitter. No wonder she was so sweet your Honey.

Then put the hare in, add a cup of the potato stock (or other vegetable stock, if you've got any). Then add half a cup of sweetish white wine. Add salt. Leave to stew for at least an hour.

Before serving add another half cup of white wine.

Then deep-fry the parboiled potatoes. Serve them separately with parsley finely chopped and sprinkled on top. That's it.

'There were no gusts when you spoke,' Leila announces. She has listened, like she was hypnotised. True, no gusts. She put it all to memory. I have observed her throughout.

'Don't you be superstitious,' I say.

Then *you* say to her that you only learnt how to cook hare

when you came to live in Tamarin. That was when the Islands had already got closed. And when you found yourself in Tamarin and you had nothing else to eat. You used to trap them. 'I was hardly older than Juna,' you say.

C losure of Islands: As from the date of this Order in Council the Chagos Archipelago, being islands which immediately before the date of this Order were included in the Dependencies of Mauritius, shall together form a separate colony which shall be known as the British Indian Ocean Territory. [*Statutory Instrument Made 8 November 1965 at the Court at Buckingham Palace.*] – Booklet about Diego Garcia and the whole of Chagos in the Prison's Library.

So I take the opportunity of asking you, 'What do you mean, Mama Gracienne, when you say the Islands were closed? What islands? When? What did this have to do with *you*?'

You stare into the middle of the cell. I signal Leila to listen. 'It's a story,' I whisper to her. 'Listen.'

'You watch, the gusts will go away,' she says.

'Impossible,' I whisper.

Then you start. And the gusts do die down. I am not superstitious.

'Sometimes I can't remember.

'Sometimes I don't understand. Sometimes I don't understand anything. For a start, I don't know how I got missed out, or maybe it was me that missed my chance. But I wasn't ever *registered* like the others were. I was never in any movement. I never joined in any of the hunger strikes. I didn't even know there were any. Or what one was. Or where it was held. Afterwards I have heard. I have learnt about them. I didn't even know the others were registered. I didn't know anything. I never got compensation. Nobody even knows I ever came from Diego Garcia. I am forgotten. Sometimes I think whatever happened to me was *then*,' you say, 'and not when I found Honey dead in her bed that night. I think when that man at the ticket office said *the Islands are closed*, it was then that my great granny first entered my soul and made me give up like that and go quiet and not be noticed. And when he just went on saying *next* like that and ignoring me, I thought I didn't exist, and that was how she, my great grandmother, got in. She found me empty or gone and she

256

moved in for a while then. Since then, she was just lying low inside of me until that night when I heard that strange coughing sound and ran and found Honey and didn't go for help and didn't call anyone and just hid everything from myself and left again.

'My mother came from Diego Garcia too, and her mother, my granny, and my granny's mother, my great grandmother. *Her* mother, in turn, had been taken there as a slave when she was only little and had brought Africa with her. My great grandmother could move into *her mother* afterwards, after her mother had died. She only did that when she went empty, she told me. *Into her mother* from Africa. But she wasn't often empty. Just at night, at full moon, when there was phosphorescence on the sea, then. *Then*, she said, she would move into her dead mother from Africa. Or her dead mother from Africa into her. It's not clear,' she says.

'And your father?'

'I didn't know him. He went off to Peros Banos island when I was very little. That's another island in the Chagos Archipelago. His mother was also from the Islands, and his granny. I don't know further back than that.'

'So, the man said *the Islands are closed*. Then what did you do, that day. You say you had babes in arms. Where are they?'

'They died that week. Both of them. The very same week. Then Aunt Paquerette found me at the hospital, haunting the whole of Casualty with my silent crying. They both had diarrhoea, the two little boys. They both died. We three had been sleeping outdoors in Porlwi so after the one died, I just stayed in the hospital in Casualty, and then after the other one died, I just stayed again. I think it was for days and days. I couldn't believe it. I refused to accept it. I wanted them back again from death. They were too small to move into me.

'The hospital got the social security to do the funeral. One funeral for the two of them. Solid little boys, they were. But their tummies had started to bulge out a bit since we had been on this main island. One was a babe in arms really, quite literally, the other one more a toddler. At the hospital they called me *Zilwa la*, the Islander, because they knew I came from Chagos, from Diego

Garcia, the nurses did. They let me sit there in Casualty. And the hospital servants would bring me meals, and cups of tea. They said my head was *tired*. *Very tired*. I suppose it was. I was tired out. Too tired to move. Because my children had died in the hospital, they said not to shoo me away yet. *Les li.* They said I would go when I was ready to go. I used the Casualty toilets and the taps. I washed my face and hands in the hand basins in Casualty. The hospital that didn't manage to save my boys saved me. For what it's worth.'

Leila gets up and kisses her.

Still no gusts.

'Then Aunt Paquerette came to Casualty one day, bringing an old, old man, a relative of hers from Bambu. She was quite young then. She asked me where to take the sick old man. She asked *me* for directions. And then she realised she had asked someone who knew less, much less than even she knew. She was startled, and this was how she began to talk to me. I helped her with the old, old man. Then, when she left the man – an old grandfather, who was sick and got admitted – she said goodbye to him, and to me she said, she just said it, as if to her such words come easily, "Come live with me until you get settled, then. In Tamarin. I live in Tamarin. Come on. What you waiting for?"

'I said, "I haven't got anything of my own. Not even the bus fare. No rent money. No food. I haven't got a suitcase of things waiting for me somewhere. I haven't got anything. No family left. I am lost. I have nowhere to go to afterwards. I haven't got . . . *nothing*. The Islands I come from are closed. What I have is there, over there on the Islands. My house, my bed, my man, my chairs and table, his boat. My pots and pans. My mother's tomb. And her mother's. And her mother's. *The Islands are in my heart and head and eyes and ears and understanding, and I am in them.* I've got nothing left."

'She said, "Well, you've got yourself, haven't you."

'I didn't tell her I had perhaps moved out of myself and into someone far away or maybe dead. Or that someone had moved into me. That my great granny had perhaps entered my soul and brought this silence with her. A calm came over me. A peace of mind. She made it seem so easy. "Come live with me until." So I went with her. That night, she gave me soup with pig's feet stewed into it. And she made faratas with flour on a griddle iron on a fire between three rocks on the ground. She used to fold the faratas and roll them out with warmed oil twice, when she made them. And I slept on a blanket. Just like I did last night. On the floor of an overhanging veranda. On the ground there was bare earth, moulded with mud and cow dung. Over me she laid a huge quilt that she had sewn from little hexagons of thrown away cloth that she scavenged from behind the tailor's workshop in Braban Street and that she had filled with the soft feathers of chickens. I can still feel those hexagons between my fingers if I concentrate really hard, like a honeycomb, each filled with two or three feathers. And it kept me warm.

'So I lived with her for three years. Not three days, nor three weeks. Not three months. But three years. *She is poor, and yet she takes me in.* I stayed with her, as if she were my Aunt. She helped me get a job washing clothes for the Cheshire Old Age Home. Every morning I went to work, and washed clothes. Look at my nails. Till now they are all curled up from all that washing I did with harsh soap. I spent half my money on bus fares in to Porlwi. Once a week, I went down to the quayside, and asked if there was any boat arrived from the Islands. There never was. I went on a pilgrimage to my mother and granny. I never found them. Nor my man. And I would also ask, is there any boat going to the Islands. *I want to go back. I want to return.* There never was. Each trip I would go and see the man in the hole in the wall, at the ticket office, and present my ticket. He would say, "The Islands are closed. *Next!*" Until he got cross and shouted, "*Tir sa depi la!*" The other half of my money I used to save up for my ground lease, a nine-year ground lease on a bit of land next door to Aunt Paquerette's. Then Aunt Paquerette helped get me a job at the salt pans, raking in salt that was the dried up tears of the sea, baskets of it. Baskets and baskets. We raked and raked. Salt of the sea. If I were to count how many baskets of salt I have raked, they still would not be equal to the tears I should have shed.

'Then I made my own house. To any passerby it might have looked like a hovel, a one-roomed tin shack, an *eyesore* I once heard a tourist say, but to me it was peace and haven and shelter and a hiding place from the cold and the rain and the heat and the sun and the wind. Inside, my house had got everything. A bed, a table, chairs, a cupboard for my things. And we are still neighbours, Aunt Paquerette and me. The police couldn't steal *me* without her knowing. She'll be here to see me, I know. She has never ever let me down. That's how she helped me the night Honey died.

'We have gone on renewing our leases. Nine years at a time. Perhaps my house will be boarded up now. Closed. Like the Islands.

'Once I had got my house, long ago when I first got it, I lived in a silent peacefulness. A man moved in soon after I built this shack. My husband, you could call him. He lived with me for years. He knew nothing but work. *A beast of burden,* he was then. A silent man. Stern and hard-working and stubborn. He and I had a dull and harsh household. With no words. And no laughter, certainly not laughter. No singing, never. He woke up every morning and chopped wood. Then he fetched water. Then he looked after a small square of plants at the back of the garden. Hard little pumpkins and bitter aubergines and sour tomatoes and skinny little onions and burning hot chillies. He hoed the earth, weeded, watered. He leant over and put manure into each plant's hollowed out basin in the earth. He sought out insects and harmful caterpillars one by one and crushed them between his broken-ended nails. Then he washed himself and put on his sugar estate uniform and drank his tea. He took his work basket with his daily or nightly food in it. He put on his hat and a plastic overcoat, got on to his bicycle and went out to work on the sugar estate. A twelve hour shift, as an irrigation worker, either nights or days, and brought the money home. He neither smiled, nor laughed. He hardly ever spoke. He just worked and worked. Sometimes I thought he thought he was an ox or some other such beast accidentally born in the form of a man. But then slowly he turned our one-roomed shack into a solid tin house with concrete floors and electric bulbs and a tap. All this in a heavy atmosphere. As if he was doing hard labour. As if he was sentenced to it.

'Then after a few years, we had Honey. Yes, he was Honey's father.

'And from when she was born, she made the gurgling sounds of pre-laughter, and she brought gaiety into our house. As if a sweet soul had escaped into the air all around us at her birth. She was coy and playful. She cooed and sang from when she was in her cot. Her endless gurgling was musical, and she never cried. She only laughed. Light came into our house, and the atmosphere changed. *He* changed too. *Dull caterpillar into beautiful moth*. He started to sit back and look at the garden in an armchair. He would sit next to me and share a bottle of beer of an evening, watching the sun go down, after work. And he would talk. Which seeds to let ripen and keep for next year. Whether he could learn to fish at his age. What Honey would grow up like. He went out to town and bought himself a brightly coloured shirt. And me a brilliant red scarf, long as my outstretched arms, with a silver thread in it. He bought a radio cassette player hire-purchase and we had music in the house. And programmes on this and that. He would bring home venison sometimes, and brightly coloured Indian sweets made from cream and honey and nuts. Life became funny in my eyes too until I myself started to giggle a lot, if I made a mistake or if he did something new. And I would laugh. And as Honey started to talk and to walk, she by her disposition made us happier every day.

'We had nothing to worry about in life.

'There was only lightness and airiness and happiness. Honey brought it in with her. Can you believe such a thing? She was always like that until her dying day.

'By then, by the time she was born, I mean, I had lost contact with everyone else from the Islands. I had got tired of spending money going to Porlwi to the man in the hole in the wall, and I had forgotten what it was like to be on Diego Garcia where there is nothing to buy anyway, where you live off fish and vegetables and coconuts and get rations of rice and lentils and oil. And where you go and dig out a big nest of turtle eggs and take one or two home to cook and cover the rest up again with sand. The Islands were closed from my heart now. Covered up with sand. And he filled my heart, in a way, so long as he was there. And Honey, of course. She was everything.'

'But, I want to ask you a question. What does it mean, *the Islands were closed*? What were the Islands when they were *open,* if that's the expression? How come they got closed, Honey's Mother?' *I have got to know now. I can't just go on guessing what this might mean.*

'Oh it's easy,' you say. 'We used to live there. It was the only country we knew. Chagos. Our ancestors were slaves, they say, from Africa and Madagascar and India and were brought to the Islands, sometimes direct, mostly via Mauritius. The Islands are part of Mauritius, you know that don't you? We used to take the outside husks off coconuts, men and women doing the same work for the same money. We got food and lodging free when the Islands were open. The old people looked after the children and got paid for it by the Company. Every year or two, one of us from each household would take the ship to Mauritius to buy pots and pans, cloth and maybe a new bed or chair and bring it back on the boat. We didn't used to get married. Brings bad luck, we'd say. But then one day, a ship came near and sent small lighters to the land on Diego Garcia where most of us lived, and this ship had brought soldiers from America. They started to build a big port there, they blew up the reef and covered the beaches with concrete. They cut down every coconut tree and blasted the coral in the lagoons up with dynamite in half of the island. We used to peep at them from the other half. Our eyes riveted. We were told to keep away from that side of the Islands, *keep away,* and they, the soldiers, were told not to talk to us. But one man did. He was called Pedro. He gave me a Hershey Bar. Maybe he thought I was pretty. I was about your age, Leila, with the two baby boys already.

'Then, we noticed people started to *not* come back. *To not come back.* First of the people close to us not to come back was my aunt, May. She didn't come back, so I told my mother I'd go on the next boat to look for her on the Island of Mauritius, and I'd take enough food for the boy too, and the little one was still on the breast. It'll be good for them, I said. An experience. Know their country, I said.'

Here she stopped a while, and I thought she may move out of

herself again. But she just sighed. Leila was right. This was the longest gap in gusts. The silence was oppressive.

'No one told us anything. So I went to Porlwi by boat. With the two little boys. Then when we went to the Company to find out when the boat would be going back to the Islands, when we went to the man in the hole in the wall, he said the Islands were closed. And I kept going back but they just said "Next!"'

'And then my little ones died and my heart broke. Aunt Paquerette picked up the pieces, and then he, my husband, came along and built up my shack into a nice house around me. And Honey came and made us happy in it. He died later. Of diabetes, I think. And then years later Honey was gone. And there's just her sweet boy now. Then I made the confession.'

She let her head fall into her hands.

We hear a terrible rumbling.

'What is that?' Leila asks. It is a massive gust, wreaking havoc in its path. *Anger has got all let loose,* I murmur, *anger has been unleashed.*

'Rest now, until lunchtime. The gust has gone. We are safe. We are together here. Lie down. Cover your eyes with her ribbon, and rest. We will do our exercises and our planning now. You have spoken of things too heavy to bear.'

Mama Gracienne slips into quiet sleep, as if her whole being is protected by a halo of peace. Meanwhile the storm goes on building up relentlessly outside and trying to get inside through every crevice.

It is hard to start.

But we must.

So we march, she and I do, then we jog, then we run, then we jump. Then when I do my bit, standing on her shoulders, I check the two tools, and I look out of the window, I see the sky a dizzy movement of high clouds. I steady myself. I worry about the tools on the sill. I feel stable up there, stable enough to get an idea.

'Can you walk a few paces until I'm under the grid over the light, do you think? In our common land?' I trust her now.

'I'll try,' she says shuffling slowly.

I balance carefully, unable to touch the ceiling properly with my hands, just running my fingertips along. And then we get to the metal grille, which is a few inches lower, and I hold on to it, with relief. It is secure. I pass my hand along the top of its criss-crossed bars. Yes, it would be a better place for the tools. Maybe I'll put them there next time.

A gust comes, and shakes the building. I hold on to the grid. My nerve gets shaken. Then, just in case, during that gust, I slide my hands right along the right hand edge. Then the other edge, and then when I am feeling the top of the third side, I find something that moves when I roll it. Tiny. Cylindrical. Hard and long. Smooth. My forefinger touches the length of it. I feel the joy before I'm conscious of what it is. *A needle.* A sewing needle. I roll it off the grid, until I hold it between my thumb and forefinger. Yes, I glance up at it. A shining needle. A number one sewing needle with a big eye. I throw it down in to the bottom corner of her part of the room under the window, making sure I miss the slop bucket because I know the lid doesn't fit properly.

'Let's go back to the window for me to hang on to the bars to get down.'

I haven't told her I found anything. I go over to where the foot of her bed is.

'Out of my room. Exercises are over!' she is joking. I don't say anything. I just pick it up and hold it in front of her. She can't believe her eyes.

You, Mama Gracienne, wake up charmed.

'Treasure,' you say. 'A tool. A gift from someone you don't even know. A heritage.'

A *third* tool. So I tell them about the other two.

We hide the needle in the corner of my bunk. We'll only put it back up there if we expect a proper search or anything. Or if we are leaving the cell, like the girls who left it for us in the first place. We are the inheritors of a vast fortune. First, the ideas get passed down to us, the messages, the *language*, as I put it. Now the tools. Including one needle. We are overjoyed. And we haven't even thought of anything to do with it yet.

'Maybe there's something else up there. Did you feel all around?'

We do our stunt again, to pass the time of day, we are so restless, but there isn't anything else. Rest is not possible for us. Only *you* could have been blessed with that half-hour's deep sleep, now over. You who have lost everything twice.

So we practise her walking about with me on her shoulders. I am practising balancing. She is practising gliding.

'So, there's not that many ways of getting out, are there. We can get out over the top of the walls, by air, we could say. Climbing, say.'

'Or flying,' she adds. She knows at once. *We can cut through one of the bars in the cell.* That would be just for the three of us. Or cut through bars in the dining hall or in the workshop. Or scale the high wall of the grounds. There's the roof of the kitchens, though. Have you noticed it, it's a bit low?

For all this, for any plan at all, we realise we will need bits of cloth strung together for hauling people out one by one. 'Or for binding and gagging blue ladies, more to the point,' Leila adds with glee.

I ask her to bite a little hole in the edge of my prison shirt.

'Just here,' I say. She does it without asking why. Then I rip it hard. The bottom three inches comes off in one fast rip.

Then I dig my needle out of the corner, and start undoing the thread in the hem of the torn-off bit.

'Should have done that the other way round,' I muse, realising I have gone and exposed myself to a few minutes of danger.

Slowly I undo a length of thread from the torn-off bit. Then I hide the torn off bit under my blanket, in the corner of my bunk.

And I thread the needle.

'Shall we hold an inauguration, Mama?' I ask you.

She cuts the ribbon.

You can also do theatre now. *Healing.*

Then I get Leila to sew my shirt up at both edges and in the middle. Looks normal again.

Now that we've got the needle, we choose one hem at a time, get the thread out of it. Then we bite a tear in one end, and rip off a layer and hide it. Then we put a new hem in our shirt. Until we have got six quite strong bits of cloth, all the same brown colour of our prison uniforms. And nobody knows but us. Then Mama Gracienne, you say, and a squall of rain and wind comes at the same time, as if encouraging you, 'My blanket's a bit long.'

'**O**r . . . to escape, I spy with my little eye, something beginning with an *h*. It's imaginary,' I say this.

'A *hole*,' she says.

'That's right. First try.' How does she know? Is sharing a cell enough to make us share thoughts?

'We can get out by digging. Under the ground,' I say.

'Nonsense,' she says, 'there's rock under the ground here.'

So I say we can dig a hole in the wall itself. Choose a stone in the wall that looks as though it can be dislodged. Slowly loosen it. Slowly notch out the cement between the rocks. We need to look for something that can give us a leverage angle. We would have to put it back in place every day. It would have to be in a place where they wouldn't notice us loosening it. In the exercise ground, maybe. We'd have to think of ways to stop them seeing us.

Leila says we could be behind someone, or behind something, or inside something while we were digging. Sick bay gives on an outside wall. Round and round our minds go.

'Have you got a plan of the prison *in your mind*,' Leila asks me. 'In your mind's eye?'

I start drawing one. *True, she's right. A map is never the same as an itinerary. We all know how to find the itineraries we need to form a sentence in our own language, for example, but only us experts get to see a common map for all languages.*

Or, I say, we can get out *through the doors* that everyone who works here comes and goes by. That would seem the easiest to me, of course.

'What?' she asks. 'That's impossible. They are locked. Locked up electronically.'

People open them, I reply.

And there's a thing called *hostages,* you add, Mama Gracienne.

As if you were one. Are one. Are you? A living hostage from Diego Garcia. Living on into another age. As bombs are lifted off from there today to bomb Serbia, Afghanistan, Sudan, Iraq. And the Prime Minister wimps about returning Diego Garcia – look at the hostages – only to stay silent in exchange for some trade quota.

And of course, you point out that we need a knife, or a gun. Everyone who mutinies takes hostages, you say, and mutineers all have arms.

By now, we are all hungry. Ravenous.

And it's my turn for a recipe. The only thing I can think of beginning with an '*i*' is innards. *The wonder of the insides.*

I nnards, curried goat's innards (or sheep's), also called Vinndu Curry: You can use the goat's liver. Take the skin off the liver and pull any big blood vessels out and throw the skin and big blood vessels away or cook them for the dog. Chop the liver up into beautiful one cubic centimetre pieces.

Then you can use the kidneys as well.

Wash them out nicely first, again removing big blood vessels, and cut them into the same size pieces.

Put quite a bit of oil into the heavy-bottomed saucepan or karay and brown lots of onion in it slowly on a low heat.

Once the onions are browned, put in garlic. Then pour in a lot of curry powder, stir well for a few minutes, until it smells cooked in the oil, and then immediately add all the innards. Stir the innards, oil and spices together and add salt.

Turn the heat up, and from time to time stir until it is frying.

Then turn the heat right down, wet your hand and shake a few drops of water into the saucepan, put the lid on and let the dish cook for long enough for the meat to be tender.

Serve small helpings, with little purris, or on quite a lot of rice, with dhal, together with a salad made of grated cucumber. When you cut the end off a cucumber, if it is not very tender, rub the stub against the end and a white substance gradually comes out. If you keep rubbing it gently for a while the cucumber gets much nicer. It's this white stuff that can make cucumber indigestible.

L eila recedes into a sulky corner. Her back resentful, facing us. She must be very hungry.
Or cross.
Whatever's the matter.
I ask her to rub my back.
She sighs, but does. Then she rubs Mama Gracienne's too.

Y ou clear your throat. Just that. An old lady clears her throat. Nothing more. Then, we both stand up as though of a common accord, and we move, without a word passing between us, nor a look, towards the cell door. Then, as if by chance, we stand as though looking out of it, although it is as opaque as any heavy iron prison door. And the peephole is one-way. Our backs are to the cell. Our backs are to the slop bucket. We get engrossed in a deep conversation, as if it is the most natural thing in the world. Perhaps about protection rackets like Secure Life insurance, or the progress of the twin cyclones. We pretend there is nothing happening.

Behind us, you move over to the slop bucket quietly, and use it in private.

A t night I dread the dark. When I was outside, darkness was a cloak of comfort around me. Imprisoned in this cell, night time now hides wild animals that prowl around me, just out of view, and the fear of Jay's death a wilder animal. Each new gust brings growls from them.

Get a grip on myself. *He still runs with the pack.* Even in prison he runs with the pack. Didn't the driver say as much. *Safety in numbers.*

Have you smuggled in your stolo-stolo? Lodged the metal bit you strike with your thumb, into a thin crack in the wall? Do you sneak it out at night and cup it into your hands. *Tor-wing, tweng tweng, tor-wing, tor-weng.*

I chase away visions of them cutting out your tongue, Jay. Your song. I chase away visions of you, Jay, and your pack, not running any more, but lying still. When I get closer I find you are all dead. And I am pinioned down, I can't *prevent, nurse, heal, attend to, bury.* A bullet in your jaw, from the underneath side by the gland in your neck – by the mumps gland – right up till lodged in your skull. And yet you are still laughing. I can hear the laughter rippling away in circles into the ionosphere.

If you die, Jay, where would all our shared experiences go?

What have we done to deserve this. Why us? *Why me?*

Self pity ends like a full stop.

Self-limiting.

So I speak to you, Jay, instead. Address you. Try keep the monsters away with *words*. Jay, Jay, are you listening? I've got some questions, Jay. Do you, the *men* prisoners in Alcatraz, *you plural*, do you guys fit the bill any better?

Are you perhaps the *real* prisoners? The ones who *deserve* it? Are you? Are you *proper prisoners*? Are you the convicts and dangerous jailbirds that exist in imaginations?

Are *you* the hardened cases? The ones who instil fear into children who stare into Black Mariahs at dark faces inside, dark hands on the mesh, dark fingers, tentacles of a sea anemone trying to pull something in, tendrils of a grenadilla plant flaying about looking for a trellis?

Why did mother earth abandon you like this? And me, too? To sleep on floors that slope towards the door for easier cleaning? Why are we forsaken, Jay?

Who built these prisons according to what plan?

Who are *they* anyway? How do *they* come to sit in judgement on us?

Can we not, in turn, get to judge them, Jay? Judge their judgements?

Their litany of laws is frightening. Offences, ingredients for a witches' broth.

Like mine. *Conspiracy to plant drugs.*

Do you, on your side, *damage property by band*? Like her. Like Leila. Commit *assault with effusion of blood*? Sleep of the just, look at her. Her hair cut all crooked like that, fallen across her face.

Or do you, like Mama Gracienne here, *confess*? Do they torture·you to get the confessions? Do muffled cries come out of the Porlwi Sid section of the CID? I saw Boni brought in. I took her in.

Do you harbour offenders? The very thing a jail does.

Or are you locked up for *loitering with intent, taking part in march without permission, forming associations of malefactors, trespassing,* or for being *rogues and vagabonds, idle and disorderly,* imprisoned for things *so vague and formless*?

One arrested for singing at a concert. Another for drinking one too many? A third for being out of a job? Another for an unsought after fight?

Only *more of you,* in the men's side? Ten times more, twenty times more, hundred times more?

I am one. An allegator. I feel my skin for scales.

What am I doing in this place?

One just walked the streets. *Soliciting.* So much for free trade. Another went to see a *backstreet* woman. One *stole* a tin of sweetened condensed milk from a supermarket, for a babe on a milkless breast. One *administered noxious substance* to her husband. Three took on their husbands' drug-peddling charges. A clutch of broken down addicts. When all they wanted was to fill up an empty space somewhere inside them with something.

Some of *them*, Jay, some of them out there? What about *them*? How *innocent* are they, Jay, and their leaders?

There are those who *declare war*.

They walk free. Maim and kill people by the hundred. By the thousand. *Collateral.* They strut around in suits and ties. *In their minds and in their eyes, is what?*

There are those who cause armaments to be made. Bombs, aircraft carriers, automatic weapons, tanks, landmines, linked in to their orders for spark-plugs, speedometers, ball-bearings and warning lights.

There are those who cause starvation. *En masse.* They lower wages and sack people, with intent. They raise prices and close factories. Leaving the little children to suffer without *give us this day our daily*. Shorten the second. What about them?

There are the *invisible*. Those who state conditions. Loans if *no hospitals*. Loans if *pay schools*. Loans if *no taxes on rich*. Interest rates. Surely there's some kind of larceny in this?

I only deal in language, Jay, and in electronics. How can I be expected to understand all this and more? Jay?

You, for no more than planting six small bushes. *Tor-wing, tweng tweng, tor-wing, tor-weng.* And they want to pull your tongue out too, I know it. The pictures crowd back into my mind.

But now, I fight them off with thoughts of *mutiny*.

Mutiny.

We prepare. Right now, Jay.

Mutiny.

I whisper the word. I whisper the noun and then the verb.

Mutiny. We'll mutiny.

And, then?

Then, Jay. Then what?

What is the point of a mutiny in *just this one neck of the woods, Jay?* In our prison, our country, our region? Would they not snuff us out like a candle? In the wind?

A small island, our earth is. So green and blue and turquoise you could cry. I've seen it through the eyes of a satellite so often.

Could it be everywhere? Our mutiny, Jay?

Round and round? Could we call it a revolution then? Turning around? Turning around what? Dancing together? Singing? Everyone the artist? Everywhere, Jay?

For us, women, there are the unborn who get involved. The inside.

But, then again, we can only do it where we can do it.

And for the meantime that means, it's here, inside the Women's High Security.

I look at these two. They have gone to sleep like kittens, while this mounting storm brings bedlam. What mutiny can we be expected to accomplish? In this pandemonium?

W hen we get to the mutiny, there will be other sections of the criminal code just lying in wait for us. I know. I hear talk of these sections amongst the old prisoners. Section this and section that. *If* we fail. Laws lying in abeyance, unnoticed. With horror, I read them in the Prison's Library. Blue One-One just walks right into our cell and threatens us with one. She brings it out of its dark hiding place to scare us with. *'High treason!'* She shrieks at us.

Then, this gets her going. *'Sedition. And inciting disaffection. Blasphemy. And outrage. Going on strike. Picketing!'* Then she adds, sarcastic, *'if financial loss incurred.'*

'Trespass! Contempt. Publishing a plot against the state. Taking command of armed force. Stirring up war. Emergency Powers, that's what!'

Just a litany, I think. Blue One-One litany.

'Stirring up hatred against a class. Inciting others to mutiny, stirring up civil war. Disclosing official secrets. Rebellion by more than twenty armed persons.'

And also *damaging property,* like Leila did, *by band.*

That's all for afterwards, if we don't succeed.

Only *past* revolutions are just. Everybody knows that. They hold a ball at the Embassy each year. Only if they *succeed,* though. Otherwise they are at first considered dangerous and mad, then gradually ill-inspired and stupid.

We must succeed.

The night gets much more stormy now. It must be cyclone warning Class Two by now, of that I am sure.

I can't get to sleep. The wind is too restless now, rising to disorganised crescendos, that then rush around and round uselessly until they peter out. And the cyclone is starting to get out of hand. Threatening everyone out aloud. *All hell is going to get let loose.*

'You awake, Mama Gracienne?' I lean over in hope. I become like Leila, a little girl without her mother, and so I lean over and say, 'You awake, Mama Gracienne?'

'I see you thrashing your limbs about,' you reply, in a whisper, as though you have been watching me all along when I was speaking to Jay, keeping the visions away.

'Got one for me beginning with a "j", Mama Gracienne?'

You turn over and look at me and say the letter 'j' is too *difficult*. You are sleepy anyway. So I suggest one beginning with 'k'. And you say, no, Leila, the Effusion of Blood, has to do one beginning with 'j'. Maybe in the morning when she wakes up, you say.

But Leila isn't asleep, and she says, 'A bad night, Juna?'

You always give her that confidence that I would not know she had. And she asks this question *a bad night, Juna?* She who would never have wanted to know or to care.

Leila hesitates. She's about to give up, say she doesn't know anything of any value to anyone, when she suddenly thinks of something and agrees.

Juice, she says, like some juice, Juna? Passion fruit and bergamot juice? Otherwise the cyclone will come blow down the fruit anyway and it will go to waste. I like saying passion fruit instead of grenadilla. *Passion fruit* thrills my ears.

You squeeze as many sour old bergamot, or grapefruit, or limes, or lemons as you can get before the cyclone gets them. Harvest them by the basketful. Same for passion fruit. Now I'll tell you the *secret of passion* fruit in juice. I don't know many secrets like this, so listen carefully

Take the pulp out of passion fruit cut in half and put the pulp into a metal strainer over a bowl. This is the secret: Add sugar to the passion fruit pulp in the strainer, and grind the passion fruit and sugar through the strainer.

When no more seems to come through, add more sugar, and grind away.

This grinding is what gets the taste out of passion fruit, otherwise it's tasteless as straw in sugarwater.

You've got to break open each little individual cell to let out its passion. Its ester. Like its spirit really.

Then when you've got nothing except dry black seeds left, you scrape the bottom of the strainer.

Add the two juices together.

If you want to serve immediately, then you add water and sugar to taste, then ice cubes. All friends invited. We could serve the whole of Block D.

If you want to keep it, pour the concentrated juice into the squares of an ice tray and keep deep frozen. Then every time you want a glass or two you just pop out one cube of frozen concentrated juice. But that is assuming that there are not weeks without electricity after the cyclone.

Who'd have thought she'd got so many recipes in her head. Green banana chips and passion fruit juice. The storm is shaking recipes out of her memory, like grenadilla seeds from the strainer, sown almost by chance when they were thrown away and then when the rain comes they sprout into elegant creepers with tendrils against the wall, reaping more ripe grenadillas. Passion fruit.

A ny person who, by any food, drink, medicine, or by violence, or by any other means, procures the miscarriage of any woman quick with child, or supplies the means of procuring such miscarriage, whether the woman consents or not, shall be punished by imprisonment for a term not exceeding 10 years. The like punishment shall be pronounced against any woman who procures her own miscarriage or who consents to make use of the means pointed out or administered to her with that intent, if such miscarriage ensues. Any physician, surgeon, or pharmacist who points out, facilitates or administers the means of miscarriage shall, where miscarriage has ensued, be liable, on conviction, to penal servitude, for a term not exceeding 20 years. [*Criminal Code 235 (1838) Sections (1) and (2)*] – Copied down from the Prison's Library.

'Which one shall we try to file off?' I ask my two cellmates this right in the heart of the mid-afternoon imprisonment which is called *rest*. Some rest. Everything is disturbed. In disequilibrium. Winds prepare their forces in the distance, hold them in, and then blow them on us, *blow, blow, blow winds, blow*. This way, then rush back again that way. Buffeting even the stone walls, causing the reinforced concrete ceilings to tremble, and sending in mists that fold one after the other, wet and sticky on us. And the temperature continues to rise.

We are all three of us tossing and turning in our confined space without hope of finding a comfortable position. Without hope of seeking one. The bunks go hard and pitiless, pressing on pointed bones of hips and shoulders, ankles and ribcages. Leila's bit of cement floor even harder than our bunks. And sloping towards the door.

And the sounds of the cyclone outside gain in uncontrollable restlessness, verging on the *shrill* now. Sudden and disconcerting gusts, rush in and press down and sideways on everything, and no sooner are the gusts in, than they begin to push and push until things start suddenly to break and to burst out. We hear them. A shutter here, a pane of glass there.

Never let a cyclone into your house, it'll pop your windows out.

The blue ladies didn't allow us to go into the quadrangle for *exercise* today as is our *right*. This adds to *our* restlessness. Our limbs are accustomed to a certain amount of exercise every day.

We were only allowed to go and empty our slop buckets and come back. We were not even allowed to wash ourselves.

We smell.

Then there came *rest*.

Which adds more to the restlessness.

The cyclone causes us to be over alert and edgy, adrenaline keeping us in the ready for emergencies and then because of the confines around us, leaves us bored and listless. Nervy and nervous. Jumpy. When she's awake, she bites her nails, and in her fitful sleep, she grinds her teeth. That's the only way you know she has fallen asleep for a few minutes. That terrible rage of tooth grinding.

Anxiety. Caged and aimless fear, imprisoned anger, culled hatred, suppressed aggression, they all come out as *anxiety*.

But at least it isn't dark.

So the spooks don't come out and get billowed around in our minds so easily.

Leila knows what I'm talking about. '*That* one, second from the left.' She is so sure of herself. Of course, she's right. That is the one that will leave the biggest gap.

She bites her nails, meanwhile, and says, 'You are all going to get your periods, the whole lot of you!'

Can she smell it?

'What you talking about? What you mean? Who is? Me?' I can't believe my ears, what is she talking about? 'Who d'you think you are? Cassandra?' As if the cyclones are bringing them on, like twin moons pulling doubly hard on all monthly creatures whether tek-teks or bigger bivalves that dig into the sand when the breakers recede.

Never cut bamboo at full moon, if you want to use the rod you've cut, or so they say. It will get infested with woodworm. What about in a cyclone?

The gusts go on getting stronger. And more frequent. Building up each time until they, the gusts, get themselves into a frenzy. The rain in each gust gets thicker, each drop bigger and the drops closer together, heavier. And it starts to fall less diagonally and more horizontally. Inbetween, thick hazes of drizzle suddenly get blown silently into our cell, like the folds of sheets.

'It's a fact. It's not a prophecy. It's a fact. How do I know? The other prisoners tell me, that's how. And I can believe it. Last month everyone did get their periods at the same time, here, the whole place was full of blood last month. Didn't you notice? It's catchy. It's to do with the smell of the sweat in your upper lips, they say. And it's coming again because it's time. As from today.'

I was already confused before the most recent elongation, with the other elongations. That's how I ended up pregnant. Not just me either. Lots of us. Every time the authorities do an elongation, I get into a tizzy and I can't be sure how to work out when I had my last periods, nor when I'm expecting the next, nor how long a new month is supposed to be. I lose sight of the moon so easily. We all become like air hostesses on international flights, who don't know how to count the days, nor in which direction to change the time on their watches at night.

At first I think *that's* what she's talking about. Some comment about the elongation. But I'm wrong. She is talking about everyone's periods coming at the same time.

I ask her if her upper lip and nose are inoculated. *Vaccinated or something?* Because she didn't say *we*, she said *you*. I am hard on her sometimes.

'Yes. Yes, they are at the moment. In a manner of speaking my upper lip is inoculated,' she laughs. 'I'm *expecting*. You see, I'm expecting.'

So, I was right.

She drops this news on purpose.

That is what she has been building up to. She is young, and doesn't know how to tell these things, how to make the space to say something in. Hard for her to find a proper cue. An opening.

'*Expecting*? Expecting what? You're only a schoolgirl!' *you* say.

I could kick you sometimes, Mama Gracienne.

Why are you so dumb? The girl only just *told* you. Can't you just listen? Let her be. As though you think green mangoes are the cause. And as though you think young girls don't *eat* green mangoes. She's not even sixteen, for god's sake.

'So what if she's a schoolgirl? Weren't you younger than that when you had your first little boy, when you were on the Island?'

I turn back to Leila again and ask if she has been getting nausea or anything.

'No, I don't feel anything,' she says. 'Doesn't make me either hot nor cold.'

I ask her if she wants to have it. 'No,' she says, 'definitely not.' She will have to tell someone, the doctor or someone, because these things in wombs don't go away by themselves just because you want them to.

She knows that, but as *you* say, Mama Gracienne, will the doctor help her? Will the doctor break the law then?

There is silence now.

None of us think the doctors will. Unless there is some advantage for *them*.

I was certainly offered no choice, but I won't tell her that yet.

She must get *her* attention.

She must either do something about it or start accepting it all by herself first.

So there is silence now. The wind and the rain even abate for a while between gusts. Oppressive heat rises from the floor, a constant mist now coming in uninvited and sinking down beside us, even between gusts, from that small cell window, and condensation meanwhile forms and makes drops that balance precariously on all four walls, then, like so many tears, begin to run down the cheeks of that cell.

I am thinking.

Cyclones are hard to think in. They are things which get into your head and turn it topsy-turvy.

Then you speak, Mama Gracienne, and you say that you for one aren't going to get your periods. You've given them up. Bless the Lord. For good, you say.

'So,' and you turn towards me, Mama Gracienne. 'It's just you! It's just you who'll catch this thing that's going round.'

I won't either, of course. But I leave it at that. Neither of them takes in my silence, or takes it up, each being too absorbed with herself. A funny cell.

What with her predicting a flood of periods, yet none whatsoever in this cell.

As if the cyclone weren't enough. One visitation. Now the curse. En masse.

97

Y ou lie with your ear to the door, Mama Gracienne, listening. You are our lookout. Only you are looking with your *ears*. Because there's nothing to *see* with your eyes, the peephole being one-way. You've got good ears. Didn't you hear Honey when she made those sounds? Not that it helped you then. You wish you had your knitting. You could sit and knit a pair of booties for Leila. *Pink or blue?* You look at your fingers, and imagine them knitting. Two purl, two plain for the ribbing. If only. You are all ears. You are our ears. It's hard to hear because during the gusts the cyclone brings noises that invade from the outside, and then during the gaps between gusts, there is an eerie thickness that muffles and absorbs sound, eats it all up, even what you want to hear like the sound of a footfall in the corridor, like a blue lady clearing her throat. Like silk stockings scraping together on a sneakily approaching blue lady's overfed thighs.

Not *now*. We don't want to be found out now. And, more than at any other time, it is at this exact point, precisely this moment, when we are getting excited, that we *can* most easily get found out, because we are more liable to make mistakes. Not that we've done anything visible yet. But still, we know our progress is remarkable. Enough to make us realise how if we hadn't done anything, if we didn't do anything, if by choice we refrained from planning things, how much we would be missing, how much we would be losing out on, how dumb we would be being. Before there is a single result, we have already transformed so much.

So our minds do vacillate. From being a jungle of wild

thoughts at war with themselves to being a place of peaceful cultivation of ideas and emotions.

'I am so glad you were cast away into our cell, Mama Gracienne,' Leila says, quite suddenly. 'Is this why you made your confession then? You knew somehow, you just felt it in your bones,' she teases, 'that your blanket would get thrown in here, and then you would get cast away in here after it, and that once you were locked up, you could get to help two girls like us in the clink?'

You laugh at us. What do you see? You see Leila, an Effusion of Blood, a girl so large and approximative, so unpredictable, a child-mother, brought like this to heel. You see me, Juna the Allegator, a small stunted creature emotionally crippled by computers that try to *represent* the world inside their very innards, a creature who suffers horrible visions at night and calls out for help in the strangled sounds of a slaughtered sheep, and for whom you brought a message in.

And we took you in.

Now you shake your head in disbelief. Now, you laugh with your head tilted backwards and your hands parted, fingers together. *Did you do it?* You ask yourself. *Will you ever know?* you ask yourself.

Never, it is lost, the knowledge is gone.

Perhaps your real laugh, the laugh you left buried on the Islands, a laugh maybe from Africa, will come back one day. Perhaps it will dig under the sea, and tunnel. Or rise up and saw a hole in the clouds and fly over. Imagine a laugh coming back and finding you inside this dingy cell. A laugh that even Honey didn't bring back whole when she got born.

You are pleased with your role. *The listener*. You smile and you laugh slowly now. *Anybody there? said the listener*.

You love watching us doing our acrobatics anyway. It's your favourite thing. Better than the television, you say. Better than the Russian circus, you say. We can be professionals when we get out one day, you say. We can travel.

It's more and more confusing when you listen now, and you pin your ear to the cell door, because when the gusts come, you hear so many new noises now. You hear the creaking of things that have never creaked before. Creaking coming from outside. Creaking coming from inside. Moans and shrieks. Hysterical rattling starts and then, when you get used to it, it stops, thus causing anxiety. Sudden banging and shattering glass, in a place that seemed to have nothing loose enough to bang and nothing brittle enough to shatter in it. Groaning of concrete beams in the lookout tower as it sways.

And the wind howls through branches of trees now, *wooow, woow,* and whistles past electric pylons, *whis-s-s-tle-le-tle-s-s-s,* and shrieks around the lookout tower, *shree-eeks-ks.* And the wind itself now starts to growl and howl, in its own right, stalking around the bare stone building we are in. A wild animal. Old, wounded and desperate. Biting its own tail now. Pulling its own entrails out.

But even then, you listen at the door for the slightest sound.

And Leila swaggers to a still position. She breathes in and out aloud. You can see her breathing but you can't hear the breathing. Then she puts her hands in the stirrup position. I climb up, on to her hip, then her shoulder, then I steady myself and pick up the file from the sill. No need to move it now.

I must report to her on everything I see. Before she gets cross. She can't stand it if I don't tell her something. If I know anything and keep it a secret, she picks a fight with me.

By chance a lull descends and wraps around everything. Swaddling-clothes around our ears and a shroud around the cornices of the building.

I report, 'It's a calm spell now.' And as I speak, the full impact of the desolation I see hits me, so I cry out, 'Look!' shouting to you and to her, as if there was any hope of you or Leila seeing. But it doesn't matter. Neither of you has had time to get to know all the leaves as intimately as I have, nor as closely. It's only me that's bereft. There are no leaves left on our lakoklis tree. It stands stripped to the bone. I mourn for those leaves. They are gone. As if there was any hope of getting them back on again. 'There isn't a single leaf left. All those new leaves that have just made all that effort. All so green. All gone. The single mad dancing leaf is gone too.'

After a test bomb blast.

A frozen northern winter.

I feel the death of this one leaf.

All its energy wiped out.

For ever.

I suddenly think of Jay. There he is in my head as I stand on Leila's shoulders, mourning the death of a leaf. *Maybe he's dead.*

Then, a relief comes over me, as my mind *moves on*. Manages to move on. It doesn't get stuck in the old rut. It moves on. On to Honey, poor Honey, with the foam between her lips. To the other girl, the girl that was Leila's roommate before me. Was she Mopey-Sue? The one who died and dried up like the wasps?

The leaf, like the dead, is gone.

My head is free now. Shaved unequally, and scratched and scabbed, but free.

The clouds race much faster up there, now, I tell her, they are such very high clouds up there. There's no abating up there at all. High up there, way up in the sky, the winds are phenomenal. Constant. The gales aren't just in gusts up there high in the sky, but are without let-up. Making clouds race vertiginously. Run wild. Let loose. Go berserk. Tear across the firmament. No calm spell up there.

Like the sea, once it's up. It doesn't quieten down for days, maybe weeks, let alone in the eye, let alone in a calm spell.

And here comes a gust. Down here. 'Can you hear it coming?' I shriek, 'Hold on!' The gust is trying to tear a branch from the lakoklis tree. A huge branch is getting wrenched round and round. Like a madman in pain, the tree contorts itself, into a ball, desperately trying to hold on to its branch, but there it goes, rent off, ripped off, flying as though it was nothing more than a tiny dry twig, off and out of my line of vision. Out of sight. Rain is pouring in on to my arms now, and on to my face. 'You'll get drenched under me,' I say to Leila, as I feel the water start to run down from my arms and my face on to my neck and down my body on to my legs, 'Prepare yourself.'

It must surely be Class Three already. The twin cyclones must surely have gone on and on rushing headlong south-westerly towards us. Hurtling. Maybe they have joined up into one. How will we know?

I've got work to do up there. I try out the file now. I am standing on her shoulders, *still* as can be. When she stands firmly on her two legs, she is strong as a horse. I try to make myself light. As if by an act of faith. Some sort of levitation.

Now I start to file. We have chosen to file the bar she suggested, second from the left because if we can get it out, then I can fit through the gap it will leave. And maybe she can too. Now I put down the file, pick up the hacksaw blade and I cut in a notch in the bar right at the bottom to get my file going. If I file right at the bottom, the stub won't tear our prison shirts nor rip our innards out when we have to squeeze over it to get out, and with luck I may be able to bend the whole thing, and then pull it out of the top by hanging on it. Who knows? I hold on to the far left bar to get a bit of weight behind my filing. And I file and file and file. I file really smoothly. I imagine it's my nails. I want them perfect, so I file really gently, really smoothly, never letting the file catch or jar. This way I spare her shoulders any extra pain. And never pressing too hard on the file.

I file and file and file until I'm tired. Or until she's tired. Then I put the file down on the ledge next to the hacksaw blade and bring myself down.

We lie on our bunks and try to think. But thoughts get to be staccato. Like those of a bird. We peck at one phrase, then at another.

Then we do it again, and again. Up, and file away. File, file, file. Never let it get stuck.

So after exercises, and before exercises, and after planning and before planning, so after meals and before meals, so after food games and before them, I am up on her shoulders. Filing. The whole day long. And you, Mama Gracienne? You are our guardian angel. You grace us with your company. You listen. You keep watch.

Mama Gracienne, you suddenly speak up. You say we are working too much, and you say we need a break. We'll tire ourselves out, you say. Stop, you say. Time, you say, for a snack. Enough is enough. *Good as a feast*, you say. You are putting your foot down, you say. You hold your hands like the referee in a football match, showing a T, for time. *Time that changes so much that it was an insolence ever to try to measure it.*

We are dead beat and starving.

There is something left in your refrigerator from yesterday, you say. It's better when it's day old. And it is *no time* to be cooking, not now. Only for slowing down and telling.

We accede.

It begins with the letter '*k*', of course.

Kale and potato. A little something to keep the wolf from the door. I say kale, she says, but you can also use mustard cress or Chinese lettuce, she says, instead. Whichever you get, whichever's cheaper. My man grew a rugged, harsh kale in Tamarin, she says, and other things. He said it was mother of vegetables – of cabbage and cauliflower, lettuce and sprouts, and of broccoli too – so it grows more easily. Wash the vegetables carefully. Cut the kale or Chinese lettuce starting at the root side, into closely shredded slices. Start at the root-end, so you can soak the root-end bits to get any soil out, then put it all in a colander to wash. If you use cress instead, you need to check for little snails as well, and not use the big central stems if they are too bitter.

I could die of hunger at this point. I could eat the snails. Imagine what it must be like for her? Leila, the angry, hungry, growing one, ravenous all the time, her wolf at the door. After all the exertion. I look over at her. She bites her nails. And looks at the crooked ends of her father-hacked hair, ready to nibble them as well.

Boil the kale and drain it. Throw away the water, unless you can think of a use for it. Boil the potatoes until they are ready for mashing. Drain them too.

Then put quite a lot of butter in a heavy-bottomed saucepan and fry onions in it until they are brown. Concentrate so that you brown them thoroughly without burning them, and *enjoy the perfume*. My Honey used to. She loved onions browning, browning, browning and then suddenly adding the garlic. She would pretend to swoon with the fragrance.

Anyway. Anyway, you throw in a dried red chilli and then add crushed garlic and a little crushed root ginger. Then add both vegetables and salt and pepper. Mash them well, and let the potato stick from time to time, to make it taste browned (like roast potatoes).

Chop up parsley and sprinkle it on top.

Then, after eating something like that, you lie back a while, and think peaceful thoughts, and then when it's gone down, then you can get back to work.

98

W hich is what we do. After our kale and potato and when late afternoon has come, I am up filing again. Filing away.

I hold harder on to the far left bar with my left hand, to get even more weight behind the file. But not too much weight. Back and forth. Back and forth. I am getting quite good at it by now. *If the ants do, why can't I? Where the bee sucks, there suck I.*

I give the other two live reports on the weather. As seen from the cell window. I tell them that another of the big branches is being ripped right off the tree and carried out of view. There is more light out there now. The clouds are so high now that the sun can still see them and reflect quicksilver off them.

Cyclones chase away darkness, you say. Hound it out. Until it flees in fear.

All night long it will be light. More than mauve now, it will remain purple. And one will be able to walk around without lighting even though it's *no moon*. So you, Mama Gracienne, you the Confession, you who should know, so *you* say. You still follow the moon. From the days of the Islands when it was your only calendar. You never let it go.

We forget about the blue ladies.

We know them only too well. In a cyclone, they will forget about us. Out of sight, out of mind. The end-of-rest bell has not even been rung. Our cell doors have stayed silently closed.

The others must be seething in their cells. Fear of floodwaters rising.

'Mama Gracienne can you sing, can you sing for us, while we

work? Leila has to stand so still, with me on her shoulders, and I have to file, so we need music.' I wish my brother Jay was, I wish.

The only song you know is to the tune of a sega, you say:

> *I am in prison*
> *The Islands are closed*
> *You are in jail*
> *The ship won't take you back*
> *Any more*
> *A-la-li-la. A-la-lay-la-la-la.*
> *She is incarcerated*
> *Bound on every side*
> *They're out on bail*
> *But not allowed to sail*
> *Anywhere*
> *A-la ley-la-la. A-la-li-la, li la.*
> *Where am I now?*
> *In the clink!*
> *Weh, weh-weh, weh!*
> *Where are you now?*
> *Behind bars*
> *Where is she now?*
> *Locked right up*
> *And where will we be tomorrow?*
> *On the main road*
> *Where will we be the next day?*
> *By the well*
> *Drinking from the fountain*
> *Of freedom*
> *And then?*
> *Swimming in the sea of love*
> *Always*
> *La, al la lay la la la.*
> *La, al la lay la la la.*

There are only some bars in your music that I file the bars on the window to. Others that I don't. I never file while you're asking a question, only for the answer. As though the answer is in the filing. You like this, it makes your singing *useful*.

You start all over again, and it's never the same the next time. *Music builds up. Note after note, sequence after sequence. Movement after movement. It adds up.*

Which makes the work go easily.

After about six more times going up, and filing until I am exhausted and until Leila's shoulders ache, and then without warning them, I am through. I have cut right through. I grab right at the bottom of it, warn Leila, lean with all my weight backwards, pull inwards on the bar with all my weight, and it bends slightly. I pull again and get it to clear the edge of the window sill. How could someone of my size and weight bend an iron bar?

'Stand clear now,' I say to Leila, 'Stand clear,' I say.

She does.

I hang with all my weight on it.

A gust builds up, and rushes at the prison building. Mama Gracienne and Leila are making clapping movements but without the noise. There's too much noise in that gust to hear any sound we might wish to make.

Your ear is still firmly to the door. How do you do it? Sing and yet listen. Clap and yet listen.

And as the massive gust makes the whole building give, it shudders, and a ripple of shaking moves right through all the prison walls, we hear it, and sure enough, the bar *gives*, and the top part comes out of the bit of wall above it, a lump of concrete still joined to it. I fall to the ground with the bar in my hands. *Did the cyclone help.* Leila asks? *Did it?*

We have a cell we can get out of whenever we want to. Potentially. For what it's worth. Even Leila can get through a space that big. Once we see it, we know. Mama Gracienne, you just shake your head in admiration, as if you are beyond escape. Beyond getting out. *Or maybe already out.*

Our cell window gives on to a small courtyard that, in turn, gives on to the central electrical and electronics room. But the central electrical and electronics room also has bars. And a glass window inside them.

Mama Gracienne, it is you that reminds us to put the bar back up in place for show, *quick*. How wise you are, the Confession. Just the kind of thing that would catch the eye of even the laziest blue lady, that, a missing bar, second from the left, in a cell window.

So, tired as I am, I jump up into her tired hand stirrup and on to her exhausted shoulders and balance it in its old place. For show.

'It is a nice *thing* too,' you say, Mama Gracienne, referring to the new crowbar we have balanced up in the window. I see that you were scared I might let it fall out.

You say we should take it with us when we go out. You feel for the cloth strips now with your soft, warm hand. You say they're for 'coming back' in again. You already know there will have to be *va-et-vient*.

'How nice of you to want us back,' I say.

Leila is hungry. She could die of hunger after all the effort of holding me up like that.

The bakeries will all be closed by now, you say, Mama Gracienne. There won't be any power for their ovens, their delivery vans will be in the garages, and their workers will be at home by now. Looking after the children. Taking the animals in. Lopping off branches. Nailing down whatever may lift up. All of which means, you say, *We*, just like everyone else, will have to cook *little purees* and we, like everyone else, will have to catch the rooster and eat him because he may get killed in any case in the cyclone. Lucky *little purees* beginning with an '*l*'.

Little purees, and chicken fricassée: The dough, you say, and you ought to know because you made them for Honey for all those years, the dough for little purees is as dry as you can make it and as hard as you can make it so that it's still rollable with a rolling pin without fragmenting into bits. (For faratas, it's the other way around, the dough has to be as wet and as soft as you can knead it so that you can roll it out without it sticking to everything, but that's another recipe for another day.)

Flour (you can use half whole wheat flour and half ordinary flour), a tiny bit of salt, so that you *can* just taste it, and an equal amount of sugar, so that you just *can't* taste it! Everything you cook has to have just enough sugar (or salt for that matter in the case of sweet things) in order to be up to the normal sugar (or salt) taste in your mouth, a taste that's always there, so although little purees aren't at all sweet, you have to add a pinch or two of sugar. Otherwise it tastes wrong. Anyway. You add a tablespoon of vegetable oil, and then the smallest amount of water possible.

Leila loves this. She lies, hypnotised head against the hard prison wall. I know what she's thinking. She's thinking the wind has quietened down to listen to you, Mama Gracienne. We listen to you.

You play with the flour, *you go on*. In the air making crumbs of it, then you knead it. *Your hands show us. Lifting up the flour and sifting it. Playing with it. Making it into one round ball again and again.* When it feels all nice, like plasticine, then you make one long snake about an inch across, and roll it nicely. *You roll out a long snake with your hands.* Then you break off one-inch round bits, break! Break, snap, snap. Then you play with each one till you make it into a perfect little ball, and then you squash it flat with your hand on the table top. *You put one hand on top of the other.* And then you roll it into a thin pancake about five inches' diameter. You may need to use either flour or oil to stop it sticking to the table or sticking to the rolling pin. Then you hang it over the edge of your empty mixing bowl. You do this to all the little *wheels*, as little purees can be called.

You put on a round-bottomed wrought iron karay (or a frying pan, if you haven't got a karay) with enough oil in it for one five-inch little puree to float freely in it.

When the oil is hot, you pick up one puree carefully with a big spoon with holes in it, and then put it into the oil. If the oil is the right temperature, the little wheel will almost immediately blow up like a balloon, and then you turn it over, let the other side cook for a few seconds, and take it out. Drain it with the spoon, and while one is draining, you can slide the next one in.

Each one doesn't take more than a minute. You put them on a plate, lined with *Le Dimanche*.

Serve with chicken fricassé already prepared as follows. Heat up a tiny bit of oil, throw in at the same time: Chicken cut into small pieces, bone and all (for the taste), finely chopped onions, crushed cumin, crushed garlic, fresh thyme, mint. Allow all to sizzle without the lid. Stir once chicken is browned, and wait for it to brown again. Then add a few very finely chopped tomatoes and salt to taste. Close lid firmly, and turn heat down. Allow to cook for . . . twenty minutes or so.

As you are saying the words 'twenty minutes or so', Leila and I have to lip-read because the cyclonic gusts have crept silently closer and this one is so violent it drowns out your voice and all other sound. At the rate these two cyclones are getting nearer, it'll have to be tonight that Leila and I will be going out.

99

A nd so it comes to pass.

That night, you watch us, Mama Gracienne. You see me put the two tools into my shirt hem for the journey. You put your hands together in a namasté greeting mixed with a prayer and you watch me climb up on to Leila's square shoulders, shoulders that must be aching by now, pinched and bruised. You watch me taking the bar out, throwing it out the window into the cyclone, in case we need it later, tying the cloth rope to the left-hand-end bar so that a rope-ladder is half falling inside half outside.

You see me disappear. Then you see her climb up the inside rope-ladder and disappear down the other side head first, feet following, climbing-tumbling down our rope and into the wildest night of storms and rain and wind. You imagine the buffeting we are taking. Do your hands stay together after having wished us farewell, because they are waiting to greet us again? Do you sometimes move them up towards your chin and in towards your heart, begging us to come back?

Leila and I fight our way through the wind and rain and flying sticks and pieces of tin whipping past. I see Leila mouthing something to me, but sounds don't travel. I signal to her that I can't hear anything she's saying. We, blinded by the stinging rain and whipping of the wind, hands up to protect our heads, grope our way to underneath the electronics room window. Her fearlessness impresses me. Strong as a horse, but nerves better than a horse's.

The searchlight is on, but it doesn't penetrate through that kind of downpour, a downpour that pours down *sideways*. The torrential rain diffuses light, like sheets of frosted glass would.

When we get there, and stand under the window we have to get into, there is rain running off the roof in cascades and down us on all sides. Living waterfalls, we stand there. Ankle-deep in a rising lake in the middle of that courtyard. All the storm drains must be blocked with branches and leaves and rubbish.

Leila is undeterred.

She stands with her feet firmly on the earth, water covering her prison sandals and the bottoms of her prison trousers. She holds her hands and arms like a stirrup once again. As if it's normal. As if she always did it. We are steeped in a strange and exciting conviction, a conviction that is all our own, and it makes a kind of calm inhabit us, and gives a weird beauty to our movements, even in that buffeting whirlpool of out-of-control weather. We should by rights be physically tired, we should by rights be suffering from exhaustion and soon from exposure, we should by all accounts be terrified. But we aren't. We are as if *there is no question any more*. We are happy. I am happy and I feel Leila is too. *No one will ever take this moment away from us. Exhilaration in our every movement.*

First I finger my shirt to check the two tools, like telling beads on a rosary, then I summon my energy with *a-one, a-two, a-three*, and with ease, I climb up yet again and then begin to put my arm muscles to an endurance test. I saw in a first notch with the saw-blade. Then I file and file, smoothly and evenly. Pressing down just the right amount. I again try not to allow the file to stick, but it keeps sticking. The water doesn't help. I free my left hand to press the bit of my left cheek next to my nose towards my nose, I give a long hard pinch, and then another really hard pinch, with my head bent down to avoid the heavy waterfall coming out of the gutter of the roof on to my head, and that's how I get some grease from my nose which I then manage to rub on to the cutting edge of the file. When Leila is tired, she touches my left leg twice, knock-knock, and I hold on to the bars to let her out, she clears out rubble from under the water for me, and then I jump down into the ankle-deep water. We cower away, trying to avoid the worst of the overflow from the roof, which is like a pounding force in front of us.

On the third time up, I find that the bar is slightly rusted on one side and it is this that will make the job possible. When I get down, I tell Leila this as she shivers next to me. Because she has to stand still she is starting to get cold. I get her to run on the spot, run, run, run, to warm up. Then up I climb again.

We do this ten times in all, I counted, until we are both so tired we should drop dead – she, shivering like a leaf by now – and then on the eleventh time up, I get right through and I haul the bar out. I balance the loose iron bar in its place again, which is difficult in that weather.

She hugs me when I get down, and picks me up in the air as if I were a child and swings me round and round. *The cyclic movement of the cyclone is getting inside of us. Two witches we are. Swinging round and round in the rain.*

To get back is risky. I remember the cut out bar from our own cell window and have to feel around blind in the water under our window for it. We are both purple. The sky a haunting white. There is no moon and there are no stars. But it is bright light in the middle of the night, on all sides, way out beyond the hedged in searchlight.

I climb on to her stirruped hand yet again, so that I don't have to weaken the roped sheet any, on to her shoulders, drop the bar in first.

I slither in, drenched, and then she clambers up the rope, just praying it won't go and break. It doesn't.

Once inside, your hands – still palms together – part to hug us both. You take our drenched clothes off us, squeeze water out of them in your vice grip into the slop bucket and hang them over the edge of the two bunks. *Have to sleep naked under your blankets*, you say.

So all is ready. Readiness.

We say nothing. There is pandemonium outside now. All the fury of the cyclone is let loose. And in the middle of that noise, a sparrow gets buffeted in. It, too, like the ribbon, falls on to the corner of Leila's rug.

No way it can survive that night.

Poor thing.

We think of the pair of canaries. Leila takes her orange ribbon hidden under the corner of her blanket, and plaits a nest for the sparrow. She cradles the bird on it, and asks me if I'll go up and put it on the ledge.

Better go free, she whispers in its ear.

So, she stands nearly naked now. And hands you the sparrow's crib, Mama Gracienne, while I, also nearly naked now, climb up on to her shoulders, and I lean down and take the crib from you, Mama Gracienne, and put it carefully up there on the left side.

Pass the bar, Mama Gracienne, I say, because we had forgotten to balance it in place.

When night comes, she and I sleep like we've never slept before in our whole lives. *The just.*

But when I wake up early, the monsters which respect nothing try to get into my mind, and I fight them out with more sleep, and in my sleep, I dream.

I dive down under the turquoise navy blue baby blue transparent green glistening surface of the water with my eyes closed, blindly, and I keep them tightly closed, using my hands to grope through the thick water and relying on all my willpower to *not look* and at the same time to *keep myself down* under the water that is pressing me upwards buoying me, so that when I get to where I want to be, when I hold on to a jutting out piece of coral to keep me down, when I open my eyes under that water I suddenly see the whole universe in perfect, purest colours emitted like vibrant rays, colours that I have never seen before so bright and delicate with a radiance so passionate, and I see things in shapes and forms that are out of this world, yet created by it, in spirals and filigrees, funnels and half-moons, pipes and plates, beehive cells and infundibulae, and two fishes glide past me, canary yellow they are, they almost fly past me, and the sea is peopled in the distance with graceful swimmers who, like dolphins, play and nuzzle one another and sway this way and that to the tune of an excruciatingly beautiful sound which is the music that the waves are transmitting from the spheres and I am one with all of them and I know happiness and want it to last for ever and ever and ever but when I turn over on my back at my most relaxed, when I have forgotten everything except this beauty and peace and ease, and when I believe I inhabit a world of truth, I look up right above me, and I see that on the surface of the water, as if through glass, there are clouds racing past in dark grey colours like coarse prison blankets, one after another, hurried and up to no good, looking deceitfully behind them, scurrying, scuttling in undignified haste, and then I see below the clouds, in the water but at the surface above me, steel blue sharks speeding into view, sharks with tinted glass for eyes and retractable fins and numbers painted with fluorescent paint on their flanks, and to my horror I see them gang up and use their electric charge to attack an unsuspecting group of fishermen I had not noticed standing quietly waist deep in the water with their lines taut waiting, causing red to start to swirl outwards, and directly without hesitation these steel blue sharks go on to maraud a party of swimmers who are laughing in the swells nearby, causing more blood to change the colour of that sea, and then they make a direct and efficient line for the children in paddle boats, butchering them in cold blood, and leaving their remains only to rip open the stomachs of teenagers on windsurfs until the whole *green one red* and in that blood, that like clouds begins to spread out and like smoke begins to hover, I see Jay reaching out for my hand and I try to reach him but I am sinking, sinking, falling through space not water.

'It's me! It's only me. It's Mama Gracienne,' I hear your voice over troubled waters, echoing over a vast distance. And then you're *shaking me*. Shaking me again. Shaking me awake.

'Those noises,' you say, 'I can't stand those noises. Not any more. Like you're being strangled or hanged by your neck. Quiet, quiet, quiet now! It's only a nightmare.' Her palms move gently down from my hairline to my jawbone, again and again in consolation.

'Sharks,' I say.

No it isn't sharks, you say.

'The sparrow,' I ask. 'How's our little sparrow?'

'It's flown away,' you say, 'it's flown on.'

And so she sings me to sleep:

> *dodo, baba*
> go to sleep my only one

dodo, baba
faraway horizon
I come from
dodo, baba
go to sleep my only one
dodo, baba
see the same old sun rising
all blue skies
dodo, baba
go to sleep my only one
close your eyes
dodo, baba
hear the sound of a mama's
lullabies

A grown woman I am and yet, like a child, I'm scared of the wind. You, the Confession, you who came in with untidy old plaits sticking out in all directions, now stroke my head, a head with only tufts of hair and scabs on a naked scalp, two women in La Salpêtrière, and you draw your palms over my closed eyes again and again and I drift, peaceful, back to sleep.

F *ood*: (1) The prisoners' dietary shall be regulated by the Minister. (2) Every convicted prisoner shall receive the prison dietary, and no other article of diet of any description except when ordered by the medical officer. [*Prisons Act (1888) Section 25*] The Commissioner may authorise an unconvicted detainee to bring in food. [*Reform Institutions Act (1989) Section 26*] – Copied down from the Prison's Library.

We wake up *unlike* other days inside. *The bird has flown.* And we wake up to expectancy today. We wake up to knowledge of our own thoughts and actions. Usually, it is the worst moment. Usually. Just when dreams and even nightmares eventually recede in the morning light, the solid fact of imprisonment comes rushing in, like the walls do, a reminder of the cruel truth, worse than the worst nightmare.

Worst there is none.

Depression usually oozes from the ceiling and weighs like a weakness of the forearms of us all. An aching weakness. A giving up. A wish to bend forwards like a foetus and to go back into oblivion.

But not so today. Not so today. Today, morning blends into the fitful, stormy night, in heads full of plans and unpredictable expectations, a day run by a cyclone out there, wild and let loose, and action in here, held in as if by the reins of sheer human will.

Surprises are lying in wait for us. Everywhere. Like a paper trail. Wonders and presents and gifts and possibilities never dreamed of. We wait for them now.

As our cell doors are opened electronically, instead of pouring out like some flowing substance like we usually do, *reluctantly to another part of the jail*, we step out and literally *prance* down to breakfast, with a lilt to our every footfall, looking this way and then around that way. We hardly even need to look at one another. We *know*. All of us do. A graceful movement in us. Swift but never hurried. Unpredictable but calm. Never before.

Not the same as all the other days. *An imprint on history.* A spoor. Possibilities.

Leashed in only by our own decision.

Never has a cyclone so consistently moved so fast. *So they say.* We hear all the details that any prisoner may have gleaned, as we begin to gather for breakfast, from the winnowing winds. Like migrating birds. In patterns. Ever changing. Chatter chatter chatter. Receive and emit. Listen and talk. Speak and be spoken to. *Two cyclones moving fast. They are moving at twenty-eight kilometres an hour. Incredible. Winds of over 300 kilometres an hour. Still in parallel. The mega-cyclonic system has never been deflected for an instant from its original direction.* It heads inexorably towards us. It is determined. Like a persistent messenger being sent. It gets worse and worse, closer and closer, more and more menacing.

We've got an ally.

In the night the cyclone warning *has* been upgraded into a Class Three warning. They play the cyclone bulletin over the intercom as we file into the dining hall. I wonder why. Why do we suddenly get this privilege of knowing? Maybe it's some clause in their insurance, to do with *force majeure.* I am sure of one thing: It is not because they like us.

The two cyclones have shown signs of becoming one. Latitude 15.7 south, longitude 62.5 east at about 600 kilometres north-east of Mauritius and moving in a south-westerly direction. Cassandra has attracted and may be uniting with Doorgawatee. Or vice versa. This means that the intensity may be expected to increase. Multiplier effect. It may become one massive eye. Moving in a general south-westerly direction. Intense tropical cyclone. Winds of unprecedented speed rush into the centre. Over 420 kilometres per hour. Rain is torrential, coming down in sheets. Visibility is low. Seas are atrocious. Phenomenal tides can be expected. Tidal waves are already covering low-lying areas. Bridges are washed away in many places. Some by rivers others by the atrocious seas. Huge trees block all roads. Coastal roads have collapsed into the sea. The earth is shifting slightly on mountainous slopes. There is land sliding in Labit. Evacuation being attempted. Huge buildings sway metres this way and that.

A massive crane on top of a building site for a skyscraper has got tied in a knot. Palm trees have snapped in half. Whole avenues of giant trees have been uprooted.

I imagine their roots now reaching for the sky like grasping fingers of dying souls, once buried heads under the ground and feet sticking out.

And the cyclonic system continues to head towards us.

The official meteorological bulletin is followed by radio announcers talking in spurts and starts, inane adjectives and then a sudden poetic skid, misplaced adverbs and then words falling into place like jewels on a string, dire warnings followed by shoddy nervous instructions. They can't remember what class of person they are talking to. *Who is the listener? Is there anybody there?* They can't be sure what kind of person they are themselves. Are they the representatives of the state? *Who is she who speaks now, over the air? Whose voice do the wind and the airwaves carry outwards in circles like this?* And so they begin to vacillate from persona to persona.

The present heat in that breakfast queue is compounded by gusts. The gusts make the heat penetrate into us instead of staying just outside us, on our skin, respectfully. The gusts get even more frequent. They get more forward and obstreperous. And stronger as time goes on. There is rain falling directly *sideways* now. *I always thought falling meant downwards* and beating inwards with each gust. Horizontal rain, under the pressure of the speed of the wind, forces its way into every window and under every door. Spraying through airbricks. At the same time, a cloud-like system starts to form inside the high-roofed mess, and rain begins to fall *inside*, and to be whipped around in every gust. And this is the first sign that the outside is becoming the inside.

There is an airlessness that accompanies all this frenzy. And any air there is in this place, is electric. Dangerously electric.

The anger about the seconds getting longer is still here. Not dissipated even by the movement nearer to us of Cassandra and Doorgawatee, who we know will unite as one soon. It is as though, while the twin cyclones approach each other and join up, our anger approaches that of the inmates near us, joins up and increases.

Rebellion is out. Suspended in every molecule of the place. Only to be breathed in by us. Vibrating in our breasts. And then exhaled, invigorated further still. And we all look *through* this rebellion. Darkly. Through air. Right through it. Rebellion is the calm. Rebellion is in the air. Rebellion is sharp focus.

And there is knowledge. Shared and unspoken. Conviction. *Convicts with conviction.* Certitude. Knowledge that later. Later we will rebel openly. Revolt. Act as though we are in tumult. Open mutiny. Overthrow something. Everything.

Suspense mounts with every gust. What could the wind blow away now? Nothing but old cobwebs. Uneven rooftops? Outgrown oppression? Madness from out of the draughty heads of our rulers?

No one in the place can hide from this suspense.

Those in power cower in their castles, which shimmer in a mirage in the gusts and start to resemble sand-castles. Castles in the air. Buildings made of dominoes. Or houses of a pack of cards.

She was right about everyone getting their periods all at once. There is pre-menstrual tension here all right, palpable in the air. Like an extra sense. An edge. A cutting edge.

She is right. Some of us twitch openly. A part of an arm twitches without shame. Or of a leg. Like a filly. We might shake it out, slowly, and then just go on standing in the queue, waiting. As though there is too much energy in our limbs. About to bolt.

And there is the smell of menstruation, already beginning to flow, as it were. Some of us have begun to let the blood flow. Have given in to the ebb and. So there is the scent, like rich perfume, which rises and hovers around us in that breakfast queue. Warm, welcoming, calming. And as it gets blown away by a gust, so more of it gets created by us.

It causes a truce amongst us. Even bullies are humbled by it and quieted.

The smell of the recurrence of time, that's all. Back around to the same spot. A spot of blood. An ooze. A tidal movement. The birth moment of each moment.

No matter what *they* change.

And this smell causes us all to move gently, quietly, slowly, our body weight from one foot to the other. A slow musical lilt. Tilt. Counterpoised. Like a bascule. The harmony of a see-saw in balance. A pair of scales with equal weights in them. Justice holding our inner equilibrium fairly and blindly.

Relative to one another, our movement is a kind of counterpoint. Almost a dance. But not quite visible. A choreographer's dream movements as she prepares to teach a new dance. Each of us with our own dance in our heads. And then we start to rock almost imperceptibly forwards and backwards, in time to an invisible inaudible beat.

From us comes a sound. Like humming. Or distant drumming. The precursor of harmony in our movements. A melody that could be born from the humming. A dance that we will dance later and a song that we will sing later. *We are the music, we are the dance.*

And we move and hum as if from inside a trance, a state of calmness.

We ourselves a bridge over troubled waters.

And even under troubled waters. Because torrents rush over the roof and off the edge into view. And we stand apparently inert, but with just a hint of wild energy held in firmly. *We are the music, we are the dance.*

In our very gentleness, a threat. In our non-violence, the menace that we have under our breath, that we can muster, the strength to pull asunder that very power that binds us like beasts in captivity. Like Samson, we may lean on pillars and push them apart. Like Kali, we may kill. And hang *their* heads like pearls on our necklace. To choose when to give birth.

And we cast our glances around, widely. Looking slightly further than one another. Not quite seeing the walls, but beyond. Hearing a faraway sound. And moving to it. Singing a faraway song that moves into us. And we smile nonchalantly. A smell and a mood unite us. A movement and a sound unite us. The tides of time have got back inside of us. Particular swells wash each of us this way and that, with the waxing and waning of the moon.

Separate from my roommates, inoculated as we three are, I am nevertheless overcome by the air outside of me. My body begins to doubt whether to stay pregnant and whether to persist in being separate from the other women. I feel the strong desire to relax, join the general movement, and let my body prepare to expel the contents of my womb. As though I could spontaneously abort. The body is linked to the mind, I know now with a forceful knowledge.

Yes, I'll do that.

We are overtly restless now. And restive. We tend to change places with one another in the queue, an unheard of thing, and to brush against one another absently. And to meander from our correct places. And as we let go, we begin, quite openly to take in one another's perfume as we dance. Making sure we get every syllable of every message absolutely correctly. As if life depends on it. Because it does. Lost senses return to us.

There is a strange quiet, when a gust passes on. Before the next one starts to build up.

There are none of the usual complaints. No mumblings. No polite conversation. No snarky comments. No spite. Certainly no silly high jinks like there usually are. No one tripping anyone else, or pretending to take a swipe at anyone else's head, or swearing at another prisoner loud across the room. No one pulling someone's hair from behind and then hiding behind someone else. No sniggering at some weaker prisoner's faults. Nothing.

And stronger than this smell of menstruation, and almost drowning this smell out, is the clear, enticing and overwhelming smell of *mutiny*. A scent to drown all scents.

It has got worse.

The fact that each second is now longer has intensified the desire to move collectively, all at once, when there is the signal. We have been attacked collectively and that's how we will defend. The very looseness of time that those in power have imposed has allowed us a certain movement.

I concentrate with all my might on avoiding responding to any false signal myself, and of preventing anyone else from doing it either.

I know it could be fatal.

The others seem to know too. Human consciousness heightened. It is now that I see Boni. She's up. I see her right at the back of the queue. The sight of her face, as people turn around in the queue and stare at her wounds, seems to intensify the mounting desire to rebel. Anger held in by her, we too must hold it in. We breathe deeply and hold our heads high. She stands like a giant behind us. Skin and jaw bones. Nail and tooth. Calm, as if presaging the eye of the cyclone and signalling to us that we must be still. Dignity in the face of.

The effect of the low atmospheric pressure is there too. As the cyclone approaches, the barometer must be falling, falling dizzily, faster and faster, below anything the human body knows. There is the pressing need to have air enough to breathe.

The rage of being confined this way during a natural disaster amplifies in us a deep sense of wonder at our enslavement. Disbelief. Defiance. It also magnifies our ability to make acute observations. Of all the senses.

It is us, we ourselves, who are the ones who give away what we make, what we think, what we own, what we are, and we do it in exchange for next to nothing. *The skin of our arses is not ours, but we see fit to give the fruit of our labour to the rich.*

We give away the power. We give away what we make. *Buttons and baskets. Electronics and aubergines. Salt-pans and bitter gourds. Soups, dried fish and marsh leaves. Book shops and cloth warehouses. Pickles and crisps. Files and needles. Hare and goat. Socks and houses. Fruit and mixed vegetables. Bread and pancakes. And carved pineapple with chilli and salt.* We make it all, and give it away. And let them bind us up as well, by the hand and by the foot. By the minute and by the hour.

Now we know.

We start filing past, taking our tea mug, balancing it on our aluminium plate next to our bread, in one hand, and preparing to pick up our two bananas, perfectly ripe today, in the other hand when we get to the end of the table. Strange mockery of the catwalk. But we decide now.

Not a single person drops her empty mug by mistake. No one bumps into anyone else's plate. Not a single hunk of bread falls on to the table or bounces off on to the ground once it has been placed on a plate. Confidence.

There is a huge woman at the front of the queue. Tall and big-boned with the muscles of a pack-horse. It is as though we consider her a rampart. Against a useless stampede, against becoming Gadarene swine. She stands firm. One hand on her hip. The other with her plate held shoulder high, mug balancing on it. Unheard of.

She is calm. All the more threatening. A menace to the whole place, we are. I see Leila, the Effusion of Blood, hungry as usual, right up front in the queue. Next to the huge woman. Nearly as tall, but not nearly as strong. Pillars like the gates to.

At the beginning of the queue they have had their mugs filled with tea. They are in front of the table with the bananas on it.

I hear a commotion. A rumble, not a roar. An angry sound. And it is moving.

Word runs along the line, the sound ripples along, as we stand in line. It moves along us like the tearing along of a breaker in the surf on the sea, from one end to the other of the bay, unfurling and thundering against the reef. Or like the muscles of a large serpent angered into movement. Or the fault line opening out as cloth miraculously gets rent in two.

'Only one banana each!' a blue lady announces, and the words run along the line, in anger, outrage.

'Only one banana each!'

T he message goes all the way to the back, reaches our anchor, Boni, and then forward again to the huge woman. 'Only one banana each!' We all start to mill around ever so slightly, picking up one another's messages. To wander and to be furious.

You stay close to Boni, Mama Gracienne. I see you. You are checking if she is all right. Her wounds hurt you. You think maybe you inflicted them. I beg of you, don't go and confess again. It wasn't you who hurt her.

Even when Boni starts to move, you shadow her. Follow along. Because this is when Boni brushes past everyone in the queue one by one and says to us, no *tells us,* to hold it in. *Rein it all in,* she says. We have to wait. She tells everyone to wait for the eye. You must all *understand.* Tells them to make plans for a mutiny. We must all understand. If we fail to understand, we will stampede. No wild-cat now. No false-start. Hold it in, she rasps from her broken face. *Do not let them tempt us to pre-empt ourselves. We will not be provoked.*

Boni cannot move fast. Next to her, there's you. You pace her. You prevent people from milling into her. Which is not necessary because in the milling mood, there is no accidental bumping. There is no shoving.

Fast, I learn from Boni. I move around, I say just those words: *Rein it in. Hold it in. Wait until the eye. Make plans for the take-over in Class Four. It is only Class Three now. Hold it in.*

'What if there isn't an eye?' one says to me.

'Then we will have to wait and see. Do not make a mistake

313

now. We will lose our chance. We are all in harmony, now. Now, hold it.'

'I am scared,' a young one says to me. 'What plans can a fool like me make?'

'Make your own plans. You are the only one that can make your plans for you. You're big enough to be here, you're big enough to make plans. *Understand?* You have to understand. You'll never walk alone now. Look around you, girl, see us all.'

Some of us move as if to begin a rush. A charge. A stampede. But others add a word of calm. Oil on water. Thus moving for, proposing that, we put tumult on hold, hold it in, until we are ready. And they insist. I also insist. Boni insists. Readiness is all.

'Rebellion must feed on hope and nurture hope. Not *now*, please not now. This would be despair. Can you understand?'

She comes up to me, Leila does, and says. 'See my friend at the head of the queue. She agrees. What shall I tell her?'

'*Yes*. The answer is *Yes*.' The cyclone is moving too fast. We have to choose our method. 'Tell her that at Class Four the cell doors will all be unlocked on automatic. You and I will see to that.' All the doors, all of them, cells and other doors. 'We'll get them unlocked electronically, you and the big one open everyone's cell door, one by one, because they won't know it's unlocked, and tell them to follow you two. Tell her to prepare to bind and gag any blue ladies who cause a disturbance. Prepare cloth strips, and keep them hidden in your clothing. Use their own clothes to bind them hand and foot. Head for the main door, go through it and then for the main gates. Once the gates are open, we will fall into three groups, one with the big one and you, the other with Boni, and the third with me. You head for Porlwi, and Boni will head in the direction of Ti Rivyer. If any groups know safe houses of their own, let them branch off. Tell them at the last possible moment, that in the eye, if the eye goes past, they must help in the general mutiny. Not just the prison mutiny. I'll be here on the inside. The inside will be part of the outside. *Moebius ring, at last.* We need them all for the *general* mutiny once they're out, make sure they realise it. They must *imagine* what to do next. *Make it up as we go along.* Remind

314

them they aren't just passengers on someone else's train.' She laughs.

I mill and I whisper, 'Hold it in, everything is going fine.'

It would be dead easy to have a total hunger strike.

But that's where we are clever. We resist the urge. We do not. It is not the time for hunger strikes.

She, the big woman at the front of the queue, casts a long look all along the line, to Boni and all the way back. Then, with general assent, she puts her hand out and reaches for one banana. She picks it up, looks at it with adoration, food for the gods, nods her head as if in warning, and walks on.

There is an agreement.

There will be a mutiny. The message is in the way she took that one banana.

Either tonight or tomorrow morning.

103

S edition: Any person who by words, writing or placards holds or brings into hatred or contempt, or excites disaffection towards the Government or the administration of justice; raises discontent or disaffection amongst the citizens or promotes feelings of ill will between different classes of citizens; shall commit the offence of sedition. [*Criminal Code (Amended 1993) Section 283(1)*] – Pasted up in the mess.

We are tense, but we are getting way beyond the reach of the cyclone now. We are all becoming *untouchable* now. Equal to anyone, and beyond the reach of our jailers. We will take our food, one by one, we will do so, slowly.

It is *her* turn now, the Effusion of Blood. Leila picks up her one banana and puts it next to her hunk of bread, and smiles slowly. If anything, she gets taller, each vertebra stretching from the one underneath it, until she raises her mug of tea, and holds it in the air, champagne, and looks at it. *A toast.* Unspoken. But, no, it isn't just a toast. She is taking an oath. She is making a vow. Her hand is steady as a rock, and her eyes sweep the mess room, causing blue ladies to look down at their once polished shoes, muddied at the edges now, and this makes them shuffle their feet.

After Leila, the Effusion of Blood, the next woman prisoner comes forward and stands in the front of the queue, bringing a swelled-up moment of increased tension. Time varies, now, but because of what *we* are doing.

She is a greedy, spiteful woman, in for poisoning the child of a neighbour who made eyes at her husband. Can we trust such a woman? Who could trust her? What will she do? Yes, she understands, she takes the one banana and she also takes the oath. The blue ladies now begin to flinch. Blue One-One gets a nervous tic, the outside edge of her right eye jerking closed and simultaneously seeming to pull out a sinew in her neck. Then the next woman comes up. What will she do about the half ration of bananas? She also takes the one banana, without any hesitation. The oath.

The blue ladies begin to stand hovering in pairs now, or even to cluster in groups of three or four. Never alone now. They huddle. *Like the wasps. Their time is up.* They keep their backs to the wall, just in case. Their sting is gone. From time to time they flutter. Or twitch an arm like a clipped wing. Sometimes their eyes flash in fearful doubts, and other times they blink in disbelief. Or they stare into the middle distance. A frown now passes through their gaze, rippling from one to another, as each prisoner refuses the temptation to revolt against the reduction to one banana a day. It unnerves the blue ladies completely. It is not normal. It bodes ill for them. They go more shifty-eyed and more shuffling. Blue One-One now emits a nervous giggle, shrill and off-note, which then echoes around the stormy mess room and seems unable to escape into silence, and instead goes on and on echoing, like cries trapped in purgatory. The weather starts to scare them now. When there is a gust, they cringe, and when there isn't one, they balk at the calm. They fear for their lives now. *They* are trapped in here now, imprisoned. Their eyes keep returning to the bars on the mess room windows. Repeatedly.

Another prisoner files past. She too takes her oath.

Whatever the storm does now is not a source of individual worry to any one of us any more. Whatever the blue ladies do now isn't either. We couldn't care less. It doesn't happen to bother us any more. We hardly look at them. And as for gusts, we start to enjoy them. As the next long wave of gust begins, right next to me, *you* who have moved up to me, Mama Gracienne, *you* of all people start to hum here with everyone around, and your humming gets catchy, and we all start to hum, in a rising tone, towards the crescendo of the gust, a kind of Mexican wave, at the height of which we all ululate.

The blue ladies jitter now and fret openly.

Meanwhile, as each prisoner gets to the front of the queue and makes a stand, the others get stronger. We are taking power in a process that has already begun and the knowledge – *conviction* even, because it is our own choice – that we will be acting soon means we are already acting, means victory is possible, means a certain degree of victory is already here with us, inhabiting us.

You come to the front of the queue now, Mama. I see you close

318

up, you still being just in front of me. This is where you stand. Your skin soft with age. I see the fine, intricate patterns of your wrinkles as they disappear into your prison shirt at the neck and at the arm. The expression on your face is mysterious.

Please don't go and confess again, I think to myself, half-worried half-smiling.

But I needn't have doubted you. You, who are wiser than us all, you who have generations of experience inside you all the time, you who have too much knowledge of the past, so much that it sometimes weighs you down, you who have past history distilled inside of you, god alone knows how.

Your great grandmother comes into you and you say words I can hardly hear, *uhuru libertad swaraj egalité amandhla*. A gust starts and you begin to hum again, as you raise your hand high into the air, you do, so we all hum, and you hold us humming, until the height of the worst gust so far, and then you hold up your bread and cry *roti*, touch your prison shirt and cry *kapra* and take in the walls around in one laconic and sarcastic sweep, you who slept in the casualty after your two little boys died, cry *aur makann*, and we all sing *donn seki to ena, pran seki to bizin, napa bizin get de kote, pu nu ras nu liberte-ey-ey*.

There is nothing any blue lady can do about us.

It is my turn, I the Allegator, the prisoner most suspected by the others, suspected of having committed a crime so base, so foul and so mysterious that they can't even understand it, don't even know what they would have to do to get charged with it, I the Allegator, stunted and bald, ludicrous tufts and lumpy scabs for a head, I, too, take my banana quietly. I raise my cup of tea.

'Hurry up!' shouts Blue One-One. She thinks I'm our weak link. I do no more than shoot a disdainful glance at her. I don't even bother to slow down to spite her.

It goes through everyone's mind, visibly, in a quiet lull, in that ominous silent space between two gusts: Suddenly they know that I am inside for conspiring with others to do something. And that right now we are all, each of us and all of us, succeeding in doing what I am found guilty of.

Long live the Allegation! One of the two bank robbers cries. Not Tiko, the other one.

Viva! Everyone responds.

Blue One-One gulps.

And so, we give our word, one by one. The urge to stampede is being harnessed, the one banana is being accepted quietly without rebellion. The refusal to rebel is itself the rebellion. One by one we take our oath.

The cyclone goes on getting nearer, inexorably nearer, just as the queue shortens with the same unflinching brave march forwards of each woman prisoner.

A gust starts in the distance again. Whistling almost inaudible, then a rumble you can't quite hear, but only feel in your gut, and then howling closer. The whole mess room, like the rest of the world, begins to shake. Each push of the gust gets stronger and stronger. The shaking gets worse and worse, rising to a frenzy, while oaths are taken calmly throughout, banana by glorious banana, unhindered by the crisis in the elements, and more than that, actually *using* the crisis in the elements.

Then, just as Boni, the last one in the queue, gets to her turn to take a banana, when all the rest of us are already sitting on the mess room benches with our one banana each, our lump of bread and our aluminium mug of tea standing in front of us on the aluminium topped tables, the gust quite unexpectedly passes on to somewhere else in the world, and all the shaking lays off rather too suddenly, causing slight consternation.

Strange. I put my head to one side. What is happening?

Why the sudden lull? Complete silence. Boni uses this silence to make her act of refusal-to-be-provoked-into-useless-rebellion into an act of drama. Her face bruised and swollen, she looks at the banana first. Then, she picks it up, and places it on her plate. Then instead of a slow toast with her mug, she leaves her mug on the aluminium table top, like you did, and raises her fist in the air. It's unanimous, she is saying. The commitment is complete now.

Before any blue lady can say or do anything, we all rise from our benches, stand up and raise our fists and hold them up in the air for a full five seconds. She lowers her fist, and then we all do and we sit down and go on as if nothing ever happened.

The blue ladies wonder if they imagined it, the whole thing. They look behind them at the blank wall, trouble on their brow, they are perturbed. They'll never get proof that it happened. They can't understand anything any more. Blue One-One looks at the two bank robbers usually so *loyal* to *her*, so indebted to Old Blue, the Keeper, but they eat as if nothing ever happened, and calmly refuse to return her look. They had raised their fists, too.

Blue One-One goes out and soon comes back with Old Blue, the Keeper, in tow. Old Blue studies us closely from the doorway, then, as if losing face, turns around and leaves Blue One-One deserted in the lull.

This lull is worse than previous lulls. We eat. We sit and eat through it. These lulls that come between each of the gusts allow an eerie silence to settle in, breed and take over. The air gets more forbidding every time. Fetid. By now, each lull has become a haunting threat, hanging over the world. The atmospheric pressure is low now, very low, palpably low, rock bottom, the humidity thick in the air, very thick, and the temperature high as the humidity allows it to get. And mixed into all this, there is a most suspicious quietness that carries in it the worst threat of all, 'I, this silence, will come to an end.' This threat is all the more unsettling because of the uncertainty of *when* exactly the silence will start to come to its end, and when all will start moving again. So we eat with a threat in each mouthful. But it doesn't get under *our* skin any more, this silence. We are impervious to it. Our eyes now start to flash this way, and then that. And, in turn, with each mouthful, we threaten. *We threaten.* We add our threat to its threat. We loiter with intent.

Our silence in reaction to this diminished ration signifies our threat of future action.

They know it. We know it. And now this lull proves it.

We eat on in near silence, chewing majestically and swallowing pointedly.

Blue ladies' emotions start to get uselessly labile, up and down for nothing, you can see the pointless vacillations succeeding one another in the corners of their mouths, which pull this way and then that, up this side and down that. Blue ladies all act as though they have constricting suit-ties around their throats. The lull gets them. Our threats completely unnerve them. Their confidence has gone, as if it had never been very firmly lodged in them. They clutch at their electronic keys in a cussed, worried way. Resentful. They look as though they might just give up soon and hand us the keys as if we are the rightful owners.

I hear a strange sound in the distance, or is it more like a strange *feeling* than a strange sound. It is a low-pitched roaring that echoes in the pit of each woman's womb. A distant and continual shuddering, which then lets up a little, then when it presses down again, it is slightly nearer than it was the time before, slightly louder than the time before, slightly more acute than the time before. And so it is approaching again. Almost imperceptibly, it gets nearer and nearer and nearer.

We chew slowly and listen. We sip at our tea. Freedom is quiet. Freedom is way beyond anything like insolence. It is independent.

We feel union. We feel the fusion of excitement with calm, the two in perfect balance, the thrill of heightened mental capacity with the confidence brought by perfect physical co-ordination.

Then the sound starts to take on the recognisable form of the discordant noises that move along with a new gust. It approaches, terrifying all ahead of it with the chaos in its wake.

Except us.

It hits the building slowly at first, and then pushes and pushes, as though pressing with the hands of an enormous giant and shaking. We smile quietly. *You* lay your eyes on all of us, Mama Gracienne, with a blessing in them, and you hold the gaze of any young one who may show signs of losing her nerve. *You* are beyond fear yourself now anyway, so you sit and eat and probably hum your confession song all to yourself. The whole place shakes. Yes, a basalt rock prison can shake when it gets pressed and pushed like that. The power of the gust builds up more and more, pressing on the prison until it is at breaking pitch.

The trunks of close-together casuarina trees cry with the pain each gust brings. Then their voices are drowned out in the generalised cacophony of the windy storm and all its wild, wet debris. By now there are hardly any leaves left on any trees. Stark branches against a dirty pink sky. Even the most tenacious of leaves are gone. Whole branches of lakoklis trees, their leaves having whipped round their stems, torn off the tree and rolled up like so many balls of cotton wool, billowing along past the high windows in gusts, thrust past the prison as if in anger, and then casting themselves dejectedly into doorways or flopping down in alleyways. Even needles are gone from casuarinas. Mulchy leaves and needles lie in corners, inside and out, inside-out. A sheet of corrugated iron whips past the high mess room window like a sheet of smart letterhead onion-paper, jerks this way and then that, and as it hits the mess room wall, there is the chilling sound of steel against concrete.

We smile again.

She, Leila, the Effusion of Blood, who though young or because young, used to seem so heavy and dull, of all people raises an eyebrow, as if amused.

Boni arranges to sit next to me. She does not have to say a word, though.

Because when the gust is at its height, what had seemed securely fitted turns out not to have been. The solid prison begins to melt into rattles and it shakes and shudders. What had seemed certain, isn't. It is in grave doubt instead. What had seemed unchangeable, *is* changeable. It actually changes before our eyes. The previously immutable itself emits its own hints of change and seems to threaten to burst with impending transformations from within as from without.

What had seemed cast in iron, is in fact only made of clay. What had seemed permanent, ephemeral. What had seemed concrete can turn to pale grey powder within seconds.

Never say never, that is all Boni says to me.

Even that which has always seemed waterproof is not waterproof any more. It is permeable. Water literally pours through our roof now. The leak that had started as a slow dripping, has speeded up, into a constant flow. The water off the roof of the High Security Women's Electronic Prison now runs down walls on to the mess room floor and out into the corridor, I don't know where it all comes from, nor where it is going. The level even begins to rise. I only know that *that* blue lady nurse said it would, *that leaky place*. Rivers of it. Rising.

'The doors will be open within the hour,' I say to Boni, not even bothering to whisper any more, 'before we get stuck in this place without electricity to open the doors with. And with the water rising inside.'

'Pessimist,' she says, crooked out of her beaten-up jaw.

As if it were part of my joke, the lights go off for one and a half seconds, the automatic switch turns us over to the generator. The electrics and electronics are all on Delco now. Instead of the apparently everlasting flow of electrical current from the mains, we are on what is so clearly finite that it depends on some small stock buried in the quartermistress's store. We listen to the hum of the prison Delco. Suddenly prison stocks are so petty. Brown shirts for prisoners, blue skirts for blue ladies, food, soap, blankets, grey paint, light bulbs, WD-40 for the locks, stationery, and a paltry stock of diesel. *Her stock of diesel must be very limited,* I lean over and whisper to Boni.

Now Boni points to something that defies a crisis. *There is life, that seems to spring through the dead prison building itself,* she says and directs my eyes with hers. I notice for the first time, a young pawpaw tree is sprouting from a crack in the wall under the windowsill of the mess, protected in this cyclone. An image comes up of the prison gone to ruin and overrun by vegetation, mainly female pawpaw trees, bearing great pulpy orange fruit full to the brim with hundreds of dark grey plumped out seeds.

And there is no one who does not have her periods now. Except for those of us who are pregnant or who have *achieved* age. Blue ladies have theirs too. They can't help it. The authorities try to help them suppress them with various pills and injections, but there they are, their periods, the minute the blue ladies lose concentration, back again.

And they have lost their cool as well, the blue ladies. They are not even sure that they are blue ladies any more, not sure in their own minds, minds where a dread has moved in, a dread that they may be some *other creatures*, creatures perhaps fractured in the past and now restrung together all wrong, turning into whelps in a storm, whelps on badly manipulated puppet strings. Their electronic keys on their belts, silent and light, weigh them down and, instead of calming them, fluster them. Especially when the floodwater rises like this. They hesitate and falter and from time to time, if you listen closely, they whimper. They look *up* to us. Even to me, stunted as indeed I am.

It's not the *storm* of the cyclone that makes them lose confidence, like the storm makes officers in charge of a cargo of slaves fear the elements as a leveller, and fear finally Death, the Leveller, himself, finishing everyone equally.

No.

It is the storm that has got *into us* today, galley slaves all. It's the fear of mutiny. That's what they can't stand. What if we break our chains and shout, over the noise of a tempestuous sea, thunder and lightening: *You mar our labour, keep your cabins . . . Hence! What cares these roarers for the name of King? To cabin! Silence! Trouble us not!*

And what with the owner of this hulk, the prison, being miles away, a paymaster who is so absent, they can't quite remember *where* he or they, is or are, and what with the generalised privatisation of prisons, they aren't even sure *who* he is or who they are any more. All they know is that once again it's a company.

They go to pieces.

Quietly. They mourn our refusal to rise up against the provocative cut in banana rations. They well nigh beg us to act like we usually act. They have lost touch.

Where will a prison company, an electronic key, a few bangles, a bit of deodorant and a short supply of diesel get you after all, in the times of a mutiny?

I can see there will be no need for any bloodshed in order to cow them. The more resourceful amongst them may even seek recruitment to our side too early for our liking. They are already looking for places to hide. The spectre of war tribunals rises from somewhere deep in the recesses of their unconscious memories and they feel on trial already. They look left and then right, hoping to find crevices to crawl into, themselves.

We could hardly do worse than they did at running this place.

We eat our meal without a sign of mutiny. In this, there is the sign. One banana served to each of us, and no complaint.

The huge one, sitting I notice right next to Leila, picks up her banana, and looks at it. Then she begins to peel it to half way down, really slowly, as if with love. Then she begins to eat it. We all in unison now take our bananas and start to peel them.

Before we eat them, at the very moment that we hold up our bananas to eat them, they broadcast the Class Four warning over the loud hailer system. The two cyclones have united into a single megacyclone. Quote. They name it *Doorgandra*. The giver and the taker, Doorgawatee, has united with the teller of the future, Cassandra.

We throw one another glances before we leave the mess. Boni signals with no more than a movement of her right arm that we must hold in our desire to mutiny until the time is ripe.

The blue ladies quake.

T he minute we three get back to our cell, I don't need to say
anything to you, you Mama Gracienne who have already
got your bits of homemade rope out ready, one length for you to
keep here, and one length for me to take along. And Leila's also
ready. Champing at the bit, as she stands there, no warm-up, no
nothing, with her hand like a stirrup, so I'm at the window. The
bar that had been balancing there has already been blasted out by
the storm. Once a cyclone gets into a cell, it pops everything loose
outwards. *In times of peace, you should never let a cyclone get
into your house, if ever you have the choice. It runs amok. It
breaks windows and blows everything out. It takes up residence
inside and makes you into a squatter in your own house.*

So I am up on her shoulders.

'Can you do it? Can you really *open the electronic doors?*'
Leila asks, standing still like that with me on her shoulders, an act
of faith. She is quite breathless with curiosity and stands calm,
physically prepared.

'Better than *breaking in by hand*, isn't it?' I like to joke with her
like this, 'or than *effusion of blood*.' From where I am, standing
on her shoulders, I turn around to you, as you stand by the door
barring the electronic peephole with your soft hand, and I ask
you to stay that end of the cell, because I'll throw in the missing
bar from outside, in case *you* need it for self-defence.

We won't meet anyone out there now.

Up, I draw myself and out down the handmade rope that looks
like one of the falling strands of a waterfall. I stand alone in the
courtyard, water up to my shins now and rising, and running

somewhere, the elements amok around me. I have to fight to keep my balance. I lean against the wall, holding on to the cloth rope. She climbs up the cloth-rope inside, *you* have come over to the inside wall for a minute to hold one end, and then she comes down after me, down the outside, me holding the other end. Visibility is next to nil the rain is so thick. Sheets of it, veils of it, loosely folded, file past. Curtain upon curtain of it. Mashed vegetation soon gets whipped on to her and on to me, by every gust. It hurts. It gets pasted on to us, plastered against us, stuck to us. It works as a disguise for us.

She is still waiting for my reply. 'Have to wait and see,' I shout to her, checking for the two tools in my shirt again. Always checking. I am hoping the passwords haven't been changed. I know it is the very same computer system and electronic prison door sub-system that I worked on, that's for sure. We grope around for the bar under the water again and she finds it under a layer of broken leaves and sticks and rubbish, that instead of flowing around have got stuck around the bar, as if preparing to begin a new eco-system when the waters subside and the sun comes out again. She gives the bar to me, and I wait for a lull, then aim it carefully and lob it up through our window and into our cell. There is so much din from the rain on our ears that we don't even hear the bar hit the floor. But we know you've got it in there with you. Not that I can imagine you using it though. Not even in self-defence. You, who confess to murder.

The rain stings more now, it comes so hard at us sideways, whirling around that barren courtyard, in fits and starts, penetrating its every crevice. We have to cover our eyes with one hand. To stop the lashing of the rain on our eyeballs. The wind during bad gusts is wicked, bending us this way and that, making us puppets trying hard to defy our puppeteers, to breathe our own life into limbs they used to control.

Or like an early run of black-and-white film. Charlie Chaplin in the hurricane on the edge of the cliff.

Turning our senseless jerks into a dance.

We run across to the electronics room, buffeted this way and that, clutching each other for balance, and being torn apart again. So covered by leaves, we look like trees moving. We get to under the window, knee deep now, and torrents coming off the roof. She puts her head inside the torrents and beckons to me to do the same. Loud sitar music, that's what it sounds like behind the waterfall. Peace behind the waterfall.

She stands with her legs firmly apart again, steadies herself against the wall, and prepares her stirruped hand. I have my cloth rope with me for getting back from the other side. I feel around in the water at our feet for the iron bar, in case it has already been blown out. Can't find it. I look up, protecting my eyes from the speed of the rain, and see that, as if by some miracle, it is still balanced in place. So, I do the same thing outside this window, up into her hands, up on to her shoulders. Only this time, when I have taken out the filed off bar, I need to break the window panes that are inside the bars to make space to get my hand through. So I wait for the noise of a gust, and in the middle of it, holding on for dear life with my left hand, I take the bar with my right hand and strike at the window suddenly with a dull knock of the bar, knowing the noise will be lost in the general pandemonium of the cyclone. Then in quick succession, I chip, chip, chip away every bit of broken glass and splintered wood near the handle. I pull the last bits of glass that are in the way out and throw them down into the wind. They speed away like splinters of glittered straw into the gale. I send my hand through, find the handle and carefully open the window inwards out of the way. I drop the bar inside *in case*. Then I tie the rope to one of the bars that's still in place, again allowing half the rope to fall down inside, and half outside. I pull myself, face down, on to the window ledge and slide down the inside wall, not unlike a snake, on my tummy, slithering in the wet, hardly being able to hold on to that drenched rope. After seconds, she follows. I tell her she needn't have but she says she wants to watch how I do it.

On Delco all the lights are dimmed, to save up current for the locking systems.

'Nothing to see really,' I say.

We are both bright, the colour purple now. Dark purple. Pure deep purple.

'You look wonderful,' she says, 'purple butterfly.' I look at myself then at her. We have leaves and flowers pasted on us head-to-toe, and the leaves and flowers and bits of skin showing between them are different shades of deep purple.

'Metamorphosis,' I laugh, and feel the decorations stuck to my naked head.

I take a long look at the computer system again, as I prepare to use it. A big outfit, and one which I suspect I already know off by heart. Who would have ever thought I would learn anything so useful in that company?

I concentrate hard as I sit down in front of the computer. It hums its familiar hum, almost lost in the storm now. It's on standby, as it should be, and I know that the blue ladies won't be in here for ages, not until lunch. They told us no more exercises. But I hand her the iron bar, and ask her to keep an eye open anyway.

'Can you do it?' she asks again. She can't believe how easy it is. She is amazed that anyone in the world even knows how all this technology works. What she did at school bore no resemblance, she says into my ear. Her wonderment makes me wonder how we, we who made these electronic creations up, ever handed them over.

'Need our heads read,' I say to her, as I type in *Begin*, 'not to have used our knowledge better all along.'

I try the first-code-key set that we had made up at work. Only the engineers and the language creation section workers like me knew. Four of us in all. There were only twenty sets of first-code-keys and then a sub-set of twenty, and so on for five rounds of further sub-sets. I had, as is my wont, made up a song to remember each series by the first letter of the song words. We told clients, all the prison companies in the world market, if you don't mind, and only their top-brass would speak to us about it, that the chances of anyone cracking the codes were minimal. *Infinitesimal*, we said at the time. And we should know. True. But we invented the thing ourselves, so I don't have to crack anything at all.

Not the first one. Bad luck. One in twenty chance. Five per cent gone. I tell her I will take my time. It's one in twenty, I tell her. Even if it's the last one, I tell her, it'll only take an hour, if it's three minutes each.

I try the second set of code-keys. Wait the required time. No luck. The third, not it. Not the fourth, not the fifth, not the sixth. Nor the seventh, nor the eighth, nor the ninth.

But, when I have typed out the tenth, the screen says, 'Now what?' which is what I'm waiting for. This means I have to come up with the next set of code-keys.

From now on it's dead easy for me, because I know which song goes with the tenth. WALOR, first letters of the song 'What a load of rubbish', that the Liverpool fans sing if their own team plays badly or starts to lose to Everton. My father was a Liverpool fan and we had all the stuff at home. I type in the ASCII value for 'W' which is eighty-seven, then the ASCII value for 'twenty-three', that is 5050, because W's the twenty-third letter of the alphabet, and that's it. Then the computer says, 'Now what, then?' So I type in the ASCII value for 'A' which is sixty-five, then for '01' because it's the first letter of the alphabet, that is 4849, and so on.

I lean over to her, like the night *you* were due to be brought into our cell, and I say, 'I've got another secret to tell you.'

She says, 'What is it this time, then?'

'It's going to say *"Bingo"* in twenty-two seconds and they'll all be open, every door in the place. Every day *they* do this kind of exercise, but the partial ones, for just the cell doors and other relevant doors, before breakfast, before exercise, before basket-making, before lunch, and before dinner.'

Sure enough, there it is on the screen, 'Bingo'.

'If only we had realised that it was us, the workers at electronic creations, that made the whole thing,' I say to her, 'And all of us taken together in all the factories made everything, for that matter. Because it's so easy, isn't it?' She says it's true. I think: Easy as if we were blind-folded and sleep-walking. But she wants to know: Are the doors all unlocked now?

'Every last one,' I say, mildly pleased that I have used the code for 'all doors', not trying to do them set by set, which could have had interesting advantages like locking some of the blue ladies up, but which is time-consuming and can be more risky.

That instant, a gust comes and starts pressing on everything, forcing, forcing, forcing itself on this part of the globe, as if to turn the earth on its axis. We stop speaking, lift up our shoulders close to our ears, still sitting in front of the computer, waiting for the worst to pass. The wind whips round, making the sound of constant thunderclaps in quick succession. Then at the strongest thrust of that gust, a huge portion of a branch, a big heavy log without any side branches or any leaves, comes flying through the small open window like a missile directed at us and lands not on us, but right on top of the computer in front of us, breaking it in half down the middle. Sparks spew out. As we jerk back out of the way, the crash sound is deafening even in the general noise of the gust. And close-by hissing from the computer subsides. The smell of burnt Bakelite.

Just like that, the whole system is ruined. In our lap.

We both start to shiver in fright. That huge branch looks ludicrous in there with us. It could have injured or even killed us. But it didn't.

'Look!' Leila cries. We see a split start to crack open in their prison wall. One whole inch wide. Brick separated from brick. Mortar from mortar. Fissure in their very edifice now.

The delight of a ripe pomegranate. Bursting open. Fruitful. Proof that everything is ready now.

Then we stare at one another in fear.

There is no sound.

Now we hear only a hush of nothing. Of *no* sound. Of no *sound*.

A blanket of silence thick and warm has suddenly cradled us. Sound is absorbed by the carpet of vegetation everywhere. Quiet. Calm. Rest. Peace. So silent.

This is the eye of the cyclone.

Suddenly I see that pencil-thin termite tunnel in the basket workshop. The hidden attack on the wooden beams of the place. So slow and sure.

And now this hurtling, dangerous, unpredictable log, flying in and crashing down on the heart of the whole computer system.

In the eye, in that purple eye, in that silence so intense it blots up the sound of breathing, I laugh in horror at the thought of failure, terror at the knowledge of the vengeance we will face if defeated. The air eats up the sound of my own laugh as it bubbles out of my mouth.

Leila takes my hand.

'*The narrow chances in life,*' I whisper to her.

'Could have been killed by that log,' she says.

'Or the computer could have been ruined *before* we opened up the doors and gates,' I reply.

Now *they* are stuck with them wide open.

Because as it happens, they can't close them again now.

Their technology is going to slow them down now.

The eye of the cyclone causes the blue ladies to become phased out, blank-minded and to talk to themselves. Some play cards, mainly vingt-et-un, while others break the regulations and chatter on cellular telephones without ceasing. They are dislocated. They are prisoners who don't even know for sure that they're locked up.

We can walk through the place, in that eye, as though we are invisible to them. Smoothly, even gracefully. Quietly.

The doors are all already unlocked, but still in place. Even the enormous portal at the front and the little door at the bottom of it, openable.

We are the dogs that have slipped the lead and continue muddling playfully at our unsuspecting master's legs. And then we run, heads back and run.

Leila is off. She runs like a wolf, low and barefooted, pointing her toes when her feet are in the air. She runs in a way that gives a new meaning to *breaking in by band*.

She canters straight to Block A, slightly sideways on, head looking this way and that, and, as planned she lopes up to Boni's cell door and quietly opens it. Then, in the lintel, she dances.

It's so easy. Round and round, dancing revolutions.

I watch Leila go, still dancing, dan*sing*, *danzing*, and inviting inmates of Blocks B and then D to follow her if they will, and then leading a loose formation, thrown into a jazz movement by the silence of the eye, out of the main portal. She and her friends no longer pushed here and then there, no longer pulled this way nor that, now dance as if in perfect syncopation, letting the rhythm from the inside out. Leila fleeing, flying, her friends fleeing flying behind her, alongside her, like so many seagulls, using the upcurrent created by each wave of their own dance. I watch her moving away. She's got green leaves, yellow acacia flowers, and flamboyants bright red, all stuck to her making her prison clothes the wings of a bird of paradise. Looking up, she sees the Secure Life, twisted out of shape and pinned against a leafless tree. I see her sing out aloud off, flying across the bridge with the others, the eye of the cyclone bringing wondrous grace to every movement of their wings. While the torrents rise to just beneath the bridge, rushing madly to the sea, which stays wild and relentless, not letting up even in the eye, the eye which allows the movements of these dancers to become more classical and permits their wings to move more like human arms in *bharat-natyam*. Then they spin along *kitchipudi* on a plate.

I run up the spiral stairway to the watchtower and follow their every movement. Down to the football field on the other side of the river, I see Leila go. They dance to the pirogue named *Sapsiway*, its timbers lapped by the swollen river. Bright clothes are being pulled out of it, as if by magicians from a hat. Each needs only a smattering of – a shocking pink shawl here pulled in close, a pair of yellow high heeled shoes there, a green hat pulled down, a navy blue and white bag slung diagonally over one shoulder down the other hip, a polka-dotted waistcoat pulled over a prison shirt like so many Smarties spilled out over a brown table-cloth, a layered skirt, amber alternating with tan, dissembles prison trousers. Or just a stray gold-coloured belt or scarlet scarf. And a plastic box inside a plastic bag tied under the back bench of the boat with a radio in it. With batteries, that I know.

I see them huddle. I see them listen. All ears.

I see them explode outwards, screaming with joy. *Must be the mutinous forces outside, controlling radio.*

Leila puts her head back and bays.

In the eye of the cyclone.

PART III

109

As it turns out, we laid down our arms prematurely. *We do this so often in history. Almost every time. It causes us to sigh afterwards. And to sift through scraps of paper, and to cry.*

In that very wind – the harshest wind that comes with the far side of the eye of the cyclone, following the eye of the cyclone – a wind that hit us like a flying wall, with no build-up of gusts like there are *before* the cyclone, nor any other warning, in that very harsh, cruel west wind that we had hoped to harness and employ, in *it*, the troops from abroad attacked.

They blasted and bombed.

Everything was scorched and broken up. *Hit by the other side of the cyclone.* From the west.

Afterwards, when it was all over, *they* had left behind them a field of vision so wintry and desolate to look at, so hot and rotting to smell, so quiet and empty and lifeless to listen to. They left us so helpless, struggling, starving, straggling, hopeless one by one back to beg, to beg for *them* to take us in, take us in as *zurnalye* or for piece work, give us handouts.

When that cyclone departed, like all cyclones, how quickly it went away.

Quite unbalanced, it is. No symmetry in it.

Arms laid down too soon.

Postscript

T hat time.

    This time, of course, I have tools secreted away all over the cell. And next to my bunk, right here in the cell, I run what amounts to ten miles a day, easily. And I'm not the only one.

In here, it's me, of all people, they call 'Mama' now.

But the vagueness of *my* mind is restricted to remembrance of the *loss* of that time. Such wonderment.

As regards preparing tools for next time, I am not vague. I spend my time sharpening them.

This time I am not just waiting for word either.

This time their high-tech is so advanced it could kill them. They are well-nigh technology-bound.

ACKNOWLEDGEMENTS

For the long conversations on Criminal Law and its use in relation to acts of a political nature, thanks to Ram Seegobin and Jean Claude Bibi. For swapping stories of our respective arrests on political charges under criminal laws, thanks to Ragini Kistnasamy, Rajni Lallah, Veena Dholah, Alain Tolbize, Ashok Subron, and Ram Seegobin. For sharing an arrest and a trial in Port Louis in 1981 with me, thanks to my seven co-accused, all women from Diego Garcia, the Chagos Islands and Mauritius Main Island; and to our lawyer, Kader Bhayat. For sharing an arrest and trial with me in Johannesburg in 1969, thanks to my twenty co-accused, all students from the University of Witwatersrand, and our three lawyers. For telling of their memories from Robben Island, thanks to Neville Alexander, Marcus Solomon and James Marsh. For a lifetime of stories about the stubborn inappropriateness of criminal law to many of those accused under it, thanks to my father, a retired magistrate.

And thanks to girl students incarcerated in a government boarding school at the same time as I was, in East London, South Africa, for our shared rebellions. Acknowledgements for all I learnt during the six months preparation and the three weeks of strike action from the cane labourers, mill workers, dockers, bus drivers and conductors, other sector workers, and militants, during the 1979 general strike movement in Mauritius. Thanks to Sylvio Cottoyé for his reports on the mutiny inside the prison when he was in it, at the same time as the strike movement was going on.

For conversations about the Creole languages and about human grammar, thanks to Prof Derek Bickerton.

For doing a double-act with me in live story-telling, thanks to Anne-Marie Sophie.

Acknowledgement to the young people of Mauritius, who, during the February 1999 riots over the death in detention of the popular singer, Kaya, forced the gates of the prison at Borstal open, thus showing the *possibility* of the kind of things already written down, by that time, in early drafts of this novel.

For reading early drafts and making wonderful suggestions, my thanks to Ram Seegobin, Ragini Kistnasamy, Rajni Lallah, Alain Ah-Vee, Roger Moss. Thanks also to Ulka Anjaria.

For giving ongoing form, humour, and love to life, my acknowledgement to everyone who nurtures organisations like *Lalit, Muvman Liberasyon Fam, Ledikasyon pu Travayer, Bambous Health Project, Muvman Lakaz*. They made the novel possible.

And for their emotional generosity and intellectual creativity as agents and publishers, Alexandra Pringle, Victoria Hobbs, Margaret Halton, Marian McCarthy.

A NOTE ON THE TYPE

The text of this book is set in Linotype Sabon, named after
the type founder, Jacques Sabon. It was designed by Jan
Tschichold and jointly developed by Linotype, Monotype
and Stempel, in response to a need for a typeface to be available
in identical form for mechanical hot metal composition and
hand composition using foundry type.

Tschichold based his design for Sabon roman on a fount
engraved by Garamond, and Sabon italic on a fount by Granjon.
It was first used in 1966 and has proved an enduring
modern classic.